The Kate Huntington Mystery Series:
MULTIPLE MOTIVES
ILL-TIMED ENTANGLEMENTS
FAMILY FALLACIES
CELEBRITY STATUS
COLLATERAL CASUALTIES
ZERO HERO
FATAL FORTY-EIGHT
(coming in 2014)

The Kate On Vacation Series (novellas):
An Unsaintly Season in St. Augustine
Cruel Capers on the Caribbean
(coming Winter/Spring 2014)

ECHOES, A Story of Suspense
(a stand-alone ghost story/mystery)

ZERO HERO

A Kate Huntington Mystery

Kassandra Lamb

Zero Hero
A Kate Huntington Mystery

Published in the United States of America by *misterio press*,
a Florida limited liability company
www.misteriopress.com

Zero Hero is a work of fiction. Names, characters, and events are
ALL products of the author's imagination (as are some of the
places). Any resemblance to actual events or people, living or
dead, is entirely coincidental. Real places have sometimes been
used fictitiously.

~~~~~~~~

Edited by Marcy Kennedy

Cover and interior design by Melinda VanLone,
Book Cover Corner

ISBN 13: 978-0-9913208-1-3 (misterio press LLC)

ISBN 10: 0991320816

To all the 9/11 First Responders,
and to those who lost their lives that day
and their families and friends.

We will never forget!

PROLOGUE

Swirling shades of gray. Searing heat. Air choked with black particles. His arms wrapped around two little bodies. The little girl limp. The boy's mouth open, eyes scrunched closed, screaming in terror, his screams inaudible over the roar of the flames and the groaning of a building tearing apart.

Stumbling down steps. Can't see. The wrenching sounds getting louder. Then the crackling voice from the radio, "Get out! Get out now! It's coming down!"

Racing down the stairs, praying. *Don't miss a step! Don't fall!* Then nothing under foot. Only space and darkness.

Airborne, twisting around to avoid landing on top of the little bodies. *Gotta protect the children!* Falling through space...

He bolted upright, gasping for breath, eyes wide and unseeing. Sweat poured down his face. His body stank of it. It took several seconds for his brain to register that it was just a dream.

His therapist's voice echoed in his head. *It's not just a dream, Pete. Stop minimizing what you're going through.*

Something she had told him more times than he could count.

But she wouldn't be saying it anymore. No more therapy sessions. His insurance had run out.

Kelly'd had tears in her eyes when she'd told him that if it was up to her she would see him for free. But it wasn't up to her. She worked at a for-profit counseling center. She'd referred him to the county health department's mental health clinic. Six to eight weeks, he'd been told, before one of their counselors could see him.

He wasn't sure he was going to make it.

CHAPTER ONE

Kate watched for the telltale thatch of silver hair above the heads of the lunchtime crowd at Mac's Place. Her lunch date was late, which wasn't all that unusual. Partners in thriving law practices sometimes had trouble getting away from the office.

She wondered if there was anything to the old wives' tale that stress causes one to gray prematurely. Rob said his hair made him look distinguished, gave him an advantage in the courtroom, but Kate knew it bothered him some. He was occasionally mistaken for the father of his petite, strawberry-blonde wife, much to her delight and his annoyance.

"Penny for your thoughts."

Kate jumped a little, then smiled up at the tall, broad-shouldered man standing next to the booth. A slight paunch, pushing against the buttons of his dress shirt, attested to his ongoing battle with middle-aged spread. He tossed his suit jacket onto the bench and sat down across from her.

She shoved an errant dark curl out of her eyes. "I'm not sure they're worth that much." She wasn't about to tell him what she'd been thinking, that his stress level might be aging him before his time. "How're you doing? How's Liz?"

Before he could answer, a short, compact woman suddenly appeared beside them.

"Holy crap, Rose." Kate clutched at her chest in feigned shock. "Oh, no, we've been transported back in time. Mac's still running the place and you're helping out. Where's your apron?"

"Very funny," Rose Hernandez said. "Mac and I needed to

meet. Got cases to discuss. Figured might as well come here, so he could touch base with the manager." Mac Reilly, Kate's friend since childhood, had grown tired of running a restaurant a few years back and was now an investigator for the private detective agency Rose and Kate's husband co-owned.

Rob grinned at Rose. "Not to mention the food is free for the boss and his bride."

She graced him with one of her brief but gorgeous smiles. "Yeah, there is that. Mac's in the kitchen. You want me to place your orders, for old time's sake?"

"Sure," Kate said.

After Rose headed for the kitchen, Rob leaned forward. "Speaking of cases, I have a referral for you, if you want it."

"What do you mean, if I want it?"

"This guy doesn't have any money, and his health insurance benefits just ran out." Rob shook his head slightly. "He was a first responder on 9/11. He's a Baltimore County firefighter but he was on vacation in New York, visiting a cousin. If he'd arrived five minutes earlier, he'd have been inside the World Trade Center when the first plane hit. Like everybody else, he assumed it was some kind of freak accident or pilot error. He started helping with the evacuation. Then the second tower was hit." Rob paused to take a sip of the water a waitress had deposited on their table.

"Long story short, Pete borrowed the equipment of a firefighter who was suffering from smoke inhalation. He was responsible for several of the lives saved that day, including a couple kids."

Rob's voice was hoarse. Clearing his throat, he picked up his unused straw and started twisting it around his thick fingers. "Now his life's become a nightmare, thanks to the insurance companies. He was okay at first. Said he was in some of the debriefing groups held in New York right afterwards."

Kate nodded. Hundreds of teams of stress management counselors had descended on New York City in the days and weeks following 9/11. Their interventions had been effective with a fair number of people. It never ceased to amaze her how resilient the human psyche could be.

"Pete didn't start having problems until the ten-year anniversary. When the media started replaying the videos of the planes hitting the towers, and the scenes from Ground Zero afterwards..." Rob dropped his gaze to the mangled straw on the table. "He's been having nightmares and flashbacks ever since."

Butterflies invaded Kate's stomach. Rob was not prone to either nervous behaviors nor poor eye contact. He'd struggled with post-traumatic symptoms himself years ago, after her first husband's murderer had tried to kill them as well, and had almost succeeded with Rob. Could this client's case be stirring all that up again?

The waitress arrived with their food. Mac's Place was famous for having the best crab cakes in Towson, no small feat in the state of Maryland. The fragrance of succulent crab meat mixed with Old Bay seasoning was as mouth-watering as always, but somehow Kate wasn't as hungry as she'd been a few minutes ago.

She was somewhat reassured when Rob swiped her pickle slices to add to his own on his sandwich. That *was* normal behavior for him.

They ate in silence for a minute. "How could his benefits run out this early in the year?" Kate asked.

"Not his yearly benefits, the lifetime cap," Rob said. "Insurance company has an upper limit of sixty visits for PTSD."

"Say what? That's only a year of weekly sessions."

"Yeah, I talked to the Baltimore County fire chief. He said they went along with that in order to get any kind of decent premiums. Since PTSD is so common in firefighters no company was willing to give better coverage for it without charging outrageously. He figured since it's almost always work-related in firefighters, most cases would be covered by their workers comp insurance anyway."

"But this is due to trauma he suffered when he wasn't officially on duty." She was starting to grasp the rock and the hard place here.

"Exactly. So no workers comp and only sixty visits. Pete got into drugs. Trying to hide from the feelings, he said. Got suspended from duty, went through rehab, but he needed to go to counseling twice a week for awhile to stay clean. That ate up most of his visits pretty fast. And here's the real kicker. His insurance required that he go to one of their specified providers. The one he went to doesn't do reduced fees or *pro bono* counseling. So no more insurance benefits, boom, they dropped him."

Kate took a bite of her sandwich to buy some time to think. She wasn't an addictions counselor, which was a fairly specialized subfield of psychotherapy. Her first reaction was to say no to this case. "Drug addiction should make him eligible for more sessions."

Rob shook his head. "That's what I'm fighting with the insurance company over. They're claiming the drug addiction is secondary to the PTSD so the cap should still apply."

"That's bull hockey."

"Of course it is, but a few insurance companies do this. Any excuse to deny the claim, hoping the patient will pay out of pocket, or drop out of treatment. They don't really care, as long as they get away with not paying."

Kate put her sandwich down. *Hell of a way to treat anybody, much less a national hero.*

"Aren't lifetime caps against the law now?" she asked.

"The insurance company's claiming that only applies to physical health benefits. The law's a little vague regarding mental health issues. I have my paralegal checking if there have been any cases filed yet, see if any precedents have been established." Rob paused and took a sip of water. "The sad thing is Pete really liked his counselor, felt she was helping him. Now he's on a waiting list for the mental health clinic at the health department."

Rob was fiddling with his straw again. "And I haven't gotten to the worst part about the insurance—"

"How long has he been off the drugs?"

"Not quite eight months."

Ah, now they'd come to the true source of Rob's hesitation. He knew she required at least a year clean and sober. She wanted addicts to be solid in their recovery before she started poking around in their psyches, maybe stirring up stuff that could rock their sobriety.

She shook her head again. "I'll try to find a colleague who will take him on a reduced-fee basis."

Rob winced. "That's the worst part. He can't even afford reduced fee now. His disability benefits have run out too, and his commander won't put him back on duty without a medical release. His previous counselor told him she couldn't in good conscience give him one. She's afraid he'll start having flashbacks while in a burning building and maybe run in the wrong direction, get himself trapped in a fire."

"She's probably right," Kate said. "Can't he get Social Security disability? Hey, wait a minute. What about that law that was passed a few years ago, to provide healthcare benefits to 9/11 first responders?"

"He's applied for the former, but the wheels grind slowly. I'm looking into the latter. It's iffy. Requirements are that he was working the scene for at least four hours that day. He's got no idea how long it was. He just grabbed the guy's gear and started running in and out of the building. When the tower came down, he and the kids he was carrying were trapped in the debris. He was knocked out. Woke up in the hospital, with a concussion and smoke inhalation. He was released the next day, and there never was any documentation that he'd participated in the rescue efforts."

"So it's just his word he was helping with the evacuation," she said, "and even he doesn't know for how long."

Rob nodded. "My staff had a hell of a time finding out what happened to the kids."

What's that got to do with the legal case? Kate's butterflies were back.

"But you did." She braced herself. From his expression, the news wasn't good.

"There were two kids transported around the same time as Pete, from that area of Ground Zero. One went to the morgue. The other one survived but his parents were killed. He's fourteen now, living with an aunt in New Jersey."

Rob paused to take a deep breath. "I just found out this morning the rest of the story with the little girl. Fran managed to track down her next of kin, an uncle. Again her parents were killed that day. Fran got permission to get the autopsy report. Little girl was already dead from smoke inhalation, before the building came down. Pete feels horrible that he didn't save her. I keep telling him to focus on all the people he did save."

He paused again, then continued, his voice thick with emotion. "I was really hoping you'd take his case. I know there are other good therapists out there but he needs the best."

She knew he wasn't trying to flatter her. She *was* one of the best trauma recovery specialists in the Baltimore area. "I'm thinking about it, but I'm also worried about you." She put her hand on top of his lying on the table. "Aren't you getting a little too invested in this client?"

Rob shoved his plate of half-eaten food away. Startled, she pulled back.

"I've never been so pissed about a case in my life," he said. "This guy, he was just a kid back then, just twenty-two. He risked his life when he didn't have to, and now everything's crashing in on him and he's getting screwed by the system."

Worry shot through her. This wasn't the first time one of Rob's clients got a raw deal. Was this getting to him because the guy was roughly the age of his own daughters?

Kate knew this case wasn't for her. She didn't have the background in addictions that was needed here. She opened her mouth to gently say no, then closed it again.

She owed a lot to this man sitting across from her. He'd stood by her through some of the roughest times in her life, and she loved him like a brother. "I'm not an addictions counselor," she finally said.

"Pete's not a typical addict. He'd never even been much of a drinker before 9/11. He used drugs for less than a year. He's in NA, has a sponsor." When Kate didn't respond, he added, "Look, I'll pay for his sessions. Just give him a chance, please."

Kate managed not to glare at him. "You know damn well it isn't about the money." Thanks to her late first husband's foresight, a sizeable life insurance payout gave her the luxury of taking *pro bono* psychotherapy cases when she felt she could help. But in this case...

She softened her tone. "I'm just not sure I'm the best therapist for him."

"You're a damn sight better than no therapist."

Kate held up her hands, palms out. "Okay, I'll meet with him one time, just to see... well, we'll see, that's all. I'm not making any promises. I think I have an opening Friday at one. I'll call you when I get back to my office to confirm that. Can you see if he can come in then?"

"I'll make sure he's there."

Kate shook her head. "Rob, you really need to take a step back from this–"

A wiry, scruffy-looking man suddenly dropped onto the bench next to Kate.

"Hey, Rob. How ya doin', sweet pea?"

Kate grinned at the man. In only a short time in the kitchen, he'd managed to splash grease and a few other questionable substances on his faded Army T-shirt and jeans. "I'm good, Mac. How've you been?"

"Not bad."

"How's married life treating you?" Rob asked, looking immensely relieved by the interruption.

Kate suppressed another grin as a pink tide crept up Mac's tanned, leathery cheeks. After two divorces, he'd taken his sweet time deciding to tie the knot again.

She slugged his shoulder. "You're blushing, you old goat."

"If I'd knowed you all were gonna abuse me," Mac grumbled. "I wouldn't have come over."

There was not the slightest glimmer of apology in Rob's expression. Kate was struggling not to laugh out loud. They both let the silence stretch out.

"What the hell am I s'posed to say," Mac growled at them. "It's good, okay?"

"What's good?" Rose asked, appearing next to the booth. With her hair pulled back in a silky black knot and her crisply-ironed shirt and khaki slacks, she presented a sharp contrast to her husband's unkempt appearance.

Mac stood up, his cheeks now downright red. "Ya ready?" Without waiting for an answer, he took Rose's arm and turned her around.

Rose cocked an eyebrow at Kate over her shoulder, but she let her husband hustle her away from their now-grinning friends.

Kate and Rob managed to restrain themselves until the couple was seated out of earshot. When they had their muffled laughter under control, Kate said, "I'd love to be able to eavesdrop on their conversation about now."

"Do you think they're happy?" Rob asked, his grin fading.

Kate narrowed her eyes at him. He was in the strangest mood today. "Yes, I do. They're as unlikely a pair as one could imagine on the surface, but I think they're well matched."

Rob nodded. "I suspect Rose is the only woman who could handle Mac Reilly."

"And vice versa."

~~~~~~~~~

One of the things Kate assessed during intake interviews was how she felt about the person. She'd discovered the hard way that if she didn't like the client, she probably wouldn't do good work with them. In Pete Jamison's case, she didn't think that would be a problem.

He was reserved and rather earnest. He answered her questions about his own and his family history without hesitation, but with minimal elaboration.

As she listened to the content of his answers, she observed the nonverbals as well. One of the hardest parts of doing psychotherapy was the mental multitasking required, especially in an intake interview.

He was clean and neat, his gray eyes clear and his sandy hair combed, although it could use a trim. On the tall side, he was slender but broad-shouldered. His clothes hung loose on him, as if he'd lost weight recently. Not too surprising. Both drugs and the PTSD had no doubt played havoc with his appetite.

When they got to the subject of the symptoms he'd been experiencing since September 11, 2011, he was more forthcoming, which surprised her a little. He even talked, although hesitantly, about his feelings. His previous experience with counseling had apparently trained him well, and his lack of resistance boded well for his motivation level.

Without prompting, he segued into his drug abuse. At first he'd taken pills to help him sleep, although that strategy hadn't always worked. He'd smoked marijuana to ease the anxiety and ward off the images that haunted his days, again with only intermittent success. Then he'd started using uppers during the days he worked, to counter the sedative effects of the other drugs.

"Did you realize what you were getting into?" Kate asked.

"Yeah, on some level. But at the time I don't think I cared. I hit bottom a month after I was suspended. I went on a total binge. Pills, alcohol, whatever I could get my hands on. A cop, a buddy of mine, picked me up off the street, literally. I'd passed out on the sidewalk in front of some swank restaurant. Butch had me by the front of my jacket, hauling me to his squad car. When I opened my eyes, I saw the dawning recognition in his."

Pete dropped his gaze to his lap. "I wanted to die. Butch just said, 'Aw, shit, man. How'd you end up like this?' Instead of arresting me, he took me to an AA meeting. I had no idea he was a recovering alcoholic."

Kate let the silence hang for a moment as she made her decision. Everything she'd seen confirmed Rob's view that Pete was more a PTSD sufferer who'd used drugs for awhile than a drug addict who happened to have PTSD. On top of that, she liked the guy and felt bad for him.

She leaned forward. "I'm not an addictions counselor, Pete. Normally I require a bare minimum of a year clean and sober before I'll work with someone."

"I'm not quite there. I''ll be celebrating my eighth month at my home NA meeting next week."

"I'm going to take a chance on you, but staying clean is a requirement for continuing with me. Are you okay with that?"

Pete nodded without hesitation, then shyly dropped his gaze again.

Kate debated for another moment. A somewhat unorthodox treatment plan had been forming in the back of her mind while they'd been talking. Normally first sessions were limited to getting to know clients and beginning to develop a treatment plan.

But her gut was telling her she needed to move faster here. This young man might still be on solid ground, but his toes were dangerously close to a crumbling cliff. He needed to know his life was turning around as of today.

"Rob found out what happened to the little girl. Did he tell you?"

Pete's head jerked up. His eyes clouded over with pain. "Yeah, she died. I'd already suspected that. She was so limp..." He looked off to the side. His Adam's apple bobbed as he swallowed hard.

"She died from smoke inhalation," Kate said. "Long before the building came down."

"That's what Rob said. I... I didn't get her out fast enough."

"Pete, you were running out of a collapsing building. Do you really think you could've moved any faster?"

He gave her a startled look. After a second, he actually let out a soft chuckle. "I guess not. Running for your life is pretty much as fast as it gets."

"The autopsy said she didn't bleed from the wounds from the building collapsing. That means her heart had already stopped at least several minutes before. She couldn't have been revived even if you'd gotten her out before the building came down." Kate paused. "Rob talked to her next of kin. Her uncle wants to meet you. Rob asked me whether that would be a good idea for you, recovery-wise."

Pete's now red-rimmed eyes widened. "Why does this guy want to meet me?"

"Rob said he wants to thank you."

"What the hell for?"

"I think I'll let him explain that. Are you game?" Kate prayed she wasn't pushing him too fast.

Pete shook his head in confusion. "Game for what?"

"He lives in Pennsylvania. If you don't have anything planned for next weekend, I think it would be good for us to go up there."

"Us?"

"It's called *in vivo* therapy. The therapist goes with you into the real life situation you need to face in order to heal." This really wasn't typical *in vivo* therapy, but one of the perks of private practice was that you could get creative, without anyone questioning why you were deviating from more orthodox treatment approaches.

She sat quietly, letting him digest and decide.

"Okay," he finally said, a little hesitantly.

"I'll set it up and call you with the details." She rose to escort him to the door. Once there, she laid her hand gently on his arm. "Pete, it's going to start getting better as of next weekend."

He met her gaze and smiled for the first time since he'd arrived. It was a quick, shy smile but she got a glimpse of the more carefree young man he had been pre-9/11.

Once he'd left, Kate paused to wonder if *she* was now getting too invested in this case. She shook her head. Probably. She owed Rob an apology.

CHAPTER TWO

Kate was helping Maria set the table for dinner. The front door banged open. Footsteps pounded through the living room and around the corner into the kitchen. "Mommy, guess what?" her seven-year-old exclaimed. "Fiddlesticks is for sale, and Daddy said maybe we could buy him!"

"I said no such thing, Edie," Skip Canfield corrected as he came around the corner after her. "And what are you doing running through the house in your riding boots?"

The little girl dropped to the kitchen floor and started yanking the muddy boots off. "Can we, Mommy, can we buy Fiddlesticks? You said I could have a horse when I was seven and I've been seven for almost two whole months now!"

Amused at her daughter's convenient memory, Kate stifled a snicker. When she'd managed to mold her smile into a more stern expression, she turned around. "We said we'd *consider* getting you a horse when you were seven, and so we will. Your father and I will discuss it and get back to you. Now go wash up. Dinner's ready. And put those stinky boots in the laundry room."

Once they were settled around the table, including Maria whom Kate considered part of the family, they closed their eyes and five-year-old Billy began to stumble through the blessing. Kate opened one eye and looked at her children as she silently added her own nightly prayer of thanksgiving. She'd had fertility problems and it was a true miracle that these two little beings even existed.

The unenlightened probably wouldn't guess that the children

had different biological fathers. Edie was a miniature version of her mother, with out-of-control dark curly hair and sky blue eyes. But her personality was pure Ed Huntington, sweet and cheerful.

Billy was a mixture of his parents. His hair was the same straight brown as his father's, but instead of Skip's hazel eyes, Billy's were light blue. Personality-wise, the little boy shared his mother's tendency to be a bit intense.

One way that intensity was exhibited was by talking several decibels louder than necessary, as he was now doing while regaling his parents with the details of his day in kindergarten.

"Inside voice, Billy," Kate reminded him for the second time.

"Sorry, Mommy," the boy said, with no discernible reduction in volume. "We're gonna have a pettin' zoo soon. Miss Sylvia sent home a paper 'bout it. We can bring in our pets as long as it's not a snake or a trantula. I'm taking Peaches."

"*Ta*rantula," Kate corrected, then grimaced at the thought of their neurotic cat surrounded by a group of excited kindergartners. "I don't think Peaches would deal with that very well. Why don't you take your gerbil instead?"

After a brief argument, Skip said, "It's the gerbil or nothing, son."

Billy slumped down in his chair, a pout on his face.

Kate decided a change of subject was in order. "Are you likely to have to work next Saturday, sweetheart?"

Skip looked at the ceiling for a moment, mentally reviewing his cases. "Don't think so. Why?"

"Because I do have to work."

He tilted his head at her. She never scheduled clients on Saturdays, unless it was a dire emergency.

"I be 'round if you need go out, Skip," Maria said.

"You've got your party to get ready for," Kate protested, giving her husband a meaningful look. For the past seven years, ever since Rose, her cousin, had sponsored her immigration from Guatemala, Maria had been Kate's live-in nanny and housekeeper. Her only activities, beyond Kate's little family, involved the extensive Hernandez clan or going to church on Sundays. This

Valentine's party, sponsored by her church's singles group, was the first social event Maria had ever expressed interest in attending.

"You'll be home long before she has to leave, won't you?" Skip asked.

"I don't know. I'm going to Pennsylvania, so it may be late afternoon before I get back."

Skip gave her the cocked head questioning look again, but client confidentiality meant she couldn't give him much of an explanation. "I'm doing an *in vivo* intervention, helping a client face his fears."

"How are you getting there?"

"I'm driving us up there."

"This guy safe to travel with alone?"

Kate had given that some thought after Pete had left her office. She trusted Rob's judgement of the man's character, and her sense of him was that he was harmless. "Yes, I don't think he's capable of hurting a fly."

~~~~~~~~~

The audio book of Janet Evanovich's latest Stephanie Plum romp turned out to be an excellent choice. Kate had figured it would be rather awkward trying to make conversation for over three hours each way in the car. And silence would be even more so. But Pete Jamieson actually laughed out loud a few times at the antics of New Jersey's bounty hunter *extraordinaire* and her sidekick, Lula.

The book was just past the halfway point when Kate turned into the entrance for the Fernville Cemetery in Columbia County, Pennsylvania. She turned the CD player off.

"I thought we were going to see the girl's uncle?" Pete said.

"We are."

Kate pulled her Prius up behind a dark green SUV parked along the cemetery road. She got out of the car and waited for Pete to climb out. Then she headed up the sloping hill in front of them, huddling into her jacket as the cold February wind gusted around her. At the top of the incline stood a middle-aged man, wearing a navy pea jacket.

Pete stopped when they were close enough to read the words

on the small marble headstone at the man's feet. *Kerrie Ann Phillips, beloved daughter, niece, granddaughter, b. December 2, 1996, d. September 11, 2001.*

Kate stepped forward. "Mr. Blake." She held out her hand. "I'm Kate Huntington. Thank you for doing this."

"Thank *you*, ma'am," the man said as he shook her hand.

Kate turned back toward Pete. "This is David Blake, Kerrie's uncle. Mr. Blake, Peter Jamieson, the man who tried to save your niece."

"Mr. Jamieson, I can't tell you how grateful I am," Blake said. "Thank you, sir, for returning Kerrie to us."

Pete stared at him, his mouth open. The unsaid words *but I didn't save her* hung in the air.

"My sister and her husband, their bodies were never recovered. We had nothin' to bury, my parents and me. It killed my dad. He died of a heart attack a month after 9/11. And my mom only lived another year after that. They said it was ovarian cancer, the silent killer the docs said, 'cause it don't hurt much 'til it's too late. But I say she died of a broken heart." The man's voice choked on a stifled sob. "At least we had Kerrie. At least we could lay her to rest."

He held out his hand. Pete stepped forward to take it.

Kerrie's uncle pulled Pete toward him and broke down in sobs as he pounded his other hand on the firefighter's back. Pete awkwardly put an arm around the man. He looked at Kate over Mr. Blake's shaking shoulder, and nodded.

Kate decided this was the best client "session" she'd had in weeks.

~~~~~~~~

Kate shook her head, trying to dislodge the cobwebs so she could focus on her aikido *sensei's* words. Not an easy task at seven in the morning on too few hours of sleep.

She'd been tired yesterday after her long day on Saturday, but also elated by the outcome of her experimental technique. Pete had talked for almost two hours on the way home, then he'd fallen asleep. They never had finished listening to Stephanie Plum's exploits.

She'd gone to bed early last night and had fallen asleep instantly. Then at two in the morning, one of those damned dreams had yanked her awake.

She'd had a reprieve for the last several months and had hoped the dreams were gone for good. But apparently not. This one was the vaguest of them—someone carrying her over his shoulder in the dark.

Something she didn't actually remember since she'd been unconscious for that part of the ordeal. Even though she'd only been taking aikido for six months at that time, what she'd already learned had been helpful in thwarting the plans of those who had kidnapped her and Skip.

She'd found that quite empowering, and since then she'd increased her classes to at least three mornings a week. She liked the defensive nature of aikido, sometimes referred to as the gentle martial art. You used your opponent's energy and momentum against them. They come at you and you dip your shoulder just so. They fly right over your back. The students didn't fight *per se* but rather took turns practicing the defensive moves until they were second nature.

In addition to the sense of empowerment, Kate's muscles were toned like they hadn't been in years. A nice serendipity that made her feel more on an even plane with her muscular hunk of a husband.

As her body went through the warm-up exercises on autopilot, her thoughts shifted to Pete Jamieson. She wasn't sure what to do for an encore. Maybe she should call today to check on him? She decided to leave it alone, just wait until his session on Thursday to see how he's doing.

The class had moved on to practice rolling properly when their opponents flipped them. Time to pay attention or she would be bruised tomorrow from landing wrong.

~~~~~~~~~

Pete Jamison knew he shouldn't be here. He could imagine what his NA sponsor would say, had said more than once. *Boy, ya gotta stay away from them slippery places. The folks ya use ta call your friends, they ain't your friends no more.*

But he had to try one more time. He walked down the street toward the apartment building, two blocks over from Baltimore Street and the notorious red light district known as The Block.

This is an eleventh step, Pete told his sponsor in his head.

He and Jimmy Matthews had been best friends since their freshman year of high school, drawn together by their shared interest in law enforcement and firefighting. They'd spent many hours in their adolescence debating the respective virtues of the two careers.

But Jimmy had ended up on the wrong side of the law. It had started as normal college drinking and partying, and had escalated from there.

Pete had gone out of state to study firefighting in Connecticut. He hadn't realized how far his friend had sunk until his return to Maryland after graduation. He came home to discover that Jimmy had started dealing to support his own habit.

Pete had made several attempts to convince Jimmy to get his act together. Finally he'd decided his friend had slipped beyond redemption.

A decade later, Pete discovered that redemption wasn't as easy to achieve as he'd assumed. Desperate to sleep without nightmares and get through the day without the flashbacks, Pete had found himself talking again to his old buddy. He had become one of Jimmy's customers.

Pete knew his efforts today would probably be futile, but he had to try. He hunched his shoulders inside his coat and reminded himself to breathe through his mouth as he entered the dingy lobby. As usual, it stank of decay, stale sweat and urine. He climbed dimly-lit stairs to the third floor.

Jimmy's face broke into a huge grin when he opened his door. "Hey, man, wha's up?"

"Hey. Gotta minute?"

"For you, always, my man." Jimmy turned back into his apartment. He spread his arms expansively, then staggered a bit to one side. "*Me casa es su casa.*" His words were slurred.

Pete's heart sank into his stomach. "Sampling the merchandise, is that good for business?" He tried to keep his voice light as he closed the apartment door behind him.

"It's what you call *quality control*, man. Gotta check it out now and then, make sure it's good shit."

Pete wasn't sure what to say or do. Why the hell had he assumed his friend would be sane and sober when he happened to come calling?

"Hey, Petey, lemme show you somethin'." Jimmy shuffled over to a table beside a battered sofa. "Got me a new piece." He turned back around.

In his hand was the biggest pistol Pete had ever seen.

"Big mutha fucker, ain't it?" Jimmy slurred, waving the .44 Magnum around. "Got me a few new enemies, since I been pimpin' girls. Bet this little baby'll make 'em think twice."

Pete fought the urge to dive behind the sofa. This had been a very bad idea indeed. His mind scrambled for a game plan.

"Hey, Jimmy, let me have the gun. I wanna take a closer look."

Jimmy waved the gun vaguely in his direction again. Pete cringed. He grabbed for the barrel and Jimmy let him take the gun out of his hand.

Pete transferred the gun to his other hand and made a show of examining it. There didn't seem to be a safety. He thought about removing the bullets but decided Jimmy wasn't quite that out of it. He probably wouldn't get away with dismantling the gun.

"Nice piece." Pete laid it down and put himself between Jimmy and the table. "Come on, let's take a walk. Talk about old times." Jimmy started to reach around him for the gun. "You don't need that cannon today, man. I've got your back."

"You sure, man?" Jimmy swayed on his feet.

"I'm sure." He was braced to get the hell out of there if Jimmy insisted on taking the .44 along. When his friend turned and staggered toward the door, Pete let out a pent-up breath.

CHAPTER THREE

The house line rang at eight-ten on Tuesday morning.

What the...? Who's calling this early?

Kate picked up the portable phone from its charger on the kitchen counter. She recognized Rob's cell number on the caller ID. "Hey there. What are you up to this early in the morning?"

"I'm at the county jail," Rob's voice sounded grim. "Pete Jamieson's been arrested."

Kate shook her head. Had she heard him right? "Pete's been arrested? For drugs?" She glanced over at the big oak table, where the children were chatting with Maria while eating their breakfast cereal.

She missed part of Rob's next comment as she headed around the corner into the living room. "Wait a minute. What did you just say?"

"Not for drugs. For first-degree murder."

"Say what?"

"He's been charged with killing his former drug dealer. And he's not in good shape. Is there any way you can get down to the jail and see him today?"

Kate perched on the edge of an armchair and tried to wrap her brain around what she was hearing. "Did he do it?"

"From what I can tell, probably not," Rob said. "The guy was also a friend of his. He was trying to talk him into cleaning up his act. Says the man was still very much alive when he left him."

Kate did a quick mental review of her schedule for the day. "I don't think I have anybody right after lunch. I'll have to double-check but I should have at least a semi-decent window to go down midday."

"I've gotta go to the office for a couple client meetings. I'll be back here by twelve-thirty. The bail hearing's at one. It would help if you were there for that, if you can make it."

"Are we likely to be done by one forty-five?"

"Yeah, probably by one-thirty. Bail hearings tend to be quick and merciless."

"Tell Pete I'll be there by twelve-fifteen, and I'll stay for the bail hearing."

~~~~~~~~

Pete was an only child. His working class, widowed father had moved to a trailer park in Florida. The assistant prosecutor contended that Peter Jamieson had very little tying him to the Baltimore area. He was a flight risk. She requested bail be set at a million dollars.

Rob stepped forward. "Your Honor, that's a ridiculous amount." The judge arched an eyebrow at him. Rob continued undeterred, "Mr. Jamieson has no history of violence. He's only had one prior arrest for drug possession. He's in therapy." Rob gestured toward Kate. "And he's been clean for eight months. He's currently on medical leave from the Baltimore County fire department. He values his career very much and is not about to jeopardize it by jumping bail for a crime he did not commit."

The judge looked at the assistant prosecutor. "Do you have Mr. Jamieson's record, Ms. Gerard? And by the way, where is Mr. Fitzsimmons today?"

"He uh, had a previous commitment related to another case," the young attorney stammered. She located the relevant paper in her briefcase and handed it to the judge.

"I'd also like to point out, Your Honor," Rob said, "that Mr. Jamieson's drug use was directly related to the post-traumatic stress syndrome he's experiencing as a result of his heroic efforts as a first responder on 9/11."

Kate felt Pete squirm beside her. She put a restraining hand on his arm.

"Mrs. Huntington is Mr. Jamieson's therapist," Rob said.

The judge glanced up from the single sheet of paper in front of him. He looked her way but didn't ask her any questions.

"Bail is set at $250,000." The judge brought the gavel down.

Kate and Rob were granted a short meeting with their client before he would be taken back to his cell. While Rob told Pete what would come next in his case, Kate was mulling over another issue. A bail bondsman would require a ten percent fee. Even she couldn't afford $25,000, but maybe she could raise it. Although she had no clue how she would do that.

When she mentioned the possibility, Pete shook his head. "I can handle being in jail. I was about to be evicted anyway. This way at least I've got a roof over my head and three meals a day."

Rob scribbled something on a sheet of paper and slid it across the table, then handed Pete his pen. "That gives me permission to enter your apartment and remove your belongings. I'll put them in storage."

"I can't afford storage."

"I've got an old garage behind my house," Kate said. "We'll put your stuff in there."

Relief on his face, Pete nodded. "Thank you."

Walking down the steps in front of the Towson courthouse, Rob put a big hand gently on Kate's shoulder. "Now who's losing their perspective?"

"Yeah, about that. Sorry I gave you a hard time. Now that I've met Pete... If anybody deserves a break from the system, it's him."

Rob shook his head. "The breaks don't seem to be in his favor here. There's no way you can raise twenty-five grand, and the bail bondsman's going to want collateral for the rest."

"I know. It's a long shot, but I've got to try. I'm scared to death what several months in jail is likely to do to him."

They had reached the sidewalk. "I'll walk you to the your car," Rob said. After a couple minutes of silence, he glanced over at Kate. "I think I want to hire Skip's agency to look into this."

She stopped walking and blinked at him. Anxiety fluttered in her chest.

"I got Pete to sign a waiver of confidentiality so we can fill him in." Rob took her hand and looked down at her, concern in his eyes. "But I won't ask Skip if you don't want me to."

Kate sighed. She appreciated that he'd asked her first but she couldn't begin to sort out how she felt about the idea. She squeezed his hand, then let it go. "I'll talk to him about it after dinner and call you. But I can't let you pay for it by yourself. *If* we decide he's going to take the case, that is."

"We'll split it," Rob said.

Kate gave him a half smile. It was the tactic she used on him to let her pay her share when they went to lunch.

~~~~~~~~~

Kate waited until Edie's homework was done and the children were in bed. She sat down on the sofa next to her husband and turned sideways, sitting cross-legged to face him.

The gold flecks in his hazel eyes flashed at her as his mouth spread slowly into one of his easy grins. She couldn't begin to imagine life without him. Her chest hurt at the thought. She reached up and brushed an unruly lock of hair back off his forehead. Her fingertips grazed his skin.

Skip's grin softened into a dreamy smile. He captured her hand and kissed her palm.

Kate stifled a small gasp. Trying to ignore the tingling sensations that gentle touch of his lips had elicited, she wrapped both of her hands around his. "I need to talk to you about a client."

She almost laughed out loud at the expression on his face as he struggled to shift gears from seduction to shop talk.

She gave him the background on Peter Jamieson, then moved on to that day's events. "He and the guy he's accused of killing, they were seen arguing on the street downtown yesterday afternoon. Rob wants to hire you to investigate."

"How do you know he didn't do it?" Skip asked.

"Can we come back to that in a minute. I'm not at all sure I want you to get involved in this case. The street they were on was two blocks from *The* Block and the murder victim was a drug dealer and a pimp. This is not in the same league as your normal cases. As much as I want to help Pete, I'm scared to death at the thought of you poking into this."

Skip pulled his hands loose from hers and gently took her by the shoulders. "Kate, I thought we'd gotten past this."

She had thought so too. Last year they'd stumbled into an international assassination plot and had spent a week running for their lives. The experience had forced them both to face their fears about losing each other.

"That was a bit different," she said. "We didn't have any choice about whether or not we were in danger. But this time—"

"Kate, this is what I *do*. It's not usually dangerous but sometimes it is. That's why I carry a gun. You were the one who told me years ago, on our first date that you refused to call a date," he gave her a small smile, "that you try not to let fear dictate what you do. That's true for yourself, but you don't always apply that when it comes to those you love."

Damn! He'd backed her into a corner with her own words. "Okay, that's playing a bit dirty, don't you think?" But she couldn't quite keep the corners of her mouth from curling upward.

"Look, darlin', why don't we talk about the case some more, and let me see if I even think I can help. Then we'll decide from there. So what makes you so sure this guy is innocent? You said you've only been working with him for a little over a week, and you know drug addicts are notorious liars."

That gave her pause for a moment. Was she being naive? She shook her head. "He's not your typical drug addict. And yeah, I've only worked with him a short time, but it's been pretty intense. He's the client I went to Pennsylvania with on Saturday. We met the uncle of a little girl Pete wasn't able to save, and then had a marathon therapy session in the car on the way home. Pete was finally starting to put things in perspective."

"So why was he downtown buying drugs yesterday?"

"He wasn't. The drug dealer was a friend of his, from high school. Pete was trying to get him to go to an NA meeting with him. In the twelve-step groups, it's the eleventh step, to try to help other addicts get into recovery. But the guy was high, waving his gun around. Pete managed to get it away from him. That's how his prints got on it."

"What was the fight on the street about?"

"Pete was trying to convince Jimmy to get his life back on track. Jimmy was yelling at him that his life was just fine, thank you very much. He had money and women, what else could he want. Pete grabbed him by the shoulders and shook him, and started yelling back. Then he realized it was all futile and walked away."

"And you're convinced this guy is on the up and up?" Skip asked again.

"Yes, I think he is, and I think you'll be convinced too, once you meet him."

"So you're okay with me taking the case?"

Kate blew out air. "I didn't say that." She looked down at her hands in her lap. "What would you do if you did take it?"

Skip took one of her hands in his. "First thing would be to talk to the police and find out what they've got on your boy. See if I can poke any holes in their case big enough to get them to rethink the whole thing. If that doesn't work, then we'd go looking for who the real killer might be."

Her stomach clenched. "Which is the point where you start messing around with some of the slimiest slime in Baltimore."

"True, but I would do so with the utmost care. Kate, I know what I'm doing. Have you ever known me to be reckless?" There was a touch of annoyance in his voice now.

Uh, oh! She backpedaled. "Of course you know what you're doing. You're excellent at what you do, which is why you and Rose have been so successful. But these are very dangerous people you'd be dealing with."

"Let's take it one step at a time, shall we? I'll have Dolph find out what detective caught the case and we'll have a little chat with him."

"Rob's going to pay for the agency's services." Kate decided not to mention she was covering half from Eddie's insurance money.

Skip looked at her and shook his head. "I'm not taking money from either one of you for this."

She grinned sheepishly.

Skip unfolded his six-five frame from the sofa, then pulled her to a stand. "I don't know 'bout you, darlin'." A bit of his native Texas had crept into his voice. "But I'm kinda depressed after all this talk of drug dealers and 9/11 heroes gettin' shafted. And you know what the best antidepressant is, don't you?" He tucked a stray curl behind her ear, then leaned down and whispered, "Great sex."

Kate smacked him lightly on his arm. But she wasn't about to disagree with him. She'd been married to this man for six years and he could still turn her knees to jelly just by kissing her palm, or nibbling her earlobe as he was doing now.

He wrapped strong arms around her. She relaxed against him with a sigh. His lips trailed across her cheek and found her mouth.

When they ran out of air, Skip swept her up in his arms and carried her into the bedroom. Once there, he put her on her feet so she could go into the bathroom to wash her face and brush her teeth. She smiled at the blend of hot lovers and old married couple they had become.

When she came out of the bathroom, he was lying in bed, covers pulled up to his waist, one arm up behind his head. She paused for a moment to admire the broad expanse of his muscular chest. Shedding her clothes and tossing them in the general direction of the hamper, she slipped between the sheets and snuggled against him. She lay her cheek on his bare shoulder and slid her hand across his abdomen.

He sucked in his breath.

She dug her fingers into the ticklish spot just above his hip.

He squirmed. "Woman, you do know how to kill a mood."

"Oh, I think we can recapture it," she whispered as her hand slid lower.

His eyes went wide.

~~~~~~~~

On Wednesday, Kate cancelled her weekly lunch with Rob

so she could go to see her priest.

Elaine Johnson came out of her office to greet Kate. In her steel gray suit, with black clerical shirt and white priest's collar, she was a formidable-looking woman. Her chocolate brown face broke into a wide smile. "To what do I owe this mid-week pleasure?"

"I have a request."

Once settled in Elaine's office, Kate gave her the bare bones of the story. Cognizant of client confidentiality, she stuck to the facts that were public knowledge, filling in as needed with vague generalizations. Peter Jamieson was a client of her lawyer friend. She couldn't admit that he was her client as well, but she knew Elaine would figure that out. Pete was a 9/11 hero. His life had been rough lately, and now he was being accused of a murder he didn't commit and he couldn't afford bail.

"A bail bondsman charges ten percent. I wanted to try to somehow raise the money. Would you be willing to let me ask the parishioners for donations?"

Elaine sat back in her chair and watched Kate's face for a moment. "Would you mind if I went to visit this young man?"

"I wouldn't, but I'm not sure how he would feel about it. I'm going there this afternoon. Let me ask him if that would be okay. And by the way, he didn't ask me to do this. When I suggested it, he said not to bother, that he'd be okay in jail."

"But you're not so sure he will be," Elaine said.

"No, I'm not."

~~~~~~~~~

When 'Dolph' Randolph entered the homicide bullpen and headed her way, Judith Anderson started to smile. The smile turned to a grimace when she saw the tall man following in his wake.

Dolph lowered his butt, which was a little broader than it had been when he was a homicide detective, into her visitor's chair. Gray now dominated the rust in her former partner's hair and it had completely taken over his bushy moustache and eyebrows. As usual, his white dress shirt and dark slacks were rumpled.

"Why such a grim look, partner?" Dolph's tone was teasing.

She scowled at him. He knew perfectly well why she was less than happy. "To what do I owe this pleasure?" She was ignoring Skip Canfield, who was now perched on the far corner of her desk.

"You caught the Matthews' homicide, I hear."

She narrowed her eyes at him. "Yeah."

"Nice when you can get a case closed that quick and easy."

Judith shrugged. It happened often enough. Most criminals were dumb as rocks.

She glanced up at Canfield. He looked like he was trying not to loom over her, but in the close quarters, it was hard for a guy his size to pull that off. "For Pete's sake, Canfield. Grab another chair."

He did as instructed, straddling the chair backwards, his arms crossed on the back. "Actually, that's why we're here. For Pete's sake." He didn't crack a smile, which told her he knew the joke was lame.

"We've been hired by Mr. Jamieson's defense attorney," Dolph said. "Of course, you could make him wait until he's filed all the proper papers, but it would be helpful if you'd let me take a peek at your case file, for old times' sake."

"No can do. The investigation is not complete yet."

"Does that mean you're considering other suspects?" Canfield asked.

"No... We have our man." Even she heard the lack of conviction in her voice.

Canfield looked her in the eye for a long moment. He broke contact just before it became a full-blown staring contest.

"You've got an arrest," he said in a low voice. "But you're not happy with it, are you?"

"Did you know the boy was a 9/11 first responder?" Dolph asked. "Saved a bunch of lives that day."

"Yeah, well, that doesn't give him license to take a life."

"And you're sure he did that, killed his friend?" Canfield said.

"Killed his drug dealer. We've only got his word for it that they were ever friends."

"Jamieson says they went to high school together. Easiest thing in the world to check out the school records."

"Doesn't prove they were friends. That's just where they met."

Canfield was staring at her again. Judith let her gaze drop to her desk, and the file she had been going over, again, when they had made their entrance. The Matthews' file. She was debating whether to take it with her. No need really. She practically had the damn thing memorized.

She suddenly stood up, startling the two men. Tall and thin, she was now looming over them. Tucking her white shirt more firmly into the waist of her slim black slacks, she grabbed the matching black jacket from the back of her chair. She ran fingers through her short cap of hair and then glanced at her watch.

Sliding the file into her desk drawer, she said, "I haven't had lunch yet. You're treating." Without looking back, Judith strode across the bullpen for the door.

~~~~~~~~~

Once on the sidewalk, Skip asked, "What's your preference, Detective?"

"Your friend's place is fine. I'll meet you there."

As she walked briskly away from them, Skip said in a low voice, "Does she ever wear anything but black and white?"

Dolph thought for a moment. "Nope. Came to a cookout at our house once. Black T-shirt, white shorts."

Once they had all settled into a booth along the back wall of Mac's Place and had ordered food, Skip said, "I never got a chance to thank you properly for bringing in the cavalry last year."

"Just doing my job," Judith said curtly.

"Ah, cut the crap, Judith." Dolph's voice was sharp. "If Skip had turned himself in like you wanted him to, we wouldn't be sitting here now, 'cause he'd be dead."

Skip and Judith both stared at him for a beat. Then Judith blew out her breath and turned to Skip. "Sorry. I guess me looking incompetent was a better outcome than you dead."

"I'm definitely partial to not being dead," Skip said.

Dolph pursed his lips. His tone mild again, he said, "So what's the deal on the Matthews' case?"

Judith leaned forward and kept her voice low. "I've got a case against your boy. Means, opportunity and motive."

When she didn't continue, Skip said, "But you're not happy."

"I'm not, but the State Attorney's office and my lieutenant are, so case closed."

Skip cocked his head at her. "Thought you said it was still open."

"Technically it is. I've been told to gather more evidence against Jamieson."

"By doing what?" Dolph asked.

"Interview some of the people who went to high school with them. Subpoena his counselors' records. Try to find a history of violence or poor anger management. Am I going to find one?"

"From what I understand, probably not," Skip said. "What exactly's giving you a bad feeling about this, Judith?"

"Another suspect who's got a lot better motive, but his prints aren't on the gun, and Jamieson's are, along with Matthews' own, and lots of smudges."

"How clear are Jamieson's prints?" Dolph asked.

"Three clear. Two partials a bit smudged."

Dolph winced.

"Yeah, but they're not—" Judith stopped talking as the waitress appeared with their sandwiches.

"They're not what?" Skip asked, once she was gone.

"Where you'd expect them to be. Two of the clear ones are left thumb and index finger on the barrel. The other one is right thumb, under the butt. Consistent with handling the gun, which is what your boy claims happened, but not with gripping it to fire."

"Rob's going to have fun with that," Skip said.

"Who's the ASA on the case?" Dolph asked.

"Fitzsimmons."

Dolph shook his head.

"Is that good or bad?" Skip asked.

"Depends on which side you're on," Dolph said. "Good for us, bad for Judith."

Skip waited until she'd swallowed the bite of tuna on rye she'd just taken. He didn't want her to choke when he delivered the bad news. "I've seen Rob Franklin in action. He's gonna blow your case out of the water."

"Already figured that out, big boy," Judith said. "That's why I'm talking to you. Of course if anybody asks, this was just a social get-together."

"Who's the other suspect?" Dolph asked.

"Frederico Gonzales, goes by just Frederico on the streets. Matthews' competitor. Except Freddie boy was there first. Matthews was the interloper, and we all know how well drug dealers and pimps like that. Frederico probably would have left him alone if he'd stuck to drugs, 'cause he made most of his sales outside the neighborhood, to old friends and acquaintances like Jamieson. But Matthews decided pimping would be fun too. Then he was definitely stepping on Freddie's toes."

"How long had Matthews been into prostitution?" Skip asked.

"A few months. He didn't pilfer any of Freddie's girls. That would have gotten him dead a lot sooner. Vice guys say he hung out at the Greyhound station and recruited the newbies coming into town. Offered them food and shelter, help getting started in a new town."

Dolph snorted. "Mr. Benevolence."

"His girls actually spoke well of him. Said he treated them okay, and none of them were new to the trade, just to Baltimore. Except one girl, who looked about twelve, but her Wisconsin driver's license says she's eighteen. This is her first gig, according to her. She says Matthews didn't pressure her though. Apparently he was about to expand his business ventures further, into the world of porn movies, and she was going to be his star."

Skip grimaced at the thought of the perverts who would buy such movies. "What's Frederico's story?"

"Mother was Hispanic, a prostitute. He came out of the oven a lot browner than her, with nappy hair, so the assumption is that his father was black. Mother died of an overdose when he was five. He ended up a ward of the state, raised in a series of foster homes, most of them black families. Disappeared onto the streets when he was fourteen. Clawed his way to the top of the heap in his slimy little corner of the world about five years ago."

"How old is he now?"

"Twenty-six. He's alibied, by the way, for the TOD time frame. For what it's worth, his homies swear he was with them all afternoon and evening, at his place."

"Why would Matthews try to horn in on the territory of an established dealer and pimp?" Skip said.

"Wait until you meet Frederico. He's a caricature of a pimp, and he's got identity issues. Pretends he's one hundred percent Hispanic, which he obviously isn't. My buddy on the City Vice squad says people tend to underestimate him, not take him seriously, which is a big mistake."

While Skip and Dolph mulled over what she had told them, Judith finished off the last of her sandwich and signaled the waitress. She ordered dessert.

"Where do you put all those calories?" Skip teased.

"Good metabolism, and lots of exercise kicking ass," she retorted.

"Wait a minute," Dolph said. "How'd you catch the case if Matthews was in the city?"

"Body was found on the grounds of Jamieson's apartment building here in Towson. A sizeable bag of cocaine was in his pockets. Gun was thrown in the bushes. That's why Fitzsimmons and my lieu aren't buying Frederico as a suspect. They figure he'd never leave that much dope and a good gun behind."

"Shit," Skip said.

Dolph just nodded. "You got anything else?"

"A little trace evidence. Matthew's hair in your boy's apartment."

"Which doesn't mean much if they were friends," Skip pointed out.

Judith shrugged as she dug into her pie.

"Autopsy?" Dolph asked.

Judith swallowed. "M.E.'s doing it this afternoon."

After paying the tab, they parted company with Judith outside Mac's Place.

"We going downtown to talk to this Frederico punk?" Dolph asked.

"Not yet. I'm going to talk to Jamieson, then touch base with Kate. If she's too spooked about the danger, I'm not gonna push it. I'm doing this as a favor for her and Rob."

CHAPTER FOUR

After handing over her psychotherapist's license, ID and car keys–the only things she had brought into the building–Kate was admitted into the Towson jail's visiting area. It was after regular visiting hours but she had referred the guard on the front window to the judge's order, arranged by Rob, that allowed her to meet with her client outside those times.

Her guard escort left her in a small room, dominated by a large metal table and several chairs, all bolted to the floor. A few minutes later, Pete was brought in, his hands and legs shackled. The guard attached the leg shackles to a ring in the floor beside one of the chairs and gestured for Pete to sit down.

"Please remove the chains from his hands," Kate said.

"You his attorney?" the guard asked.

"No." She looked at Pete. He inclined his head in a slight nod. "I'm his therapist. Remove the shackles."

The guard still looked resistant. "He's accused of murder, lady."

Kate narrowed her eyes at him.

He produced the key and removed the shackles from Pete's wrists. "We're watchin' you, bub. No sudden moves."

Kate resisted making a snarky remark. There was no point taking her frustration with the legal system out on the guard. He was just doing his job.

The door slammed shut with a clang. "How are you holding up?" she asked.

Pete shrugged his shoulders. The too-big orange jumpsuit barely moved. No doubt as a firefighter he had once been muscular but drugs and inactivity had shrunk his frame. He looked almost frail, his face haggard and pale.

"There's a lot of testosterone in the air around here," Kate said after a moment.

"I can handle it. I hang out with firefighters and cops, remember?"

"Did you get any sleep last night?"

He shook his head.

She let the silence hang for a moment, then said, "Pete, you don't have to worry about my feminine sensibilities. I'm a trauma recovery specialist. I've heard it all. If anything happens in here, that you need or want to talk about, *I* can handle it." She intentionally reflected his words back to him.

"Kate, nothing happened *because* I didn't sleep. I'm an addict. I've been in jail before."

She paused for a moment. "Okay, can you let down your guard now so we can talk about how to cope with all this emotionally?"

He sighed. For the first time since he'd entered the room, she saw a hint of life in his hollow eyes. "Yeah, give me a minute to shift gears."

Kate gave him a small smile. "Pete, I'm still trying to get to know you. So let me put something out there and you tell me if I'm wrong. You kind of remind me of a turtle. Not because you're slow, quite the opposite. My sense is that you're a gentle soul, but you can retract into a hard shell when you need to, and that shell protects you."

After a couple of seconds, Pete nodded. "That's about right."

"I believe you when you say you can handle it," Kate said. "But it could be months before your case goes to trial. That's a long time to have to stay inside that shell."

Pete nodded again without saying anything.

Afraid the guards would come back, Kate jumped to the crucial issue. She'd come back to how he was coping if there was time. "I am going to try to raise the funds to get you out on bail." She paused. When he didn't object, she continued, "I've asked the priest at my church if I can ask for donations from my fellow parishioners. In my opinion, if anybody's a worthy cause, you are. She wants to meet with you before she'll agree to that."

Pete looked away from her. He stared at the side wall of the room.

"I'll tell her not to come if you're not comfortable with it. I'm not trying to evangelize here, and neither is she. I'm just looking for a way to get you out of jail."

His eyes cut back to her. "A female priest?"

"Episcopal."

A slight nod. After a beat, he said, "I was raised Catholic."

Kate knew what that phrase implied. He hadn't said that he *was* Catholic.

"So was I," she said. "You're not practicing now?"

"No." A pause. "I guess you'd say I lost my faith, after 9/11."

"A lot of people did."

"I'll talk to your priest. But I don't see you raising twenty-five grand by passing the plate on Sunday."

"There are a few deep pockets in the congregation, so we'll see. A bail bondsman will want collateral though. I'm not real sure what to do about that."

"I have a piece of land, in western Maryland, with a trailer on it. I bought it a few years ago, thinking it would be a good investment, and a place to get away in the meantime. It didn't quite work out that way. I've only been there twice. The second time, I left after one night."

Kate intentionally paused, then said, "Too much time alone isn't always a good thing, with PTSD."

Pete nodded. "It's for sale, but the market's dead out there right now."

A key rattled in the door. "Time to go back into my shell," he said, with a small smile.

Kate returned the smile. "Elaine will probably be by tomorrow or the next day. I'll try to get over here tomorrow as well." She stood up as the door swung open.

"Hang in there," she whispered, then walked out of the room. Pete didn't need a witness to the humiliation of being locked back into those shackles.

~~~~~~~~

When she stepped through the outer door of the sally port that separated the jail itself from its lobby, Skip was standing at the guard's window.

"I don't care if you're the king of Persia, mister," the guard was saying. "No more visitors tonight." As Kate walked toward the window, he put her license and keys into the tray in front of him and hit a button. The tray pushed past the metal plate covering the small opening at the bottom of the window.

Kate retrieved the items and the tray retracted. "I can vouch for this man. He does work for my client's lawyer."

The guard shook his head. "Sorry, ma'am. They'll be taking the prisoners into the dining hall soon for dinner. No one's allowed in or out while they're out of their cells."

Skip cocked his head and gave a half shrug. Kate knew the gesture well. It meant the issue wasn't worth fighting over. "Makes sense," he said. "I'll come back tomorrow."

"It's better if you get something in writing from the lawyer," the guard said.

"Will do. Have a good evening, officer."

Skip walked Kate to her car, parked on a nearby side street. "I got lots to tell you when we get home."

"Me, too," she said, standing on tiptoe to peck him on the cheek. "See you in a few minutes."

Once at home, Kate checked on Billy, who was playing with his matchbox cars in his room. Then she stuck her head in the kitchen doorway. Waiting for Edie to take a breath in her monologue about her day, Kate said to Maria, "Skip and I need to confer about a mutual case for a few minutes." To Edie, she added, "Help Maria set the table, okay?"

"Sure, Mommy," the little girl said, then picked up where she'd left off. "Susie's really mean to Jill and I don't think it's fair..."

Kate shook her head as she headed for the living room. That was her Edie, the little diplomat. She'd probably end up

Ambassador to China someday.

She and Skip settled on the sofa. They gave each other a synopsis of what they'd found out that day. Then Skip said, "Next step, after I meet with Jamieson tomorrow, is to have a chat with this Frederico guy." He was watching her face, his own expression neutral. He lifted his eyebrows, the unspoken message, *It's up to you.*

Confronting a pimp and drug dealer in downtown Baltimore– this was what she'd been afraid of. But surprisingly her reaction wasn't as intense as she'd expected it to be. Worry gnawed at her stomach and made her heart beat faster, but it was not much worse than the worry she carried around every day until Skip was safely home each evening. Would the day ever come when she'd be able to stop worrying?

She let out a small sigh. *Yeah, when he's retired.*

"I'll take plenty of back-up," Skip said. "This guy's not going to mess with us. He's got too much to lose. If he goes to jail for an assault beef, somebody'll move in on his turf while he's gone."

Kate snorted. "Those guys are shooting and knifing each other all the time. Don't you listen to the news? They might as well rename Baltimore *Murder City*."

"Going after another pimp or drug dealer is one thing. Messing with a bunch of middle-class white boys from the suburbs is something else. I'll make it clear from the get-go that the police know we're there and why."

She let out another sigh, then nodded. "We'll call Rob and fill him in after dinner."

~~~~~~~

Skip spent the first part of the morning tying up loose ends for a couple other cases. Then he headed for the Towson jail, faxed letter from Rob in hand. At a little before eleven, he and Peter Jamieson were facing each other across a metal table. He had not asked the guards to remove the hand shackles.

The guy didn't look so hot. Skip was still debating between the I'm-your-buddy or the hard-ass, ex-cop approach, when Jamieson said in a flat voice, "I know you've got no reason to believe me, except Kate's and Rob's say-so that I'm a good guy."

Okay, he'd let Jamieson set the tone. He kept his own voice neutral. "Actually those two people's opinions weigh pretty heavily with me. Tell me what happened Monday."

Pete told him the story of going to visit his friend, and the argument on the street corner when his frustration had gotten the better of him.

When he'd finished, Skip asked, "How'd you get downtown?"

"Bus. Car got repossessed last month. Couldn't keep up the payments on disability."

"The body was found outside your building. Was Matthews coming to see you?"

Pete shrugged. "He must've been, but I wasn't expecting him."

"Cops tell you he had a bag of cocaine in his pocket?"

Jamieson's face registered mild surprise. "No, but that would explain why they kept implying that I'd panicked and run away. And by the way, I never used cocaine, just weed and pills. Mostly pills."

"When and where'd they pick you up?"

"Walking on York Road around two-thirty in the morning, a couple miles from my place."

"What were you doing there?"

"It's what I do, when I can't sleep. Can't drink, can't take pills, so I walk until I'm exhausted."

Skip took a small notepad out of his shirt pocket and jotted down a few things. "What time frame did they say, when they asked about an alibi?"

Pete looked at the ceiling for a moment. "I think it was four or four-thirty, until ten."

"Did you have an alibi for any of that time?"

Pete shook his head. "Home alone."

"What time did you go for your walk?"

"Two. I wait until the bars are closed."

"Are you an alcoholic?"

Pete hesitated. "Some hard-core NA people would say I was,

but I only used alcohol when I couldn't get my hands on anything else. Booze takes too long."

"Too long for what?"

"To reach a state of oblivion."

~~~~~~~~

As Skip headed for the offices of Canfield and Hernandez to pick up Dolph and Mac, he mentally rehashed the interview with Jamieson. He was inclined to agree with Kate. This guy seemed to be on the up and up.

Once they were headed downtown in his Expedition, he handed Dolph a list of questions. "Call Judith, would ya? See if she's still in a generous mood."

Ten minutes later, Dolph disconnected. "Matthews was last seen alive at four-thirty, by one of his girls. 911 call was at ten-thirty-six. Guy said he'd seen a dead body lying beside a building. Judith went from the scene to track down Matthews' girls. The same one who last saw Matthews alive was one of the witnesses to the argument with Jamieson. BOLO went out around one. Vigilant boys in blue spotted him at two-thirty-two."

"Did she know that Jamieson claims he never used cocaine?"

"Yep. She'd asked him what he used. He said he *used to* use pills and weed. Her buddy in City Vice is Tyrell Cooper. She's calling him to see if he's available to meet with us."

Skip let out a low whistle. "No wonder Judith's not happy about this case. They're enough holes in it to drive a fleet of trucks through."

Mac grunted in agreement from the back seat just as Dolph's phone rang. He listened for a few seconds, then said, "Thanks, sweetheart," and disconnected.

Skip grinned. "You get away with calling Judith *sweetheart*?"

Dolph chuckled. "Only when I'm not in the same room with her. We're in luck. Cooper's waiting for us at his precinct."

"What's the deal on Fitzsimmons? How long's he been in the State Attorney's office?" Skip asked.

Dolph pursed his lips, calculating. "For about three years before I retired, so eight years total. He's got a lot more ambition than brains. His goal is to rack up as many wins as he can in a year, but he always falls short. Mainly 'cause he jumps on cases like this one, thinking they're a slam dunk, when they're not."

"Lemme guess," Mac's gruff voice came out of the backseat. "Always somebody else's fault when he loses a case."

Dolph nodded, his expression grim.

Mac opted to stay with the truck when they arrived at the precinct downtown. "In this neighborhood, won't be much left if there ain't nobody guardin' it."

As they entered the detectives' bullpen, Skip noticed a tall, skinny guy sitting in one of the desk chairs. Café-au-lait skin, scraggly beard, dreadlocks, old T-shirt, baggy jeans. He was lounging back, hands clasped behind his neck, ragged sneakers up on the corner of the desk. *That guy's gonna get his ass kicked when the detective who owns that desk comes back.*

As they wandered among the mostly empty desks, looking at name tags, the guy stood up and approached. "You looking for me?"

Skip wasn't able to completely hide his surprise. The guy smiled. "One of the few perks of working Vice. It's always casual Friday. I'm Tyrell Cooper." He shook first Dolph's and then Skip's hand, then waved toward metal chairs in front of his desk.

Dolph grinned as he sat down. "How'd Judith describe him?" He cocked his head toward Skip.

"Small mountain with a pretty-boy head."

Dolph laughed out loud. Skip gave him a mock scowl. "You undercover?" he asked Cooper. Undercover cops didn't usually hang out at the precinct, in case some no-good from the street was brought in and saw them there.

"No, but it helps to blend in," Cooper said.

"Did Judith fill you in?"

"Not really. Just said you were private. Headed to meet Frederico and wanted some background on him."

Skip and Dolph exchanged a glance. She apparently hadn't told Cooper she was trying to undermine her own case.

"What's your interest in Frederico?" the detective asked.

"Paternity suit," Skip said.

Cooper snorted. "Good luck with that."

"What are we going to find when we get to Frederico's place?" Dolph said quickly, before the detective could ask more questions.

"If you get past the front door, there'll be a half dozen home boys hanging around him, all Hispanic. Frederico's half black, but don't mention that fact if you like living. He'll come across as not all that bright but don't let him fool you. He's got ten times the street smarts of the rest of these bastards, which is why he's king of the hill. Either of you know Spanish?"

"I do," Skip said.

"Don't let on that his accent sucks, and whatever you do, don't speak Spanish back to him."

Skip nodded. "How risky is it, going into this guy's crib?"

"Don't go to his apartment. He won't be there this time of day. He'll be at Santiago's. It's a hole-in-the-wall Latino café. But to answer your question, he's a lot of bark and not much bite if you're the heat, even private. It's his own people that have reason to fear him. He rules with an iron fist. Just you two?"

"Got another man in the truck."

"He as big as you?"

Skip shook his head. "Nope. On the short side and scraggly-looking. Ex-Green Beret."

"Three's about right," Cooper said. "Any more and Frederico would interpret the crowd as a sign of fear, not strength. You need anything else?"

"Don't think so. Thanks for your help, Detective," Skip stood up and offered his hand.

Cooper stood. "Tyrell," he said, shaking Skip's hand. He held Dolph's for an extra half a beat. "Tell Judith I'm happy to help. Hope you guys can save her bacon."

Skip waited until they were across the bullpen and out the door before saying, in a low voice, "Did she tell him what's going on?"

Dolph shook his head. "Educated guess. Matthews' case has been all over the news last couple a days, along with the info that Jamieson's a 9/11 hero. If this goes to court and he's acquitted..."

He shook his head again, this time in disgust. "That weasel Fitzsimmons'll look for a way to make it Judith's fault, not his."

~~~~~~~~~~

Skip pushed through the door of Santiago's first, Dolph close on his heels. Mac slid in behind them and moved to the right. Skip spotted a dingy curtain over a doorway to a back room. He caught Mac's eye and tilted his head in that direction.

Mac nodded slightly, his gaze now glued to the curtain.

The lighting was poor. Just three of the hanging fixtures had bulbs that worked, casting shadows across the laminated tables and red-vinyl cushioned chairs. Someone, a long time ago, had tried to make the place cheery. But the fake flowers in little vases on the tables were now covered in dust, and the once brightly colored red, orange and yellow striped curtains were gray with grime, the stripes blurred together.

Skip had been in worse dives, but he couldn't remember when.

Two men were standing in the shadows at the back of the room. Another three sat at a table. The one in the middle had to be Frederico. They had half-empty glasses of beer and greasy empty plates in front of them.

A swarthy-skinned old man hurried out of the shadows. "Sorry, *señores.* We are closed," he said in a Spanish accent thickened by anxiety. "All filled up. Private party."

"We're here to talk to the guest of honor," Dolph said. "Detective Cooper suggested we drop in for a visit while we were downtown."

Skip scanned the faces of the men in the room, as best he could in the dim light. Three of them were Hispanic. The fourth guy, standing near the doorway to the backroom, was tall and beefy. He was the only one wearing a suit. Skip couldn't see his face very well. He was swarthy but Skip would bet money he wasn't from Central or South America.

Frederico was tall and lean. He wasn't as flashy as some pimps Skip had known but he dressed the part–a black silk T-shirt over the dark purple pants of a track suit. The purple jacket hung on the back of his chair. Several gold chains adorned his chest and there were three earrings in one ear, two in the other.

His parents' genes hadn't mixed well. A wide flat nose separated chiseled cheekbones on a broad face the color of spicy mustard. His black hair had been straightened but frizzed at the ends.

"I don't recall invitin' no *gringos* to my party," he said, in the bad Spanish accent Tyrell Cooper had warned them about.

Careful to keep any hint of Texas out of his voice, Skip said, "Sorry for the intrusion. We're looking into the Matthews' homicide. Just have a few questions."

"Don't think we got no answers today, white boy," one of the other seated men said.

Frederico shot him a glance. "Ya got badges?" he said to Skip.

The men in the room tensed as Skip reached for his back pocket. He slowed his movements, carefully pulling the leather case containing his P.I. license out and flipping it open. He took a step toward the table and held it out. "We're private."

Another of Frederico's underlings leaned forward and silently mouthed the words on the license. He burst out laughing. "Dis here *hombre* iz *Reginald* William Canfield, de *tird*." His accent was genuine.

Frederico's face broke into a big grin, exposing teeth that had received very little dental care. "Yer shittin' me."

The other guy leaned over and took the license case from Skip's hand. "Nope. He's Reginald, de tird, alright."

Frederico kicked the leg of the only empty chair at the table. It flopped over on its back with a bang. No one flinched.

"You amuse me, Reggie, de turd. Ya got five minutes."

Skip picked up the chair and straddled it backwards. He wanted easy access to the gun at the small of his back, covered by his windbreaker. His hand snaked out and retrieved the license case that Frederico's man had dropped on the table.

Four minutes later, they had nothing, other than confirmation that the man's Spanish accent was indeed fake. It seemed to come and go.

Frederico denied having any interest in Jimmy Matthews'

encroachment on his territory. "He's a minnow. I'm a shark. Why I be worried 'bout him? He's not even worth takin' a bite out of."

"Even when he started collecting girls at the bus station?" Dolph said.

Frederico shrugged. "Long as he kept his hands off a mine, I got no beef wid him. Plenty a johns to go 'round."

Skip pushed a bit. "So it's just a coincidence that Matthews ends up dead a few months after he sets up shop on your turf?"

"Look, I got more important things to do den worry 'bout some white boy, thinks he's hot shit. 'Sides, de girls, dey just a sideline for me."

Skip caught movement out of the corner of his eye. The big guy in the shadows had twitched. Now he was edging toward the backroom doorway.

Might be time to get outta here. Skip stood up slowly. "Thanks for your time."

Mac stayed by the door until Dolph and Skip had gone through it. Then he backed out after them.

"Who the hell was the big guy?" Dolph said, in a low voice, once they were on the sidewalk headed for Skip's Expedition.

"Good question. He sure as hell isn't Hispanic," Skip said.

They were almost to the truck–Skip had already hit the key fob button to unlock it–when they heard a shout. "*Amigos*, look out!"

A barely audible popping sound. Dirt flew up from the patch of scraggly grass next to the sidewalk. Dolph and Skip whirled around, guns drawn. Another pop. A chunk of cement flew up from the sidewalk and bounced off the side of the truck.

Mac was several feet behind them. He crouched down and started running in a zigzag pattern.

Skip raised his gun but he didn't dare try to provide covering fire. In the city, a stray bullet could kill an innocent bystander blocks away. His eyes scanned the dilapidated buildings. *Where the hell's the shooter?*

Another pop.

Mac's eyes grew wide. He pitched forward into Skip's arms.

CHAPTER FIVE

Skip hefted Mac onto his shoulder and ran around the back end of his truck, putting it between them and the shooter.

Dolph had yanked the back door open. Skip laid Mac on the back seat. Dolph now had the front door open and was crouched behind it, prepared to return fire. But there were no more shots.

Skip crawled into the passenger seat, then across to the driver's side. Dolph jumped in after him and slammed the door. The pop of a fourth shot was drowned out by the roar of the engine starting. The bullet ricocheted off the driver's door.

Skip jammed the truck into drive and took off. Dolph scrambled over the console between the seats. He tore at Mac's clothing, trying to find the wound.

A block away, Skip took his eyes off the road just long enough to glance in the rearview mirror. All he saw was the back of Dolph's head. "How is he?"

"Bleedin' like a stuck pig. Find a hospital."

~~~~~~~~~

Kate reached over and took Rose's hand. The younger woman did not resist. That in itself spoke volumes.

They had been sitting on the hard vinyl couch for what seemed like hours. Skip slouched in a nearby chair, his long legs stretched out in front of him, a hand over his eyes. But Kate knew he wasn't asleep.

Dolph was downstairs, in a small room commandeered by the City police to take statements. Skip had already given them his.

Kate tried to think of something reassuring to say to the

woman next to her. But her mind kept wandering. To her parents' backyard in the summertime, she and her siblings and Mac catching fireflies and locking them in mason jars, with holes jabbed in the lids for air. To Sean Reilly's empty bar on Sunday afternoons after church, where they played hide and seek while the adults lingered over their lunch.

She saw in her mind's eye a scrawny kid yelling at her. Mac had talked his parents into buying him sweet potato fries at the Maryland State Fair. He'd never heard of such a thing and he had to try them. He'd yanked two out of the container and stuffed them in his mouth when Kate tried to grab a few as well. The flimsy cardboard container had slipped from his hand, the fries scattered on the ground.

For months, Mac had acted like he hated her guts, calling her a big fat sweet potato–the taunt that had eventually morphed into the endearment *sweet pea*. Then one day she'd fallen off her bike and had almost been hit by a car. Mac had raced out into the road....

The rest of the memory blurred as Rose pulled her hand free and jumped up. A doctor was coming down the hall toward the waiting area. Kate was on her feet and both women raced in his direction. He had stopped at the nurses' station for a whispered consultation.

"Ms. Hernandez," he said, looking past Kate, a grim expression on his face.

How did I get in front of her? She turned back. Rose stood, frozen, three paces behind her. Skip's hands were on his partner's shoulders.

"May I speak to you alone?" the doctor said.

"Is he alive?" Rose whispered.

"Yes."

Rose wobbled. Skip grabbed her arms to hold her up.

Kate realized the doctor wasn't going to say much else in front of them. *Damn HIPAA law!* Out loud she said, through clenched teeth, "What is his condition?" Hospitals would release at least that much information.

"Critical."

Kate's own knees threatened to give out.

Skip turned Rose around and steered her back to the waiting area. He nudged her down onto the couch as the doctor took the seat he had vacated. The doctor looked up at them. "I'm sorry. I know you're worried too," he said softly.

Kate grabbed Skip's arm and tugged him down the hall. The sooner they were out of earshot, the sooner the doctor could tell Rose what was going on.

Skip wrapped his arms around her and buried his face in her hair. She felt his lips moving against her scalp and realized he was praying. She clung to him, too scared to even find the words to pray.

After a few minutes that felt like an hour, the doctor approached them. He nodded in the direction of Rose, still sitting in the waiting area, staring into space. The doctor walked away without saying anything.

Dolph was standing in front of Rose, looking confused. He was juggling four styrofoam cups in his hands. He put the coffees down on a side table and flopped into a chair.

Kate's eyes stung. Her heart was in her throat as she and Skip raced back to the waiting area.

She sat down next to Rose. Skip dropped onto the floor, cross-legged in front of them.

"Is he going to be okay?" Kate asked. The look on Rose's face terrified her.

"He's not sure. Mac..." Rose stopped, cleared her throat. "He lost a lot of blood. Bullet grazed his kidney. Doc said he'd be able to..." She stopped again, looked at the ceiling, blinking hard. "He'll know more in the morning."

Kate fought down the sob that was building in her chest. *He's alive! He's alive!* she repeated to herself. There was still hope.

"Where is he?" Skip asked.

"Still in recovery. Then he'll be in the ICU."

"You want to go there and wait?" Skip's voice was rough with emotion.

Rose shook her head. "Doc said it'll be hours before he's

conscious. Told me to go home and get some rest." She tried to snort, but it came out as a choked sob. "Rest! Not while that bastard's still out there."

Kate glanced at her watch. It was only five-twenty, even though it felt like it should be midnight. Rest was definitely not what Rose needed right now.

Kate stood up. "Let's go down to the cafeteria."

Rose frowned at her. "I'm not hungry."

"Neither am I. But I figured that's as good a place as any to have a war council."

Rose's mouth twitched in an attempt to smile. That's what Kate had dubbed their brain-storming sessions eight years ago, when she and the Franklins, with Mac's help, were trying to track down Eddie's killer. Rose had been a rookie cop back then, assigned as Kate's police protection.

"I'll let the nurses know that's where I'll be."

Kate watched as Rose shuffled away. Blinking back tears, she got out her phone to try Rob again. He'd been in court all afternoon but he should be getting her voicemail messages about now.

~~~~~~~~~

Rob looked across the cafeteria table at the fire in two sets of female eyes, one pair chocolate brown, the other blue. The sight was a little scary, even though that fire wasn't aimed at him. He swallowed hard. How could this happen? Mac was the invincible one. They *never* worried about Mac.

A wave of guilt washed over him. He'd started all this, dragged the others into it. Because he felt bad for Pete Jamieson. Kate was right. He'd lost his perspective. Worse than that. He wasn't sure what he was doing anymore, or why the hell he was doing it.

Liz slipped her hand onto his thigh under the table. He wrapped his own hand around hers and squeezed gently. She squeezed back.

A second wave of guilt, not quite as strong. *Get a grip, Franklin!* Instead of worrying about his own angst he should be trying to help the others decide what to do.

"How do we get this bastard?" Rose said through clenched teeth.

"I don't think any of Frederico's people pulled that trigger," Kate said. She tapped her pen against the small note pad she had pulled out of her purse.

Rob tugged on the pad. She relinquished it and he pulled several blank sheets out of the back of it. Maybe if he took his own notes, he'd be able to focus better.

"I'm inclined to agree, darlin'," Skip said. Dolph nodded.

"Tell us again," Kate said. "Every detail."

Rose growled under her breath.

"Bear with me, Rose. There's something haywire about all this."

"Maybe a couple a somethings," Dolph muttered.

Rob started making a rough diagram of the scene, as Skip and Dolph took turns telling the story again.

~~~~~~~~

They repeated Judith's and Tyrell Cooper's comments about Frederico, then described the man's physical appearance and went through the encounter at the café again.

Kate didn't hear anything that disproved her theory. She sat back in her chair. "I'd bet money that Frederico is dyslexic, or he never learned to read."

"So?" Rose's tone was belligerent.

The others seemed to be digesting that piece of information.

"So we've got a butt-ugly man, who lost his mother at a young age, was raised in foster homes as a black kid, and is now trying to reclaim his Hispanic roots. Plus he can't read. We're talking major insecurity here. Yet he's smart enough to become the alpha wolf in his pack..."

Dumb like a fox, Mac's voice echoed in the back of Kate's head. Her eyes stung. She blinked hard.

"He's done a credible job, he thinks, of convincing you that he's got no motive to kill Jimmy Matthews, and you are leaving. As Detective Cooper pointed out, he's savvy enough to know not to mess with you all, but every minute you're there it's a delicate balance for him. He has to maintain his stature and authority with his men, but he doesn't want a major confrontation with you. So why would he raise your suspicions again by taking pot shots at you?"

"Pot shots?" Rose said angrily.

But Skip was nodding. "Those shots weren't meant to hit us. The first kicked up dirt near our feet. If that guy hadn't yelled, Mac wouldn't have started weaving, to make it harder to hit him. He veered *into* the line of fire."

"Then no more shots until you're all in the truck," Kate said. "And then it hits the door, not the window, which is a pretty good sized target on your truck. And the more logical place for the shooter to aim, if he'd actually wanted to hit you."

"Not that it would've done any good. The glass is bulletproof," Skip reminded her.

She barely nodded, not seeking reassurances this time. Something had shifted inside, she wasn't sure what. Now was not the time to sort it out, however. The detachment normally reserved for therapy sessions had kicked in, but she knew her emotions would break through it eventually. She wanted to make use of the detachment for as long as it lasted.

She tapped her pen on her pad again. "Question number one, who shouted 'watch out'? Question two, who was the shooter and what was his motivation?"

"To scare us off," Skip answered the last part of question two.

"Maybe you were just in the wrong place at the wrong time," Rob said without looking up from his diagram. It happened often enough in Baltimore City. Innocent bystanders got caught in the crossfire of drive-bys and drug deals that went awry.

"Unh-uh," Dolph said, "Gun had a silencer on it. Not the norm in drive-bys. And one or two shots might be strays. Four, unlikely. The guy shouted, '*Amigos*.' Makes me think it was one of Frederico's men. A total stranger would more likely just shout, 'Watch out.'"

"What are we going to do, guys?" Rose was gripping the edge of the table, her knuckles white.

They all stared at her. They'd never known Rose to lose control, not once. But then again, no one had ever shot her man before.

"We investigate." Skip's words were matter-of-fact but his tone was gentle. "Tomorrow we go downtown and try to figure out the answers to those questions."

"I feel obligated as an officer of the court," Rob said, "to point out that the city police might not appreciate that."

"I'll clear it with Cooper in the morning," Skip said. "I doubt he'll object as long as we don't get in the way of his people."

"Once Mac is stable, I'm going undercover, in Frederico's operation," Rose said.

Not *if* he's stable, but *once* he's stable, Kate noted. Rose wasn't brooking any other possibilities.

She was a beat slower than her husband registering the other implication of what Rose had just said. His mouth had fallen open.

"There's only one job he'd hire you for," Skip said. "And you know what the interview would involve. Are you willing to do *that*?"

Rose dropped her gaze to the table top. Kate realized she was staring at her ring finger. At the ruby, surrounded by small diamonds, that Mac had given her when they'd gotten engaged, and the gold band that now sat beside it.

Kate's detachment slipped. She fought down the sobs threatening to erupt. Her first impulse was to reach out to pat her friend's arm. She stopped the hand halfway there. Rose would resent comforting right now.

"No," Rose finally said with a shudder. "And I'd probably strangle the bastard if I was in the same room with him."

Then she looked up, excitement now mixed with anger on her face. "But I can pretend to be a hooker, new to town, hang out on the street corners with the ladies. It'd be totally natural for me to ask questions about the local pimps."

"And nobody knows a pimp's business quite like his girls," Dolph said.

"You and I are her back-up," Skip said to him.

Rose stood up. "I'm going up to the ICU."

Kate started to say she'd go with her, but it occurred to her that Rose might prefer to be alone. She made it a question instead.

"You want me to sit with you?"

Rose shook her head. "I'll call if there's any change."

~~~~~~~~

When they got home, Maria had just finished supervising the kids' baths. Kate helped her get them ready for bed, then Skip took over for story time. Outside Billy's door, Maria said in a soft voice, "You two no eat. I warm dinner up now."

"That's okay," Kate replied. "I'm not all that hungry. We've imposed on you enough tonight."

Maria looked up at her, eyes narrowed and lips pursed. She headed down the stairs to the kitchen instead of upstairs to her third-floor apartment.

Kate sighed and followed her down. At the bottom of stairs, Maria turned. Tears were pooled in her dark eyes. "Iz not impozing! Mac iz *mi* cousin. He iz *familia*. You all... *mi familia*." The last word came out on a choked sob.

Kate once again fought to shove her own emotions down as she gathered the weeping woman into her arms. In all the chaos, she *had* forgotten Mac was related by marriage to Maria. Despite her best efforts, Kate felt tears trickling down her cheeks.

After a moment, Maria pulled away. She took a tissue from the pocket of her brightly patterned house dress and swiped at her eyes. "You catch who did dis. Not worry 'bout de children. I watch de children, day *and* night."

"Thank you, Maria," Kate said, squeezing her hand.

"I warm food now. Skip come down, you two eat!"

"*Si, Mama.*"

Maria gave her a mock glare, then headed for the kitchen.

When Kate and Skip were settled at the kitchen table, Maria stood over them until they picked up their forks and started eating. Then she went up the stairs to her rooms.

As soon as she was out of sight, Kate put her fork down again. The food was sticking in her throat.

Skip gave her a concerned look. "I know you're worried about me pursuing this, but–"

"You have to pursue it now. They shot Mac!" She shocked

herself with the vehemence in her voice.

"Mac's tough. He'll pull through."

Kate stared at her barely-touched food without responding. She was trying to capture the half-formed insight she'd pushed aside earlier in the evening. "I think I had some kind of epiphany tonight," she finally said.

Skip paused with his iced tea glass halfway to his mouth. "About what, darlin'?"

"Mac is as dear to me as my own brothers, and yet I've never worried about his safety. His sanity, yes, several times, especially right after his parents died, but never his safety." Kate paused to take a sip of her own iced tea. "I worry about you and even Rose and Dolph sometimes. But never about Mac."

"And yet he's the one who got hurt," Skip said.

Kate nodded. "I don't need to say it all again. We have nothing to fear but fear itself; life is too short, yada, yada. We've had the conversation a dozen times before. And some things did shift for me last year. But this feels deeper, more solid. I refuse to live in fear anymore."

Skip gave her a lopsided grin. "Does this mean my sweet Kate is about to morph into kickass Kate?"

"Actually, yeah. And I think part of the shift is because of the aikido. It's pretty empowering to know you've got a good chance of being able to defend yourself, if someone attacks you."

Skip nodded.

She knew he'd be able to relate. He'd no doubt felt something similar when a late growth spurt had taken him from the short scrawny teenager the bullies loved to pick on to the biggest, strongest kid in his high school.

"Just remember, discretion is still the better part of valor," he said.

"Oh, don't worry." Kate gave him a reassuring smile. "I'm not going to go looking for trouble. I'm just not going to waste my emotional energy worrying about what hasn't happened yet." Her smile faded as she thought about Mac.

"We got enough to worry about with what's already happened,"

Skip spoke her thoughts, his own expression grim.

Tears sprang into her eyes for the umpteenth time. This time, she didn't bother to suppress them. "Dear God, let him be okay," she whispered.

"Amen." Skip picked up her hand and trapped it against his chest under his own.

Despite her brave words, she found the strong beating of his heart reassuring.

CHAPTER SIX

Kate wasn't too surprised that she hadn't slept well. By unspoken agreement, they hadn't made love. Skip had rubbed her back instead, until she'd drifted off into a fitful sleep. She'd jolted awake several times. The bad dreams and the tears were all just a blur this morning.

She went to the hospital before work rather than going to aikido class.

Rose was sitting next to Mac's bed. "No change," she said, barely glancing up before returning her gaze to her husband's face.

Mac lay so still, his tanned leathery skin tinged with gray. Kate could hardly bear to look at him.

Focusing on Rose, she said, "Liz called this morning. She took a personal day so she could do whatever she could to help. I suggested she put together a hooker outfit for you."

Rose looked up a second longer this time, a ghost of a smile on her lips. "Perfect job for her." Liz loved to shop, Kate had mixed emotions about the task and Rose loathed it.

"She said she'd go for things a bit long on her and a little loose. Should then be appropriately too short and snug on you." Liz was one of the few people shorter than Rose, and she was much more slender than Rose's solid and somewhat voluptuous build.

Rose just nodded without looking up.

"I gotta get to work." Kate started toward the door, then turned back around. She'd never questioned Rose's ability to look out for herself before, but the woman wasn't thinking entirely straight right now. "If... *Once* Mac's stable, if you go downtown, please be careful. These people are ruthless."

Rose turned dark hollow eyes on her.

"If you get hurt..." *Or worse!* Kate banished that thought. "Mac's gonna feel just as bad as you do right now."

Rose opened her mouth, then closed it again. She nodded. "Pray for him," she whispered.

"Of course."

~~~~~~~~~

At eleven-fifteen, Kate was thinking she should have followed Liz's lead and taken the day off. She was having trouble concentrating on what her client was saying. Fortunately Jeanette mainly needed to vent about her boss today. The man was a psychological replica of her father, and he managed to push her buttons at least once a day. Jeanette was job-hunting.

After seeing the young woman out at the end of her session, Kate checked phone messages. Two cancellations. She took that as a sign that she was not supposed to be working today. Grabbing the files of the other two people scheduled, she skimmed through the notes of their last sessions to see where they'd left off.

Neither seemed to be in a bad place. Unless something crucial had come up during the week, they shouldn't mind postponing their sessions.

She made the phone calls, then headed back to the hospital.

When she arrived, Mac was awake, but just barely. Rose was filling him in on what had happened. His eyes drifted closed and he tried to lick dry lips. Kate poured water from the plastic pitcher on his bedside table into its matching cup, then held the straw so he could sip from it. He swallowed twice, then let go. "Thanks, sweet pea," he croaked out, as his eyes fluttered closed again.

Kate gestured for Rose to come out into the hall with her. "Has the doctor been around?"

"Twice," Rose said. "He sounded a lot more optimistic the second time, after Mac had opened his eyes. He said it'd be slow going for awhile. Bullet tore through a lot of tissue. We're supposed to keep Mac as quiet as possible. Not let him get out of bed or move around much."

Kate snorted. "That won't be hard today, but by tomorrow, all bets are off."

Rose smiled for the first time in twenty-four hours, although it lacked her normal wattage.

"Skip was here a little while ago. He wants to get started investigating, but..." Her eyes cut to the door of Mac's room.

"I cancelled my afternoon clients, so I can sit with him," Kate said.

Rose still looked conflicted. She glanced at her watch. "I guess I'll catch up with Liz and see what she's come up with."

"I'll call if there are any developments," Kate reassured her, then hesitated. Rose wasn't much for demonstrations of affection, but Kate suspected she could use a hug. She put her arms around her friend.

After a moment of startled rigidity, Rose relaxed and hugged her back.

"Be careful," Kate said again as she let go.

~~~~~~~~~

Liz stepped back to examine the results of her efforts. "You look like a proper slut to me."

Rose frowned at her image in the floor-length mirror on the back of Liz's bedroom door. She was wearing dark brown silk short-shorts, dark stockings and black pumps with very high heels. The strapless black push-up bra was covered, just barely, by a low-cut peach tube top.

She felt like her boobs would pop out if she breathed hard.

A white lace jacket, which left plenty of skin showing through, completed the ensemble. Fake-gold chains hung around her neck.

Liz pointed to one of the clip-on earrings dangling from Rose's earlobes. "Hope nobody looks at those too closely. They're plastic. Came from a dress-up set for kids."

Rose nodded, knowing that was the best Liz could do. Her ears weren't pierced. She took off the two pieces of jewelry she normally wore, besides her watch. She squeezed the rings inside her fist for a moment, then dropped them into Liz's palm.

"Hang onto those for me."

Liz cleared her throat. "You bet," she whispered. "Wish I could do more."

"This was a big help. Thanks."

Rose kicked off the shoes and pulled sweats on over the outfit. She sat down on the side of Liz's bed to put her sneakers back on. "Gonna carry the shoes for now. Hopefully I won't break my neck when I have to walk in them."

Liz put a hand on Rose's shoulder. "Be careful."

Rose contemplated those two words as she drove to the agency office to meet Skip and Dolph. She'd said them often enough herself–to her employees, to Kate, and even to Skip at times. But she couldn't remember the last time someone had said them to her. Now *everybody* was.

She and Mac never said them to each other. They both knew the other would be insulted. When one or both of them were going into potential danger, that was the only time they said "I love you" to each other. By mutual agreement, they wanted those to be the last words exchanged between them, should the worst ever happen.

Had she said them to Mac before she'd left the hospital? She couldn't remember. Probably not since Kate was there.

She blinked several times, refusing to let the grittiness in her eyes turn into tears. "I love you, Mac Reilly," she said out loud.

Then she took a deep breath and consciously loosened her death grip on the steering wheel. They had a job to do. They needed to clear Jamieson.

And she was gonna find the bastard who shot her husband.

~~~~~~~~~

At a little after three, Skip stuck his head inside the door of the café. It was empty. Good. Rose wanted to see the place for herself but they didn't want Frederico's people associating her with them.

He made a come-on gesture behind him. Rose, in her sweats and a baseball cap, followed him through the door. Dolph brought up the rear.

Skip felt an odd sensation in the pit of his stomach. Was he coming down with something? Hopefully not. Maybe it was just a reaction to the malodorous bouquet of the less-than-clean restaurant.

The wizened little owner came out of the kitchen, wiping his hands nervously on his apron. He looked relieved when he saw them. "*Buenos dias, señores, ey señora.*" He made a small bow in Rose's direction. "De *hombre* who got shot yesterday, he okay?"

"He's alive," Skip said. "Did you see the shooter?"

"Oh, no, *señor*. I in back, cook food." The little man shook his head, but Skip could see the lie in his shifting eyes.

"Big guy, in the suit, slipped through that door just before we left." Dolph tilted his head toward the doorway with the dingy curtain. "He go outside?"

"No see him, *señor*."

Skip seriously doubted that. "He had to walk right past you."

The man was silent, rubbing his palms on his apron.

Rose headed toward the curtained doorway. The little man started to step into her path.

"I wouldn't try to stop her," Dolph said in a mild voice.

He and Skip followed her into the kitchen. A door on the side wall led to the outside. The horizontal bar across the middle allowed it to be pushed open quickly from the inside while it remained locked from the outside. No doubt a requirement by the city fire marshal, although the thick layer of grime and grease said the place hadn't been inspected any time recently.

Skip wondered if the owner was trying to kill Frederico with food poisoning. Or maybe he was hoping the kitchen would catch fire, then he'd take off through the side door and watch his nemesis burn.

They went through the door into an alley. It stank of garbage. Dolph held his nose. Rose kicked a small box out of her way. A rat ran out and scurried away.

They picked their way through the trash to the alley entrance. "My truck was there." Skip pointed to a scraggly tree next to the curb. "Just in front of that tree."

Rose nodded. "This was probably where the shooter was. Clear line from here. No way he missed you all by accident, unless he's the world's worst shot."

Dolph pointed down the block to a narrow opening between two buildings. "Guy who shouted might've been there."

They went back through the front door of the café. The owner was sweeping the floor. "Someone called out to us yesterday," Skip said. "Told us to look out. Who was it?"

The old man hesitated, no doubt weighing whether it was safe to answer. "Frederico send man after you. Hiz *número tres.* He go out, then I hear yelling."

Skip nodded. "*Gracias, señor.*" Skip extracted a twenty from his wallet and tried to hand it to the man.

"*¡Vaya, señor!* I no want you money. *Su amigo,* I pray for him."

Skip pocketed the bill, then extended his hand. "*¡Muchas gracias!*"

The old man went still for a moment, then he wiped his palm again on his grimy apron and shook Skip's hand.

~~~~~~~~~~

Standing next to Rose's car a block away, Skip said, "So he sends his number three guy out to watch us. Maybe just to make sure we truly leave. And the guy shouts a warning. Says to me the shooter was not acting on Frederico's orders."

Dolph and Rose both nodded. She beeped her car unlocked.

It took a moment for Skip to figure out how to collapse his big frame into the back seat of the small sedan. "Feel like a damn pretzel," he muttered as they pulled away from the curb, Dolph at the wheel.

Several blocks from Jimmy Matthews' apartment building, Dolph pulled over to the curb and Rose got out. She had shed the sweats, revealing the results of Liz's efforts. Skip let out a low teasing wolf-whistle.

"Shut up, partner," Rose muttered. She strolled away, shivering and wobbling on the unfamiliar high heels.

The temptation to call her back and get them all the hell out of here flitted through Skip's mind. He squelched the thought.

"Hope she doesn't have to run in those," Dolph said as they watched her turn the corner.

"She'll kick 'em off and use 'em as weapons if things go south," Skip said with more confidence than he felt. The queasy feeling in his stomach was back, and he couldn't blame it on *Señor* Santiago's smelly café this time.

Dolph pulled out and slowly followed, hanging back a half block. When Rose joined a group of four scantily-clad women on a corner, he moved over to the curb again. She chatted with them for a few minutes, then strolled away when two men approached the group. Further down the next block, she stopped to talk to two other young women. Their body language seemed a bit hostile. Rose moved on.

Dolph waited for a break in traffic and then made a U-turn. Going around the block, and then up two blocks, he turned again and pulled over to the curb. They were now several hundred feet beyond where Rose was talking to another group of three women, all of whom looked a little worse for wear.

Rose suddenly kicked off a shoe, then stooped down and pretended to shake a pebble out of it. That was the signal to pick her up.

Dolph glanced over his shoulder and eased the car out into the street after a cab rumbled by. Skip crouched further down in the backseat, out of sight. He stuck his head up just enough to peek out the tinted side window.

Dolph stopped adjacent to the group of women across the street and lowered his window. "Hey, *señorita*." He slurred his words as he leered at Rose. "Wanna go for a ride?"

Rose stepped to the curb and called over to him. "It's like a cab stand, mister. Ya take the next in line."

"First I heard a that rule. I likes my women on the tan side, ya know what I mean." Dolph let out a lusty chuckle.

Rose looked over her shoulder at the other women, two black and one white. They exchanged glances just as a delivery truck stopped behind Dolph and blew his horn. The white woman—who

looked to be pushing fifty but was probably a decade younger–
shrugged plump shoulders clad in a sheer black blouse.

Rose flashed the women a grin, then checked the traffic and
wobbled across the road. Dolph raised his window. "How do they
stand the cold in those outfits?"

Rose slid into the passenger seat and slammed her door. Her
teeth were chattering.

Ignoring the truck driver who was now waving his hand out
his window, middle finger erect, Dolph started moving the car
sedately down the street. He was keeping an eye out for any of
Frederico's men.

When they were several blocks away, Skip sat up.

"Frederico's taken over Jimmy's girls," Rose said, "and
they're not happy about it. The unanimous message was that I
should get myself right back to the Greyhound station and get
outta town."

"Were you able to find out anything about the guy in the
suit?" Skip asked.

"Not much, but one of the ladies said the first thing Frederico
did, after informing them that he was their new pimp, was to pass
them around to his men. But the, quote, 'big guy with the stick up
his ass' didn't participate. My sense is the take-over of the ladies
was rather matter-of-fact, no gloating or posturing, just Freddie
boy announcing they were his now."

The three of them rode in silence for several minutes,
pondering what Rose had found out.

Finally Dolph said, "Got more questions than answers out
of that deal."

"Yup," Skip said.

Rose just nodded as she leaned down to strap her ankle holster
back on under her sweatpants.

~~~~~~~~~

First thing Saturday morning, Kate called Mac's room at the
hospital to check on him. Rose picked up and reported that the
patient was recovering, slowly but surely.

As Kate hung up, she realized, with a pang of guilt, that

she'd forgotten all about Pete since Mac had been shot. She wondered how he was doing. Skip agreed to watch the kids, so after breakfast she headed for the jail.

She sat at the metal table–trying to hide her shock at the sight of her client–while the guard went through the routine of locking the leg chains to the ring in the floor, then releasing Pete's hands from their shackles. One of his eyes was blackened, his lower lip puffy and sporting a large cut only partially scabbed over.

Once the door clanged shut behind the guard's burly back, Pete said, "The other guy looks a lot worse."

"What happened?"

"Some guy tried to pound on me. But don't worry, I've got a protector now." When Kate looked at him in horror, Pete hastened to add, "I didn't have to trade any favors to get his protection. Seems Bubba heard a rumor I was a '9/11 hero'." He made quotation marks in the air. "Are you responsible for that rumor?"

"No. My guess is Rob planted a bug in the warden's ear that it would be bad PR if anything happened to you on his watch."

"It wouldn't take long for that information to make it into the rumor mill." After a moment of contemplating his fingernails, Pete added, "I'm not sure I'm real comfortable with this, trading on the hero thing. It feels wrong."

"I can understand that, but we need to keep you safe."

Pete nodded, then looked down at the table top. "Doesn't sit right though. I'm not a hero."

Kate leaned forward. "Pete, I'm wondering if you were standing so close to the trees you never saw the forest."

He looked up. "What do you mean?"

"You were there, at the Twin Towers, pulling people out, then running back in. From your perspective, it felt like you didn't do enough, because you couldn't save them all. But that's not how the rest of the country experienced 9/11. We were in our offices, our kitchens or living rooms, watching on TV as the second plane hit, and then the buildings came down, and people were running away. We were in shock, unable to believe that this was happening in our country. And there was nothing we could do.

Helplessness is a terrible feeling, Pete. The worst one humans ever have to deal with. You felt like you couldn't do enough, but we couldn't do *anything*."

Pete was silent, watching her intently.

"I was convinced that tens of thousands of people died in those towers," Kate said. "And that's before I'd even heard about the Pentagon and the plane in Pennsylvania. I actually felt *relieved* later that day, and the next, when the estimates of those killed went down and then down again. I thought it was downright miraculous that we *only* lost three thousand souls that day. Not to discount those people's lives or what their families suffered, but it could have been so much worse. And you, Pete, were one of the reasons why it wasn't worse. So get used to the idea that the rest of America thinks you're pretty damn special!"

After a moment, Pete gave her a small smile. "Still don't feel like a hero, but I get what you're saying."

~~~~~~~~~

Skip caught himself. He'd been about to ask Maria if she'd mind watching the kids while he went to visit Mac. Then he remembered what Kate had told him. Instead, he asked Maria if she wanted to go with him to the hospital. They could take turns staying with the kids down in the cafeteria.

Maria's visit was short. She returned to the cafeteria before the kids had finished the ice cream Skip had bought them. She was beaming. "He grouchy. Good sign."

Skip grinned at her. He handed over a twenty-dollar bill. "They can each spend ten dollars in the gift shop, but *not* on candy."

"Cool," Billy said with enthusiasm, as his sister bounced in her chair.

"Finish ice cream first," Maria said.

Skip hoped they wouldn't be disappointed. Ten dollars didn't usually buy you much in a hospital gift shop. He headed for the elevators.

He took two steps into Mac's room and froze. The women had reported the patient was improving, but he looked like hell.

His wiry body seemed downright frail in the big hospital bed. His eyes were closed, the eyelids thin with blue veins showing through. The white towel draped over his chest was only a couple shades lighter than his skin. He looked like an old man, wearing a bib to catch his drool.

Fear ricocheted through Skip's nervous system. For a moment, he thought Mac was dead.

The patient's eyes opened. They brightened when he saw Skip. "Hey, boss man. How ya doin'?"

"I'm fine." A lie. His heart was galloping a mile a minute. "I wish you wouldn't call me that."

Mac was two years older than Skip's forty-four, and on a toughness scale of one to ten, Skip considered himself an eight and Mac an eleven.

Mac gave him a lopsided grin as his right side rippled under the bed covers.

Worry gnawed again at Skip's gut. Had Mac suffered some kind of stroke or nerve damage?

"Damn nurse keeps wrapping me up like a mummy. Can't even get my arms loose."

Letting out a short bark of relieved laughter, Skip stepped over to the bed and pulled the sheet and light blanket loose. Mac disentangled his arm and shook his hand.

Rose came into the room carrying a pair of scissors. "Finally convinced the nurse I wasn't a homicidal maniac and could be trusted with sharps... Oh, hiya, Skip."

"Hey, partner, how you doin'?"

"I'm fine but the patient's annoyed 'cause he missed his haircut this week."

Mac might go two or three days without shaving but the one aspect of his appearance about which he was meticulous was his hair. He kept it trimmed in a precision military buzz cut.

"Ah, thus the towel," Skip said. He noted that indeed Mac's hair was rather ragged looking, and there was a good bit of gray now sprinkled in with the light brown.

Are we gettin' too old to do this shit? He pushed that thought aside as Mac asked him about the investigation.

~~~~~~~~

On Sunday morning, Kate and Skip were sitting in their usual pew, three rows back from the front. Kate patted her stomach, willing the butterflies to settle down. She should have her head examined. Did she really think people would donate money to bail someone accused of murder out of jail?

Maybe she should...

Too late. Elaine had finished her other announcements at the end of the service and was now looking in Kate's direction. "I had an unusual request this week from one of our parishioners. I'll let her explain but I wanted to tell you all that I've met with the young man in question. I'm inclined to agree with Kate's assessment of him and the situation. However, as I said, it's an unusual request so each of you should do as you see fit."

Kate stood and smoothed down the jacket of her suit. "I'll try to condense this as best I can. A young man I know has been arrested on murder charges. I believe he's innocent and my husband's agency is looking into the case." She summarized Pete's life-saving efforts on 9/11. "Now he's in jail, with no money for bail, and that's not a good environment for him." She stopped to swallow the lump growing in her throat. "He's a gentle soul, and it will be months before his case comes to trial. The ushers are going to pass the plate again. Anything you feel you can give would be helpful. I know it's a lot to ask, to take my word for it that he's innocent."

"And mine," Elaine said. "But you don't need to feel obligated to give."

A voice came from the back of the church. "Well I think we should feel obligated to give." A woman Kate didn't know stood up. "I lost my dad on 9/11. My parents owned a business in the World Trade Center. On the ground floor. My dad shoved my mom out the front door and then he took off for the fire stairs to try to help others get out." The woman stifled a sob. "They never even found his body."

The lump in Kate's throat was now too big to swallow.

"I lost friends on 9/11, in the Pentagon," a male voice called out.

Another woman stood up. Kate knew her in passing, Jane or Janet something.

"Most of you don't know this since I've only been coming here a few years, but I was widowed on 9/11. My husband was on the Pennsylvania plane. He was one of the ones who rushed the cockpit. Like the guy whose call to his wife ended up on the news, he called me... from his cell..." Tears were streaming down the woman's cheeks. "Told me to tell the children..." She waved her hand in the air, unable to continue, and sat down. The people on either side wrapped their arms around her.

Kate swiped at the tears on her face with the back of her hand. Skip dug out his handkerchief and handed it to her, even though he was sniffing a bit himself.

Doris Baines stood up.

Kate stifled a groan. The woman was the most negative person she'd ever known.

"Will this young man take off when he's out on bail?" Doris asked. "I mean, just because he's a 9/11 hero doesn't mean he didn't do what the police think he did."

Kate had to admit she had a point, at least from the perspective of someone who didn't know Pete. "I don't think he'll go anywhere. His support system is here in Towson. And he'll have his day in court. But in the meantime, I'm very concerned about what being in jail will do to his mental health. If he's innocent, as Elaine and I and several other people believe he is–"

"Including the arresting officer," Skip muttered beside her.

"If he's innocent and being locked up for months destroys him..."

Skip took her hand and gave it a squeeze.

A murmur of dissatisfaction had been growing in the sanctuary. Kate didn't know if it was aimed at her or Doris.

Elaine raised her arms in the air, the white sleeves of her robe looking a bit like angel's wings.

Kate caught the expression on the priest's face. *Make that an annoyed angel's wings.*

The murmur subsided. Elaine nodded to Sym, the head usher, and the ushers started passing the alms basins around the pews. "I don't think we need to have a long debate about this. Give as you're willing. If you have questions for Kate, ask her during coffee hour. I'm sure she'll be happy to take your donation then as well." She frowned at Doris when she didn't take the hint to sit down.

Doris held up her hand. "I just got one more thing to say. I think we *should* help this young man."

Laughter rippled through the congregation as Doris resumed her seat.

Jim Sutton, the church treasurer, stood up. "Checks should be made out to Kate, not the church and these donations are not tax-deductible."

"Spoken like a true accountant, Jim," a voice rang out. Another ripple of laughter.

Jim smiled. "And I wanted to say that my son is a firefighter. It scares the you-know-what out of me every day, but I'm also extremely proud of him. Firefighters are the bravest people on this planet. They run *into* burning, collapsing buildings!"

"Or they're the craziest," someone said *sotto voice*.

Jim chuckled good-naturedly. "Yeah, well, that's what we've got Kate for."

Kate smiled in his direction, her vision blurred by fresh tears.

One of the ushers had grabbed the basket normally kept in the back of the church for canned goods for the local food pantry. Sym took it and dumped the overflowing contents of his alms plate into it. The other ushers followed suit, then went back to passing the plates along the pews. They were only halfway to the front of the church.

"Thank you," Kate tried to say, but it came out as a breathless whisper.

Skip stood up and wrapped an arm around her shoulders. "Y'all have left my wife speechless," he drawled. "You've got no idea how rare a phenomenon that is."

Laughter erupted.

CHAPTER SEVEN

Sunday afternoon, Skip sat at the kitchen table enjoying the peace and quiet. It was one of those unusually balmy days Maryland was sometimes blessed with this time of year–referred to as the February thaw. Winter usually came back with a vengeance afterwards. But one learned to savor the mid-winter sample of the springtime that would come eventually.

Kate had said it was a sign that everything was going to be alright. She'd taken the kids to the park near their house.

Skip took a sip of coffee and flipped the Sunday paper over to the sports section, but his mind was on his wife.

He couldn't have been more proud of her this morning. After the round of testimonials there wasn't a dry eye in the house. Wallets and checkbooks appeared in people's hands, and more than once the collection plates were held up as someone finished writing out a check. The ushers had dumped everything into the basket and Elaine had blessed it.

Between the collection and a donation from the priest's discretionary fund, Jim had thought they'd raised at least ten thousand dollars. He and some of his volunteers were going to count it and call this evening with a final figure.

It wouldn't be enough to get Jamieson out of jail, but it was progress in the right direction.

Skip's mood sobered as his mind turned to his hospital visit yesterday. His stomach knotted at the memory of Mac, so pale and weak in that hospital bed. He stared sightlessly at the basketball scores while trying to sort out whatever the hell was going on.

Kate was right. Mac was the last person he'd have expected to get hurt. It had shaken both of them. Kate was ready to kick ass, and he was... *what?*

The image of Mac falling toward him, surprise and pain in his eyes, came unbidden into his mind. Sweat trickled down his sides. His palms felt clammy.

Shit!

This strange emotion he was feeling was *fear*.

He shook his head to dislodge the image. He flipped the paper over to the next page, the local news section, and stared at it without really seeing it.

Had he lost his nerve? He was laid-back by nature. Mr. Unflappable, Dolph called him. In dangerous situations, there was a shot of adrenaline of course. It sharpened his senses, put him on full alert. But a calmness came over him that cleared his head, helped him think fast on his feet.

It had saved his life more than once. But now... Could he trust it to be there the next time he needed it?

He shook his head again. The picture in front of his face finally registered. It was an artist's drawing. The guy looked familiar. He scanned the accompanying story. The face belonged to a floater, found in the Patapsco River near the Baltimore harbor on Saturday. The medical examiner believed he'd been in the water less than forty-eight hours, although the cold temperatures made it harder to judge time of death.

The niggly feeling of familiarity was just beginning to bloom into full recognition when Skip's cell phone buzzed in his pocket.

"You see the picture in the local section?" Dolph said in his ear.

"Yeah, just now. It's Frederico's guy in the suit."

"Son of a bitch. Wonder what the hell this means."

"Hell if I know." Silence as they both contemplated this development. Then Skip said, "Are we getting too old to be chasing bad guys?"

"What? Where's that coming from?"

Skip didn't answer him. He wasn't real sure where that had come from.

"I'm pushin' sixty," Dolph said, "and I don't feel like I'm too old yet. I do like being private though. We get to pick and choose which bad guys we chase."

"Then why are we chasing slimeball pimps and drug dealers?"

Silence, then Dolph said, his tone matter-of-fact, "'Cause a young man who deserves better is getting the shaft."

Again, Skip didn't answer him.

"You want to pay Frederico another visit tomorrow?" Dolph said. "Would be interesting to find out how his man ended up in the river."

Skip was wrestling with himself. "I've got a concern."

"What's that?"

"Mac getting shot, it, uh..." No way could he admit to this man, who had stepped into the role of father figure, that he was afraid. "It's got me more cautious."

A pause. "Caution's a good thing. I think Mac's shooting shook us all some."

"Uh, I'm concerned that I might be too cautious, maybe hesitate at the wrong moment."

"My advice is to get back up on that horse right away."

Skip's head agreed with that idea. His stomach clenched at the thought. "Maybe you shouldn't go, Dolph."

A longer pause. "Don't be puttin' your *concerns* on me, son."

"No, it's not that. I know you can handle yourself. It's... You matter to me. I don't want my hesitating to put you in jeopardy."

Dolph cleared his throat. "You matter to me too, son. And I don't think for a minute that you're gonna freeze under pressure. You'll be a little scareder than you're used to, but you'll do what you gotta do."

He wished he shared Dolph's confidence in that. Apparently he wasn't going to be allowed to back away from that damned horse. "Uh, thanks for listening. See you in the morning."

"Not a problem. See you tomorrow."

~~~~~~~

Dave Samuelson stretched his long legs out in front of him and tried to get comfortable. The Sunday evening train was far from full and the seat across from him was vacant, giving him a little bit of breathing room. Dave hated small spaces.

He was in a rare introspective mood, pondering where his life was going. He thought about his wife and the tow-headed toddler he'd bid farewell to just a little over an hour ago. Nell had said she'd miss him, but he knew she didn't mean it. He'd seen the relief in her eyes.

His marriage had been a career move. His employer expected it. Married men were more reliable, more stable when they had a family to provide for. But Dave didn't really care what happened to his family. Maybe it would be different if he had a son. A boy he could raise to be like himself, to carry on his name.

He snorted, drawing a mildly curious glance from the woman sitting across the aisle from him. Of course, the name the boy would carry wasn't Dave's real name. It had been so many years since he'd used his real name, he probably wouldn't answer to it now.

His mind shifted to his current assignment. He was to be a liaison of sorts with his employer's new affiliate.

His boss had informed him that a plan had been set in motion to resolve the problems this affiliate was experiencing. Dave's job was to observe the situation and come up with a Plan B should Plan A not work. He was confident he could do the job. Reading people was one of his talents, and he liked a challenge.

He hoped the assignment would last awhile. He was looking forward to the freedom of living anonymously in a hotel room. No doubt the affiliate would be willing to provide some entertainment.

But tonight would be devoted to work, not play. He had some research to do.

~~~~~~~~

By eleven-fifteen Monday morning, Skip and his men were in position inside Santiago's café. After checking the place over to make sure they were the only ones there at that hour, Skip had intentionally taken the chair Frederico had occupied the previous Thursday. His instincts told him it was the right tactic. Claim the man's territory to show he had the upper hand, and then willingly give it back to him.

But Skip's stomach was rebelling at the idea of being seated when his adversary came through that door.

Dolph leaned against the wall a few feet away to his left. Another Canfield and Hernandez operative, Manuel Ortiz, stood three feet behind his chair. Manny wasn't all that tall but he was built like a stone wall—thick chest, powerful biceps, muscular thighs.

At eleven-fifty, Frederico and two of his men came through the door, laughing. Skip only caught a few words. Apparently one of them had just told a lewd joke.

They froze when they saw they had company. Three more home boys spread out along the wall on either side of the door.

Skip made himself stand up slowly. He bowed toward the chair he had just vacated with an it's-all-yours gesture. Letting a bit of Texas creep into his voice, he said, "Good ta see y'all again, *señor*."

Frederico narrowed his eyes.

Skip backed up until he was standing beside Manny. He faked a smile and gestured again to the chair.

Frederico moved partway toward the table but didn't sit down. "Wha' ya doin' here, man? I done answered yer dumb questions."

"Yes you did, but there have been some interesting developments since then."

Frederico just glared at him from several paces away.

"First, your man shoots at us." Skip was surprised his voice sounded so calm when his heart was pounding in his chest. "Then that man ends up floating in the Patapsco. So excuse me if I'm confused."

Frederico's rigid posture relaxed slightly. "Now I don't know how dat dumb fucker ended up in de harbor, but it weren't no man of mine dat be shootin' at ya."

A surge of anger had Skip closing the gap between them in two strides. Towering over the shorter man, his voice now had a hard edge. "Then why's one of my men in the hospital, missing part of his kidney?"

Frederico's men had started to move forward, but a hand signal from him stopped them. He gave an elaborate shrug. "Look, man, I done took care of yer problem for ya." His voice was impatient. "Now go away."

Skip took half a step back and digested that for a moment. So the big guy was the shooter, operating without Frederico's say-so, and Freddie had killed him for it? Seemed a bit drastic just to enforce his authority.

He considered probing some more but Freddie's expression said he wouldn't get an answer. "You only took care of one of my problems, *amigo*. Pete Jamieson's still in jail for a crime he didn't commit."

Frederico shrugged again. "Can't help ya there."

Skip paused, then nodded slightly. He took another step back and then circled around the other man, without turning his back on him. Two steps from the door, Dolph and Manny in tow, he said, "You let me know if you hear anything 'bout that, ya hear?"

One of Frederico's men muttered to Manny, "*Oye chico. ¿Porqué estás con ellos?*"

"I ain't your *chico*," Manny growled back.

Frederico's men stiffened. Both he and Skip made the same slight gesture with their hands. The homeboys backed away, their body language protesting. Skip shoved Manny out the door.

Back in Skip's truck, Dolph asked, "So how was the ride, son?"

"Bumpy."

"It'll smooth out."

Hope so. Skip willed the knots in his stomach to relax as he steered away from the curb.

~~~~~~~~~

Inside Santiago's, the man behind the faded striped curtain in the kitchen doorway had a small smile on his face. His eyes, however, were calculating.

CHAPTER EIGHT

With a packed schedule on Monday and a mad dash over to the hospital at lunchtime to check on Mac, Kate wasn't able to get to the jail until after five.

The guards dealt with her with the boredom of routine. When the door slammed shut, Pete's face collapsed into a haunted look.

Kate tried to keep the alarm from her voice and body language, partly because she knew the guards might be watching through the one-way mirror behind her. "What's wrong?"

"Bubba's in the hospital. Some guy attacked me, on our way back to our cells after dinner last night."

Kate made herself take a moment to digest that. "What guy?"

"Just some guy. He and I'd never exchanged a word. Makes no sense why he came at me like that."

"He came at you with what?" Kate asked.

"A knife."

"How the hell'd he get a knife in jail?"

"Good question," Pete said. "It wasn't some jury-rigged shiv either. It was a real knife. Bubba got cut up pretty bad before the guards got there to separate them."

There was guilt and worry in Pete's tone but she decided to wait to address those. She had a much greater concern. "He came at you how? What started it?"

"I was toward the end of the line, heading back to our cells. Guy was in front of me. He suddenly just turned around and shoved me. Yelled something like, 'Get the hell off me.' Then the knife came out. I deflected the blow, got cut some." He rolled up his left sleeve to show her a gauze bandage. "Bubba grabbed the guy's wrist and they started wrestling for the knife. Then the guy tried to claim I'd pulled the knife and he'd grabbed it away from me. Fortunately the guards believed Bubba and me over him."

"Holy crap," Kate muttered under her breath, as she processed the implications.

She jumped up and strode over to the one-way mirror. Rapping her knuckles against it, she yelled, "I need a phone. Now!"

Pete's mouth fell open.

Nothing happened. She went to the metal door and banged on it.

A few seconds later, the door opened and a guard stepped in. "You done?"

"No! You have an inmate in the hospital who ended up there defending my client from a knife attack?"

"Uh, yes, ma'am."

She was about to question why Rob hadn't been called, and how the hell did the assailant get a knife, when she caught herself. Taking her anger out on the poor guard wouldn't accomplish anything.

"I need a phone to call my client's lawyer. Now, please."

The *please* was pure form. Her tone said it was not a request. The guard opened his mouth. She narrowed her eyes at him.

He closed his mouth without saying anything and left the room.

Kate turned to Pete. "Are you able to handle solitary confinement, at least for a day or two?"

"Uh, yeah, I guess so."

The door lock rattled and the metal door opened. The guard handed the portable phone in his hand to Kate.

"Thank you." Kate dialed Rob's cell phone and filled him in as succinctly as she could.

Rob got the implications even faster than she had. "Alleged killer dies in a jailhouse brawl. Case closed."

"Hell of a risk that guy was taking," Kate said.

"Probably worth it if he was getting paid well enough," Rob

said. "And with Pete dead, they might've believed the lie that the knife was Pete's and he'd started it. Try to get the guards to let him stay there with you until I call back. Tell them I'm contacting the Director of Corrections." He disconnected.

"I don't understand. What's going on?" Pete asked.

She leaned forward and lowered her voice. "Rob and I think the knife attack was a hired hit. He's calling the jail's director now."

Pete's eyes went wide.

"I told you my husband was going to look into Jimmy's murder," Kate said. "Try to find out who really did it. Somehow he's shaken something loose, we're not sure what. He went downtown to talk to Jimmy's competition, a guy named Frederico. Since then, uh, things have happened that seem to be aimed at discouraging Skip's interest in your case." Kate didn't want to mention Mac getting shot. Pete would feel guilty about that as well.

"So you think this wasn't just some random attack 'cause I looked at the guy the wrong way?"

"If he'd taken a swing at you with his fist, maybe. But a knife attack. That'll get this guy a lot more years in jail than whatever sentence he's already serving."

Pete sat back in his chair and stared at her for a moment. "Bubba saved my life. What if he dies?" Worry clouded his eyes.

Kate took a deep breath. Time to switch gears and go into therapist mode.

"Do you fear dying in a fire, Pete?"

Once again, he gave her a startled look. "I don't get it."

Kate tried a different tactic. "What's Bubba in jail for?"

Pete still looked confused. "Second degree murder. Barroom fight. He was drunk. He pled not guilty just to delay going to the federal prison. Conditions are better here, he said."

"So he's been in prison before. Did you get the impression he fights a lot?"

"Oh, yeah. He said so. Says he likes a good fight, gets the juices flowing."

Kate nodded. "So fighting is what he does and the potential

consequences don't scare him all that much. If you rescued somebody from a fire, and then ended up dying from injuries from that fire, would you want that person to feel guilty?"

Pete cocked his head to one side. She could see on his face that he'd gotten it, even before he shook his head.

The phone lying on the table rang. She answered it.

"Couldn't reach the director," Rob said without preamble. "Deputy director's on his way."

"That was fast."

"To quote him, 'we take security and the safety of every prisoner very seriously.'" Rob's tone was derisive. "He's going to put Pete in the Protective Custody Unit, with a hand-picked guard on the door. How's he likely to handle being isolated?"

"We already talked about that. He'll be okay, for now at least."

"Good. I'm going to ask for an emergency hearing tomorrow, to revisit the bail situation. Might help if you could be there."

She stifled a sigh. Tomorrow's afternoon schedule had been left open so she could help Billy's teacher with the petting zoo. She didn't get all that many opportunities to participate in school events, and she hated to give this one up. But Pete's safety and sanity were more important.

"I've got tomorrow afternoon off anyway. I was supposed to help in Billy's classroom."

"Okay, I'll try for early afternoon."

"That'll work. Maria can take Billy's gerbil in and help out in my place until I can get there."

~~~~~~~~~

At noon on Tuesday, Skip, Dolph and Rose were once again cruising the streets in Frederico's territory. They spotted a group of scantily-clad ladies standing at the next corner. Dolph pulled over.

This time Skip was going to talk to them. Rose was in the backseat. She pointed out three of the women who had been Matthews' before he was killed.

Skip was secretly relieved they weren't confronting Frederico today. Nonetheless, he was fighting the unfamiliar feeling gnawing at his gut. He'd always been a big believer in listening to his gut instincts, but now he wasn't so sure. Were there signs of true danger he'd missed, or was this irrational fear?

Just talkin' to some prostitutes here, he reminded himself.

But he didn't get very far with them. They answered his questions in monosyllables, if that. He reached into his back pocket and took out the wallet that contained only a dozen of his business cards and a few ten dollar bills. Several folded over fifties were in his front pocket. He handed out the cards. "Any of you ladies think of anything, you give me a ring. If it turns out to be helpful there's a fifty in it for you, maybe more."

Starting to shove the wallet back into his pocket, Skip noticed the youngest of the group giving him a speculative look. He couldn't quite read it. He didn't think she was sizing him up as a john. This must be the one Judith had told them about. She looked no older than twelve.

He pulled the wallet back out and held it up, meeting the girl-woman's gaze. "A fifty, or more, for information. Even something little might help. You never know what you might know that would be useful to us."

He pocketed the wallet and turned to walk away, his senses now on high alert.

He'd only gone half a block when he felt what he'd been expecting, the feather-light touch of someone trying to pick his pocket. He reached back and clamped down on a thin wrist, then pivoted around.

But it wasn't *who* he'd expected. He was looking into the emaciated face of the tall, black girl who'd identified herself as Gazelle.

"What do you think you're doing?" Skip said in a conversational tone, as she tried desperately to twist her arm loose.

"Nuthin'. Lemme go!"

"Nothing, huh? Looks to me like you were trying to pick my pocket."

"No, no, I was just gonna ask if you wanted some company, tha's all."

"Gazelle, my wallet's half outta my pocket. You were trying

to steal it.""

"Oh, no sir, I weren't. I just be behind in my quota." Her eyes, already wide with fright, went wider. She'd said something she hadn't meant to say.

"Your quota?"

"Of johns."

"Of johns or wallets?"

"No, sir, of johns. But if you don't want none, I be gettin' back to work."

"What does Frederico do with the wallets, Gazelle?"

"Don't know what you're talkin' 'bout." She yanked harder and Skip was afraid he might break her wrist.

"I could get you arrested for assault and theft. Those are a little tougher raps to get out of than soliciting." He expected her to relent and start talking, but she didn't.

"I didn't steal nothin' an' you can't prove nothin'. Now lemme go." Her voice was a low hiss now.

He let her yank her wrist free. Skip had never seen a woman run in platform shoes with three-inch heels before, but she was steady on her feet as she took off down the sidewalk.

Back in the car, he filled Dolph and Rose in on the exchange.

"Curiouser and curiouser," Dolph said.

"Yup."

~~~~~~~

Rob and Kate stood on either side of Pete, in his orange jumpsuit and shackles, in front of the judge's bench. The prosecutor, a bailiff and the two guards who had brought Pete over from the jail were the only other people in the courtroom.

Rob had briefly made his case for lowering the bail amount to $150,000. He'd told her beforehand he thought that was the lowest amount the judge would go for.

Now the prosecutor was repeating his spiel about Pete being a flight risk.

The judge raised his hand to stop the flow of words. "Thank you, Mr. Fitzsimmons, for that recap. This is more than a little unusual, Mr. Franklin. I don't really see how your client's cell mate getting knifed in a fight should affect my ruling regarding bail."

"Your Honor," Kate spoke up. "My husband is a private detective. He's been checking out another possible suspect for Mr. Matthews' killing. When he started investigating, he and his operatives were shot at, we assume to discourage him from continuing that investigation. We think this knife attack is related. If Mr. Jamieson dies in a jailhouse brawl, end of case."

"So you don't think the police have the right man?"

ASA Fitzsimmons started spluttering but the judge held up his hand.

Kate resisted the temptation to point out that the police detective on the case didn't think she had the right man.

"Mr. Jamieson is innocent until proven guilty," Rob said. "Until his day in court, the system is required to keep him safe. You set bail based on the possibility that he is a flight risk. Mrs. Huntington and I are sure enough he is not, that we are willing to post his bail and I will take personal responsibility for him until his court date."

The judge raised an eyebrow. "You've got $150,000 to post bail for this young man?"

"No, sir, but we have the ten percent fee a bail bondsman requires."

"I would assume, Mr. Franklin, that you know you will not get that money back."

"Yes, sir," Rob said.

"Some of the money is ours," Kate said, "but most of it came from the parishioners at my church, and my priest's discretionary fund."

Now both of the judge's eyebrows were in the air. "You collected fifteen thousand dollars by passing the plate on Sunday?"

"Well, almost, sir. It's a big church, with some deep pockets. A little over ten thousand was collected from the congregation."

The judge shook his head. "Now let me get this straight. You two are putting up a sizeable chunk of your own money to get this man out of jail, because you are that convinced of his innocence."

His tone was skeptical.

Kate was suddenly afraid he would think they'd lost their professional perspectives. They had! But that didn't change the reality that Pete was in danger if he stayed in jail.

"Mr. Franklin, this is not a very lucrative approach to running a law practice," the judge was saying.

Kate jumped in. "Yes, sir. We're convinced he's innocent, and we're also doing this because Mr. Jamieson saved lives on 9/11." She felt Pete squirm and nudged the side of his leg with her knee. "As Americans, we owe him a debt of gratitude that money can hardly begin to cover."

The judge looked at the lawyer and the therapist for another long moment. Finally he said, "I'm lowering bail to $100,000. Give your priest his money back, Mrs. Huntington. Mr. Jamieson, you'd better not let these people down."

"No, sir. I won't," Pete said.

The judge motioned to the guards. As they moved across the courtroom, he leaned forward and said in a low voice, "Mrs. Huntington, if I ever run for office, I want you to be in charge of my fund-raising."

Kate smiled up at him. She opted not to point out that her priest was a woman.

~~~~~~~~~

Kate thoroughly enjoyed the rest of her afternoon. By the time she'd arrived at the kids' school, the petting zoo was in full swing. Watching Billy's class play with each other's pets and learn about the different animals had been a blast.

The two clouds that had been affecting her mood lately had lifted. Mac was definitely on the road to recovery, and Pete Jamieson was out of jail and safe.

After Rob had made the arrangements with a bail bondsman, he'd called Judith Anderson. She'd given him permission to put Pete in a safe house, as long as she was kept apprised of his location. They'd consulted with Skip and had decided Pete's place in western Maryland was relatively safe. The trailer had been parked there by the previous owner without bothering to get a permit, so on paper it was undeveloped land.

Skip had seemed hesitant but he'd finally agreed to send two bodyguards out there with Pete. One of them was Manny Ortiz. Kate knew he was excellent at his job. He'd been her guard on a couple occasions in the past.

When the dismissal bell rang, Kate gathered up Billy and his gerbil and went to collect Edie from her classroom. As the three of them started across the parking lot, Billy insisted on carrying Harry's cage.

"Okay, but be careful," Kate said, pausing to make sure he had a good grip on the handle. Edie began to tell her mother about her day.

Kate tried to pay attention to the girl's chatter while monitoring Billy's handling of the gerbil cage. Suddenly the light dimmed. She looked up, thinking maybe they were in for a storm.

A man was coming toward them, his tall, broad-shouldered body casting a long shadow in the afternoon sun.

Just as he came abreast of them, Billy tripped on a crack in the sidewalk. The man reached out and snagged the gerbil cage before it could tumble out of the boy's hands. "Whoa there, son."

"Thank you," Kate said, as she took the cage from him. She peered in to make sure Harry was okay. The gerbil gave her an accusatory look. She lowered the cage and made eye contact with Harry's rescuer. He was quite handsome in a generic, boyish-good-looks way.

"No problem. Phil Talbot." The man extended his hand. Kate juggled the cage over to her left hand so she could shake his.

"We're new in town. My daughter's just started here."

"Oh, what class is she in?" Kate asked to be polite.

"Gosh, how embarrassing. I don't know her teacher's name. My wife deals with all that, meeting the teachers and all. She's in third grade."

"What's her name?" Edie piped up.

"Ashley. Would you watch out for her and try to show her the ropes?" Mr. Talbot asked her.

"Sure," Edie said. "I'm in second grade. We have lunch at

the same time as the third graders. I'll look for her tomorrow in the cafeteria."

"That's terrific," Talbot said. "Can I tell her your name?"

"Oh, I'm sorry. I'm Kate Huntington-Canfield." It was a mouthful but she always used both names at school, since Edie's last name was also officially Huntington-Canfield. "This is Edie and Billy."

"Well, it's a pleasure to meet you, Mrs. Huntington-Canfield, and Edie and Billy. You take care now."

Kate caught herself turning to follow the man with her eyes as he walked away. He had a nice butt.

Stop that! She chuckled to herself. *Well, if the guys can look, why can't I?*

Halfway to the family van, she glanced back over her shoulder again. The handsome Mr. Talbot was standing on the school steps. He sketched her a small salute, then turned to go into the building.

Kate was glad there were no adults around to notice her blushing.

CHAPTER NINE

Skip's gut was churning with some very unfamiliar sensations. He stared, unseeing, at the paperwork on his desk.

He and Kate rarely fought, but the conversation earlier about how to keep Peter Jamieson safe had been rather tense. Now not only were they spending a good bit of time investigating the case for free but they were paying to guard him. Kate had offered to cover that cost, had insisted even, but he'd said no. Maybe he should let her pay for them. Maybe then he wouldn't resent this case so much.

That was a big part of the problem. He didn't know where to point his resentment. Pete was a nice guy and he certainly didn't deserve what was happening to him. So getting mad at him just made Skip feel worse. But he sure as hell didn't want to be pointing his anger at his wife for getting them into this mess. It wasn't her fault either.

Bottom line, he wanted out of this case. They should have listened to Kate's instincts at the very beginning. He had no business dealing with these slime bags.

He tried again to focus on the paperwork in front of him, but memories kept intruding from his state trooper days. Several times he'd dealt with men as bad as or worse than Frederico. It hadn't particularly bothered him back then.

I was younger then.

He shuffled the pages of the report on his desk, then signed off on it even though he hadn't really read it properly.

Hell, he knew age wasn't the issue. Difference was he was

brave back then, and now he was scared. He wanted to run as far away from this case as he could get.

Ain't no shame in sayin' no, son, his dead father's voice echoed in the back of his head. He started to smile, but his daddy's ghost wasn't done with him yet. *Think 'bout whether ya wanna do a job first, but once ya give yer word, ya gotta finish what ya started.*

He would definitely think twice next time before doing a favor for a friend.

Wait! That wasn't the way he wanted to be. Rob was far more than just a friend; the Franklins were like family. The kids even called them Uncle Rob and Aunt Liz. And Rob had saved Kate's life on two different occasions. Skip would give him his last pint of blood, without thinking once about it.

Skip shoved the paperwork into a desk drawer and stood up. He was going home early and take a nap. That was about the only decision he felt capable of making today.

~~~~~~~~~

Dave was stretched out on his hotel bed, his laptop balanced on his thighs. He was no longer feeling all that chipper about this assignment.

His cell phone rang. Grabbing it from the nightstand, he checked caller ID, then quickly answered. "Good evening, sir. How–"

"Plan A didn't work. What do you have in mind for Plan B?"

"I've been doing some research, both online and on the ground. The main cause of our affiliate's problem is an interesting specimen. But I have a concern."

"Which is?"

"Based on his history, there's a real good chance that efforts to discourage him may backfire and just make him more persistent. Our affiliate is of the opinion we should leave things be. I'm inclined to agree."

Silence for a moment. "You're suggesting doing nothing? What the hell am I payin' ya for if you're gonna just sit down there and do nothin'?" The voice had lost its polish and gone up in pitch. The man now sounded like the young upstart that he was.

Dave suppressed a sigh. "Sir, I know it's frustrating to not have the situation completely under control. But short of eliminating the problem completely, which would be likely to attract more undesirable attention, there is no definite way to control it. And I do think there is a good chance the problem will go away of its own accord."

"I sent you there to come up with a Plan B." The voice in his ear was a low growl now.

"Yes, sir. I've laid the groundwork for a way to do that, but again, it may or may not work."

A brief pause. "What do you have in mind?"

Dave tried to keep the words calm as he pushed them past gritted teeth. He hated talking about specifics over the phone, even if both parties were on throwaway cells bought with cash. No point in voicing that concern again. He'd just further aggravate the man on the other end of the line.

"First, he's taken the case *pro bono*—"

"What's that?"

Man, you really are a dumb shit.

"He's working for free, as a favor for a friend."

"Humph."

He had to admit he shared his boss's opinion of that behavior. *Never do nothin' for nothin'*, Dave's old man used to say.

"Second, his vulnerability is his family..." He really didn't want to admit to a specific crime over the damn phone. "Uh, I can convey the message that this case is really not worth it to him."

A long pause. "Okay."

Good, maybe the fool had heard him last time and wasn't going to totally micro-manage this assignment.

He decided to try one more time. "Again, sir, both our affiliate and myself believe any action at this point could backfire."

"Just do it. If it don't work, move on to Plan C."

"Yes, sir."

Dave disconnected, then popped a couple antacids. The nagging questions from the train were back. What the hell was he doing working for this idiot?

Well, he'd give Plan B his best shot. If he succeeded, he'd probably get a fat bonus. And if he didn't...

Dave opened his browser and went through the steps to access a highly protected website. Once in, he stared at the screen for several minutes. The zeroes at the end of the balance in his offshore account were very comforting.

~~~~~~~~

On Wednesday, Kate realized her life was actually getting back to normal. With Mac on the mend, she didn't feel the need to race to the hospital every day, and no more visits to Pete in jail.

She walked into Mac's Place with a bounce in her step.

Her mood deflated a notch when she slid onto the bench in their favorite booth. Rob's slouched shoulders and shadowed eyes suggested all was not well in his world.

"How ya doing, Kate?" His smile was half-hearted.

"I'm good. What's up with you?"

"I'm okay."

Yeah, not.

A waitress appeared next to their booth. She had waited on them several times before. "You all want your usual?"

They both nodded.

"So, you did good yesterday at the hearing," Kate said, not sure how else to draw him out. Something was obviously wrong.

"I doubt I'd have pulled it off without your input."

"I think you'd already convinced the judge. I just wanted to make sure, in case he was wavering."

The waitress was back already with two iced teas. She deposited them and straws on the table, then hurried off again. The noise level was rising as the restaurant filled with the lunchtime crowd. Raucous laughter broke out at a nearby table of construction workers.

"He was right, you know," Rob said in a low voice.

Kate wasn't sure she'd heard him correctly. "Who? About what?"

"The judge. It was crazy that we were willing to put up our own money."

Kate shrugged. They probably were a little crazy. But they could both afford it, to save a man's life. And as it had turned out, they didn't need to put up their own money.

"And now I've staked my reputation on this guy," Rob said. "What if we're wrong and he takes off?"

Ah, the bigger issue. His good name was much more important to Rob than money.

"I doubt he will. But if he does, I don't think the judge is going to hold it against you that you took a chance on the man."

He gave her a look that was almost accusatory. "You're the one, right from the beginning, who said I might be losing my perspective."

"Yeah, I did. But after meeting Pete and starting to work with him, I got why. He's a sweet guy who deserves a break. I think we'd be going above and beyond for him even without the hero piece."

"I sure as hell wouldn't be putting up my own money for bail."

She paused a moment, then said in a gentle voice, "Is this really about the money?"

He looked away.

The waitress chose that moment to deliver their crab cakes. Rob stole her pickles as Kate slathered tartar sauce on the bun of her sandwich.

She took a bite, letting the silence stretch out. She was half expecting him to change the subject.

He'd piled the pickles on his own sandwich but then he just stared at it. "I don't think it's even about this case. I don't know what's going on."

Finally he picked up the sandwich and took a bite. After a moment, he said, "I'm making some progress with the insurance mess. Pete's Social Security disability's been approved but it'll be at least a month until he actually gets paid." Rob seemed to get more grounded as he talked. "Fran's got more patience than I do. She's been pestering the health insurance company. I think she got disconnected at least a dozen times as they transferred her around."

Kate nodded. She had to deal with insurance companies way more than she wanted to. It usually took a minimum of three calls to get even a minor problem straightened out.

"Fran finally got the name of the person to talk to about getting a denied claim re-evaluated. I spoke to the guy this morning and he said he would look into it to determine if it had been denied in 'error.'" Rob made quotation marks in the air.

Kate snorted. "Did you threaten to sue?"

"No need. Companies tend to sit up and take notice when I add *attorney* while introducing myself." He gave her a small smile.

"Sounds like excellent progress." She decided not to press him about whatever was eating at him. He'd talk about it when he was ready. "What's going on with the criminal case?"

Rob's face clouded again. Maybe she should have left that topic alone as well.

"The detective sent me copies of the autopsy and the crime lab reports. There are a few things I think I can use. If you read between the lines in the autopsy, it sounds like the M.E. isn't completely convinced Matthews was killed where he was found."

"What are the chances of acquittal?"

He grimaced. "Not as good as I'd like them to be."

Kate's jaw dropped. "But the evidence is so shaky."

"Who knows how a jury's going to read this. There's a possibility they may be harder on him *because* he's a hero, a *fallen* hero."

Rob stopped and took another bite of his sandwich. His expression was thoughtful. "I think what's bothering me about this case," he said after a moment, "is that, in criminal law, you don't assume your client is innocent. Your goal isn't even to prove that. It's to plant seeds of reasonable doubt that he *might* be innocent."

"When did the legal system become so cynical?" she asked.

A corner of Rob's mouth quirked up. "Probably somewhere around the Middle Ages."

"So what's the problem?"

Rob shook his head, then took another bite of his sandwich. She polished off her own crab cake while she waited for him to continue.

"When I took Pete's case *pro bono*, I was helping a good guy deal with a civil law matter. Now the cynical lawyer side of me keeps wondering if he's not completely a good guy, that maybe he was, at the very least, trying to buy drugs that day."

"I've had a similar reaction," Kate said. "Several times I've asked myself why I'm expending so much time and energy on this guy."

"Not to mention money," Rob said.

"Yeah. Addicts can be so manipulative, so I get to wondering if we're being duped. And then I see him and realize again that he doesn't really present like an addict. He's a guy with PTSD who used drugs to help him cope."

"How convinced are you that he won't use again?" Rob asked.

"Before he was arrested for murder, I'd have said there was a very low chance. Now..." She shrugged. "Even out of jail, these are not ideal circumstances for clean and sober. He's isolated from everything familiar and under a lot of stress."

As she poured dressing onto her salad, she added, "Hopefully Skip will find something soon that will give Judith Anderson enough ammo to reopen the police investigation."

"Yeah," Rob said. "Then we can go back to *just* helping him with insurance companies and PTSD."

~~~~~~~~

As Kate was closing up her office at the end of the day, her mind turned again to Rob. He'd been in such a strange mood today. Things were looking up in Pete's case, for the most part, and yet Rob had seemed almost depressed. She hoped their talk had been at least somewhat helpful.

On her part, it had fertilized some seeds of doubt. They really were going out on a limb for this guy. She believed what she'd told Rob, that Pete was worthy of their help and their trust. But still...

She intentionally shifted mental gears as she crossed the street in front of her office building and started across the parking lot. Time to put aside clients, including Pete, and focus on her family.

Her steps slowed as she neared her Prius. A man was leaning against the driver's side door.

It took her a few seconds to recognize him out of context. "Mr. Talbot! What–"

"Sorry to bother you," he said, standing up. "If I could just have a few minutes of your time. It's about my daughter."

Kate laid her briefcase on the hood of her car and dug in her purse for her keys.

"Ashley isn't dealing well with the move," Talbot said. "I heard you're a therapist. I was wondering if I could... I mean I'd be happy to pay for your time."

Kate stifled a tired sigh. The man had obviously looked up her office address. "I'm not a child or family therapist, Mr. Talbot."

Wait! How would he know where I normally park?

She took half a step backward. "I'll be happy to give you a referral."

And how would he recognize my Prius? I was driving the family van yesterday.

She tensed.

Talbot's worried expression morphed into a predatory leer as he lunged. He grabbed her arm, just above the wrist. "If you scream, I'll have to shoot you."

CHAPTER TEN

Terror exploded in Kate's chest. Her knees turned to jelly. She instinctively pulled back, resisting as the man began dragging her across the parking lot.

This can't be happening!

"We're going for a little ride. I hate to mess up that nice face of yours but I gotta smack you around a little, so your husband learns to stay out of things that aren't his business." A one-handed fumble with a key fob elicited a beep from a dark nondescript sedan several rows away.

It is happening! Her mind scrambled to remember what to do.

He was dragging her toward his car as she continued to mutely resist.

She pulled back harder, then suddenly she shifted her weight and lunged toward him, throwing him off balance as she twisted her arm the way she'd been taught. Pulling against the weakest point of his grip, where fingertips meet the thumb, she broke loose. He stumbled backwards.

Kate took the stance that was ingrained from hundreds of hours of practice—arms partially extended, knees slightly bent, ready for the next move. Talbot—or whoever he was—righted himself and lunged for her. She sidestepped, hooking her leg around his ankle to yank him off his feet. He landed hard on the asphalt, his forearm taking the brunt of it. She heard a muted snapping sound.

He howled in pain, rolling over onto his back. Then he scrambled to his feet.

Terror shot through her again, immobilizing her brain. He wasn't supposed to get up!

But her body was instinctively poised for action–knees bent, arms in position.

He stared at her for a second, then started toward her.

A male voice yelled, "Hey, what the hell's going on?"

Kate fought the urge to look away. *Eyes on your opponent, always*, her *sensei*'s voice reverberated in her head.

But her assailant did look away, just for a second, as he was lunging for her.

Her well-trained body seemed to move on its own while her mind watched from a distance. Stepping to one side, she planted a hip against his, grabbed his shoulder and shoved him on past her. He didn't go down this time but she'd thrown him off balance. His own momentum carried him several feet away before he could stop and whirl around.

Footsteps pounded toward them.

Her assailant glared at her, then clutching his left arm against his ribcage, he darted for his car.

She got a good look at his back license plate as he raced out of the parking lot, tires squealing. She repeated the numbers over and over to herself.

Her rescuer stopped beside her, huffing for air. "I called the police," he gasped out and held up a cell phone.

Kate tried to take a deep breath, without much success. Her chest was tight, her heart racing. "Do you have a piece of paper?"

The man shook his head.

Kate looked around for her purse. It lay beside her car, half its contents spilled out on the asphalt. Stooping down, she located a small pad and a pen. She'd forgotten two of the digits in the middle of the plate number but she wrote down those she could remember.

Two cruisers, sirens blaring, turned into the parking lot. "Sir, you might want to put your hands in the air," Kate said, "just in case they assume you're my assailant."

The man, looking a bit rattled now, did so. "You're pretty

calm for somebody who just got attacked."

"Yeah, it probably won't last."

The uniformed officers were now out of their vehicles and cautiously moving toward them.

"It's okay, officers," Kate called out. "This is the guy who phoned 911. The man who attacked me is gone." Her rescuer lowered his arms.

"Are you okay, ma'am?" one of the officers asked. "Did you get a good look at his face?" He took out his notepad.

Kate felt the calm detachment slip a notch. She really didn't want to go over this a half dozen times. "Yeah, I'm fine. Uh, this is related to an ongoing case. Could you contact Detective Judith Anderson, please, and see if she can meet us at the station?"

The officer gave her an odd look, but he keyed his radio to relay the message through dispatch.

The second cop had ushered her benefactor several yards away and was taking down his statement. Kate saw the man gesture toward the space where Talbot's car had been. She walked over and extended her hand. "Thank you. If you hadn't intervened..." The detachment slipped another notch. She shuddered.

He smiled as he shook her hand. "Something tells me you still would've mopped up the pavement with him."

She wasn't at all sure about that but she returned his smile. "Well, thanks again."

He sketched a salute, reminiscent of Talbot's from the school steps, and headed for his car.

Kate was barely able to hide her reaction to that innocent gesture. Suddenly, the adrenaline was gone, and the rest of her unnatural calm along with it.

~~~~~~~~

Skip usually enjoyed the alone time that driving provided, but his own thoughts had not been good company lately. He tried to think about other things but his mind, like a tongue seeking out a sore tooth, insistently came back to the Jamieson case, stirring up the anxiety and knots in his stomach that now accompanied all thoughts about that case.

I'm turning into a damn coward.

As he turned onto his street, he saw Dolph's car parked in Kate's usual spot. Rose's car was in front of his. "What the hell?" he muttered.

He pulled up in front of the house and climbed out of his truck. Dolph got out of his car and walked toward him. The grim expression on the older man's face made Skip's blood turn to ice.

"What's the matter?"

"There's been a development," Dolph said. "In the Jamieson case. We need to go meet with Judith right away."

"It doesn't look like Kate's home yet. Let me go tell Maria I'll be late."

"Rose already talked to Maria. She's staying here with her and the kids. Kate's meeting us at the precinct."

"What the hell's going on?"

"Kate's fine. Nobody's hurt."

Somehow those words made him more scared, not less. "What the hell's happened?"

Dolph held out his hand. "Let me drive, son. I'll fill you in on the way."

Reluctantly Skip relinquished his keys. He was pretty damn sure he wasn't going to like what he was about to hear.

~~~~~~~~

Judith had just finished taking Kate's formal statement when Dolph and Skip entered the detectives' bullpen and headed in their direction. Skip pulled Kate from her chair and wrapped his arms around her.

She could hear his heart pounding. Leaning back in his arms, she looked up at him with a lopsided smile. "I'm okay, sweetheart. You know that kickass Kate we were talking about. Well, she had her debut today." She was trying for more confidence than she felt but wasn't completely able to keep her voice steady.

Skip looked down at her without returning her smile. Instead he crushed her against him again. She was both comforted and somewhat unhinged as his warmth surrounded her. She started to shake. His arms tightened. They clung to each other for a few minutes.

When he finally let her go, she felt a bit more grounded. She looked around. Judith and Dolph were gone. The few other detectives still at their desks were studiously ignoring them.

"Come on." She took Skip's hand. "They've gone to the conference room."

Once they were all settled in chairs around the table, Judith said, "The partial plate number was enough. Matched a car that was reported stolen at four-thirty this afternoon. But it could have been taken as early as one-fifteen. That's when the owner returned to his office from lunch. Kate's given us a description of this guy, but there's not much that really makes him stand out. About six-two, average build, blue eyes, blond hair, good-looking. I want to have you sit down with a police artist before you leave, Kate. He's on his way in."

Kate nodded. "This is related to Pete's case. The guy said so."

"What did he say?" Skip's voice was tight.

Kate looked at him, trying to judge how close to snapping he was. This laid-back giant she was married to had a tendency to go ballistic when his family was threatened.

"That he was going to beat me up, as a warning to get you to back off."

"What happened?" The muscles in his clenched jaw twitched with tension.

"He grabbed my arm. I twisted away from him and used my aikido to keep him from getting his hands on me again." She softened her voice. "He's the one who ended up hurt. He broke his arm when he landed on the pavement."

Skip picked up her wrist from the table and gently rubbed his thumb over the bruise that was beginning to show.

The sweet gesture was almost her undoing. She blinked hard and tried to take a deep breath. Her chest was tight.

"Had you ever seen this guy before?" Dolph asked.

She'd gone over all this with Judith but they needed to know as well. Another attempt at a deep breath was a bit more successful. She cleared her throat. "I met him yesterday, outside the kids' school. He said his name was Talbot, and his daughter went there."

"I'll call the school tomorrow," Judith said. "But I somehow doubt there's an Ashley Talbot enrolled there."

"So he's been checking you all out," Dolph asked.

"Yeah, but that meeting was also to get me to trust him so he could get close enough to grab me," Kate said.

"It would've worked with a lot of women," Judith said. "He would've had them in his car before they'd had a chance to suck in air to scream. Pretty brassy of the guy to try this in broad daylight."

"And to let her get a good look at his face," Dolph added.

"Do you think he planned to... kill Kate?" Skip's voice shook.

"No," Judith said. "I think he assumed she was an easy-to-intimidate woman whom he could attack and then threaten her with dire consequences if she went to the police."

Kate had worked with enough rape survivors to know what kind of threats–that he'd come back and kill her, or hurt her kids. Her breath caught in her throat at that thought. Had he planned to rape her too? She shook her head. Best not to go there.

"Besides, if he'd wanted her dead, he could've shot her from the safety of his car," Dolph said.

Kate narrowed her eyes at him. *You're not helping, Dolph!*

She shot a glance at Skip. His jaw was clenched but he didn't look like he was going to blow.

He turned to her. "I'm gonna have Rose assign a bodyguard to you."

She wasn't sure how she felt about that idea but before she could respond, Dolph said, "A bodyguard might just force him to use more deadly force."

Judith nodded. "My gut says he won't come after Kate again. She showed him that she's going to fight back. He's trying to scare you all off without drawing too much attention. Which has had the exact opposite effect. I've got a call in to Tyrell Cooper. I want to know what the hell is going on here that someone is so all-fired determined to get you to back off."

"This guy today, maybe he's Matthews' killer," Dolph said.

"Maybe." Judith's cell phone rang. She glanced at the caller ID, then hit the button for speaker before placing it on the table. "Hey, Ty, we've got a situation here." She told him who was present in the room and then rapidly filled him in, half of it in cop-speak that Kate only partially understood.

"Man, you guys sure know how to mess with a man's evening, don't you?" the voice from the phone said when she was done. But Tyrell's tone held no rancor. "Doesn't sound like Frederico's style. He sticks to his comfort zone. I can't see him sending somebody out to the suburbs to do something like this. Besides, if he wanted you out of this that badly, Skip, you'd be dead by now."

"Do you all have him under surveillance?" Skip asked.

"No, not enough manpower to watch all the pimps and dealers. But... I seem to recall a rumor I heard awhile back about him branching out. One of his men bragging about how they'd all be rich, 'cause his boss was getting into bigger and better things. Let me see if I can find out any more about that."

"That would fit with something that happened yesterday, when I was talking to Frederico's girls," Skip said. "One of them tried to pick my pocket. I got the impression he's making his girls turn in a certain number of wallets a day, as well as their other proceeds."

"Credit card fraud," Judith said.

Dolph sat up straighter. "He said something about the girls just being a sideline, the first time we talked to him."

"If that's what's going on," Tyrell said from the phone, "it would explain a lot. That can be a pretty lucrative racket. I'll call you all if I come up with anything." He disconnected.

Skip turned to Judith. "Any chance that all this gives you enough leverage to get the case reopened?"

"I'll run it by my lieutenant, but I'd say odds are 50/50."

Skip leaned forward in his chair. "Look, if we keep Pete under wraps until the case comes to trial, isn't there a good chance he'll be acquitted?"

Judith looked around the room. "If anybody asks, I never said this. I think again we're talking 50/50."

"I think Rob would agree with you," Kate said. "And I'm not

comfortable with leaving Pete in a safe house for months, waiting for his case to come to trial. With nobody for company but his guards, and he can't contact his family or friends."

Or go to an NA meeting.

Judith stood up. "The artist should be here by now. Kate, you want to come with me. We'll see if we can get a nice picture of this guy."

The police artist did not use pad and pencil as Kate had expected. He sat them down at a computer monitor and started asking her questions about the shape of the man's head, his features, the length and curliness of his hair, etc. He jotted notes, then he hit a few keys on his keyboard and an image came up on the screen–the shape of a face with no features. "Let me know which one comes closest," he said, as he slowly moved through a series of such outlines.

When she stopped him, he asked, "Is that the right shape or does it need some tweaking?"

"Maybe a little fuller in the cheeks."

He hit some keys and the cheeks puffed out a bit more.

After an hour, Kate and the police artist had fine-tuned the sketch as much as they could. The face peering back at them on the computer screen was handsome, the small crow's feet around the eyes the only thing that belied the boyish shape and smoothness of the skin.

"He's a pretty boy, ain't he?" the artist said with a slight smirk.

"Yeah, and that's what worries me," Kate said. "He's too... generic. He looks like every classically handsome man I've ever seen. Hell, he even looks a little bit like my husband."

Judith was standing behind her chair. "I'm afraid you're right. It's gonna be hard for someone to pick him out of the crowd based on this picture, but I'll circulate it with the uniforms, with a be-on-the-lookout bulletin. Let me put together some mug shots for you to look at. Can you come in tomorrow?"

Kate groaned. She was exhausted. "I've got a full day tomorrow but I could come by after work."

"That's fine. It'll give us time to pull out just the guys that match this description. Otherwise it would take forever to go through all of them." In a rare gesture, Judith put a hand briefly on her shoulder. "Good job of defending yourself. If only all women would take self-defense classes."

"Thanks, but it was at least half dumb luck," Kate said as she twisted around to look up at the detective. Judith's face sagged with fatigue.

Kate felt a surge of empathy for this woman who was trying so valiantly to keep the bad guys under control. She stood and extended her hand to shake Judith's. Softly she said, "There's a lot of evil in the world, Detective. Thanks for all you do to keep it at bay."

CHAPTER ELEVEN

On Friday morning, Skip was trying once again to get caught up on paperwork, and to *not* think about the Jamieson case.

He was almost used to the knots in his stomach that accompanied any such thoughts, but now he had a new set of worries. His wife was in danger.

He'd insisted on picking Kate up at her office the previous evening to take her to the police station. She'd seemed mildly annoyed but she'd gone along with the plan. They had stopped for Chinese carry-out on the way, then Kate had spent two futile hours pouring over Judith's mug shots.

He ground his teeth. They needed to somehow move this damned investigation forward.

The next sheet of paper in his in-box brought home another reality. An invoice that should have been paid last week had gotten mixed in with the reports from their operatives. Between his preoccupation and Rose spending most of her time at the hospital with Mac, the agency was suffering.

Skip had turned to his computer to pay the bill online when his phone rang.

"Canfield."

He could just barely hear the timid voice on the other end. "Mr. Canfield, I may have some information for you."

Hope surged in his chest even as his stomach churned.

"May I have your name, ma'am?" He kept his voice gentle, not wanting to spook the caller.

"I'd rather not say over the phone," the breathy voice

whispered. "It's about Jimmy. I was one of his girls. Can you meet me?"

"Sure," he said, ignoring his stomach.

She gave him an address. It was just a couple blocks from where he'd talked to the prostitutes on Tuesday. "I'll be outside. You need to act like you're a john. I... I don't want to end up like Jimmy."

Skip looked at his watch. He needed time to arrange back-up; he wasn't about to go down there alone. "I'll be there around one-thirty. That work?"

"Okay," the quiet voice agreed and hung up.

~~~~~~~

Skip pulled over to the curb half a block from the address the caller had given him. Several young women were standing on the sidewalk further up the street. Their outfits, which just barely covered the essential parts of their anatomy, proclaimed their profession. He squinted against the glare of sunlight coming through the windshield. The only one in the group who looked familiar was the young-looking one who had given him the speculative look on Tuesday.

"It's party time," Dolph said with a slight grin. He seemed amused at the thought of Skip pretending he needed to pay for sex.

Skip scowled at him and got out of the truck.

When he reached the cluster of women, they gathered around him. One started stroking his arm. "Aren't you the handsome fella now," she purred in a rather deep voice.

Skip gave her a hard look. Was she a *he* in drag?

Before he could decide, he was rescued by a voice cutting through the chatter. "Sorry, ladies. He's one of my regulars."

Although it was a bit louder and more strident, Skip recognized the voice from the phone. The girl-woman who'd been eyeing him on Tuesday elbowed her way through her sisters of the street. They responded with good-natured obscenities.

She took Skip's arm. "You got a twenty," she whispered.

He produced the fifty he'd put in his pants' pocket before leaving the office. He had locked his wallet in the glove box of his truck this time but he had a couple more bills on him.

Her eyes widened a bit, then she took the money and slipped it inside her push-up bra.

"Ooh-la-la," another prostitute said "You ever get tired of Roxie, Big Boy, you keep me in mind!"

"Come on, honey. Let's go up to my place." Roxie tugged Skip toward the doorway of a rundown apartment building.

He took a closer look at the place. Maybe flop house would be a better description. While pretending to be besotted with little Roxie, Skip scanned the entranceway for signs of an ambush.

His mouth was dry but some of his old calm seemed to be kicking in.

According to plan, Dolph was staggering down the sidewalk toward them, pretending to be drunk.

Roxie led Skip inside and started up a set of stairs. The odors smacked him in the face—mold, urine, stale sweat, and a few others he couldn't name. He swallowed to quell a wave of nausea, then breathed through his mouth.

On the second floor landing, Dolph stumbled past them and rounded the next corner of the stairwell, as if he were headed up to the next level. But once Skip and Roxie were inside her room, he would move back to her door to stand watch.

Skip surveyed the sparsely-furnished room. It contained just a double bed, a dilapidated dresser and a small table. There was a door that probably led to a bathroom. The sheets on the bed were gray. He was fairly sure they hadn't started out that color.

He gestured toward the bed. "Have a seat, Miss Roxie." He let some Texas creep into his voice. It always seemed to charm the ladies.

Roxie shook her head. "You sit. I'll stand."

Skip eyed the bed. "How 'bout we both stand."

Roxie bit her lower lip, then shook her head again. "I didn't realize you were so big." She took a couple steps back, putting the bed between them.

Skip gingerly sat down on the corner of the sagging mattress. The possibility of bed bugs crossed his mind. He pushed the thought aside.

Roxie moved around in front of him but stayed several feet away. "Sorry I had to bring you up here, but if that bastard Frederico got wind I was talkin' to you, I'd be floatin' in the harbor."

"I understand, ma'am. And the fifty's yours to keep, for the information."

"I'll have to give most of it to Frederico, or he'll wanna know what I was doin' today, instead of makin' him money."

"There's a bit more where that came from, if your information is useful. So you're one of Frederico's fillies now?"

Roxie curled her lip. "Yeah, whether I like it or not. The bastard killed Jimmy and now he's taken over his girls." Her eyes filled with tears. "I liked Jimmy. He never beat us. Left us 'nough money to live okay."

"You know for a fact that Frederico killed him?" Skip asked.

Roxie dropped her gaze to the floor. She gave a half shrug that threatened to dislodge the strap of her skimpy top from her shoulder. "He's been talkin' like he did. To some of us girls, at least."

"What has he been saying?"

"Oh, ya know, things like, 'Now that I'm rid of that dumbass Matthews' and shit like that."

Not exactly a full-blown confession.

"Do you have any proof that he killed Jimmy?" Skip hoped this wasn't a fool's errand. He most likely wouldn't be able to sell Judith and her lieutenant on re-opening the case just on the say-so of a skittish prostitute.

"Not yet, but I'm gonna try to get a recording of him talkin' 'bout it. Ya gotta understand." Her voice took on a pleading tone. "I ain't doin' this for money. I want justice for Jimmy. But I gotta get out of town. Once I get the evidence, that is. Even with Frederico in jail, his boys'll probably come after me. And nobody else will be willin' to... ya know, work with me, 'cause I turned in my pimp."

The young woman's words were plausible but the whole speech sounded rehearsed. Skip was keeping a close eye on the bathroom door that was sitting slightly ajar. "How much do you need?"

"Couple hundred would get me a bus ticket, and help me get settled someplace new."

The figure was much too low. The bus ticket would eat up almost half of that, and rooms in flop houses might be cheap, but they weren't free. She should have started much higher, to give herself some bargaining room.

When he didn't respond right away, Roxie made an offer that was no doubt intended to sweeten the deal. "You're cute. I wouldn't mind throwin' in a little bonus." She gave him a seductive smile that looked bizarrely out of place on her child-like face.

Skip managed to fake a return smile. "Well now, Roxie, that's a temptin' offer, but I'm a married man."

Roxie's expression said quite eloquently that she didn't see how that had anything to do with anything. She took a step closer to the bed.

He felt a surge of pity for this girl who believed her sexuality was the own leverage she had in the world. "*Happily* married," he said gently. "I may be able to come up with a few hundred for–"

Suddenly she was in his lap, straddling him and grinding her hips. Her miniskirt hiked up to reveal the absence of underwear.

Skip had grabbed her by the shoulders to lift her off of him, when he noticed a disconcerting sensation. He stood up, dumping her on the floor, her skirt now around her waist, leaving her privates exposed.

Skip towered over her, his fists clenched. "You should be very glad I don't hit women," he said through gritted teeth.

A scrapping noise came from the direction of the bathroom. He glanced over. The crack between door and frame was twice the width it had been a few moments ago.

He drew his gun. Roxie let out a shriek. He kicked the door. The center panel splintered as it crashed open.

A scantily-clad young woman sprawled backwards against a filthy toilet. A disposable camera fell from her hand.

Skip started into the bathroom, then his survival instincts prevailed. He stopped to quickly scan the tiny room for other occupants. The woman scrambled to her feet. She reached down for the camera but Skip put his foot on it.

She looked up at him, calculation rather than fear in her face, then she ducked to the side and darted past him.

Skip whirled around. Roxie was opening the door to the hall. Her friend shoved her aside and ran out. Roxie tried to follow but Dolph stepped into the doorway, blocking her way.

Skip hit the button on the back of the camera and looked at the image. He was standing over the exposed Roxie, his pants exhibiting a definite protrusion.

His cheeks burned. Stifling the roar that was building in his chest, he dropped the camera on the floor and smashed it with his heel.

A modicum of sanity returned. Realizing there might be a still-intact memory card, he picked up the shattered camera and jammed it in his pocket.

In the bedroom, Dolph had his hand wrapped securely around Roxie's arm. She was squirming and hissing at him to let her go. He ignored her and cocked his head at Skip.

"Other gal was taking pictures from the bathroom." Skip's voice was a low growl. "Of this little tramp givin' me an unsolicited lap dance."

Roxie turned eyes wide with fear toward him. "This wasn't my idea. Frederico put me up to it. He said we were to get compromisin' pictures of you, so he could make you stop investigatin' Jimmy's murder."

"What happened to the pics?" Dolph asked.

"Smashed the camera. Pieces are in my pocket."

"Please, Mr. Canfield," Roxie begged. "Can you give me enough money to get outta town? Frederico's gonna beat the shit outta me if I don't produce those pictures."

Under other circumstances, Skip would have been concerned for the young woman's safety. Now all he felt was scorn. "You can keep the fifty. I don't want it back after it's touched your skin."

Her waif-like face morphed into a twisted mask. She snarled at him, "How dare you act like I'm dirt, Mr. High and Mighty. You're the *pathetic* one. You're no better than the others, ready to poke your little thingie wherever you can."

Skip clenched his fists. His mind searched for the right retort, but a small, saner corner of his brain realized this creature had no concept of a world in which men were willingly faithful to their wives and had no desire to 'poke their thingies' wherever they could.

Bile rose in the back of his throat. His stomach churned. He just wanted out of here. In two strides he was past Roxie and out in the hallway. He took a deep breath, then wished he hadn't. The hall didn't smell so good.

Out of the corner of his eye, he saw Dolph give the hooker a final shake, then let her go.

As they headed down the stairs, Roxie shrieked from above them, "You're pathetic bastards, both of you!"

CHAPTER TWELVE

Dolph snuck another sideways glance. Skip was staring at the road ahead, his mouth so tightly clenched Dolph feared he might crack his jawbone.

They were halfway back to the agency office and the younger man still hadn't said a word. Dolph broke the silence. "So we got Freddie trying to convince us that Matthews wasn't worth bothering with, but now this Roxie gal says he put her up to getting pics of you to stop you from investigating."

Skip grunted.

"What happened before I joined the party?"

For a moment he thought he wasn't going to get an answer. Then Skip said, "Roxie acted like she was all broken up about Matthews. And she claimed Frederico was saying he had killed him, but the words she quoted were kind of ambiguous."

"What were they?"

Another moment of silence, then Skip shook his head. "Can't remember exactly. Something along the lines of now that he was rid of Matthews."

Dolph mulled that over. "So could be he *got* rid of Matthews, or he was just glad to *be* rid of Matthews."

"That was my take on it." Skip's voice sounded almost normal, although his jaw was still tight. "But either way he's trying to get us to leave it alone. I don't care what Tyrell thinks. Freddie was behind that bastard coming after Kate."

"Speaking of Tyrell, lemme call him. See if he can get any more out of Roxie."

"Tell him to hurry. She's probably gonna be on the next bus out of town. Oh, and Dolph, uh, try to avoid saying too much about the picture-taking, would you?"

Dolph cocked his head at him. Skip's eyes were glued to the road but a red tide was creeping up his cheeks.

"I can probably work around that." Dolph dug in his pants' pocket for his cell phone.

~~~~~~~~~~

After he dropped Dolph off at the agency office, Skip went home. He knew he wouldn't get any work done the rest of the day, and he couldn't wait to get out of these clothes.

At home he gave Maria and the kids a perfunctory greeting. Edie ran to him to show him a drawing she had made in school.

"Don't touch me, Pumkin. I'm really dirty." Skip held a hand out to stop her from hugging him. She cocked her head to one side.

"I'm all sweaty. Worked hard today." He tried to keep his voice gentle. "I gotta take a shower. I promise to look at your picture later, okay?"

"Sure, Daddy." Her little face brightened.

In the master bedroom, he undid his belt and dropped his pants on the floor. After peeling off shirt, underwear and socks, he headed for the shower.

When Kate got home, his skin was still a bit pink from where he'd scrubbed it. His clothes and sneakers were banging around in the washing machine.

He sat on the living room floor, leaning against the sofa and pretending to focus on what Edie was telling him about her day at school.

"Hi, sweetheart." Kate leaned down to kiss him. "You're home early."

"Daddy worked really hard this afternoon," Edie informed her mother.

"Oh, yeah?" Kate said in a bemused voice.

"I was sweaty when I got home. Told her not to hug me 'til I'd had a shower," Skip said.

"And he washed his clothes, includin' his shoes!" his

daughter added.

He gave the little girl a repressive look. Sometimes Edie was too smart for *his* good.

"I'll explain later." He didn't want to say anything in front of little ears.

~~~~~~~

But the explanation never happened. Skip was unnaturally preoccupied over dinner, failing to even fake that he was paying attention to the children's chatter. Kate's concerned glances didn't seem to register. When she offered to read the children their stories after bath time, he just nodded.

After finishing Edie's story, Kate leaned over to kiss her. The little girl wrinkled her brow. "Mommy, what's wrong with Daddy?"

"He just had a bad day at work. It's one of those things you have to deal with sometimes, when you're a grown-up."

Edie pondered that for a moment. "Do I *have* to grow up?"

Kate laughed. "Not for quite awhile yet, sweetie. Now sleep tight."

"'Night, Mommy."

Downstairs, Skip was sitting on the sofa, staring into space. Kate sat down and snuggled against his side. He put his arm around her shoulders.

"Rough day?" she said softly, half question, half statement.

"Yeah, but I'd rather just forget about it."

Kate debated for a second, then opted to let it go. Sometimes the best thing either of them could do in their respective professions was compartmentalize. She knew her ability to leave work at work, most of the time at least, was what kept her sane.

She dropped her head down on his shoulder and laid her arm across his waist. "This is my favorite part of the day." She chuckled softly. "Well, second favorite. My favorite is when we go to bed."

When he didn't respond, she dug her fingers into the ticklish spot just above his hip. "Lighten up, Canfield."

"Stop that." He batted her hand away.

Kate sat up and looked into his face. "Boy, you did have a rough day, didn't you?"

"Sorry, darlin'." He dropped his gaze. "Didn't mean to take it out on you."

"It's okay. Everybody's allowed to be grumpy sometimes." She snuggled up against him again. "Want to watch some TV? Lose ourselves in brainless entertainment for awhile?"

"Not really."

She looked up into his face with a suggestive smirk. "Want a massage?"

The smile he gave her was more sad than cheerful. "I'll take a rain check."

Okay, something was seriously wrong here.

"Maybe we should just go to bed early then." She didn't get the lascivious grin she'd expected, but Skip did agree that was a good idea.

When Kate came out of the bathroom, he was already in bed, his forearm across his eyes to shield them from the light. She slid between the sheets and turned off the lamp on her nightstand.

Considering his mood, she hadn't expected to make love. When he rolled over and wrapped his arms around her, she tried not to let her sigh of relief be obvious.

Slowly he began to stroke and kiss various parts of her body. He was always a gentle and considerate lover but tonight he seemed to be slower and more methodical than usual. She was trying to figure out what that meant when a wave of sensation swept over her. His kisses had trailed down over the tender skin of her belly and his tongue was doing slow circles around her belly button.

She moaned and arched her back, digging her fingers into his hair. His lips trailed fire even lower and she struggled for control. She tugged on his hair, signaling it was time to leave foreplay behind.

But he ignored the signal. His lips touched the very core of her. She groaned and writhed as a surge of sweet agony ripped through her. He hung on, kissing and probing, one long slender hand supporting her buttocks that were now in the air.

Finally the waves subsided into gentle ripples of warmth flowing through her. He eased her down on the bed and trailed his lips back up to nuzzle each breast. Then he settled down on his side and held her tenderly against him.

Encircled by her husband's warm arms, Kate's eyes drooped. Her body felt like jello.

No. Jello is cold and I'm definitely not cold.

More like warm and flowing, like hot fudge sauce. She giggled a little at the image of her body melting into a puddle of fudge sauce and Skip lapping her up.

Skip's arms tightened slightly around her and he kissed her hair.

She had almost drifted off when a guilty realization jolted her awake. How totally selfish of her.

She felt Skip's body tense a little as she rolled over in his arms. She put both hands on his broad chest and stroked the smooth skin. It quivered under her fingers. She smiled. She could still make him quiver with the lightest of touches. It took a moment to realize that his quivering skin was the only reaction she was getting.

She wrapped one arm around his slim waist and pulled him closer against her as she kissed his chest, then nuzzled the side of his neck.

He gently disentangled himself and rolled over on his back, staring at the ceiling.

The remnants of her warm afterglow evaporated. Anxiety fluttered in her chest. She laid her hand on his shoulder. "It's okay. It happens," she whispered.

He shook his head slightly.

"Never?"

"Well, once," he said softly. "A long time ago."

"I'm sorry, sweetheart."

He glanced over at her. "What are you apologizin' for? It's not your fault."

For having fun when you weren't.

"Something happened today, didn't it?"

His mouth thinned into a grim line as he stared at the ceiling. "I don't want to talk about it."

She knew she shouldn't push him, but she did anyway. "Maybe you should. Maybe it'll help to get it out."

This time his glance held a hint of irritation. He didn't answer her. After a moment, he swung his legs off the bed and stood up. "I'm gonna take a shower. I'm kind of sweaty."

Kate stared at her husband's naked back as he headed for the bathroom. He *never* took a shower after making love.

What could've happened that would make him react this way? Her hand went to her mouth as one horrible possibility occurred to her. Women came on to her handsome husband on a regular basis. She tried not to be insecure about it, but...

That didn't happen. You know it didn't! her rational brain was saying even as her chest ached and a sob grew in her throat. Unable to stay still, she jumped out of bed and put on her robe.

He had a strong sex drive. They made love almost every night.

What if that isn't enough anymore? A little voice said in the back of her head.

Stop that! Get a grip.

She plumped the pillows up against the headboard, then sat down and leaned her back against them. Noticing her arms were crossed, she intentionally uncrossed them. *Open body language. I* don't *want to start an argument!*

Skip came out of the bathroom. He had wrapped a towel around his waist–also not his usual behavior. He walked over to the chair in the corner of the room and picked up his robe. He donned it and dropped the towel on the floor.

His eyes darted toward her, then away. Her heart was in her throat as he came over and sat down on his side of the bed, his back to her.

"You need to tell me." She struggled to keep the tears out of her voice. "I hate to push you, but my mind is conjuring up all kinds of possibilities."

He glanced back over his shoulder. "I didn't cheat on you."

"I didn't think you had," she lied.

He leaned his elbows on his knees and put his face in his hands.

Kate made herself keep quiet while he sat that way for a full minute. Then the story came out, in bits and pieces.

"It was disgusting. One minute we were talking, and the next she was wiggling on my lap, and..." He was silent for several seconds. "Another gal was in the bathroom, taking pictures."

Kate sucked in her breath.

"I destroyed the camera. Stomped it to pieces. She said Frederico had put her up to it."

Kate rolled halfway over and put her hand on his broad back. She wasn't sure what to say. It did sound disgusting, but still... why had the experience rocked him so?

She flashed to a memory from college—a party her freshman year. A strange boy had rubbed himself against her butt on the dance floor. It had freaked her out a bit. She'd gone home and showered, and washed her dress. She'd probably thrown her underwear in the washer for good measure.

Still his reaction seemed extreme. She'd been a naive eighteen-year-old. He was a forty-four-year-old ex-cop.

She rubbed her hand across Skip's back. His muscles were tight under the terrycloth. She moved over to kneel behind him and started massaging the knots in his shoulders and back. They gave no signs of relaxing. If anything, his shoulders tensed more.

Understanding suddenly dawned. She resisted the urge to smack herself in the forehead. She'd been a trauma recovery specialist for two decades and it had taken her this long to realize what had happened?

Her stomach unknotted. This she knew how to fix.

"Skip, turn around and look at me," she said in the voice she used when giving the children medicine—gentle but firm, brooking no arguments.

He threw one leg up on the bed and turned halfway toward her, looking over his shoulder.

"All the way around," she said, spinning her finger in a circle.

Sighing, he turned the rest of the way around, sitting cross-legged in front of her. She put her hands on his thighs, covered by the terrycloth robe.

"You've never had unwanted erections before?" she asked gently.

He dropped his gaze. After a moment, he said in a tight voice, "All the time, in my younger years, when a pretty gal walked by. This was different."

She waited for him to continue. When he didn't, she prompted, "How so?"

"I wasn't... I didn't find her at all attractive. The whole set-up was... I was thinking about how I might pick up bed bugs from the grimy bed, and how sad she was. And then she jumped on me. I was repulsed..." He trailed off.

She picked up one of his long slender hands and held it between hers. "I can't begin to tell you how many times I've listened to rape and incest survivors shamefully admit that their bodies sometimes responded to what was being done to them. Even as their minds were reeling with disgust and a dozen other negative emotions."

He was staring at their clasped hands.

"Our bodies are primitive, and rather simple things in a way," she said. "Expose them to certain kinds of stimulation and they may respond, without being all that discriminating about the source of that stimulation."

"So if my body's so damned simple and primitive," he said through clenched teeth, "why did it respond to *her*, and now it *won't* respond to you?"

She frowned. "I wish I had a good answer for that one, but it seems to be the way things work. Those same rape and incest survivors often can't respond later to the men they love." She paused. "At least not until they forgive themselves, and their bodies."

Skip was still looking at their hands. He gave his head a small shake.

She reached up to comb the hair back off his forehead. Then she slid her hand down his cheek and under his jaw to nudge his face up. He closed his eyes and his Adam's apple bobbed as he swallowed.

After a moment he opened his eyes. "So I have to forgive my body. How the hell do I do that?"

"You start by admitting that you're pissed at it for betraying you that way."

Skip digested that for a moment. Then he tried to smile at her but didn't quite pull it off. "Comes in handy sometimes, being married to a therapist."

He glanced past her shoulder at the alarm clock on her nightstand. "Well, despite the roller coaster ride this evening has been, we're still going to be able to get a good night's sleep." He started to shrug out of his robe.

"Not so fast, buddy." She ran her hands over his muscular chest, then shoved the robe further down on his arms to trap them against his body. "That's just the first step."

"Kate, I, uh, really don't think–"

"Thinking is not required. We're not leaving things this way. You know how you have to get back on the horse when it throws you?"

"Heard that line a few too many times lately," he muttered. "Kate, I–"

She put a finger on his lips. "Hear me out. I don't work with sexual dysfunction *per se*, but I did take some classes on sexuality in grad school. There are some techniques that go all the way back to Masters and Johnson. The idea is that you let yourself just relax and enjoy, with no, um, assumptions it's going to lead to intercourse or orgasm. As a matter of fact, you're prohibited from having intercourse in the first exercise. So the pressure's totally off."

"So you think we should do this first exercise tonight?"

"As you pointed out, the night is still young."

"Okay, what do I do?"

"Not a damned thing." Hands on his shoulders, she turned him around and gently shoved him back on the bed. She shrugged out of her own robe and straddled his waist. "This time, I do all the work."

He tried to reach for her but she was kneeling on his robe and he couldn't move his arms.

Kate decided she liked that set-up, for now at least. "Huh-uh. You lie still now."

She continued the massage she'd started on his shoulders, kneading his chest muscles slowly with gentle hands.

He stared up at her for a moment, then his face softened and he closed his eyes. "I could get used to this," he murmured.

Finally she'd kneaded the tension out of his upper body. She lightly kissed his shoulder, then lifted one knee slightly to tug his robe off that arm. Draping it across his chest in front of her, she began massaging his bicep.

She felt a quickening in her abdomen. *Whoa there, sugar. You've got a long way to go yet.*

Ignoring her own body's reaction, she massaged his arm and hand until they were as limp as a noodle. Then she repeated the process with the other arm. When that one was also completely relaxed, she touched her lips to his palm, a feather light kiss. His eyes sprang open and he started to reach for her.

She put her hands on his forearms and leaned her weight forward, pushing him down into the mattress. "Lie still!" But she was smiling down at him.

He bit his lower lip and closed his eyes again.

She swung her leg off of him and knelt beside him.

"Are you sure we're not allowed to make love?" he whispered.

"Absolutely *verboten*," she said softly. Passing over his rock-hard abs for the time being, she moved down to massage his legs.

Note to self: let's do this again some time.

"What happens if I fall asleep?"

"I'll wake you up."

She rubbed his feet for awhile, until she thought he might indeed be almost asleep. On her knees, she scooted back up to his waist. The movement brought him around. He opened one eye and looked up at her, his smile dreamy.

She smiled back and placed one hand on his belly. Both eyes shot open and he sucked in his breath.

"Shh, relax." She began to knead his abdominal muscles, carefully avoiding the full-blown erection now waving at her. He closed his eyes, but his periodic gasps told her he was nowhere close to falling asleep on her now.

Her hand stopped moving but stayed on his belly as she leaned over and trailed kisses across his chest. His eyes shot open again.

She threw her leg over him, just below the rib cage, and took both his hands in her own. She pinned them to the mattress on either side of his head, then leaned down to once again touch her lips to his chest.

His body bucked a little, almost dislodging her.

"Relax and enjoy."

He groaned and closed his eyes.

Keeping his hands pinned, she moved her body a little further down, lifting some of her weight off of his stomach. They had completed the first exercise and she was moving on to number two, but she wasn't planning on telling him that. She trailed more kisses over his torso.

His eyes still closed, he gasped. "Dear God, you've got to stop."

"Do you really want me to stop?" She murmured, then resumed the trail of kisses from one large tan nipple across to the other.

"Yes, no, I don't know." He was now squirming under her, but his eyes were still closed.

She gritted her teeth as she almost lost control. When she could trust her voice again, she whispered, "Okay, I'll stop *that* now."

Keeping her face close to his chest, she lifted her weight completely off his stomach. He moaned at the loss of contact with her. She licked one nipple. His body bucked again. She licked the other.

"Dear God, that's worse," he forced out through clenched teeth.

Or better.

A quick glance to make sure he still had his eyes closed. She let go of one of his hands to use her own for another purpose. She guided him into her and settled her weight on his hips.

His eyes flew open. This time she let him pull her down against him as they started moving together.

She raised her lips to his and kissed him fiercely.

After a moment, he twisted his head gently to the side to break the kiss. "I thought we weren't allowed to do this."

She lifted up on her elbows, her breasts just barely brushing his chest, and looked down into his eyes. She grinned. "We're not. I'm cheating."

His laugh was cut short when she tightened around him.

CHAPTER THIRTEEN

Dolph's phone buzzed in his pocket as he was leaving the office on Wednesday.

"Tyrell's had no luck locating Roxie, but one of his snitches came through," Judith said before he could even say hello.

He recognized the tone—brusque with an undercurrent of excitement. Something was starting to break their way.

"Turns out our Freddie Boy's connected to some guy in Scranton, PA. At first, Ty got the run-around from the PD up there, then he's suddenly talking to their chief, and then the local FBI office."

"Whoa," Dolph said.

"Yeah, they tap-danced for awhile, then agreed to an info exchange. Looks like Freddie might be in bed with a guy who's trying to resurrect a defunct mob family in Pennsylvania."

"Who's the mobster?"

"Tony Donati, son of Benito Donati, who was a capo under the last boss of the Bufalino family. That boss, one William aka 'Big Billy' D'Elia, is currently a guest of the federal prison system, as is Daddy Donati."

"Is that what did in the family?" Dolph asked as he headed out of the building. "Usually somebody else steps into the void when the boss goes to prison."

"Yeah, except this time, the boss turned state's evidence on some of his own people, to get a lighter sentence."

"*That* would strike a lethal blow."

"Yeah. D'Elia gets out in 2014. Tony's daddy will be a guest of the government for quite awhile after that. Meanwhile, Sonny Boy's been running daddy's operation, pretending to be just a legitimate businessman."

Dolph hit the button on his key fob to unlock his car. "What businesses does he own?"

"Just one. Benito's Plumbing Supplies of Scranton, PA."

He climbed into his car but didn't start it yet. "I'm assuming since you're telling me all this that it's okay to share it around."

"Definitely. Ty's gonna try not to foul up the FBI's investigation, but he wants Frederico off the streets of Baltimore. He said the more people investigating this, the better. Just be discreet. His lieutenant's a lot more territorial than he is. Anything you guys find out, let him or me know right away."

"You got it."

"Hot-diggity. We're finally cookin' here."

Dolph laughed. "Did I just hear you say 'hot-diggity'?"

"No, and if you say I did, I'll deny it." Judith disconnected.

Rose picked up the receiver of her desk phone. "Hernandez."

"I've only got a few minutes," Dolph said. "Today's my anniversary, and if I don't get home on time, there'll be hell to pay." By the time he'd finished filling her in, she'd realized the excitement in his voice wasn't about his anniversary.

Rose got online and looked up Benito's Plumbing Supplies. The website looked normal–promotional hype on the home page, catalog, order forms, etc.

She moved the cursor across the screen to close the window. As it passed over the P in plumbing, the arrow turned into a hand. She moved it over the letter again. Sure enough the P changed color as the index finger of the little white hand pointed to it.

Rose clicked on the link. A login box appeared. She looked it over thoroughly but could find no place to register. Apparently one had to already have a username and password to go any further.

She started to call Dolph, then remembered his anniversary. She looked at her watch. Five-forty.

Liz should be home from work by now. She was an excellent

hacker, much to Rob's dismay, although Liz did try to keep things legal. But if she thought it was for a good cause, she was willing to bend the rules a bit.

Rose called the Franklins' home number, hoping it was early enough she wouldn't be interrupting their dinner.

When Liz answered, Rose gave her a brief rundown of Tyrell's information and what she had found on the website.

"Don't click on that link again!" Liz said. "Are you at home or at work?"

"Still at the office. Why?"

"My guess is that link goes to a hidden page. It may be the illegal side of his business. And they may have something on there that tracks back to the IP address of your computer."

"Like a cookie?"

"A bit more sophisticated than a cookie."

"Is that legal?"

"Oh, yeah. Not that it would stop these guys if it wasn't."

"True... Crap!" That wasn't the word Rose was thinking. "So they may know now that our computer was taking a look at their site."

"Maybe. More likely they'd just be able to tell the general geographic area."

"Is there a way to get past their login box without raising red flags?" Rose asked.

"Why don't you come over here? I can set up my computer so it can't be traced and we'll take a look."

"On my way."

At the Franklins, Liz answered the door and ushered Rose into the family room. A laptop was sitting on the round table on one side of the room. "Hang on while I turn down the oven. Rob just called to say he was running late. You're welcome to stay for dinner."

"Thanks," Rose said. Liz was one of the few people who cooked better than she did herself.

Liz looked back over her shoulder as she headed out of the room. "When's Mac getting out of the hospital?"

"Friday," Rose called after her. She heard the sound of an oven door opening, then clunking shut again.

Liz came back around the corner from the kitchen. "The roast shouldn't dry out too much."

"Roast, as in beef, as in red meat?" Rose said, one eyebrow cocked at almost a forty-five degree angle.

Liz, the health nut, chuckled. "It's Rob's favorite. Pot roast with all the trimmings. I make it once every two months. Hey, I'll pack up the leftovers for you to take home, for Friday's dinner. You'll have your hands full with Mac, without worrying about cooking."

Rose wasn't too sure that hauling away the leftovers would endear her to Rob's heart but she agreed anyway. "Thanks, that would be a big help."

"Now, to the computer." Liz gestured for Rose to join her at the table. "My laptop's rerouted through a service that masks the IP address. It'll look like this inquiry is coming from someplace overseas. What's the website address?"

Rose handed her a slip of paper.

Liz typed in the address, then started clicking on various links on the site. She would move the mouse, click, lick her lips or make a tsking sound, then move the mouse again. Rose sat across from her, trying not to fidget, but patience wasn't her strong suit.

Finally Liz said, "They've got a pretty good firewall but I think I've found a back door into their login program. If I'm right, I should be able to insert a username and password into the existing list."

"And if you're wrong?"

"They'll probably assume that somebody in Korea or Russia was trying to hack into their system."

Rose got up to move around behind her.

Liz typed something, then clicked the mouse to exit that page. "Okay, here goes." She moved the mouse over the P and clicked, then typed in the fake username and password she'd planted. She clicked on the login button and a page appeared.

Rose grinned. "It worked!" Without taking her eyes off the

screen, Liz lifted a hand in the air. Rose high-fived her.

They both stared at the screen. On a plain white background was a list of what looked like codes, combinations of letters and numbers, underlined in bright blue, indicating they were links.

It was getting harder for Rose to curb her impatience. Now that they were in, her hand was itching to grab the mouse away from Liz and go exploring. "Click on one," she said.

"Not so fast." Liz reached over and pulled a pad of paper closer to her. "Hand me that pen, please."

Rose gritted her teeth but she grabbed the pen from the far side of the table and handed it to Liz.

Liz wrote the first letter of each code horizontally down the page. She moved over an inch and wrote the next part of the code there, then the third part and so one, in columns down the page.

"First letter is male or female," she said.

Rose looked at the computer screen. "Yeah, they're all M's or F's." She took a deep breath. Liz was right. They needed to be methodical. A wrong step could get them dumped out of the site, and then locked out.

"Then a number," Liz was saying. "Mostly two digits but a couple are one digit. I'm guessing age. Then another capital letter–C, N, A or H. Race?"

Rose pointed at one of the codes. "Here's an A with a little r."

"Arab." Liz tapped the pad with the pen. "Small b is next, then two capital letters that vary, then a small c and another two caps that vary." She circled the bNO in the first code. "Born, New Orleans."

"The *c* is for current location."

"SW. Seattle, Washington?"

Rose leaned further over Liz's shoulder and ran her finger down the next column on the screen. "SR, then a number between 1 and 5. What the hell could that be?"

"Let's find out." Liz moved the mouse down and clicked on the fifth code down. "First one would be too obvious that we're just exploring."

A fresh page sprang up. The title read *Asian Male, 39*. Below that was a picture and *Born: Seoul, Korea; Current: Detroit, Michigan.*

"Damn, we're good," Liz said.

Rose pointed further down the screen. "Security Rating, three."

Liz hovered the mouse arrow over the words "Security Rating." A tiny HELP appeared in a bubble. She grinned and clicked on it.

A new window opened, with another login box. *You must enter your password again* was across the top.

"In case someone's hacked in without a password." Liz entered the fake password again.

Rose stared at the new page that came up. A security rating of one was *fabricated ID; forged documents.* A five was *real ID, live; real documents, unreported.* Three was *real ID, dead; documents forged.*

"Shit," she said, as the implications of what she was seeing sunk in.

"Yeah," Liz agreed with the sentiment.

"Why would *real ID, dead; real documents* be a four and not a five?" Rose asked.

Liz thought for a moment. "Because dead people don't have credit ratings."

"Ah, a five could be used to set up false accounts with credit card companies."

"Yes, and I'm thinking the documents are unreported on the fives because they were obtained in such a way that the owner would be unlikely to report their theft."

"Such as a prostitute's john."

"Bingo," Liz said. "This is more than credit card fraud. This is an identity theft supermarket."

She right-clicked over the page. Nothing happened. "Yeah, I didn't think you were going to let me print that page," she muttered. She jotted down the information on a fresh sheet of the pad. Then she closed the window.

She was back on the Asian man's page. Halfway down the page was a box labeled *Notes.* In the box was typed: *immigrated, age 3; naturalized, age 10; deceased, age 16.*

"How sad," Liz said. "His parents bring him over from Korea for a better life, and he probably wrapped his car around a tree a few months after getting his license."

Rose didn't respond. She was looking at the bottom of the page. "'Please select the product you wish to purchase'," she read out loud. "'Then enter your account number in the indicated box.' Interesting. The ID by itself is a lot less than the ID plus documents."

"A good forger is apparently pricey," Liz said.

"You think the username or password is the account number?"

"No, and I think this is as far as we go. At this point, we're a shopper who decided against this product. We try to enter a bogus account number and who knows what'll happen."

"You think the FBI knows about this?" Rose asked.

"Probably. If we figured it out this easily, they no doubt have computer people who could do the same."

"I wonder why they haven't shut them down yet?"

Liz shrugged. "Looks like Donati is their main man, but maybe they're trying to throw out a wide net and get as much of his organization as possible." She clicked back to the original list of codes and pointed to the screen. "The codes for current addresses are all over the country. Freddie isn't his only supplier."

Rose pulled her phone out and found Tyrell Cooper's number in her contacts. "No wonder they were trying to keep us from snooping around in Freddie's business. This operation has got to be worth millions."

~~~~~~~

At seven the following evening, a sizeable group of people was gathered around the big oak table in Kate and Skip's kitchen. The Franklins and Dolph had been the last to arrive.

"Thanks for letting us meet here," Tyrell Cooper said to Kate. "I didn't want to risk somebody seeing you all trooping into my precinct and report that back to Frederico."

"No problem." She was more than happy to host the meeting.

Finally they seemed to have enough pieces of the puzzle to begin to fit them together.

"I'm just a volunteer consultant," Judith said. "I haven't figured out how to bring my lieutenant into the loop without him telling me this is none of my business."

Kate and the others nodded their understanding. Keeping her supervisor in the dark was the lesser of the evils for Judith right now. If Pete Jamieson's case came to trial, there was no good outcome for her. An acquittal would be a black mark on her record. A guilty verdict would mean she'd have to live with the knowledge that she'd probably sent an innocent man to prison for most of the rest of his life.

Tyrell leaned forward, putting his elbows on the table. His dreadlocks fell forward on either side of his face.

Billy had found them quite fascinating when the detective had first arrived. The little boy had asked if they were his fur, prompting Maria to shoo the children up to their rooms. Kate smiled at the memory, then Tyrell's voice brought her back to the present.

"Here's the deal. I've got the feds to agree to let me handle the local operation."

"What'd you have to promise them, your firstborn?" Dolph said.

"Almost as bad. If we're successful, I turn Frederico over to them. He'll probably turn for them and testify against Donati. Then it's off to witness protection."

Rose snorted. "I give that less than six months. He disappears and ends up dealing and pimping somewhere else, with one of his own stolen identities, no doubt."

Tyrell shrugged. "But he's no longer Baltimore's problem."

"Somebody else will fill the void quick enough," Rose said.

Tyrell sat back in his chair. "I'm a street cleaner. Street gets dirty, I clean it. Gets dirty again, I clean it again. Lots of job security."

"Tyrell wants to set up a sting," Judith said, her tone slightly impatient. "Have one of you go talk to Frederico's girls again, with a wallet full of bogus credit cards, license, Social Security card."

Dolph raised his hand. "I'll do it. Skip's too obvious at this point."

Skip leaned forward. "Frederico's seen you with me."

"Yeah but the gals haven't. Except for Roxie, they've only seen me in the role of a drunk and a john."

"My people couldn't find Roxie," Tyrell said. "She's probably long—"

Skip interrupted. "No!"

Kate stared at him. His jaw was clenched and his eyes had turned the muddy brown they became when he was upset.

"Why not?" Dolph said.

"Because this isn't your mess."

"It isn't yours either, son, but you decided to take it on."

The two men glared across the table at each other. "I make my own choices," Dolph finally said in a low, hard voice. "Nothing's gonna happen to me." His tone softened. "I go downtown, with plenty of back-up, stagger around mumbling to myself. Let them pick my pocket, then stagger off."

Kate looked from Dolph's face to Skip's as they locked eyes again.

What the hell's going on with these two?

She had no idea but she decided to intentionally break up the battle of wills. She wanted to know how this was going to help Pete. "Is this likely to uncover anything useful regarding Jimmy Matthews' murder?"

"Won't know 'til I get Frederico into an interrogation room," Tyrell said. "Now that we know what he has to hide, I'm inclined to believe he didn't kill Matthews. He wouldn't want to draw attention to himself that way. But I'll bet good money he knows who did the shooting."

"Why do you want to use a civilian for this?" Skip's tone was challenging.

"I suggested it," Judith said. "We can't use any of my people and all of Tyrell's guys the hookers know are cops."

"The vice squad in the worst part of Baltimore doesn't have any undercover cops?"

Tyrell raised an eyebrow at Skip. "Got three," he said in a mild voice. "One's out on sick leave. Two are in the middle of other assignments."

"Freddie's men have seen Dolph with me," Skip pointed out again.

"I'll disguise my appearance some," Dolph said. "I'd bet money that Donati's man killed Matthews, out of fear he'd discover the more lucrative part of Freddie's operation and want in on it."

Kate suspected he was changing the subject on purpose.

Tyrell nodded. "Or maybe he did discover the identity theft racket. Matthews was a loose cannon. Naive, and he sampled his own goods too often."

"By Donati's man, you mean the floater or the guy who came after Kate?" Rob asked.

"The floater," Judith said. "Pretty Boy's his replacement."

Kate was trying to fit the pieces together. "So Donati's man followed Matthews out to Pete's place, somehow got his gun away from him and shot him with it."

"He might've seen them fighting that afternoon," Rose said. "And figured Jamieson would make a good patsy."

"How'd he end up in the harbor?" Liz asked.

"He shot Mac." Skip's tone had returned to normal but he was still frowning. "Frederico probably decided *he* was the loose cannon and got rid of him. Last time we talked to Freddie he said that he had, quote, 'taken care of our problem.'"

"So what we've got here is Dolph doing the sting, and then hopefully Freddie will spill his guts about who killed Matthews and shot Mac." Rose gave her typical succinct summary. "The asshole's already dead so case closed and Jamieson's off the hook."

"And Freddie's off the streets of Baltimore." Tyrell turned to Liz. "Mrs. Franklin, are you willing to monitor the illegal website for us? The feds will be doing their own monitoring, of course, but I want to know what they know when they know it. I could probably get our geeks set up to do it..." His voice trailed off, implying that he wasn't sure they were up to the task.

"No problem, as long as you call me Liz."

Tyrell grinned at her. "Thanks, Liz. My lieutenant's authorized consultant fees, but I'm afraid the rate isn't very generous."

"Don't worry about it. I have plenty of sick leave accumulated." Liz grinned back at him. "I feel a cold coming on."

"It'll probably be Monday, or maybe Tuesday, before I can get the fake cards and license. Let's plan on doing the downtown operation on Wednesday. Liz, I'll need you to start monitoring Thursday morning. Might take into Friday to catch them at it."

Liz and the others nodded.

"Geez, does this mean we can have a normal weekend?" Rob said.

Kate snorted. What she needed to do this weekend was anything but normal.

After they'd seen the others out, she turned to Skip. "Speaking of this weekend, is there a way I can get out to western Maryland to see Pete?"

Skip grimaced. "Be easier to set up a phone call."

Kate shook her head. "It's hard enough to judge how people are doing emotionally when I can see them face to face. Over the phone, he'll tell me he's fine and I won't know whether to believe him or not."

Skip thought for a moment. "It's not safe for you to go out there by yourself." He held up his hand when she started to bristle. "I'm not being over-protective here. I'm concerned about somebody tailing you to find out where he is. Give me a minute to think this through, okay... Rose is gonna have her hands full, with Mac coming home from the hospital tomorrow, and Dolph and his wife are going away this weekend."

"And Manny's already out there." She was starting to see the problem here.

"Yeah, that's pretty much everybody I totally trust to successfully spot and then shake a tail," Skip said. "I'd have to take you. Which means asking Maria to watch the kids all day Saturday. It's almost a three-hour drive each way."

Maria had just come down the stairs. "Kids had der baths. Dey ready for stories. What you need do on Saturday?"

Kate was about to shake her head but Skip was already explaining to her in Spanish what they wanted to do.

~~~~~~~~~

Dave stretched his long legs out on the hotel bed and stared morosely at the muted TV. He couldn't remember the last time he'd been in this bad a mood. Instead of enjoying his freedom from Nell and the brat, he was sporting a cast on his arm and spending his days hanging out in the smelly kitchen of a dive in Baltimore.

He glared at the pint of whisky on the nightstand, but he dared not touch it until after the expected phone call from his employer. He picked up the bottle of ibuprofen instead. Wincing as he pried the cap off, he shook two out to swallow dry.

Tonight, he hadn't taken the Percocet the private urgent-care clinic had prescribed. He planned to get rip-roaring drunk later, and prescription pain killers didn't mix well with alcohol.

Plan B had backfired alright, just not quite in the way he'd feared. Canfield hadn't come sniffing around the affiliate's operation lately but his bitch wife now knew Dave's face. He'd planned to intimidate her into not reporting his attack by pointing out just how easy it would be to get to her kids. But he'd never gotten that far.

His juvie record was sealed and he'd managed to avoid arrest as an adult, so no mug shots in the system. And no distinctive features that would distinguish him from any other good-looking guy. Very few people in Baltimore even knew he existed. The chances the cops would catch up with him were slim, but he still didn't like the idea that this Huntington-Canfield bitch could identify him.

Anger ballooned in his chest–at her, at his dumbass employer, and if he was honest, at himself. He'd made too many assumptions.

He started to reach for the whiskey, then stopped himself.

Each night, when the inevitable call came, he'd managed to appease his employer, but he knew he wouldn't be able to stall forever.

Not only was this whole assignment royally screwed up, he was pretty sure he was having some kind of crisis, at age thirty-five. What the hell was he doing? He had a wife and kid he didn't want, to please a boss who was at least twenty IQ points dumber than him. Not to mention the asshole's 'what have you done for me lately?' attitude.

His cell phone chirped on the bed next to him. He picked it up and checked caller ID.

Speak of the devil.

"Good evening, sir," he said into the phone.

"Is it?"

His mind scrambled for the right thing to say. He finally settled on, "Moderately so, sir. The problem seems to have lessened, although I'm not sure it's completely resolved." He didn't want to be called home yet, not with loose ends still dangling.

"My affiliate is not happy. Says he doesn't like having that, quote, 'blue-eyed prick' hangin' around."

Ask me if I care.

Dave forced a fake chuckle into his voice. "I do believe my predecessor fit in somewhat better than I do."

"Has anyone besides my affiliate's people seen you with him?"

"No, sir. I keep a very low profile." *As in, I stay back in the stinking kitchen!*

"We've had some strange activity on the website. Customers looking without buying. Could be some high school kid thinks he's a hacker. Could be... the problem. The business is at a precarious turning point. A lot of money is at stake. It's important that nothing disrupt things right now."

Dave waited, knowing there was more.

"I'm contemplating going for Plan C, just to be on the safe side. I don't like loose ends. Do you have the details worked out?"

Adrenaline surged. *Hot damn!*

He did not have the details worked out but he wasn't about to tell Mr. Micro-management that. "Yes, sir. Do you want me to move forward with it?" He held his breath. If he believed in

God, he would have prayed.

"Can you make sure it looks like an accident?"

"Goes without saying, sir."

"Then yes, go with Plan C."

"Consider it done, sir."

Dave waited until he was sure his boss had disconnected before dropping the phone on the bed. "Yes!" He pumped his right fist in the air. He didn't even care that the movement sent a jolt of pain through the other, injured arm.

Just so happened his employer's loose ends coincided with his own.

Grabbing the bottle of whiskey, he struggled with the cap. Here he'd thought he'd be drowning his sorrows and he was celebrating instead. Of course, he still had to figure out how to pull Plan C off, but he'd worry about that tomorrow.

CHAPTER FOURTEEN

On Saturday morning, Kate was having mixed emotions. Guilt and anxiety on the one hand, excitement on the other. Not only had Maria agreed to watch the kids today, she'd suggested they stay over until Sunday and make a weekend getaway out of the trip. They'd both immediately said no, unwilling to leave her and the kids alone in the house overnight. Talbot, or whatever the hell his name is, was still out there somewhere.

But Maria'd had an answer for that too. "I take *niños* to *Tia* Rita wid me. *Tia* have all dose empty rooms now her children gone. She be happy to have full house again." Maria spent many of her weekends with Rose's parents, visiting and helping her elderly aunt and uncle with chores and errands. It seemed like a busman's holiday to Kate, but Maria seemed content with this routine.

Kate had still been reluctant to dump the children on her and her relatives for the whole weekend but Maria had insisted.

Now Kate was finishing up the packing while Skip was taking the kids and their nanny to the elder Hernandez's house.

It would be so good to have some time, just the two of them, after all the crap that had been going on lately. She put the last of her things in her overnight case and carried it out to the living room. Glancing at her watch, she calculated how long Skip had been gone.

Assuming there had been no one trying to follow them, they should have arrived by now. Skip would be saying goodbye to the kids and trying to extract himself from Rita's insistence that he sit and have a cup of coffee with them. Kate could almost hear Maria intervening, telling her aunt in Spanish that Skip didn't want to have coffee with them–he wanted to go home, collect his lovely wife and be off on their romantic weekend together. Julio would let out a sly chuckle and give Skip an exaggerated wink. The women would laugh as Skip bid them *adios.*

A loud bang from the back of the house. She jumped, then ran for the laundry room door. It was securely locked. Hand over her pounding heart, she peered between the security bars over the window. Another bang. She let out a small shriek, then laughed at herself when she realized the March wind was knocking a large pine branch against the garage.

In like a lion. Out like a lamb, hopefully. We need to prune that tree.

She tilted her head, trying to see more of the yard.

A hand grasped her shoulder.

Her shriek was much louder this time. She ducked out from under the hand and whirled around, bringing her hand up, fingers stiff, to strike at her assailant's neck or face.

The face in front of her registered just as Skip's hand caught her wrist. "Whoa there, darlin'."

"Holy Mary, Mother of God." Kate crossed herself. "I almost took your eye out. Don't sneak up on me like that."

"I thought you'd heard me come in," Skip said.

"That tree's banging against the garage." She pointed out the window. "And I wasn't expecting you back this soon."

He chuckled. "Maria suggested I not come in. Said she'd make my excuses to Rita and Julio that we wanted to get on our way."

Kate patted her chest, trying to calm her still racing heart. "Everything's packed and ready to go. Shall we?"

~~~~~~~~

Skip took a circuitous route through Towson, actually heading south for awhile instead of north toward the Baltimore Beltway. He glanced in his rearview mirror again and frowned.

Was that the same car, or a different one that just looked similar? No front license plate so not registered in Maryland.

That didn't mean all that much. Almost every nearby state, and Washington D.C., only required back plates.

He slowed for a traffic light that had just changed to yellow, then quickly turned right and accelerated. At the next corner, he turned right again, barely slowing for the stop sign as he made sure nothing was coming on the cross street.

Kate glanced back over her shoulder. "Either you're in the mood for a traffic ticket or someone's following us."

"Can't tell for sure. Plain dark sedan." In his peripheral vision, he saw her shudder. They'd been followed by plain dark sedans before. He knew she still had nightmares sometimes about one of those car chases.

"When did we pick it up?" she asked.

"Couple blocks from the house, if it's the same one. He fell back a few cars for awhile. Could've turned off when I wasn't looking, and this is some other innocent soul running their Saturday morning errands."

He slowed almost to a crawl as he stared at the rearview mirror. "Nope, it's a tail. Just came around the corner a block back."

He nudged the accelerator, gradually picking up speed. At the next corner, he slowed and quickly looked in both directions. There was a pick-up truck coming on his left, half a block away. He whipped his Expedition into a left turn and hit the gas.

The driver of the oncoming truck gave Skip the finger as they buzzed past him. The guy sped up and almost slammed into the dark sedan that screeched to a halt just in time.

Skip made several turns in rapid succession, moving through the side streets of the Towson business district, then turned south again on York Road. Several blocks past Towson University, he was convinced he'd lost the guy. He turned right into a residential neighborhood, hoping this street came out on Charles Street. They were in luck. Another turn and they were finally headed in the right direction.

Kate spoke for the first time in several minutes. "Gee, that was fun." Her tone said *not* loud and clear.

He grinned over at her. "Almost as good as a carnival ride."

"Almost made me as nauseous. That was some fancy drivin', sir."

"Thank ya, ma'am. Funny, it's been, what, twenty-two years since the police academy, but it all kicks back in when needed."

"They taught you to drive like a maniac?"

"You learn how to do stuff a lot wilder than that. Those car chases on TV are a bit exaggerated, but you definitely know how to handle a vehicle by the time you get out of the academy."

"Good skill to have," Kate said.

They chatted about various things as they headed around the Beltway, then onto I-70 for the long trek to western Maryland. By unspoken agreement, they avoided the topic of The Case, as it was now called in their household. Granted Kate would be working for an hour or two while she met with Pete, but they were determined to make the most of their getaway.

"Want to stop here for lunch?" Skip pointed to the exit sign for Hancock, Maryland. "Or do you want to wait 'til we get to Cumberland?"

Kate's stomach growled. They both laughed.

They ate turkey club sandwiches at an old-fashioned lunch counter, then started out again. There had been no more signs of nondescript dark sedans.

They were now on I-68. A comfortable silence settled around them.

The road was a giant roller coaster. Long slow climbs followed by equally long but not nearly so slow descents into valleys. Often the ground fell away on one side of the highway or the other. The land was mostly undeveloped, although you could sometimes spot a house, or even a street of houses, tucked in amongst the trees on the hillsides. Bare-limbed deciduous trees lined the roadway in the valleys. Evergreens dominated the hilltops.

"Why do evergreens survive better than deciduous trees at higher altitudes?" Kate asked.

"An excellent question, for which I have no answer," Skip said cheerfully. He was starting to enjoy himself. The further they drove, the more the stress of the last few weeks seemed to slide away behind them—even though they were driving toward the source of that stress.

No, that wasn't fair. Pete Jamieson wasn't the cause of the stress. Whoever killed his friend, Matthews, was.

Nope, not going there, brain! Searching for something else to think about, he glanced over at his wife. She was looking out the window, a relaxed smile on her face.

Note to self: thank Maria for suggesting this.

It dawned on him that he hadn't felt afraid during his evasive driving. His calm was back.

Hmm, might not be back for good. Have to wait and see.

He glanced at his wife again. She was now watching him, with the same dreamy smile she'd bestowed upon the trees and valleys. He picked up her hand and turned his eyes back to the highway. As he lifted her fingertips to his lips, he voiced his earlier thought. "This was a good idea."

They held hands in companionable silence as the miles went by. Skip let go to nudge his blinker on. He took the exit for MD 546, headed for the small town of Finzel, Maryland.

He almost missed the entrance to Pete's land. A for-sale sign, splattered with mud, marked the dirt track cut between the trees.

"Good thing this truck's all-wheel drive." They bounced along, in and out of muddy ruts.

The trailer was surprisingly new-looking, a large camper, probably twenty-five or so feet long. Skip couldn't imagine what vehicle had been used to haul it back the dirt road. He parked behind a red pick-up.

Kate looked out at the stretch of mud between them and the trailer's door, then down at her tailored pantsuit. "I was going for a compromise between casual and professional. Should've worn jeans and my hiking boots."

"Wait a sec." He got out and walked around to her door, the mud sucking at his shoes. He opened the door and then scooped her up in his arms.

"Hope Pete isn't looking out the window," she said. "This will blow my professional image."

"These aren't exactly normal therapy conditions to begin with."

"True."

~~~~~~~~~

The inside of the trailer was surprisingly roomy. The bedroom even had a real door. Skip was now behind that door, ostensibly taking a nap, after asking Manny and the other guard to wait outside.

Kate was relieved. It was more privacy than she'd hoped for.

Pete gestured toward the dinette area at the far end of the trailer. "Want some coffee?"

"That'd be good." She settled herself on the padded bench on one side of the table.

Pete poured two cups from a carafe on the counter and brought them over. "Is this a therapy session?"

"Not if you don't want it to be. I just wanted to see how you were doing. And Skip said the cell phone service was pretty sketchy up here."

"Yeah, one of the guys has to drive out to the road to check in."

Kate filled Pete in on where things stood in the investigation.

When she'd finished, he said, "I don't get it. Two cops believe I'm innocent but I'm still under arrest."

"It's frustrating, I know. But Detective Anderson can't drop the charges until we have some proof. At this point, it's just a plausible story."

Pete nodded.

"Is it hard being out here?"

"Not as hard as I thought it would be. The guys have been real good about ignoring my nightmares."

"How often are you having them?"

"Not as often. Not even every night." He paused. "And they're not as bad. It's more like things are happening at a distance."

After another pause, Kate said, "And when you wake up?"

"I usually wake myself up. I call out to the people in the dream. 'Look out,' or 'Run!' My heart's racing, but I'm not covered in sweat like I used to be."

"That sounds like progress. How are you feeling otherwise?"

Pete shrugged. "Better. Not so guilty. Mostly just sad, that we couldn't get more people out."

Kate noted the use of *we*. He was part of the team again. "Pete–"

"I know, I know, I saved a bunch of people that day." The knuckles of his hands, gripping his coffee mug, were white. "But there were a lot more who died that shouldn't have."

That hadn't been where she'd planned to go, but anger was a good sign. Far better than depression. "Who are you angry at about that?" she asked in a soft voice.

He looked at her for a long moment. "Not myself, not anymore. And in a weird way, not even the terrorists. Maybe Osama bin Laden. Mostly I'm pissed at how fucked up the world is, that anybody'd think it's okay to do something like that. That God's actually gonna reward them for killing innocent people."

Kate just nodded. She waited a beat, then said, "I feel the same way."

Pete took a sip of coffee. Kate followed suit, giving him time to digest the idea that his reactions to 9/11 were now normal.

"If I go to trial, do we have to play on that whole hero thing?"

"Why does that make you so uncomfortable?"

"'Cause I wasn't doing anything special. I was just doing my job. Well, it wasn't my job that day, but I was just doing what I'd been trained to do. Look, if you'd been there, you would have tried to comfort people. Would that have made you a hero? No, you would've just been doing what you do."

"I don't run into burning buildings."

"Yeah, but what you do, it's pretty intense. It's gotta be hard."

"It's intense at times, but no, it doesn't feel all that hard to me."

He cocked his head to one side.

"When I was a kid, everybody told me their troubles," Kate said. "Even my brother Jack, who's two years older than me. I think I was ten, the first time someone told me I should be a psychologist when I grew up. I didn't even know what that was.

I was two years out of graduate school before it dawned on me that most people couldn't see what I saw. Couldn't read people's emotions like I can or understand the odd, convoluted logic of the unconscious mind like I do."

He was watching her intently.

"I'm talented at what I do. But I always took that talent for granted, because it came easily to me. It was no big deal."

"And my talent," Pete said, with a small smile, "is that I'm crazy enough to run into a building that everybody else is running out of."

Kate grinned at him. "Exactly. It doesn't feel like a big deal to you because it's what comes easily to you, but the rest of us are damned impressed. Because we know we couldn't do that."

Pete was quiet for a minute, staring into his coffee cup. When he looked up at her, his eyes had some of their old haunted look in them. "I don't think I can do it anymore."

She paused, then asked, "Run into burning buildings?"

"Yeah. I think I've lost my nerve."

"Think about this before you answer. Are you afraid of the fire, or of your own reactions?"

He only paused a second. "Not the fire."

"You're afraid of having flashbacks."

He nodded.

"I think that's a legitimate fear. It's why your previous therapist wouldn't sign off for you to go back to work, remember?"

"Yeah, I was kinda pissed at her, even though I knew she was probably right. But I thought maybe once I was there, at a fire, I would somehow be okay."

"You might be, but then again you might not. And the problem is, there's no way to really test that. There's no shallow end when it comes to burning buildings, is there?"

Pete stared at his cup again. "I don't think I can be a firefighter anymore, and I don't know what to do with that. It's all I've ever wanted to do."

"Firefighters don't always fight fires."

He looked up, startled.

"Think about other jobs people do for the fire department. You could train to be a paramedic, a dispatcher. You could teach at the fire academy. You could go around to schools and talk to kids who want to be firefighters, and tell them what it's really like. And those are just the things occurring to me off the top of my head. My guess is there's a dozen other jobs you could do that would contribute to the department. Make it possible for them to continue to fight fires."

"You've got to have special training, get certified to teach at the academy."

"So get the training."

He snorted. "And live on what in the meantime?"

"Pell grants, student loans, scholarships."

Pete's eyes lit up. "I'd like to teach. And go to the high schools and talk to the kids."

"Hey, I can't think of a better way to serve the department then by passing the torch–no pun intended–to the next generation of firefighters."

Pete grinned at her.

~~~~~~~~

As Skip drove the Expedition down the winding mountain road, he glanced over at his wife. "You look like the cat who ate the canary, darlin'."

"Pete and I had a very good session."

"Excellent. So we can now focus exclusively on each other for..." He twisted his hand on the steering wheel to see his watch. "Say, the next eighteen hours."

"Sounds like a plan. Where do you want to stop?"

"I checked out a few places online. There's one that looked promising in Berkeley Springs, West Virginia. Forty some miles east and then a bit south of Cumberland."

"Are they open this time of year?"

"Yup. There's a warm mineral spring there. Attracts folks, year round. It should be a good stopping point for another reason."

"What's that?"

"Far enough away from where Pete is that I can use my credit card to take you out for a nice dinner."

"You think these guys could be monitoring our credit card activity?"

"Probably not. But to be on the safe side, I gave Manny most of my cash, for groceries and such."

"I'll reimburse you from the bail money fund."

"No you won't. I know you've already used up what came from the collection. That's your money."

"*Our* money, sweetheart."

~~~~~~~~~

Dave sat in the stolen car, the driver's seat pushed all the way back. He stared at the Canfields' house. It had the closed-up feel to it that said its occupants were on vacation.

His laptop was balanced on his knees. There was more than one way to locate prey. He'd hacked into two sites and had them both open in side-by-side windows.

His broken arm ached. He took his eyes off the screen long enough to grab the bottle of ibuprofen from the passenger's seat. When he looked back at the computer, he felt a jolt of excitement. He wasn't sure what the abbreviation for the merchant meant, but he recognized the location.

Opening another window, he went to Google maps. A grin spread across his face.

Plan C was falling into place. It would mean a few cold hours waiting on the side of the road, but an Expedition with a dinged-up door shouldn't be all that hard to spot.

Soon all loose ends would be tied up in neat little bows.

CHAPTER FIFTEEN

Kate lazed in bed the next morning while Skip took a shower. This getaway, even though brief, had been just what they'd needed. And based on his performance last night, Skip didn't seem to have any lingering effects from the prostitute incident.

But she couldn't shake the feeling that something else was going on with him, something subtle she couldn't put her finger on. A light rapping on their door announced that breakfast had arrived. Kate put on her robe to answer the door. She thanked their hostess for the in-room service, a perk of arriving when business was a little slow.

The shower went off as she poured a cup of coffee. She poured one for Skip as well.

How to bring the subject up? It was all so vague. Something had shifted but she wasn't sure what. Nor was she sure it was a bad shift. Then again, she could just be imagining things.

Skip sat down across from her at the small table by the window. His robe gaped open across his broad chest. Kate was enjoying the view as she handed him his coffee.

"Thanks, darlin'." He took a sip, then dug into the heaping plate of bacon and eggs in front of him.

She ate a couple bites of egg. "Sweetheart, are you feeling guilty about Mac getting shot?" She figured it was as good a place to start as any.

His hand froze, a piece of toast halfway to his mouth. "Where's that coming from?"

"I don't know. You've seemed a bit off lately."

He snorted. "Life hasn't exactly been normal lately." He bit into the toast.

"True." She chewed on a strip of bacon. Was the shift just in her?

"Is it bothering you that I've become a bit more kickass, as you put it?"

He forked eggs into his mouth and chewed. She was starting to fear that he was indeed bothered by it when he finally said, "Nope, but it's required some adjustment. I keep reminding myself I should treat you more like I do Rose, and assume you can take care of yourself. Unless I've got a specific reason to be concerned."

"Like not wanting me to come out here by myself?"

He nodded.

She scooped up a forkful of her own eggs. The shift, it *had* started after Mac got shot.

She tried again. "You sure you're not feeling guilty about Mac?"

"I did some at first. Then I realized if Mac knew I felt that way, he'd be royally pissed. In his mind, he was just being a good soldier, covering my back."

"You're right. He'd be downright insulted." She thought about probing a bit more, but decided against it. She didn't really want to break the mood of their romantic getaway.

And she was finding the sight of his muscular chest way too distracting. She hastily finished her breakfast, then got up and circled the table. Sitting down on his lap, she laid a hand on that bare chest. The skin quivered under her touch.

Skip had been in the process of bringing his coffee cup to his mouth. He put it down instead and turned to look at the clock on the bedside table. "We don't have to check out until noon."

Kate kissed the side of his neck.

~~~~~~~~

At twelve-thirty, they were zipping along the highway, having paid their bill and thanked their hostess. On a chilly Sunday, few people were out and about. They had the road to themselves. They started down one of the long roller-coaster hills. Skip let the truck get up to eighty before he tapped the brakes.

He glanced over at his wife. Kate had laid her head back against the headrest, a small satisfied smile on her face.

A car suddenly appeared beyond Kate's window. He hadn't noticed it coming up behind them. Must have gotten on from the entrance ramp they'd just passed.

The car kept pace with him, which was kind of irritating. They were the only two vehicles on the road and this guy had to ride right beside him. He glanced over again. The male driver was alone in the car. A baseball cap, pulled low, cast his face in shadow. He was staring straight ahead, oblivious to Skip's irritated glare.

Opting to ignore the guy, Skip went back to daydreaming about the pleasant evening they'd had the night before. He'd taken Kate to a nice restaurant, recommended by their B&B hostess. The bottle of red wine they'd shared had been decent and the food was indeed excellent. They'd lingered over dessert, thoroughly enjoying the absence of demanding little people.

Definitely have to remember to thank–

The steering wheel jerked violently as the screech of metal against metal assaulted his ears. Adrenaline shot through his system. He slammed on the brakes.

Kate fell forward against her seatbelt, hands flying out in front of her.

Did the jerk fall asleep at the wheel?

It took a second to register that the car had not gone on by.

The dark sedan's fender bounced off of his again, pushing the truck toward the left shoulder of the road. The shoulder that had only a two-foot high guardrail separating it from a sheer drop-off.

Skip wrenched the steering wheel to the right to compensate. His gut twisted.

The sedan hit him again.

Kate was peering at the profile of the driver. "It's him!" she yelled. "I think it's Talbot!"

Skip shoved the accelerator to the floor. The powerful truck engine thrust them past the car.

He gritted his teeth. His gun was in the low console between the seats, but he dared not take a hand off the wheel.

They hit the bottom of the hill doing ninety-five and swooped up the beginning of the incline with a sickening stomach drop. Skip glanced in the rearview mirror. The sedan was trying to catch up. He let up slightly on the accelerator, until it was almost abreast of them, then he slammed on the brakes.

The tail end of the truck fish-tailed as the sedan flew past them. It kept going up over the crest of the next hill.

Skip looked in his mirror. Still no other cars around. A loud grating noise was coming from the front right fender area. He pulled over onto the left shoulder and put the truck in park.

"Are you okay?" His eyes weren't on his wife, however. He glanced back and forth between the crest of the hill and his rearview mirror, as he tried without success to slow his racing pulse.

"Yeah." Kate rubbed her shoulder where the seatbelt had grabbed her. "I couldn't tell for sure, but I think that was the guy." She sucked in air. "The one who attacked me."

Skip nodded, still surveying their surroundings as he unbuckled his seatbelt. "Stay in the truck. He may come back." He retrieved his pistol and tucked it into his waistband at the small of his back.

"Huh-uh. He could ram the truck and send it over the edge."

"Good point." They both climbed out. Careful not to look down, he edged his way along the narrow strip of gravel between the truck and guardrail. "Keep an eye out while I check on the damage."

He crouched down beside the right fender. Kate stood nearby, her head swiveling back and forth as she scanned the highway in both directions.

The fender was buckled in against the tire. They probably wouldn't get far before the friction wore a hole in the sidewall. And it looked like the tire was tilted inward at the top. Could mean the wheel or the axle was damaged.

Skip sank back on his heels. *Wonder how far it is to the next exit?* He started to stand up.

Kate grabbed his arm and yanked him the rest of the way to his feet. "He's coming."

Skip followed her line of vision. If there'd been any doubts this was Kate's assailant, they were gone now. The sedan was racing down the hill at them, going in the wrong direction on the highway.

Bile rose in Skip's throat. *This guy's crazy!*

They ran toward the back of the truck. He spotted an area just ahead where there was a strip of ground beyond the guardrail. He shoved Kate in that direction. "Get over the rail and duck down!"

She scrambled over the guardrail and clung to one of its posts.

Skip ran past her position and leaped over the railing, onto the narrow strip of ground on the other side, just as the sedan roared past them.

The dirt gave way under him. He grabbed for the guardrail, his feet scrambling for a foothold.

Pain shot up his arm. His hand reflexively yanked away from the source, a sharp spot on the upper edge of the metal railing. He started to slide down the steep incline as his other hand strained toward a post just beyond his fingertips.

Kate's scream echoed across the valley.

His body was bouncing off rocks and scrub bushes sticking out of the hillside. He grabbed for the bushes, finally connecting with one of the sturdier ones just as one foot landed on something solid.

He teetered for a moment, then leaned in against the cliff. His body came to rest against the rocky surface, his throbbing fingers wrapped around the base of a bush protruding from a crack. His toes were on a narrow ledge.

He looked up. His head swam with vertigo. He quickly lowered his forehead to touch the cliff again. The rock was cool against his sweaty skin.

He raised his head more slowly this time. Kate was looking down at him, her face too far away to read her expression. But he was quite sure she was as terrified as he was.

He swallowed hard. "I'm okay," he called up to her. "I'm on a ledge. There's a rope in the back of the truck."

Her face disappeared.

"Wait! Kate, come back!"

Her face reappeared. "My spare gun's locked in the glove box. Same key as the ignition. The bullets are in the bottom of the center console. Get it and load it."

~~~~~~~~~

She found the rope and the gun with no problem. The bullets were another matter. She considered abandoning the search. How long before the roots of that bush let go?

The sight of that sedan bearing down on them flashed into her mind. She started pulling things out of the center console with both hands. At the very bottom was the small box of cartridges. She dropped two on the passenger's seat as she hurried to cram the bullets into the revolver. Snapping it shut, she stuffed it and the box of bullets in her jacket pockets.

After a quick scan of the deserted highway, she stepped carefully over the guardrail near where Skip had fallen. Her heart thudded against the wall of her chest. Hanging onto the railing with one hand, she leaned out over the edge.

He was still there, looking up at her.

She let out her breath. "Got the rope," she called down.

"The gun too?"

"Yeah."

She knelt beside the guardrail and tied the rope around a post, tripling the knot to be on the safe side. Then she tossed the other end over the side of the cliff.

"Got it," drifted up to her. She blew out air again, then climbed back over the guardrail to more solid ground.

She started to turn around and froze. Someone was silhouetted against the sun, walking down the hill a few hundred feet behind them.

Walks like a man. She couldn't make out the face but she caught the telltale bright blue casing on his arm. *A cast!*

Further up the hill, a dark sedan was parked on the shoulder.

"Stay down there! He's coming back!"

Kate raced to the Expedition's driver door. She opened it as far as she could against the guardrail and crouched on the other side of it, fumbling in her jacket pocket for the .38.

Why isn't he coming at us again with the car?

The rumble of an engine answered her question. A pick-up truck was headed down the far slope. If he'd tried to run them over again, there would be a witness this time.

Had he seen Skip go off the edge of the cliff and thought she was now alone? She didn't know what the hell he had in mind, and she wasn't inclined to wait to find out.

She prayed Skip would keep his head down.

The pick-up truck slowed. The figure on the shoulder waved a hand, signaling that the truck driver should go on. He would help the poor folks in the stranded SUV.

The truck picked up speed again.

Kate briefly considered trying to flag it down. She'd have to expose herself to do that and 'Talbot' might have a gun. She wrapped both hands around the pistol and steadied her wrists in the V created by the open door and the windshield frame.

The pick-up truck had just passed her when she fired. The gun roared. Her arms flew up and she rocked backward. The recoil was greater than she was used to when she practiced with her own .32.

But a puff of dust rose from the spot where her bullet had hit the gravel shoulder, ten feet in front of the man. Right where she'd been aiming. Despite her fear, a brief zing of excitement rippled through her chest.

The man froze. The truck engine roared behind her as its driver sped up.

"I'm okay, Skip. Stay down there."

The figure on the shoulder stood still for what felt like an eternity but was probably just a few minutes. Then he started moving again.

Kate braced herself, adjusting for the greater recoil, and fired a second shot. Another roar, another puff of dust, closer to his feet this time. He froze again.

Her ears were ringing. It sounded like Skip was yelling from miles away. She could just barely make out the words. "What the hell's going on?"

"Jackass is trying to decide if I'm serious."

The man stood still again. Did he think she was just a bad shot or was he assuming she didn't have the nerve to truly shoot him?

"Come on, you sexist fool," she muttered. "Get over yourself and go back to your car." She didn't want to shoot another human being, but she knew in that moment she would if he kept coming.

As if he'd heard her mental challenge, he took a step forward.

Aware that the revolver only held six bullets, Kate aimed carefully for the center of his torso. She was about to squeeze the trigger when he turned and bolted back toward his car.

She let out her pent-up breath but kept the gun trained on him.

Should she try to shoot out his tires as he went past or let him go? What if he tried to ram the Expedition?

Before she could decide what to do next, a deep voice came from behind her. "Don't move, lady. Drop the gun!"

CHAPTER SIXTEEN

Kate jerked her head around, her gun still aimed at the retreating figure on the shoulder.

A Maryland state police car was facing her, lights flashing. A state trooper stood in front of it, his gun extended toward her.

Kate hastily raised her hands in the air. "We're the victims, Officer." She heard a car engine behind her and looked around. The sedan was headed toward them, in the far right lane. "The driver of that car, he tried to kill us!"

The trooper kept his eyes and his gun on her as he signaled for the sedan to pull over.

It picked up speed instead.

"He's getting away! He tried to kill us." She waved her hand in the direction of the car now cresting the next hill. Unfortunately the gun was still in that hand.

"Lady, put the gun down on the ground. Now!"

"Do it, Kate!" Skip's panicked voice yelled from behind her.

She stooped down and put the .38 on the gravel.

The trooper now had his gun trained on Skip, who was pulling himself over the guardrail. When his feet hit the gravel shoulder, he staggered a few steps. Blood dripped from one of his hands and he was covered in dirt.

Kate glanced back at the trooper. Doubt flashed across his face but his gun was still aimed at her husband. The bubble of anger that had been building in her chest exploded. She kicked the Expedition's door closed and ran toward Skip, putting herself between him and the trooper.

"Stop, lady!"

She turned around, hands on her hips. "That man tried to kill us and you're standing here pointing a gun *at us*, while he's getting away."

"I'd appreciate it if you'd lower your gun, Officer," Skip said from behind her. "I know this looks suspicious but we really are the good guys."

The trooper lowered his gun partway but made no move to holster it. "Are you armed, sir?"

"Not anymore. My gun fell out of my waistband when I slid down that cliff."

Kate's throat tightened. *His granddaddy's pearl-handled gun was gone?* She blinked away tears and ran toward Skip again.

"Ma'am, *please* stand still," the trooper yelled.

Kate whirled around and glared at him. "Can't you see he's bleeding?"

"Officer, you really don't want to take her on when she gets like this," Skip said.

"*Gets like this*. What the hell's that supposed to mean?"

Suddenly she was shaking and couldn't stop. The world tilted.

Skip grabbed her before she could fall. He wrapped strong arms around her. "Sh, sh, it's okay, darlin'. We're safe now. I'm not going to bleed to death and the trooper's just doing his job."

"Guess I'm not all that kickass after all," she mumbled against his chest.

He kissed the top of her head. "You're okay. It's just the adrenaline wearing off."

"May I see some ID, sir?"

Skip turned sideways without letting go of her. "I'm a private investigator. License is in my back pocket."

"Please take it out, sir. Slowly."

Skip's chest rose and fell under her cheek. His sigh ruffled her hair. With one arm still around her, he fished out the leather case containing his P.I. license and carry-concealed permit and tossed it to the trooper.

The shaking had stopped but she wasn't quite ready to let

go of her husband. She dragged in a deep breath. Dirt and sweat never smelled so good.

The trooper examined Skip's credentials, then walked all the way around the Expedition. He stopped at the right front fender, then looked over at them. He stooped down. When he stood again, he said, "You folks come sit in my car and tell me what this is all about while we wait for a tow truck."

"How'd you get here so fast anyway?" Skip asked as he turned Kate toward the police car.

One corner of the trooper's mouth quirked up. "I'd just set up a speed trap up the road a piece. Guy in a pick-up pulled himself over and practically jumped in my arms. Said some fool was back here shootin' at somebody."

~~~~~~~~~

They were both crammed into the front seat of the tow truck along with its husky, good-ole-boy driver. He wore a quilted vest over a plaid flannel shirt and jeans, and he was chawing away at something. Skip hoped it was gum.

He sniffed discreetly. Yup, peppermint, not tobacco. Maybe the guy was trying to quit smoking.

Kate was jammed against the door. She had her cell phone to her ear, attempting to succinctly explain to Rob all that had happened.

Trooper Ellis had believed their story. It was too outrageous to be fiction. But he'd been reluctant to let them keep the gun Kate had fired at their unknown assailant. Skip had been equally reluctant to be unarmed, out here in the middle of nowhere waiting for a ride, with a killer on the loose. Finally he'd called Dolph who'd called Judith Anderson. She'd vouched for them.

The trooper had produced a first aid kit, then left them in his car while he retrieved the gun from the ground and Kate's purse from the truck.

Skip was grateful not to have an audience as Kate cleaned his injuries with alcohol swabs from the kit. He'd winced and cussed a lot. None of the scratches or cuts were all that deep though, and thankfully it was his left hand, not his right, that was now wrapped in white gauze.

His spare gun was in his waistband holster, digging into his back. He found the discomfort reassuring.

The driver swung into the lot of a closed body shop. He stopped the tow truck and got out. Skip slid out after him and walked around the cab to help Kate down.

She had just disconnected. "Rob'll be here as soon as he can."

"You folks gonna be okay?" the driver asked. He set about unhooking the Expedition from his rig.

Kate nodded but Skip wasn't so sure. He looked around. The body shop was one of only a half dozen business establishments lined up along the country road. They all seemed to be closed on a Sunday afternoon.

The knots in his stomach were back. Was he being overly paranoid? He didn't know. He'd lost his internal compass for judging how dangerous a situation truly was.

"Is that café open?" he asked the driver.

The man turned a beefy forearm over and looked at his watch. "Not for awhile yet, but Shirley's probably still in there cleanin' up from lunch. I'll walk on down with ya. She'll let ya sit in there 'til yer ride comes. She can probably rustle up some coffee too."

"That sounds heavenly," Kate said. "I'll call Rob back and tell him to look for us there."

"No." Skip's tone was sharper than he'd intended. What if their attacker, or this gangster he worked for, had the equipment to intercept cell phone calls and track their locations via the GPS chips in them? "Turn your phone off. We'll just watch for him. The town's not that big."

Kate looked at him for a moment, then understanding dawned on her face. She fished her phone out of her purse to turn it off.

The tow truck driver gave them a funny look but didn't say anything.

At the café, he introduced them to the owner and explained

that they'd had an accident on the highway.

Shirley was a middle-aged woman with frizzy blonde hair and a voluptuous figure that was moving toward fat. She fussed over them sympathetically as she got them settled at a table. Then she went to fetch coffee.

Kate let out a loud sigh.

"You know what's funny," Skip said. "I'd just been thinking how relaxing this weekend had been, when that bozo tried to run us off the road."

Shirley came back with two steaming mugs. She set them on the Formica-topped table, then pulled a handful of creamers out of her apron pocket. "You folks hungry? Grill's closed down but I can heat up some soup, and I've got homemade pie."

"That sounds wonderful," Kate said. "What kind of soup?"

"Cream a chicken or split pea. Got apple, peach or Boston cream pie."

"Chicken soup and peach pie, please." Kate flashed her a grateful smile.

"Nothing for me, thanks," Skip said.

Kate gave him a concerned look as Shirley walked away. "You sure? It's been a long time since breakfast."

Skip shook his head. "Not hungry." He took a sip of coffee, trying to ignore her narrow-eyed gaze.

"I'm okay," he insisted.

Her eyes said she didn't believe him.

He felt a tug of guilt. His father's words echoed in the back of his head. *It ain't easy, son, for us men to share how we feel. But you gotta tell your woman when somethin's botherin' you. They got this sixth sense, and if you don't tell 'em what's goin' on, well, they'll just keep pesterin' you 'til you do.*

He took a deep breath. "You remember what we were talking about this morning?"

Kate nodded, watching him over the edge of her mug as she sipped her coffee.

"After Mac was shot, my reaction was kinda the opposite of yours. I started feeling something I'd never really felt before.

Took me awhile to figure out that it was fear."

Kate frowned and cocked her head. "You'd never felt fear before?"

"What I used to think was fear was really caution. It was... more intellectual. And usually when I'm in a tight situation, I get this calm that comes over me. I'm extra alert and thinking fast."

"That's fear," she said, "or rather the adrenaline triggered by fear. Just the right amount to keep you on your toes."

Skip shook his head. "Yeah, it was adrenaline, but it wasn't from fear. I think it was more excitement. But when Mac was shot, it was like you said. If he can get hurt, then anyone can. And suddenly I was afraid. Truly afraid. Cold-sweat, knot-in-my-stomach afraid."

"It shook your healthy denial," Kate said.

"What?"

"Denial, the defense mechanism. We tend to think of it as a bad thing, when we pretend something isn't happening. But it has its good side too. Every day, we walk out of the house assuming nothing bad's gonna happen to us that day. That's healthy denial. It allows us to function."

"But bad stuff does happen."

Shirley arrived with soup and pie. Kate thanked her, then turned back to him. "Yeah, and when it does, it shakes that healthy denial." She paused, then continued in a low voice. "That's what happened when Eddie was killed. Why I've been so paranoid that something would happen to you. If one husband could die so suddenly and senselessly..." Her voice trailed off.

"Do you want me to change careers?" he said after a moment.

"No, because then the bad guys have won. They've made us change our lives, out of fear. Besides, what else would you do?"

"I don't know, but the thought crossed my mind, the first few days after Mac was shot. I was pretty shook. Kept wondering if we all are getting too damn old to be chasing bad guys. And I was afraid I'd freeze up in a bad situation and make things worse. Maybe get Dolph or one of my men hurt."

"Was. Past tense?"

"Yeah, well, I thought it was getting better, until today."

Shirley stopped by their table. "Soup okay?"

"Oh, yeah, it's great." Kate ate a spoonful.

"I usually take a break 'bout now, but you all are welcome to stay here. I'll leave the door unlocked for your friend."

"That's okay," Skip said. "I'd rather you lock it. We'll watch for him and let him in."

Shirley looked at him funny before turning away. No doubt this was the kind of small town where locking doors was optional.

Kate put her hand on top of his. "Of course, you were scared today. You were hanging off the side of a cliff, listening to gunshots, with no idea what was going on." She cocked her head to one side. "You didn't stay down there out of fear, did you?"

"Hell no. Every fiber in my being wanted to scramble up that cliff and see what the hell was going on."

"That's what I thought. Why didn't you come up?"

"I don't know." He scrubbed a hand over his face. "I *was* scared spitless, both that I might fall off that cliff, and I was terrified for you." He shook his head. "A couple weeks ago, I would have climbed right up there and done whatever it took to protect you."

"Well I'm glad you didn't because then you would've been between me and him, and he could've had a gun and shot you."

"All that occurred to me."

Kate ate another spoonful of soup. "So you were scared spitless, but you were still thinking about all the possible scenarios? And thank you for trusting me, that I knew what I was doing, by the way."

Skip leaned back in his chair. "I did trust you. That's something else that's changed. Not that I didn't trust you before, but I would've assumed you didn't *know* what to do. Actually I think that shift started last year. We've become more of a team, when we're in a tight spot. Like Rose and I are."

"Thank you. That's the nicest compliment I've had in quite awhile."

He grinned at her. "Not every woman would consider it a

compliment to be compared to Rose."

She smiled and scooped up the last of her soup. Then she traded soup spoon for a fork and dug into her pie. She rolled her eyes in pleasure. "I love peach pie."

Skip used his coffee spoon to swipe a chunk of peach out from under the flaky crust.

"Hey, hands off my pie. I thought you weren't hungry."

"My appetite's improving. Hm, that is good."

Kate took another bite. "You know, it's not just that you and Rose are a team. You actually take turns being in charge, depending on who's in the best position to know what needs to be done."

"Yeah, we do, don't we? Hey, wait. That's part of what was going on today. You were in the best position to know what to do, and you sounded confident, like you had a plan. I knew you had a gun, and I'd lost mine." He snitched another chunk of peach from her pie. "But I don't know about this fear stuff. It's a damned uncomfortable feeling."

"Welcome to the human race, sweetheart." Kate took another bite of pie and paused to savor it. "Wait! Wait!" She started bouncing up and down in her chair.

"What?"

"I just figured something out."

"Who Talbot really is?"

Her face fell. "No, unfortunately. But I realized why Mac and Rose are so well matched."

He chuckled. "You just gotta figure out what makes people tick, don't you?"

"Occupational hazard. One of the differences between men and women is that women tend see each other as equals. More 'we're all just one big family working together.' While men tend to be more hierarchal. And if you look back at the tasks men and women did in more primitive times, that makes sense. Women had to work together to tan the hides and preserve food for winter, while men were the hunters and warriors. They needed to have a pecking order of who's in charge."

"That explains why police departments are so hierarchal."

"Yeah, and it's not wrong unless it's too rigid. As Rose said one time, you can't stop and hold a committee meeting when you're in a tight spot."

Skip laughed.

"Actually Rose is a lot more macho than many men I know," Kate said.

"Me too," he agreed.

"The only guy in the world who could snag her was one who was tough enough she'd respect him, but he'd better not try to boss her around. Meanwhile, Mac's a total male chauvinist. His first two wives wanted to be treated as his equal, but he saw them as subordinates and ordered them around."

"But Rose orders *him* around. She's his boss." Skip scratched his head, knocking loose a fine cloud of dirt that drifted to the tabletop.

"Yeah. See most men don't necessarily have to be at the top of the hierarchy. They just need to know where they stand. Mac doesn't get the concept of men and women as equals, *except* in the context of comrades-in-arms."

"Ah, so Rose is his equal as a comrade-in-arms. And he's okay with her being his superior at work 'cause that's how the hierarchy works."

"Yeah, both of those set-ups make sense to him. It's like what you said earlier. When he got shot, he was just doing his job, defending you, his commanding officer. If you'd expressed guilt about him getting hurt, he'd have been pissed because you'd be violating the hierarchy."

"I guess that's what I got instinctively, without really knowing why it would piss him off."

"Of course you get it instinctively. You're a guy."

"So how come you two get along? You're not one to suffer sexist men gladly."

"Oh, there's no way Mac and I would be friends if we hadn't grown up together. I'm essentially his younger sister. So I'm in a different category than other women."

He grinned at her. "You're the only person I know who gets excited over figuring out what makes somebody tick."

"Of course I get excited about that. It's what I do."

Skip sat back. That had struck an interesting chord inside of him. "So it's okay that I get excited when I'm in a dangerous situation?"

"Sure it is. You're not a thrill seeker. You don't go looking for danger. But when it happens, that excitement gets the adrenaline pumping. It makes you good at your job."

He smiled across the table at his wife. That made all kinds of sense.

~~~~~~~~~

Dave Samuelson's mind was scrambling for a course of action as he drove back toward Baltimore on I-70. He needed to ditch this car. Unfortunately, he was out in the middle of nowhere, with only small towns as a source for a new stolen car. Towns where everyone knew each other and he would stick out like a sore thumb on a Sunday afternoon. He'd have to take his chances that the state trooper hadn't caught his plate number.

Having made that decision, he moved on to the next. He figured he had maybe forty-eight hours before his employer realized he hadn't gotten the job done. There really wasn't any way to salvage the situation. Any additional attempts on the Canfields, even if they looked accidental, would be viewed with suspicion, and might just bring more scrutiny down on Frederico's operation. That would not make his boss happy.

It was definitely time for him to resign without notice. He really didn't want to take Nell and that squalling brat of hers with him. Was it worth the risk to go back to Scranton to clean out his bank accounts? Probably not. He could withdraw some of the money from an ATM, just before he took off. Might as well leave the rest for Nell.

Besides, he'd been socking away money in the Cayman Islands for the last three years. It was enough to live off of for awhile. He'd have to change his identity again, but that wasn't a big problem.

Where to go? South. He was tired of winter. Maybe Central America or the Caribbean.

And what would he do for a living? Hire on with the local thugs?

Dave shook his head. He let the idea that had been percolating in the back of his mind for a couple months bubble to the surface. He'd go solo, hire out as a hit man. Good money, minimal risk. You come in from out of town. Nobody knows you. You've got no connection to the target. Do a little research. Do the job. Get out. One hit a month would allow him to live in style.

Dave grinned. This whole debacle might end up being a blessing in disguise.

His mind came back around to Canfield and his wife. The bitch could identify him. Having no mug shots on file had served him well. It would continue to be an asset in his new career.

Yet another good reason to get shuck of Tony Donati. It was only a matter of time before the idiot's operation came to light, and then he, Dave, would be a "known associate." Oh, yes, this decision was feeling so right.

But what to do about the Canfield woman? Was it worth the risk to try again to get rid of her?

Dave blew out air, then shook his head. He'd get his escape south planned out and then see what he could pull off just before he left town.

There was also the matter of the prostitute Frederico had sent to his hotel room a couple times. Yet another loose end. That one should be easy enough to fix.

CHAPTER SEVENTEEN

On the way back to Towson in Rob's car, Kate and Skip made calls to fill everyone in on what had happened. Rose offered to pick up the kids and Maria from her parents' house and bring them home.

"That'd be a big help," Kate said, "if you don't mind leaving Mac alone."

Rose snorted, then lowered her voice. "He's the world's worst patient. If I don't get out of here for awhile, I'm gonna kill him." She disconnected.

Kate grinned at the phone.

Her smile faded as Skip repeated what Dolph had told him. "Tyrell Cooper's been talking some more with the feds. They sent him some pictures of guys they've seen coming and going at Donati's in Scranton. One of them looks like our guy. Tyrell wants to do a photo line-up."

"When?"

"Now."

"Now?" Kate heard the whine in her voice.

"Yeah. He's coming out to Judith's precinct. Wants us to meet him there in half an hour."

"Pizza or Chinese carry-out for dinner?" Rob asked from the driver's seat.

Kate just leaned her head back against her headrest and groaned.

~~~~~~~

On the table in an interview room at the Baltimore County Police Department were eight photos, turned face down. "I'm

going to turn these over one at a time, Mrs. Huntington-Canfield."
Tyrell used her full formal name for the benefit of the recorder.
"Look at each one carefully. Take your time. Only identify one
of them if you are sure he is the man who assaulted you."

As the third photo was turned over, Kate's stomach heaved.
For a moment, she thought she would lose the piece of pizza she'd
eaten before they'd started. "That's him."

"Wait. Let me turn the rest of them over," Tyrell said.

Kate dutifully looked at the other five, then pointed to the
third photo again. "That's still him."

"Are you sure?"

"Absolutely."

"Let the record show that Mrs. Huntington-Canfield has
identified a photo provided by the Federal Bureau of Investigation
of a known associate of Antonio Donati of Scranton, Pennsylvania.
The man in the photo is known as David Samuelson, also of
Scranton, Pennsylvania."

Tyrell reached over and pushed the off button on the recorder.
"Good job, Kate."

"So what happens now?"

"Judith can get an arrest warrant for assault and attempted
kidnapping. And we update the BOLO with his alleged name and
this picture instead of just a sketch." Tyrell made a come-on-in
gesture at the one-way mirror behind Kate's chair.

Judith, Skip and Rob piled into the room. Tyrell handed Judith
the photo. "As good an ID as you're gonna get from a photo
line-up. He's Donati's man."

Judith grinned. "Not for long. Soon his ass is gonna belong
to me." She left the room to update the BOLO and write up the
warrant request.

"I'll call the feds. See if I can find out anything more about
him," Tyrell called after her.

She waved the photo in the air by way of acknowledgment.

"Can I go home now?" Kate asked. "I'm wiped."

"Sure," Tyrell said. "Once we pick him up, we'll need you
to do a live line-up."

"Not a problem." Kate stood up.

Skip took her hand as they walked across the police station parking lot with Rob. "Judith's gonna have a couple patrol cars outside our house, until after the sting on Wednesday."

"Good. That'll make it easier to sleep tonight."

~~~~~~~~

Kate was drinking her first cup of coffee and trying to get awake. She hadn't slept well. She'd had one of the dreams again, only this time the man carrying her over his shoulder had a face— that of the man in the photo line-up, David Samuelson.

She slurped some more coffee, hoping the caffeine would clear her fuzzy head. The house phone rang.

As usual, Rose cut right to the chase. "Been thinking about the kids and Maria, and about my grouchy husband. Got a two-birds-with-one-stone idea for you."

"Hunh?" Kate mumbled, not at all sure what her friend was talking about.

"Be safer for them if someone was inside the house, as well as the cruisers on the street. Mac's not supposed to move around too much yet. I'm afraid to leave him alone all day. Figured I'd bring him over on my way to the office. He can be the inside eyes and ears for the cops, and Maria can make sure he doesn't overdo."

Kate breathed out a sigh. "That's an excellent idea. We'd already decided to keep the kids home from school. They've met Samuelson and would assume he's a good guy if he approached them. The only way I could change that would be to scare them to death by telling them the man tried to kill their parents."

"Might not be a bad idea to scare them some."

Kate sighed again. She probably should warn them, but they'd already had their innocence shaken a few too many times in their short lives. "Bring Mac on over," she said into the phone. "Maria will love the opportunity to fuss over him."

Rose let out a low chuckle before disconnecting.

Forty-five minutes later, they were getting Mac settled on the living room sofa. He slipped his gun under the pillow Kate had given him, then leaned back against it.

Kate wasn't sure how she felt about having an unlocked gun in the house with the kids home.

He caught her expression. "Don't worry, sweet pea. I won't leave it unattended. Where I go, it goes."

Kate nodded as Rose handed her cousin a bottle of pills. She rattled off something in Spanish. Maria rolled her eyes and put the pill bottle in her apron pocket. Kate surmised Rose had warned Maria that Mac might resist taking the medication.

She smiled to herself. She'd love to stick around to see who won that battle, but she needed to get to the office.

"Behave," Rose told Mac as she pulled the front door closed behind them.

On the porch, she put a restraining hand on Kate's arm. "I'm following you to work and there'll be a guard in your waiting room today."

Kate opened her mouth to protest, then thought better of it.

~~~~~~~~~

Dave Samuelson was multitasking–packing his belongings, watching the noon news, and trying to decide on a new name.

He had credentials, a driver's license, Social Security card, credit cards and even a passport, for two different additional identities. They were part of the emergency kit that he carried with him at all times. But they'd been provided by his employer's forger. So he'd have to hire someone else to make new documents in a completely different name.

He had used the credit card from one of those identities to book a flight to Costa Rica for tomorrow afternoon. From there he would hire a private charter plane, with cash, to take him to his new home, in Belize. Today, to be on the safe side, he was moving to a different motel, one near the airport.

He'd grown fond of the name David, having answered to it for nearly a decade, but maybe he would make that his middle name. What last name should he go with?

He paused in his packing to plug "common surnames in Belize" into Google on his laptop. Wikipedia informed him that over half of the twenty-two most common ones were not Spanish.

Excellent! Hmm, Smith or Jones are too obvious.

Yet the more unusual ones would probably elicit too many questions from others with the same surname, curious to know if he was a relative. Williams sounded promising.

"Hi. My name's John David Williams," he said to the mirror over the desk. "But I go by Dave." He flashed a boyish grin at himself and then went back to his packing.

He was stuffing the last of his underwear into his oversized duffel bag when a name mentioned on the TV had his head jerking up. He grabbed the remote and turned up the volume. He'd been watching for the face of a black hooker named Gazelle. That was not the face he now saw on the screen.

"This man is wanted for assault and attempted kidnapping. He is believed to be armed and dangerous," the news anchor's voice said.

Dave was staring at a photo of himself.

~~~~~~~~

Monday afternoon, Skip was once again working on paperwork. He could have sworn he'd only left a couple reports in his in-box on Friday, but somehow they'd multiplied like bunnies over the weekend.

He was tired and cranky. Kate had awakened them both at three a.m., in the throes of a nightmare.

She'd eventually settled back into a fitful sleep, but then his mind had turned to the loss of his granddaddy's gun. Twice, it had been confiscated by the police as evidence after a shooting, once when he hadn't even been the one who fired it. He'd been lucky to get it back. But this time it was truly gone for good, at the bottom of a cliff in western Maryland.

He pulled his back-up gun out of his desk drawer and held it in his hand. It didn't feel all that different, and yet it did. It was relatively new, actually a better gun. But the older one had been his grandfather's and then his father's. It was more than a gun or even a keepsake. It was a connection to the strength and courage of the Canfield men who had come before him.

He shook his head. How silly to get maudlin over a pistol. He put the .38 back in his desk drawer.

Shifting in his chair, he tried to get more comfortable. There were very few parts of his body that weren't bruised from his close encounter with that cliff yesterday. He was washing down an aspirin with a swig from his water bottle, when his desk phone rang.

He grabbed up the receiver. "Canfield."

"When you were poking around downtown," Tyrell Cooper said in his ear, "did you happen to talk to a tall, skinny, black hooker?"

"Goes by Gazelle? Yeah."

"Shit!"

Skip's stomach sank. "What happened?"

"Two of our uniforms found her this morning in an alley, bullet hole in the side of her skull. No money on her so at first it was assumed she'd been robbed of her evening's wages."

"Gazelle was the gal who tried to pick my pocket. She let it slip that the girls are expected to turn in a certain number of wallets a day."

"Were there witnesses to that?"

"The other ladies with her would've seen me grab her arm, and her trying to pull away. So they might've guessed at what happened. But no one was close enough to hear what we said to each other. And I seriously doubt she told them."

Silence on the line for a moment. "It doesn't feel right to me. I can't see Freddie killing off a source of income just because she tried to pick your pocket and failed."

"Me neither," Skip said. "But she did seem pretty damn scared when I figured out about the wallet quota. Suddenly she seemed a lot more afraid of something other than me or being arrested. She almost broke her wrist trying to twist free."

Skip toyed with the idea of trying again to discourage Tyrell from using Dolph for the sting operation. But if Dolph got wind of it, he'd be furious.

"Thanks for the info," Tyrell said. "I'll let you all know when

I've got the details ironed out for Wednesday."

"Okay." Skip hung up the phone and stared at it for a moment. He wished he could shake the feeling that this sting wasn't going to go well.

He saw Gazelle again, in his mind's eye, running away from him in those ridiculous shoes. Her life hadn't been much but these greedy bastards didn't have the right to take it.

He went back to his paperwork, now glad for the distraction. His cell phone rang. *Now what?*

"Pete's gone," Manny said when he answered it.

"What the hell?"

"I went out to make a circuit around the trailer. Todd was sleepin'. I was only outta sight of the door for maybe five minutes. When I came back inside, he was gone. We're almost out to the main road. No sign of him, and no fresh vehicle tracks in the mud. But there's lots of woods to hide in around here."

"What's your take on it?" Skip asked.

"He left on his own. He's been antsy all morning."

Skip ran fingers through his hair, then grabbed a hunk and gave it a yank. "Can you stay out by the main road where you've got phone service? I'll call you back in a few minutes."

"Sure, Boss."

He glanced at his watch. Five of three. With any luck, he'd catch his wife between clients.

"Kate Huntington."

"We've got a problem. Your boy's slipped his leash."

"What?"

"Pete's gone and all signs indicate he left of his own accord, on foot."

"Holy crap! Hang on, lemme tell my next client I'll be a few minutes."

While Skip waited for Kate to return to the phone, he tried to shove aside his anger so he could sort out the best course of action. What was with this guy? They were giving him all kinds of *pro bono* services. Hell, they were buying his groceries and paying to guard his ass, and he just slips off when he's feeling restless? Not to mention the small matter of attempts against their lives because of him!

"We need to find him," Kate said in his ear.

"Maybe, maybe not."

A couple beats of silence. "What do you want to do? Drop the case?"

The word *Yes* was on his lips. They'd invested so much in this case–money, sweat, risk. Mac had been shot, almost killed. *They'd* almost been killed yesterday. Enough was enough. Time to end the craziness.

Gazelle's emaciated face swam in his mind's eye. He tried to ignore the lump of guilt and sadness in his throat.

Bottom line, he had two men out there waiting for instructions.

"I need to go out there. See for myself what's going on. But yeah, I might tell my men to come home."

"I'm going with you."

"Why?"

Another beat of silence. "For the same reason. I need to see what's happening with Pete, if we can find him. Decide what to do. And we can't just leave him stranded out in the boonies with no transportation. If nothing else, Rob promised Judith and a judge that he'd be responsible for him."

"Okay. We need to leave as soon as possible."

"My four o'clock client's in pretty good shape right now. I'll call and see if she can reschedule. But I've gotta give my three o'clock her full hour. It'll be about four-fifteen when I'm done here."

"I'll ask Rose if she and Mac can stay at the house this evening, until we get back," Skip said. "And I think I'll run home and check on things, then pick you up at your office. That'll save us some time."

"Thanks, sweetheart. See you later."

Skip disconnected.

As he headed out to retrieve his rental truck from the parking lot, he called Rose to fill her in, and then Manny to tell him to sit tight.

At the house, he greeted Mac, who was channel surfing, then

checked on the children.

Rose was in the kitchen, talking to Maria. "Just did a circuit of the house. Everything's secure," she said when he entered the room. "How're you doing?"

"I'm fine." His tone was sharper than he'd intended.

Rose cocked an expressive eyebrow at him.

Damn it! His partner knew him a little too well.

"I've been in better moods. Depending on what we find out there, I may pull our guys off this case."

Rose processed that for a second, then nodded.

She walked with him to the front door. "Sorry to disrupt your evening," he said.

Rose snorted and tilted her head toward Mac, stretched out on the sofa, remote in his hand. "It's not like I had big plans."

~~~~~~~~~

Dave sat in another nondescript stolen car, this one light tan, a block down from the Canfields' house. The anger that only Nell had ever seen fully expressed was now raging inside his head. He took a deep breath to steady himself. Things were spinning out of control, but that just meant he needed to be more careful.

Aside from the desire for revenge, he'd decided that Kate Huntington-Canfield was a true threat. Yeah, the cops had his picture and his fake name, but other than that they had squat. They wouldn't be able to convict him of anything if the only person who could definitively identify him and testify against him was dead.

Dave pulled down the visor and looked in the mirror. He practiced a more reserved smile than his normal boyish grin. The expression matched his newly-dyed brown hair and black-rimmed glasses. The brown contact lenses were a bit annoying, but he'd get used to them.

His overall plan was intact. He'd still be able to come and go in the U.S. as needed to pursue his new career. He'd just have to use disguises and other identities. But first he was gonna deal with the bitch who'd screwed things up for him. He ground his teeth.

The red Explorer with the rental car sticker in the back window had been parked in front of the house when he'd arrived. Dave figured it was Canfield's replacement for the Expedition he'd tried to send over a cliff. There were quite a few other cars parked on the street, but no sign of the wife's blue Prius.

Dave sat up straighter. Canfield had just stepped out of the house. He came down the front porch steps and headed toward the Explorer.

Excellent. Now he just had to wait for the wife to come home from work.

He didn't have a concrete plan yet, but something would present itself. He had to make sure her death looked like it had nothing to do with him though.

He pulled his Glock out from under the driver's seat and put it in his left hand. The weight of it made his arm, inside its cast, ache. He gritted his teeth while his right hand fished inside his jacket pocket. Whatever he ended up doing, he definitely didn't want to draw the neighbor's attention.

His hand closed around the object he sought. He pulled the silencer out of his pocket and attached it to the customized barrel of his gun.

CHAPTER EIGHTEEN

As Skip drove them around the streets of Towson for a few minutes, checking for tails, Kate noted the clenched jaw. Finally he pointed the truck toward western Maryland.

He was silent, staring straight ahead. She really didn't know what to say either.

Or feel for that matter. Anger and disappointment were doing battle in her chest while anxiety gnawed at her gut. No, it was more than disappointment. She felt hurt, as if Pete had done something *to her.*

She blew out air. Boy, had *she* lost her detachment with this case. She'd practically canonized Pete just because he'd saved lives on 9/11. No, that wasn't being totally fair to herself. She'd assumed it would be relatively easy to get the competent young man he once was to shove the addict aside, especially when her first intervention worked so well. It was a mistake an experienced addictions counselor probably wouldn't have made.

Staying clean and sober had been part of their original contract. She should probably try to find an appropriate referral for him. Yeah right, who the hell was going to take on a recovering addict who was charged with murder and had no money?

The evening rush hour had just barely started. It hadn't taken long to get around the Beltway to I-70. Now they were zipping along through Howard County. The still wintry March sun was beginning to set in front of them. Kate caught her breath at the beauty of the sunset—the sky aglow with oranges and reds.

Skip frowned and lowered his visor.

"I'm sorry I dragged you and the agency into this," she said.

"It seemed like a good idea at the time."

She couldn't tell if he meant that sarcastically or not. "I guess we shouldn't get too mad at Pete until we find out what the deal is."

Skip just glanced sideways at her.

"Guess that boat's already sailed, huh?"

"And you're not pissed?" he said.

"Yes, I am, but... I guess I'm just used to putting my own feelings on hold while I do what's best for the client. I could really use a sounding board for that right now."

"You know he's slipped. He went looking for drugs."

"Maybe, maybe not." Kate paused, trying to gather her thoughts.

Skip snorted. "That's what addicts do."

"Okay, hear me out, please. Pete's a combination of two people at this point. The earnest, responsible person he used to be, before the PTSD. And the addict he's become. If the addict took over for awhile and made him sneak out on your guys, that doesn't necessarily mean he's totally slipped."

Skip opened his mouth. She raised her hand in a hold-on gesture.

"I thought you wanted a sounding board?"

"I do, but I haven't finished. What all this does mean is that Pete can't take being out here. He's not dealing well with the isolation. He needs to be where he can get to a meeting, or call his sponsor."

"He's had the option of going to a meeting all along. I told the guys to take him to the one in town if he asked."

"Did he know that?"

"Well, no, but I figured he'd ask them if he wanted to go."

Kate shook her head. "The old Pete would, maybe even the recovering addict Pete might. But addict Pete is going to assume they'd look down on him for needing a meeting, for feeling shaky. He'd try to suck it up and hang on."

"Until he couldn't anymore. And if he's feeling shaky, addict Pete would be front and center." His tone had lost most of its hard edge.

Kate breathed out a soft sigh. "Most likely. And addict Pete might also lie to himself. Tell himself he's going to find a meeting when he's really looking for a way to get high."

"Thus the sneaking away from his guards," Skip said. "Instead of just saying he wanted to go to town to catch a meeting."

Kate nodded. "I'm not suggesting we should forgive him for screwing up and dragging us out here, but he's fighting a battle. Today, the enemy is winning. If he feels like the battle's completely lost no matter what he does, he won't keep fighting."

"That's what you've been afraid of all along. That he'd give up."

Kate swallowed a lump in her throat. She forgot sometimes just how astute her husband could be. "Yes. He wasn't totally on solid ground, before all this started. And he's also lost his friend. I'm quite sure he hasn't really grieved for Jimmy Matthews yet."

"When I first interviewed him in jail, he told me that when he couldn't get drugs, he'd drink."

She nodded again. "So we need to find out if there's any local drug trafficking, and also where the bars are."

They were silent for a few minutes. Then Kate said, "If he's slipped completely then maybe we should both find a way to extricate ourselves from the case."

If I can find someone crazy enough to take it.

"We still need to bring him back to Towson though" she said. "There's the little matter of Rob having to answer to Judith and a judge regarding his whereabouts. But assuming for a moment that he hasn't slipped and we decide to keep helping him, where could he stay and be safe?"

"Rob's house?" Skip suggested.

It was the most logical solution. They had plenty of room now that the girls were grown. But she found herself shaking her head.

Skip glanced over at her. "You don't like that idea?"

"It might work. But I've been concerned all along that this case... that Rob's lost his perspective some with Pete."

As have I now.

"How so? He takes on *pro bono* cases all the time."

"Yeah, I know. Most of them are my clients. But this one's been way too personal for him. He almost lost his temper at the bail hearing. I've never seen him be anything but totally in control in the courtroom."

"Can't think of anyplace else, except a motel. Not sure that'd be an improvement over where Pete is now, and he might not be as safe."

"True. I guess we should wait and see how he's doing. If it feels like a bad idea to leave him out here, I'll call Rob."

~~~~~~~

Why hadn't the Canfield woman come home yet? The lights had gone out in the upper-level windows of the house a half hour ago. No doubt, the kids were in bed now, and maybe the Mexican maid as well.

He'd gotten out and walked around the perimeter of the house. The only light was a dim one coming from the front window of the house. Probably left on for the Canfields. He'd checked the garage, just to make sure the woman's Prius wasn't parked in there all this time. But it was full of boxes and old furniture.

He went back to his car. As he sat, watching the house, a plan began to form in his mind. If he could get into the house without waking the maid, he could take a few valuables, then lie in wait for the bitch and make it look like she interrupted a burglary. Canfield might come home first, or they might come in together. That was fine. He wouldn't mind taking them both out, for all the trouble they'd caused him.

A niggling voice in the back of his mind told him this wasn't a great plan. Rage surged, threatening to take over. He was getting tired of sitting out here in the fucking cold.

With effort, he tamped down the anger. He needed to think the idea through more, fine-tune it.

Hopefully the kids wouldn't wake up. He wasn't fond of kids, but he'd prefer not to have to kill them.

~~~~~~~

Just past Hancock, Maryland, Skip took the exit for I-68. "How 'bout putting that fancy new phone of yours to good use.

See what you can find in Finzel. I don't remember seeing much in the way of business establishments when we drove through there."

Kate tried to recall the layout of the tiny town. "Me neither. It was mostly houses."

She punched buttons for a few minutes, then blew out air. "One of these days, I need to sit down and figure out how to use this properly." After another few minutes, she decided she wasn't finding much because there wasn't much to find.

"Doesn't look like they have their own police or sheriff's department. Finzel truly is just a wide place in the road. I can't imagine where Pete would find drugs there."

"Any bars?"

"Just one, on Finzel Road about halfway between the highway and the town. It's the only one he could have conceivably walked to."

"He could hitchhike."

Kate groaned. Frostburg was less than ten miles from Finzel, and it was a college town. Lots of bars, and probably places to score drugs as well.

They almost missed it. A car coming the other way lit up the front of a muddy brown building that was obviously not a house. There was a sign on the roof but they were past it before Kate could read it.

"Turn around. I think that might've been it."

The sign read *Cindy's Tavern*. The parking lot was deserted.

Skip backed into a parking space so that his headlights fell on the building. He plucked his gun from the console between the seats and leaned forward to tuck it into his belt. "Stay here."

He came back around the corner of the building in less than two minutes. Kate stepped out of the truck, leaving her door open.

"Definitely closed, maybe permanently."

She had opened her mouth to answer him when a voice from behind her had them both spinning around. "Kin I help you all?"

Skip's hand had flown to the small of his back, and was no doubt resting on his gun butt. Kate squinted at the vague figure by the side of the road. The voice could have been male or female.

"We're looking for a friend of ours," Skip said. "Thought he might have stopped here."

"Place is closed." A match flared, a hand cupped around it as the owner of the hand lit a cigarette. A brief glimpse of a weathered face with gray stubble before the match went out. "Your friend a young guy? Sandy hair, needs a haircut."

"Sounds like him," Skip said.

"He was hanging 'round here earlier. I thought you might be him and his buddy coming back, maybe to try to break in."

"His buddy?"

The end of the cigarette glowed brighter as the man took a drag. "Some guy stopped and picked him up."

"What kind of vehicle, and which way did they go?"

"Toward the highway. Old junker, light colored. Didn't pay no 'ttention to the make or model."

Kate's heart sank. Pete could be anywhere by now.

"Did you see the driver?" Skip asked.

The end of the cigarette moved back and forth as the man shook his head. "Pretty sure it was a guy though."

Kate had a thought. It was a long shot but... "Sir, do you happen to know if there's an AA meeting around here tonight?"

The end of the cigarette jerked. A pause, then, "Yes, ma'am. At the Methodist church. Ain't that far from here but kinda complicated gettin' there."

He gave them directions that sounded like he was sending them in circles. "Do you happen to know the street address?" Kate asked. She had her phone in her hand, ready to punch it into the GPS function, which she had found, miraculously, without much effort.

"Pocahontas Road. Don't know the number."

They thanked him and climbed back in the Explorer.

After three right turns, the last two within a block of each other, Skip said, "We're headed back the way we came."

"This thing says it's two hundred feet ahead, on the left."

Skip ducked his head forward to search for a street sign. "Yup, there it is. Pocahontas Road."

The church was near the corner, a simple but modern red-brick structure. Only a small white steeple identified it as a church. The front was dark but over a slight hill they could see a lighted parking lot. It held a dozen cars.

Skip pulled around to the side of the building. Two people came out of a door.

Skip lowered his window. "Excuse me," he called out.

"No!" Kate hissed. "Don't ask about a meeting."

"Oops." He waved at the two men who had stopped by their cars. "Never mind."

He parked the Explorer and they climbed out. Kate spotted a light-colored, older model car with rust spots on the side and a dented fender. She dared to hope it was the junker the old man had described.

As they neared the door, a young woman, bundled up in a coat and scarf, came out.

"Did we miss the meeting?" Kate asked.

"Yeah, it just ended." The woman hurried off toward the cars.

"Now how come you could ask but I couldn't?" Skip whispered as he opened the door for her.

"I didn't ask if it *was* a meeting."

Warm air hit them as they entered what looked like a parish hall. Several rows of folding chairs were lined up near the front. A few people were standing around chatting. They approached the two nearest men. Their backs were to them, heads bent, talking low.

"Excuse me, gentlemen," Skip said. "We're looking for a young man, a friend of ours."

The two men turned around. One of them was Pete.

Kate almost cried out in relief.

~~~~~~~

The show they'd been watching went to commercial. Rose glanced over at her husband. He'd fallen asleep propped up in the corner at the other end of the sofa. It didn't look like a very comfortable position, but she opted not to wake him.

Deciding to make another circuit of the house, she got up

carefully.

As she neared the back of the house, she heard banging in the backyard. Pulling out her .32, she eased into the laundry room and over to the back door. She cautiously looked around the edge of the window in the door. A tree branch was banging against the garage.

Letting out her breath, Rose leaned down to return her pistol to its holster.

When she stood up, a man's face was framed in the window, a gun with a silencer pointed at her.

She jumped back, letting out an involuntary yelp. Her hand was halfway back to her ankle holster when the end of the silencer rapped sharply against the glass. She froze. The man mouthed, "Open the door."

Rose's mind was racing. There were bars on the window, but the glass wasn't bulletproof.

"Don't make me shoot the lock," the man called through the glass. "If the kids wake up, I'll kill them."

She didn't have to fake a look of horror on her face. If she tried to get to her gun, he'd shoot. He might not hit her, but things would get messy from there, and if Maria or the kids came downstairs...

He was probably assuming she was Maria, an unarmed nanny. Best to let him continue to think that. She made sure the safety chain was on the door and then unlocked the dead bolt and turned the knob. The man pushed against the door. She pushed back.

"I let you in, *señor*," she imitated Maria's accent, "but please no hurt de children."

The man smiled and her suspicions were confirmed. Under the dark hair and glasses was the boyish face of David Samuelson.

"I just want your valuables and then I'll be on my way."

Rose rapidly backed away from the door. "Please no hurt us, *señor*!" she yelled to alert Mac. She dove sideways into the living room. Curling into a ball to reach her ankle holster, she rolled across the floor.

A crash as Samuelson kicked in the door.

In the next instant, he was framed in the doorway of the laundry room, gun out in front of him. He pivoted in a half circle, scanning the room for her. She raised her gun to shoot.

A cannon went off, deafening her.

CHAPTER NINETEEN

The interior of the Explorer was silent, the atmosphere somewhat tense. Pete and Manny were in the back seat. The other guard was following them in his pick-up truck.

Skip turned the radio on. Country western music kept them company until they were almost to the Baltimore Beltway.

A buzzing sound came from the console between the front seats. Skip reached for a button on his steering wheel, that wasn't there. Damn, he missed his own truck, and especially its Bluetooth that was synchronized with his cell.

"Could you get that for me?" he asked Kate as he turned the radio off.

He glanced over. She was looking at the caller ID. Then she said into the phone, "We found Pete. We're taking him to Rob's and–"

When she stopped talking, Skip glanced over again. Kate's face had gone completely white.

He went cold inside. "What's wrong?"

She turned toward him, her eyes wide. "Samuelson broke into the house. Mac shot him."

He swerved across the empty lane to his right and off onto the shoulder. His heart racing, he took the phone from Kate and hit the button for speaker.

Rose's voice sounded tinny and far away. "Made a mess of your rug."

"Are the kids okay? Was anybody hurt?" Skip yelled.

"Everybody's fine," Rose said. "Well, the kids are a bit shook.

Edie more than Billy."

Skip pulled onto the highway again and shoved the accelerator to the floor. "We'll be there in fifteen minutes," he shouted over the whine of the Explorer's straining engine and the blood pounding in his ears.

Manny's hand landed on his shoulder. "Easy does it, man. The kids need you alive, and I'm kinda fond of my own skin as well."

Eighteen minutes later, Skip stopped the Explorer in the middle of Linden Lane. The street was partially blocked by two cruisers and an unmarked police car, lights flashing on all of them. Kate shoved her door open and raced for the front porch.

She heard Manny yelling behind her. "We'll get Pete to Rob's house, Boss."

A cop on the porch stepped into her path and put out his arm to block the open doorway. "This is a crime scene, ma'am."

Skip growled and started to move around her. The officer tensed. Kate put a restraining hand on Skip's arm. He looked like he was about to deck the cop.

Judith Anderson yelled from inside the house. "Let them in, Jackson. They live here."

"Yes, ma'am." The officer stepped aside.

Kate ran into her living room, then stopped, trying to process the overload of stimulation. Crime scene technicians swarmed around the back section of the L-shaped room. The rug had been partially rolled up, exposing wood floorboards stained with blood. There were some rusty red marks on the walls as well.

Two uniformed officers stood off to one side. Rose was dictating a statement to a female officer sitting in one of the armchairs, typing on a laptop. Judith Anderson stood in the middle of the semi-chaos, barking out orders and waving her arms, like a conductor trying to control errant parts of a rebellious orchestra.

"Where are my children?" Kate demanded in a loud voice.

Rose broke off her dictation. "They're okay. Maria has them upstairs. She's reading them a story."

Skip took off for the stairs. Kate started to follow, then caught sight of Mac, sitting on the sofa gritting his teeth. His face was gray under his tan. The bottom half of his faded green T-shirt was dark red.

"Mac! Dear God!" Kate raced to his side.

"Incision hurts a bit," Mac wheezed out. "But I'm okay, sweet pea." His face turned grayer from the effort to talk.

Rose closed the distance to the sofa in two strides. "The hell you are!"

Skip nudged both women aside and scooped Mac up in his arms.

"Out of the way!" Rose yelled at the uniforms, even though they were already scattering to either side of Skip's path.

"Jackson, take him in your car!" Judith barked.

~~~~~~~

Afterwards, Kate had no memory of how they'd gotten Mac into the back of the police car. Skip had yelled something from the sidewalk about checking on the kids and then following them.

She was sitting in the cruiser's front seat praying. Rose knelt on the floor in the back, a bloody towel in her hands, putting pressure on her unconscious husband's oozing incision.

Where'd the towel come from? Kate had no idea.

Officer Jackson got them to Greater Baltimore Medical Center in less than six minutes. Judith had apparently radioed ahead. A nurse and porter were waiting with a gurney beside the driveway leading to the ER. They had Mac hooked up to an IV by the time they hit the doors to the entrance.

Kate and Rose jogged after the gurney. Another nurse stepped into their path. "I need some information."

"He was in here last week. Gunshot wound," Kate gasped out, as she kept moving forward. "The incision opened up."

The nurse backed up in front of them. "Who's *he*?"

"Mathias McKenzie Reilly," Rose barked, as she tried to dodge around the nurse.

The woman put a hand on Rose's shoulder. "Was he still breathing in the car?" Her voice was gentle.

"Yeah."

"Then he should be okay. We've got him now."

Rose and Kate both stopped trying to push past her.

"How long ago did the incision open up?"

"An hour maybe," Rose said. "He shot a guy who was breaking into her house–"

The nurse held up a hand, then jotted something on a clipboard.

"He's going to be okay?" Kate heard the tremor in her voice.

The nurse didn't answer her. "Either of you ladies his next of kin?"

~~~~~~~~

It was after two in the morning by the time they got home. Skip thought he might have to carry Kate up the porch steps, she looked so beat.

A uniformed officer was standing on their front porch. "Detective Anderson assigned me to watch the house tonight, just in case the perp wasn't acting alone. She said to tell you that he's stable at St. Joseph's Hospital."

"So's our friend who shot him," Kate said.

"How much damage did Mac do to the bastard?" Skip asked.

"Took a chunk outta the guy's left shoulder, but he's okay."

"Damn!" Skip said.

A corner of the cop's mouth quirked upward. "I'll be in my car out front if you need me. Goodnight, folks."

Once the officer was down the steps and almost to the street, Kate mumbled, "Ain't much that's good about it."

Skip gave her a small smile. He was surprised at his lack of guilt over wishing Mac's aim had been truer. He opened the door and stepped aside, waiting for Kate to enter.

The living room had been straightened up–no doubt Maria's doing. The conflicting smells of bleach and lemon oil drifted across the room. He walked over and examined the walls and floorboards. "She got out most of the blood."

Kate just nodded. He followed as she stumbled into the kitchen and squinted at a note on the table. "Apparently there's food in the fridge for us."

Skip chuckled softly at her bleary-eyed expression. "You're

not hungry?"

"Famished, but I'm not sure I can stay awake long enough to eat."

"Sit down. I'll get it." He put the casserole of meat and beans in the microwave to heat while gathering the rest of the ingredients for burritos. He put together one for Kate first before making one for himself.

"The last couple days have been a bit more exciting than I care for," Skip said between bites.

"Amen to that. I have no clue how I'm going to get through tomorrow, and I've got a couple clients scheduled who are in rough shape."

Skip glanced at his watch. "We got by on less sleep than this sometimes when Billy was a baby."

Kate just made a noise that sounded like "humph," her mouth full of burrito.

"I've got a meeting with a potential new client tomorrow morning," Skip said. "But I'm gonna try to come home early and catch a nap. I need to be on my toes on Wednesday."

He made himself another burrito and bit into it.

"You still worried about Dolph?" Kate asked.

"Yeah. I've got a bad feeling about this operation." As if on cue, his stomach knotted. He put the burrito down on his plate.

"To paraphrase a very wise man I know," Kate said. "He's been doing this for years. He knows how to handle himself."

Skip grunted. Those words weren't all that comforting when he was on the receiving end of them.

"How are you feeling?" Kate asked.

She didn't have to say which feeling she meant. "I guess I'll get used to being less than brave eventually."

"I can't recall who but somebody famous once said, 'Courage is the mastery of fear, not the absence of it.'"

"Mark Twain. My daddy used to quote him a lot. But his favorite quote on the subject was from John Wayne. 'Courage is being scared to death... and saddlin' up anyway.'"

"So you know there's no shame in being afraid, as long as the fear doesn't take over."

Skip took a bite of his burrito to buy himself a minute to think. "The problem is," he finally said, "I thought I was feeling fear before, and overcoming it. I didn't realize that it was more than just a rush of adrenaline and a... a mental sense of caution. It's a lot harder to push past than I'm used to."

"Welcome to normal."

"Well, it's not normal for me. I hope it goes away soon."

"Skip, I don't think it will. I think you'll just get used to feeling it and doing what you need to do anyway. That's what the rest of us do."

He grimaced. "Was that meant to be a pep talk? If so, it needs work."

Kate gave him a tired smile. "Part pep talk, part reality check."

CHAPTER TWENTY

The next morning went by in a blur. Kate wasn't real sure how she stayed upright on such little sleep, much less managed to say anything that made sense to her clients. But no one ran screaming from the room.

At lunchtime, Kate called Rob's house. Manny answered.

"How's it going?"

"Not bad so far. Having cable TV is helping."

"Is Pete handy?"

"Sure. Lemme put him on."

After they had greeted each other, Pete asked, "Is it really necessary for me to be in a safe house now, with Samuelson arrested?"

Kate could hear a slight whine in his voice. Not a good sign. Addict Pete had not been completely quelled by just one AA meeting. "Skip thinks you should stay out of sight until our other bad guy is under wraps as well. But I had a thought about something you could do in the meantime."

"What's that?"

"The stuff we talked about on Saturday, was that what got you worked up?"

"No, I felt real good about all that, and I slept the best I have in ages Saturday night. But Sunday I just started feeling restless. I don't deal well with boredom. Never have, even before all this started."

Kate digested that. Yes, he felt good about their discussion of career options but it still may have exacerbated the restlessness.

"Getting tired of having your life on hold?" she asked.

"Oh yeah."

"Here's what I was thinking. You could borrow Liz's computer to do some research. Find out what other kinds of jobs are available in the fire department, and what credentials you'd need to teach at the fire academy. And you might look for a meeting near there as well. You can't go to your home group just yet, but I think you could go to one where nobody knows you, as long as your guards go with you."

"I like both of those ideas."

"Let me talk to Manny again for a minute. I'll touch base with you this evening."

When the guard came back on the line, Kate said, "I think he needs a meeting. Today. He's going to look on the computer for one nearby that he hasn't been to before. Would one of you guys be willing to go in with him and pretend to be a recovering addict? You don't have to share anything obviously. But I don't think you should let him out of your sight just yet."

"Not a problem. I could use a meeting myself."

Kate stared at the phone for a beat, then she heard Manny saying, "I've been a member of AA for a long time."

"I never would've known."

"Thanks. That shows how far I've come."

"I'm honored that you shared that with me, Manny, and I will consider it confidential information."

"No need. Skip and Rose know. That's how I got kicked off the force and ended up a bodyguard."

That gave Kate pause. Heavy drinking was not that unusual amongst cops, when they were off duty. Which was not surprising considering the stresses of their jobs. One would have to be a hardcore drunk to get fired from the police force.

A low chuckle came over the line. "Someday I'll tell you about it, over a Coke."

Kate laughed. "I'm buying."

Manny dropped his voice. "Uh, I think I owe you an apology. I should have seen the signs in Pete and kept a closer rein on him."

"Don't take that on yourself, Manny. He's a grown man."

Another low chuckle. "You sound like my sponsor. I'll see that he gets to a meeting today, and I'll let him know I'm in recovery too. Might make it easier for him to ask for support if he gets shaky again."

"Thanks. You're a gem, Manny."

~~~~~~~~

Skip never did get his afternoon nap. Tyrell called a meeting to make sure everyone knew their roles during the sting the next day.

While driving to the meeting, Skip called Rose, then put his cell phone on speaker and dropped it in his lap. Damn, he missed his truck!

"How's Mac doing?" he shouted when she answered.

"He's stable. They're probably sending him home either today or in the morning."

Rose sounded unusually tense. But then again this was the second time in two weeks she'd come close to losing Mac.

"Can Dolph borrow your car tomorrow?" Skip asked. "I'd feel better if he had the advantage of bullet-proof glass and steel-reinforced doors, for as long as he's in the car at least."

"Yeah, but I'm gonna be there." Rose's angry voice reverberated inside the Explorer.

"Uh, I thought you'd want to stay with Mac."

"He's fine. Just weak from blood loss. I want in on this."

"You sound pretty pissed, partner."

"We're gonna bring this Donati bastard down. He's behind Mac's shooting and he sent Samuelson after *mi familia.*"

Rose sounded more upset about the invasion of his home than he was. He felt mostly relief that Samuelson was behind bars. "Okay. I'm headed for a meeting with Tyrell Cooper now. I'll tell–"

"Where?"

"Judith's precinct."

"I'll meet you there." Rose disconnected.

When Skip walked into the conference room, he did a double take. Dolph had cut his hair into a buzz cut. He hadn't shaved off the mustache but he'd tamed it considerably. His normal rumpled dress shirt and slacks had been replaced with a pale green polo shirt and crisply ironed black Dockers. Wire-rimmed sunglasses completed the makeover.

Tyrell was grinning at Skip's reaction. "Doesn't he look the part of an elderly wuss?"

"Hey, I'm not that old!" Dolph protested.

Skip smiled in spite of himself. "No, but you do look like a wuss."

Once Rose arrived, they quickly covered the basics.

"I've been undercover with some of these women," Rose said. "Pretending to be a hooker new to town. I'll wear my get-up just in case I need to be out on the street at some point."

"Good idea," Skip said. "Where will your people be, Tyrell?"

"I'll have a half dozen men, in plain clothes, nearby, but they can't get too close. The hookers know their faces, know they're cops."

Skip turned to Rose. "We got anybody who could help out?"

"All our guys are too big and beefy," she said. "They'd look like cops to these ladies."

"Manny'd fit in," Skip said. "Some of Freddie's men have seen him with me but the ladies haven't."

Rose nodded. "I'll put somebody else on Pete for tomorrow. Free him up to help with this."

Tyrell placed a plastic bag on the table in front of him. He pulled out a brown leather wallet and tossed it to Dolph. "Driver's license, three credit cards, all in the name of Charles Bevins. Pictures of his grandkids. One hundred and two dollars in various sized bills. A Social Security number has been established in Mr. Bevins' name as well, but of course he doesn't carry that number on him."

"Of course," Dolph said. "Don't want to be too obvious."

Tyrell reached in the bag again and brought out a fistful of tiny electronic gadgets. "Miniature radios." He turned to Dolph and Rose. "You two will have to skip the earpieces. But the wireless mics look like a shirt button."

~~~~~~~~~

Rose tried to get comfortable. She was scrunched down in the passenger seat of her own car. They wanted anyone who might be watching to think Dolph, in the driver's seat, was alone, as they cruised down The Block.

"We've got a problem," Dolph said.

"What?" Skip said from his own scrunched-down position in the backseat.

"Roxie apparently didn't leave town."

Rose peeked up over the dashboard. "Go on down another block or two."

After a couple minutes, Skip–the only one with an earpiece–said, "Tyrell's shifting his people over."

Rose pointed to a group of women on a corner half a block away. "I talked to them before. They're Freddie's."

Dolph pulled over to the curb. He reached into the pocket of the navy windbreaker he wore over his green polo shirt.

Rose felt a quiver in her gut. She was starting to share her partner's bad feeling about this operation. "I've got an idea. Let me approach them first, Dolph, then you stagger up." She pushed her sweat pants off to reveal her hooker costume. "I think we can play this out so you don't actually have to go with any of them and then fake falling asleep."

Dolph had taken a small swig from the pint of whiskey in his hand. He nodded as he swished it around in his mouth. Dribbling some whiskey on his fingertips, he mimicked a woman applying perfume to her wrists and behind her ears. "Do I smell bad enough?"

Rose leaned over and sniffed. "Nope. Rub some on your chest, under your shirt."

Dolph lifted his shirt and did as suggested. The odor of cheap booze filled the car. He glanced up at the rearview mirror. "Lighten up, son. I'll be fine."

Rose looked back over her shoulder. Skip's expression was far from light.

She exchanged her sneakers for the high heels and wiggled out of her sweatshirt, then donned the white lace jacket. She touched the button mic to make sure it was still secure. Leaning down, she removed her ankle holster and palmed the small gun it held. Then she slid out of the car.

Turning away from both the car and the ladies on the corner, she slipped the snub nose .32 into the only spot on her scantily-clad body where it wasn't likely to show. Adjusting her tube top, she looked down, checking for bulges. Satisfied, she headed down the sidewalk.

Once she had the women engaged in conversation, Dolph got out of the car and moved in their direction, weaving a bit.

The older, busty woman said, "Here comes that guy who likes 'em tan."

Rose's gut clenched. She'd thought Dolph's disguise was good but this gal had spotted him from half a block away. She hoped Freddie's men weren't as astute as his hookers.

She rolled her eyes at the older woman. "Last time he couldn't get it up, and then he passed out."

"Did he pay you?"

"Sure. I told him he was wonderful." Rose flashed a grin. The other woman smiled back.

Dolph staggered into the middle of the group. "Hey there, aren't you a hot tamale?" he slurred. He extended his arm to throw it around Rose's shoulders and missed.

She grabbed him to keep him from falling.

Slouching against her, his head lolled onto her shoulder. He licked her skin through the lace of the jacket. "Ya tastes good."

Rose narrowed her eyes at him and made a mental note to dock his pay for that. Then she caught the movement she'd been hoping for. The older woman was deftly sliding the wallet out of Dolph's back pocket.

Catching Rose watching her, she mouthed, "I'll split the cash with you."

Rose flashed her a grin, then said to Dolph, "Come on, sugar. Let's find you a cab so you can go home and sleep it off."

"But I wanna sleep with you," Dolph whined.

"I know. Next time." Rose started to turn him around to lead him away from the group.

"Oh, ya wanna dance first. S'okay wid me." Dolph tried to grab her hand and started into a drunken waltz.

Rose more forcefully dragged him down the sidewalk.

Luck was with them. An off-duty cab was parked at the curb. Rose opened the back door and made a show of stuffing Dolph inside.

"Hey, I'm eatin' my lunch here," the cabbie protested.

Dolph pulled a twenty from his front pocket and handed it across the back of the seat. "Drive around the block and pull over when I say. Then you can finish your lunch."

~~~~~~~~~~

Kate had also caught a case of the worries from Skip. She was hoping her lunch date with Rob would distract her.

Not sure her nervous stomach could handle the richness of a crab cake, she'd ordered the Maryland crab soup instead. They made small talk while they waited for their food. When the soup arrived, its mixed bouquet of tomatoes, celery, crabmeat, and Old Bay seasoning smelled heavenly. Kate took a small bite. It burned her tongue.

Waving her hand in front of her mouth, she watched with an indulgent smile as Rob piled extra pickle slices on his sandwich. He'd also ordered sliced tomatoes, no doubt in deference to Liz's nagging that he eat more fruits and vegetables. He added them to the wobbly pile and jammed the top bun down to hold it all together.

"So are you really okay with having Pete and his guards at your house? We kind of sprung that on you out of the blue."

Rob swallowed a bite of his sandwich. "It's okay for now. It's a big house."

Kate dipped her spoon into her soup and took a small sip–still hot but bearable. She watched Rob as she took another spoonful. He didn't seem inclined to elaborate.

"Are you sure you're okay with it? The boundaries in this

case have gotten awfully blurry."

Rob shrugged and took another bite of his sandwich.

Was she imagining things or was he avoiding eye contact? A thought popped into her head.

"Rob, remember what you said awhile back, about a jury maybe being harder on Pete *because* he was a fallen hero?"

"Yeah."

"Okay, so putting aside for a minute the fact that he's sleeping in your guest room, how would you feel about Pete if he were your average recovering-addict client you were defending on drug charges? Would you be all that surprised or upset that he'd had a near slip?"

"I'm not upset," Rob said.

"You're not?"

He looked down at his plate and muttered, "Sometimes it's hell being friends with a shrink."

She resisted the urge to say something, scooping up more soup in her spoon instead.

After a moment Rob raised his eyes to hers. "Something inside me... *deflated* is probably the word for it. When you called Monday night, I just thought, 'Shit, after all we've gone through for this guy.' But yeah, on a deeper level I guess it's also about him being a hero, so I expected better from him."

Kate let out a soft snort. "Part of my job is helping clients look at things in a different way, but sometimes they teach me a new perspective. Pete's shown me that he's not a hero. He's just a guy who did something heroic, because he knew it was what needed to be done. In his mind, he was just doing his job, *pro bono* if you will. Like you and me taking on his case for free."

Rob paused for a moment, his expression thoughtful, then he gave her a small smile. "Okay, I'll let him down off his pedestal."

Kate came back around to her other concern. "I really am kind of worried that we've gotten the boundaries too blurred here." She let the topic hang out there to see what he would do with it.

Rob put his half-eaten sandwich down on his plate and

carefully wiped his fingers on his napkin. "I think I'm having a mid-life crisis."

After a startled moment, she realized that wasn't the *non sequitur* it seemed to be. "You're losing your ability to detach," she said softly.

He nodded, then turned his head to stare across the room.

Kate watched his broad face, which was starting to get a little jowly. His Adam's apple rippled in his thick neck as he swallowed.

"I think I've already lost it," he finally said. "I can't... I'm not dealing very well anymore with the way the system can let people down. The decent ones so rarely get true justice, and the obvious scumballs all too often get off easy."

"Is this just about Pete's case?"

"No. It's been building for awhile. But his case brought it to a head. I want to yell at all of them, the judges, the cops. Even Judith Anderson, who's trying her best to do what's right. I wanna yell at her, 'Just tell your lieutenant the prosecutor's an ass!'"

Kate covered his beefy hand, resting on the table, with her own.

"I don't know how much longer I can do this." There was a hitch in his voice. He still wasn't making eye contact. "I could probably afford to retire early. But what the hell would I do with myself? I'm too young to retire."

Kate was at a loss, not sure what to say. He wasn't just a bit stressed out. He was in full-blown burnout.

She fell back on basic Counseling 101. When you don't know what to say, empathize. She gave his hand a squeeze. "I'm sorry you're going through this, that your work's gotten so difficult." It sounded a little lame to her own ears.

But it seemed to work. Rob finally looked at her. His eyes were red-rimmed. "You know what scares me the most? It's getting easier now, because I've stopped caring."

CHAPTER TWENTY-ONE

After he heard Dolph give the cabbie instructions to drive around the block, Skip let out his pent-up breath and flopped down on the backseat of Rose's car. His gut had been wrong. The sting had gone off without a hitch.

His pulse had just about slowed to normal when a strange man's accented voice came through his earpiece. "Man who runs things 'round here don't like no freelancin'."

Skip bolted upright, eyes darting around, trying to locate Rose. She was standing near the entrance to an alley, surrounded by three Hispanic men.

"Okay, well I'll just move along then," Rose said in his ear.

Skip's mouth had gone dry. He sat frozen, his brain stalled.

Another male voice. "That ain't how it works, mama." Skip saw one of the men reach out toward Rose's face.

She batted the hand away.

The man grabbed her wrist. "Don't make me break it," he growled.

Skip's brain kicked back into gear. Rose would be weighing her options, trying not to blow the operation in order to get out of this mess.

One of the men was dragging her toward the alley. She pulled back, digging in her heels. "You better let go of me. I know how to defend myself."

Male laughter. "Yeah, then when ya gonna start?"

"Hold your position, Canfield," Tyrell yelled in Skip's ear. "She's telling us she can handle it. She doesn't want to blow things."

Skip tried to speak but his mouth was too dry. He worked it to produce some saliva, then said into the button mic on his shirt collar, "I'd already figured that out."

Rose and the three men disappeared from sight. Manny was moving rapidly down the sidewalk toward the alley entrance. "Three men dragging Rose into an alley," his low voice came through Skip's earpiece.

"See de way dis works is," one of the thugs was saying, "we takes you to see de man. He likes you, den yer his."

Skip ground his teeth. Under normal circumstances, Rose could defend herself. But unarmed against three lowlifes who'd have no qualms about beating her up, raping her, maybe even killing her and dumping her body in the harbor.

"Oh, you big bad-ass *hombres*, ain't you?" Rose said. "Takes three of you to manhandle one girl. Those ain't very fair odds."

"Din't yer mama never tell you? Life ain't fair."

Skip slipped out of the car. Heart pounding, he loped up the block toward the alley.

He jumped when Manny yelled in his ear. "Hey, leave the lady alone!" Then Manny moved around the corner, out of Skip's sight.

"She ain't no lady and dis ain't yer business," a voice snarled in his ear.

Manny came into view again, backing around the corner, hands out in a placating gesture. "Hey, I didn't mean nothin'."

A low growl in his ear as Skip saw a man come around the corner after Manny. He poked a finger at Manny's chest. "You better watch whose bizness you be messin' wid."

As soon as the man had cleared the corner and was out of sight of the alley, Manny grabbed his arm and gave it a wicked twist. In the next instant, the guy's face was against the sidewalk and Manny had one knee in the middle of his back.

"That oughta improve the odds some," he said as Skip slid to a stop next to him.

Manny wrapped plastic restraints around the man's wrists. "Other two dragged Rose into the back of a building," he told Skip and the others listening in.

Skip realized the entrance to the alley looked familiar. It was the one behind Santiago's Café. Long brown fingers landed on his shoulder. He whirled around.

"You stay back," Tyrell said in a low voice. "You stick out like a sore thumb down here."

"Look, there's no reason why you and I can't go in there," Skip said. "Ask some more questions about Matthews. Break up the party and get her outta there. They won't connect us with one wallet in a whole pile turned in this evening."

Tyrell hesitated. Then he shoved the man Manny had captured in the direction of one of his plain-clothes cops. He gestured for Skip and Manny to follow him.

Rose's voice came through their earpieces. "So you must be the big, bad Frederico. Is this greasy spoon all you can afford?"

"Watch yer mouth, bitch." The voice belonged to one of Frederico's men.

"Lemme go. I know the drill. I'm his girl now. No big deal."

Tyrell scanned the now empty alley, then moved past it to the street corner beyond. Skip and Manny followed him.

"Yer a meaty little mama, now ain't ya?" Frederico's voice. He did not sound displeased.

"I just got two rules," Rose said. "I only do one dude at a time and I don't perform for no audience."

"You don't make de rules 'round here, bitch."

"No, I do!" Frederico said. A long pause. Then he spoke again, his voice now amused. "Yer cute *and* spunky." Another pause. "You two, *vamoose!*"

Manny winced.

"Don't let on he speaks lousy Spanish," Skip whispered.

Tyrell peered around the corner. After a few seconds that felt a lot longer, he said, "Two men just came out of Santiago's." He held up his hand in a wait gesture as the men sauntered off. "Put your earpieces in your pockets. Let's go."

Skip, Tyrell and Manny went through the door of the café fast, then spread out across the room.

The wizened owner was standing in the kitchen doorway,

looking hopeful. Skip assumed he was hoping they'd arrest Frederico. Then his brain processed what he was seeing.

"Get this bitch away from me!" Frederico squeaked out.

Rose was crouched in front of him. His purple track pants were pooled around his feet, along with a pair of black silk boxers.

Rose had her .32 nestled against his testicles.

Skip heard Tyrell snort under his breath. Then he yelled, "Drop your gun, lady!" He pulled his service revolver out from under his jacket.

Rose stood and raised her hands. She backed away from Frederico, trying to look scared but not quite pulling it off.

Fortunately, Frederico wasn't looking at her. He was busy pulling up his drawers.

"I said drop the gun," Tyrell barked.

Rose stooped and put her pistol on the floor, then backed away from it, her hands in the air again.

Tyrell stepped forward. "You pressing charges, Frederico?"

"Can't ya all just put her on a bus outta here?"

"Can't make her leave town, but I'll have a little talk with her." He took Rose's arm and shoved her in Manny's direction.

Manny escorted her out the door.

Skip stepped over to scoop up Rose's .32. He slipped it into his jacket pocket while trying to let his pent-up breath out slowly, so it wasn't obvious just how relieved he was.

"We got some questions for you, about Matthews' murder," Tyrell said.

"I done talked to white boy here 'bout dat," Freddie said as he adjusted himself. "And de county cops. Gettin' tired of talkin' 'bout it."

"I told Baltimore County I'd do some follow-up so now you're gonna talk to me. How long was Matthews pimping girls?"

"Don't know. Maybe tree months." His fake accent–forgotten while his manhood was at risk–was now back.

"He was stepping on your turf for months and you didn't do nothing. You're losing your touch, Freddie."

Frederico glared at Tyrell. "Couple a me *amigos* paid him a visit, tole him to back off."

"That's it? They just had a polite conversation?"

Frederico curled his upper lip. "Sure. Dat's all."

Tyrell said nothing, letting the silence stretch out.

Frederico was a good bit more nervous than usual. Was that because he didn't have his men around, or because Rose had come close to blowing his balls off?

Skip felt his mouth trying to twitch up at the corners. They'd be teasing Rose with this story for years to come at Canfield and Hernandez.

"Matthews was a gnat," Frederico finally said. "Buzzin' 'round. Annoyin' as hell but weren't worth nothin' more'n a swat now 'n then."

Tyrell paused. "You'll call me if there's anything comes to mind that might help us solve this case, you being a law-abiding citizen and all?"

"Thought de case was solved. You got dat white boy who done it."

"County's convinced he did it. Me, not so much." Tyrell waited a beat, then turned and left the café. Skip was on his heels.

Out on the sidewalk, they didn't say anything until they were around the corner. Skip realized he had no idea where his ride was and neither Rose nor Dolph had an earpiece. "Can anybody tell me where our stars are parked?" he whispered into his collar button as he replaced his own earpiece.

"Three blocks west of your position," one of the cops said in his ear.

"Thanks."

Tyrell flashed Skip a quick grin. "Good job, everyone," he said into his own button mic.

Skip returned the grin. *Hot damn, we did it!*

Now all they had to do was wait to see what popped up on that website.

He sketched Tyrell a small salute, then headed across the street. Keeping an eye out for trouble–this wasn't a part of town where you let your guard down–he walked the three blocks over, then turned left. There was a bounce in his step.

Kate had been right. He was getting used to his new normal. He'd felt the fear but it hadn't stopped him, and now he was enjoying the satisfaction of a job well done.

Rose's nondescript white sedan was parked halfway down the block, with Dolph at the wheel. Skip shoe-horned himself into the passenger seat, then handed the .32 over the back of the seat to the woman crouched down behind him.

"Where the hell'd you have that hidden, Rose?"

"Not saying 'til we've ditched these mics."

CHAPTER TWENTY-TWO

Kate was considering writing a diet book. The first page would contain one sentence. All the other pages would be blank. The one sentence would read, *Spend your lunch hours making phone calls.*

As the phone rang in her ear, she prayed she was doing the right thing. She'd been waging a battle with herself all morning. She feared she might be throwing Pete under the bus. But then Rob's strained face would pop up in her mind's eye. He did *not* need a constant reminder of this lousy case sleeping in his guest room.

"Hey Liz, you got a minute?"

"Got a whole bunch of them. I'm just sitting here staring at this website."

"Nothing happening yet?"

"Oh, there's some activity now and then, but nothing related to our fake plastic yet."

"Uh, I was calling to let you know that I've rented two hotel rooms for Pete and his guards."

"It's okay for them to stay here. Hopefully it'll only be for another day or two."

"I know, but I kinda sprang all that on you, and I never intended it to be more than temporary. He's my client so I want to take responsibility for this."

"If I recall correctly, he was Rob's client first."

Damn! She should've thought this through better ahead of time. Now she'd said too much.

"True, but I'm a little worried about that. It isn't healthy for either therapists or lawyers to get too close to a case."

Liz chuckled. "Okay, Ms. Pot. I'll tell Mr. Kettle when he gets home that you moved the boy and his guards elsewhere."

Kate stuck out her tongue at the phone, then said into it, "Thanks, Liz. Can I speak to Manny for a minute?"

"He's sleeping. You want the other guard?"

"Um, no, it needs to be Manny, for reasons I can't explain. Tell him I'm sorry to disturb him."

It was several minutes before Manny's voice, slightly rough from sleep, came on the line. "What's up, Kate?"

She told him about the hotel rooms. "I know that's going to make your job harder, but I don't want to be imposing on Rob and Liz any longer."

A moment of silence, then Manny said in a low voice, "Rob hasn't been looking so good lately."

This time she smiled at the phone. The more she got to know Manny Ortiz, the more impressed she was. "Yeah," was all she said.

"Some things'll be easier. The actual physical guarding. What floor we on?"

"Third. Inside corridors."

"Good. I'll keep him safe from bad guys," Manny said. "Can't promise 'bout the rest."

"I know. It's going to be harder for him cooped up in a small room. Just do the best you can. Get him to a meeting whenever it's safe."

"Okay."

"And Manny, if he crashes and burns, it's not your responsibility. It's his."

"I know that, but thanks for the reminder. Uh, Kate, that goes for you too."

Again, she smiled at the phone. "Thanks. I probably need the reminder more than you do."

~~~~~~~~

Manny disconnected and handed the cell phone back to Liz. It immediately rang again.

"Ms. Franklin," Tyrell Cooper said in a tight voice, "I sure hope you're still on that site."

"I am. And it's Liz. What happened?"

"The feds' geek got shut down. Keeps getting an error message that it's an invalid password. They may shut you out too."

"Don't give up yet," Liz said. "They may assume it's just some random hacker." She scrolled down the page on the screen in front of her. She'd been timed out once for inactivity and had to re-enter her password. She didn't want that happening now.

The page jumped. "Hold on. There's some activity. Hmm, ninth new identity they've added today. Wonder why they're so slow. They must get several wallets from Frederico's operation every day, and he's not their only supplier."

"They may be checking them out before they put them up. At least to make sure they're not felons."

"Makes sense." Liz grabbed her pen and wrote down the new code: M58CbSFcBM-SR5. "This one may be ours, but I don't dare jump on it right away."

"Can you click on a couple of the older ones? Make it look like you're shopping."

"Oughta work. Hang on." She put the phone on speaker and laid it on the table. Then she clicked on one code, read through the information, paused, then went back and clicked on another. After another pause, she went back to the main page of codes. By this time, another new one had come up, so the one she wanted was no longer the top of the list.

"Okay, here we go," Liz said to the phone. "Caucasian male, fifty-eight, born San Francisco, currently residing in Baltimore, Maryland. And I have just successfully taken a screen shoot of this page, complete with blurry picture of some nerd who looks vaguely like Dolph."

"Woot! I owe you a bottle of champagne, Liz. Off to catch me a slime ball."

~~~~~~~~

It was standing room only inside the stuffy observation area next to the interrogation room downtown. Skip wiped the sweat off his forehead with his fingers, then rubbed them on his jeans.

In the interrogation room, Frederico was trying to look cool and uninterested while Tyrell Cooper identified himself and his prisoner, for the sake of the recording devices, then repeated the Miranda warning.

"So what have you got to say for yourself, Frederico?" Tyrell asked.

"You ain't pinnin' dat white boy's murder on me." No fake Spanish accent—a sign that he was not as calm as he was pretending to be.

"That isn't what this is about. We've got a lot on you. You're going away for a real long time." The detective outlined the list of charges and the evidence they had on him.

Then Tyrell sat back in his chair and examined his fingernails, a bored expression on his face. "And we know you've got ties to some Mafia-types up in Pennsylvania. Guess they won't be too happy that you got yourself caught."

The beads of sweat on Freddie's forehead were visible even in the observation room, but he was silent.

"The feds want you too," Tyrell said. "Can't decide whether or not I'm gonna let them have you."

Skip leaned past Dolph to whisper to Judith. "Tyrell didn't tell the Feebies yet that the fish swallowed the hook?"

"He probably did. But Freddie doesn't know that," she whispered back.

Tyrell's lieutenant, a beefy guy with milk chocolate skin and a shaved head, frowned at them over his shoulder. They fell silent.

Meanwhile Tyrell and his prisoner were having a staring contest. Frederico was losing.

"So say I got somethin' to tell ya. Wha'd I get in return?"

Tyrell shrugged. "Depends on what you've got."

"I kin give ya the dumbfuck dat went after the big guy an' his lady."

Tyrell shook his head. He glanced down at his fingernails again. "Got plenty on him already." After a long pause, he added, without looking up, "Guess I might as well turn you over to the

FBI up in Pennsylvania. They put you in jail up there, you'll be a lot closer to your friend, Mr. Donati." Left unsaid was the distinct possibility that Donati would put a hit out on him to make sure he didn't talk, and Freddie would be a sitting duck in jail with no homeboys for protection.

Frederico's mustard-colored face took on an unbecoming green tinge. After a long pause, he said, "I can turn state's evidence. Go in dat witness protection thing."

"Maybe. Or we could keep you down here awhile. Give you some extra security until they finish rounding up Donati's people."

Frederico nodded and sat back in his chair. "I might have somethin' for ya."

Tyrell looked up from examining his hands. "What I want is Matthews' killer."

"I ain't coppin' to dat."

"Fine, then tell me who did it."

"Don't know."

Tyrell suddenly leaned forward and got in Frederico's face. "I don't believe that! You either killed Matthews or you know who did, and you're letting an innocent man go down for it. A 9/11 hero no less. You're not only a dumb motherfucker, you're unpatriotic."

"One last time, De-tec-tive. I din't kill dat white boy an' I don't know who did."

"Who shot Mac Reilly?"

It took a second for Frederico to wipe the surprise from his face. *Nice move, Detective!* Skip silently cheered Tyrell on.

Now Freddie's expression was calculating. Skip figured the man would tap dance around who Mac was for awhile.

But Frederico didn't waste time with that. "What I get if I give you dat?"

Tyrell flashed him a grin. "Let's just say it would establish good will."

"You keep me outta de federal system. I do my time here in Mar'land."

"Can't promise the first. Should be able to swing the second."

"And you no be slappin' me wid no accomplice rap on dat shootin'?"

"Not unless you ordered him shot."

"No way. I jes wanted dem white boys to get lost. But that dumbfuck had to go and shoot at dem."

"Which dumbfuck we talking about, Frederico?"

"De white guy dat *mysteriously* ended up in de harbor. He was Donati's man."

Skip nodded inside the observation room.

"Okay, you're halfway home," Tyrell said. "But I still want Matthews' killer."

"Can't give ya what I ain't got."

Tyrell stood up.

Frederico was now examining his own fingernails, mimicking the detective's earlier nonchalance. "Guess I'll jes hafta cut me a deal with de FBI."

"I don't think so," Tyrell bluffed. "You got nothing they want." He left the room.

The others spilled out of the observation room. Tyrell's lieu just nodded at his man and walked away.

"How long can you fend off the feds?" Judith asked Tyrell.

"They're a little busy right now in PA. Said they'd send somebody down to fetch Freddie tomorrow." Tyrell shook his head. "I'll go at him again in a little bit, and let you know if I get anything."

~~~~~~~~

The family was sitting down to dinner when Skip frowned and pulled his phone out of his pocket. Kate could hear the low purr as it vibrated in his hand.

"Sorry, darlin'. It's Tyrell." He got up and walked away from two curious pairs of little ears.

"Go ahead and say the blessing, Billy, and you all start eating. Daddy and I'll be right back." Kate got up and followed Skip into the living room.

He disconnected and then blew out a long breath. "No dice. Frederico's not going to confess to Matthews' murder and he claims he doesn't know who did it. Tyrell thinks he's telling the truth."

"Crap. Where does that leave us?"

"Back at square one, I'm afraid. Dolph and I'll go see Judith tomorrow. See if she thinks she has a shot at officially re-opening the police investigation."

Kate wanted to scream. Deciding she should quell that urge before returning to the kitchen, she walked over and flopped down on the sofa.

Skip joined her, dropping an arm around her shoulders. "At least it's safe for Pete to go home now. No doubt it was Donati's people who were trying to kill him, to make the investigation go away."

Kate winced.

He cocked his head at her. "I thought that would be good news."

"Pete doesn't have a home to go to, remember. He got evicted." She chewed on her lip, thinking. Part of her was quite resistant to taking on any more responsibility for Pete. But if he slipped back into addiction she wasn't sure what impact that would have on Rob's psyche at this point.

And she hadn't thought this far ahead. She'd been so focused on the hope that the sting operation would result in something that would clear Pete, so he could get on with his life.

"Can we leave things as they are for a couple days?" she asked. "You could take the other guard off. Just leave Manny with him."

"Why? He's not in danger anymore."

"Well, yeah, he is, from himself. He's still shaky right now. If we turn him loose in the world, homeless." She shook her head. "Who knows what'll happen."

Skip sighed. "Darlin', don't you think we've already done enough? If he uses again, that's not our problem."

"Well, yes and no." She turned toward him and took his hand in hers. "As his therapist, it is my concern, but no, it's not my job to house him. I have some other... concerns though, and I'm not totally comfortable talking about them." Let him think she was referring to Pete's confidences, not Rob's. "I'll make some calls tomorrow, start the wheels turning for emergency housing for him. In the meantime, I'll pay Manny's wages."

Skip sighed again. "Okay."

It was a sign of how frustrated he was that he didn't argue with her about the money.

~~~~~~~~~

Skip and Dolph were once again treating Judith Anderson to lunch. She started shaking her head before Skip had even finished asking his question.

"Already talked to my lieutenant this morning. I really only had two suspects, Jamieson and Frederico. Lieu's viewing these recent developments as more evidence that Freddie Boy didn't do Matthews. He came to the same conclusion we did, that Freddie wouldn't want to draw attention to himself."

"Who else did you interview about the case?" Dolph asked.

"Besides Freddie's people and Matthews' girls, just the guy who found the body."

"Who's that?" Skip asked.

This time Judith had brought the file with her. She rummaged through it and pulled out a sheet of paper. "Paul Polinski. Said he'd been working late. Drove past Jamieson's building. Saw a guy running away and got curious. So he stopped his car and investigated. Found Matthews and called it in."

Skip held out his hand. After the briefest of hesitations, Judith handed over the witness report. He read it, then skimmed through it again. "Wait a minute. This guy works downtown and lives in Pikesville. Towson's a bit out of his way."

Judith took the report back. "Damn! How'd I miss that?"

"'Cause you had no reason to suspect this guy then," Dolph said. "You thought you had an open and shut case against Jamieson." He took the report from her, got out a pad and pen, and jotted down the guy's work and home addresses and phone numbers. "This guy married?"

"Yeah, he had to call his wife to tell her he was running even later than expected."

Skip drummed his fingers on the table. "Here's what I don't get. Why would this forty-something office worker stop to investigate when he sees a guy running away in the dark? I'd think he'd either ignore the whole thing, or stay locked in his safe little car and call the cops."

Judith blessed them both with a rare smile. "Gentlemen, I believe you have yourselves a new lead to follow. Pass me the dessert menu, please."

~~~~~~~~~

Paul Polinski was an adjuster for a small insurance company Skip had never heard of. He and Dolph had gotten past the company's receptionist by saying they were following up on a police investigation. It was the truth. Could they help it if she assumed that meant they *were* the police?

Polinski ushered them into his office and closed the door. He was doing a reasonably good job of pretending he was calm, but his palm was sweaty when he shook their hands.

He moved around his desk to sit behind it. "How can I help you gentlemen?"

The visitor's chair squeaked in protest when Skip shifted, trying to get more comfortable. "We're following up on that murder in Towson, the body you found..." He let the thought dangle to see what Polinski would do with it.

The man's Adam's apple bobbed as he swallowed hard. "That was horrible. Just awful. I'd never seen a dead body before. But I couldn't just leave the guy lying there."

Odd phrasing. "How'd you know he was dead?"

"Well, I checked of course, for a pulse, like they do on TV. Got blood on my hands. Kinda freaked me out." He twisted his hands together.

That jived with the witness report Judith had shown them, but there was something going on with this guy. He'd had weeks now to get over being freaked out. Why was he so nervous?

"The guy who ran away," Dolph said. "What did he look like?"

"Look, I already answered all these questions before. Why do

I have to go through all that again. I've got work to do."

"I'm so sorry, sir." Dolph started to stand up. "Of course, we can meet you at home later."

The man put out his hands. "No, no. That's okay. I, uh... I guess I just... I really don't like thinking about it. It was pretty scary."

No way was this guy brave enough to get out of his car to investigate a possible crime in the dark. But Skip wasn't ready to confront that yet. "The guy who ran away?" he prompted.

"Oh, yeah. He was a little taller than average. Thin. Broad shoulders. Lightish hair, some red in it. I didn't see his eyes."

Twice the details that were in the witness report, and way more than he was likely to make out in the dark as the guy ran away from him. His description might have been tainted by the reports of Pete Jamieson's arrest, and the pictures of him in the paper.

"So the guy's running away and you decided to investigate," Dolph was saying. "What made you think you should do that?"

"Well, he was acting so suspicious. And I, uh, thought maybe he'd hurt somebody. You know, like raped a girl or something. It didn't dawn on me that he might've killed somebody."

Skip nodded as if the man's actions made perfect sense. "So once the cops came and you gave your statement, then what'd you do?"

Polinski visibly relaxed. "I went and picked up... uh, some food, you know, to take home so my wife wouldn't have to cook that late. And then I went home."

"Hmm, what kind of food?"

"Chinese."

Skip nodded again. "You remember the name of the restaurant?"

Polinski shook his head a bit too vigorously.

Skip leaned forward. "Tell me, Mr. Polinski, what were you doing in that part of Towson when you work down here and live in Pikesville?"

Polinski reared back in his chair. His eyes went wide.

When he didn't answer after a few seconds, Dolph said, "Skip,

I really do think we shouldn't be taking up the man's time here at work. We'll stop by your house this evening, sir. Say about seven?" Again, he made as if to stand up

"No, no!" Polinski threw his hands out again, then closed them together in supplication. He looked around nervously as if he expected his wife to walk through a wall. "Look, I was coming from my girlfriend's place, okay?"

Skip took out a notepad and pen. He clicked the pen. "And this girlfriend's name is?"

"Ro..Rochelle." He squared his shoulders with false bravado. "And I'm not telling you her last name. I don't want her dragged into this."

Skip made a show of writing on the pad. "Rochelle... That spelled with one L or two?"

The man visibly relaxed. "Uh, two."

"Thanks for your time, sir." Skip stood up. "We just needed to complete the file. You've been a big help."

Polinski shrank back in his chair and then gathered himself to stand and shake their hands.

Once outside the building, Dolph snorted. "That dude hasn't got the nerve to swat a wasp, much less get out of a car in the dark to check out a suspicious situation."

Skip nodded. "I think we'll come back around five and see where Mr. Polinski goes after work."

"Shall I call Judith in the meantime and tell her what we got out of him?"

"By all means. Any time she wants to take back this lousy investigation, it's all hers."

~~~~~~~~~

At five-fifteen, Mr. Polinski exited the insurance company's building and headed for a paid multi-level parking lot a block away. Skip drove into the lot and followed him up to the third level where the man climbed into a pale blue compact car.

Dolph shook his head. "He even drives a wimpy car."

They drove on by as Polinski started his car. Skip circled around and followed the blue compact to the attendant's booth.

Polinski paid, then rolled down the ramp and turned right.

"Hey mister, you was only in here for six minutes," the attendant, a kid with long stringy hair, said to Skip.

"Turned in by mistake." He handed over a five-dollar bill.

"I still gotta charge ya the four-dollar minimum."

"No problem. Keep the change." He could see the kid scratching his head in his rearview mirror as he went down the ramp.

He turned onto the street just in time to see Polinski turning left at the next intersection. Skip caught the light as it went to yellow and quickly turned to follow him.

"He's headed further downtown," Dolph said.

"And I've got a hunch where he's going," Skip said.

Ten minutes later, they passed a group of ladies of the evening on the sidewalk. The blue compact had pulled over to the curb a half block ahead.

A small figure darted past where Skip was creeping forward in the bumper-to-bumper traffic. Roxie jogged up to Polinski's car and opened the passenger door. She climbed in.

"Looks like we're having another little talk with Miss Roxie tomorrow," Dolph said.

Skip's stomach clenched at the thought.

CHAPTER TWENTY-THREE

Kate had thought Skip seemed preoccupied all during dinner. This was confirmed when he answered Edie's question with a distracted, "Sure, Pumkin."

"Really, Daddy?" The little girl let out a squeal and started bouncing in her chair.

Skip's look of confusion morphed into chagrin. "Uh, oh. What'd I just agree to?"

"Settle down, Edie," Kate said firmly. "First step is to look into whether or not owning a pony is feasible for us."

Edie's face fell. "What's *fizzable* mean?"

"Whether or not it's practical. First we need to look at whether we can afford to board a pony somewhere, and is there a place close enough that will take good care of it."

Edie's look turned stubborn.

Billy's eyes darted from one parent to the other and then to his sister. "Can I be excused?"

"Yes, you may, son," Kate said. Billy made his escape.

Kate turned back to her daughter. "Young lady, if you're trying to convince us you're mature enough to be responsible for a pony, than you need to show us you can take this in steps."

Edie was obviously trying to rearrange her expression, but couldn't seem to figure out what *responsible* should look like.

Kate suppressed a smile. "I will talk to Miss Linda at Meadowbrook Farms tomorrow, when we go for your lesson."

Edie nodded solemnly. "May I be excused, please?"

"Yes, you may."

Edie got up and walked sedately to the stairs and up the first few steps. Then she took off running. They heard her bedroom door slam, followed by a muffled "Yippee!"

Skip snorted. Kate and Maria burst out laughing.

"Sorry, darlin'," Skip said. "That'll teach me to pay closer attention to their chatter."

"It's okay. She would've worn us down soon anyway."

Maria stood up. "You want me do baths?"

"That would be a big help," Skip said. "I need to tell Kate some things about the case." Those two words, *the case*, had become family code for anything related to Pete or to Mac's shooting.

Maria headed for the stairs. Skip and Kate started clearing the table.

She told him about her frustrating lunch hour, spent making phone calls. "I finally ended up with the right person at Social Services. She's checking if Pete's eligible for housing assistance." She rinsed a plate and handed it to him to put in the dishwasher. "Did you get anywhere with Judith today?"

"Yes and no. She's not able to re-open the police case but we did come up with a new lead." He filled her in on the interview with Polinski, who turned out to be a customer of Roxie's. "So the question remains," he said, as Kate handed him the last of the plates. "What was Polinski doing in Towson that night?"

"Maybe he does have a girlfriend, I mean besides Roxie."

"I doubt you'd say that if you'd met this guy. He's not exactly a ladies' man."

She let out a soft snort. "You'd be surprised at the number of women who are attracted to the pathetic types."

Skip shook his head. He took her hand and headed for the living room sofa. "At this point, not much would surprise me about women and why they do what they do."

"Hey! Watch it, bub."

Skip sat down and pulled her down next to him. "Seriously, I'm trying to figure out what motivates these gals downtown, the prostitutes. Why would they choose to make a living that way?

Are most of them addicts, doing tricks to pay for drugs?"

Kate shook her head. "First off, they don't think they have a choice, for a lot of reasons. Secondly, the doing tricks usually comes first. They start using drugs as a way of dealing with the misery of their lives. And then they're that much more stuck."

"What do you mean, they don't have a choice?"

"Well, they do, but they don't realize they do. Most, if not all of them, come from extremely dysfunctional families. Some of them are the children of prostitutes. Almost all were sexually and/or physically abused. Often so badly they ran away as teenagers. Or they got pregnant, and the same father or stepfather whose been messing with them for years calls them a slut and kicks them out of the house.

"When they run out of whatever money they started with, they've got no place to turn. The thing they know how to do best is use their bodies to survive. And their pasts have programmed them to feel helpless, to believe they can't get away from bad things."

"I knew they're often runaways, but I always figured they started turning tricks because it was better money than waiting tables," Skip said.

Kate shrugged. "They may tell themselves that, and indeed it probably is better money, until some pimp gets his hooks into them and starts taking most of what they earn."

Skip winced. "Yeah, and we saw firsthand the other day what happens if they go elsewhere and try to freelance."

"Another sleaze ball like Frederico informs them they're his, and reinforces that message with a rape and a beating. And then there's Stockholm syndrome."

Skip dropped his arm around Kate's shoulders. "I've never quite understood how that works."

"Me neither really. I mean I know the theory. If you're dependent on your captor for survival, you bond with him or her, maybe even convince yourself it's a loving relationship. But I have trouble truly understanding it. I think it's one of those things you can only relate to if you've experienced it."

"I'm *not* looking forward to going downtown tomorrow," Skip said. "I know I should feel sorry for those women, but they're... kinda hard to be around."

Kate snuggled against him. Soon enough the kids' baths would be done and they'd have to read stories and give out goodnight kisses. Those were normally tasks she enjoyed, but tonight she was exhausted.

"At least it's not dangerous anymore," she said. "Now that Frederico and his thugs are off the streets."

Skip snorted. "It won't take long for another scumbag to fill the gap."

~~~~~~~~~

The Canfields' Saturday did not pan out as they'd anticipated. As Kate and the kids were getting ready to leave for Edie's horseback riding lesson, the house phone rang.

Kate stepped back into the kitchen to answer it.

"He's gone again," Manny said.

Kate stifled a curse. "What happened?"

"He's been antsy for a couple days now. We went to a meeting yesterday and he seemed to be better. Then he had a nightmare last night. I got up and we talked for awhile. He seemed okay earlier this morning. I laid down to take a nap and when I got up, he was gone."

Kate ran a hand through her curls. She needed time to think what to do, and two pairs of curious eyes staring up at her weren't helping. "Hang on a second... Maria, could you take the kids to Edie's lesson?"

"*Si*, no problem." Maria took a last swipe at the already spotless counter top, then started herding the children toward the front door. "Come, *mis niños.*"

Edie was resisting being herded. "But Mommy, you were gonna talk to Miss Linda."

A stab of maternal guilt. "I know, sweetie. I'll call her later this afternoon. I'm sorry but I've got a situation with a client that I need to deal with."

Edie gave her a dirty look but she let herself be led out the door.

"Sorry, Manny. I'm back. You got any clue where he might have gone?"

"He said something yesterday about some stuff he had in a storage unit in the basement of his old building. That he'd forgotten to tell Rob about it, and now it was probably gone."

"Did he say what was there?"

"No, but I got the impression some of it had sentimental value."

"As good a place as any to start looking for him."

A pause on the line. "Uh, as you said before, he's a grown man."

Kate thought about that for a moment. Her logical brain was saying let him go. Then Rob's depressed face swam into her mind's eye. She blew out air.

Dear Lord, get me through this case with a positive outcome and I promise I'll never ignore my limitations again.

"It's a bit more complicated than that," she said into the phone. "Rob and I promised both a judge and Detective Anderson that we'd be responsible for him."

More silence on the line.

"It seemed like a good idea at the time," Kate echoed Skip's line from the other evening.

Manny chuckled. "Okay, I'll meet you at Pete's old place."

~~~~~~~~~

Skip was feeling more than a little off kilter. He'd thought he had his fear under control, but the idea of going down to The Block again, which was exactly where they were headed, had his stomach in total rebellion.

He wasn't happy about working *pro bono* on a Saturday anyway, and especially on a case he was no longer all that committed to. And he most definitely was not looking forward to interviewing smelly, brash prostitutes... for whom he should feel sorry when he really wanted nothing to do with them.

And to add insult to injury, his damned rental wouldn't start this morning.

"This is a mess," he muttered.

"What?" Dolph asked from the driver's seat.

"I said, this is a mess. We've spent I don't know how many man-hours on this case, for which we're not getting paid. The client's an addict who's hanging on by a thread. We've been shot at, cussed out, driven off the road."

Exposed to unwanted lap dances!

"What the hell are we doing here, Dolph?"

The older man glanced over at him. "Following up a lead," he said in an infuriatingly matter-of-fact tone.

"Yeah, well, I don't give a rat's ass anymore. Turn around."

Dolph kept driving toward downtown. "We're almost there."

"I said, turn around!"

Dolph's eyes never left the road. "This has been a tough case. But my gut says we're close to a break-through. We need to stay the course, son."

Skip's stomach churned. Dolph's words echoed in his head, reminiscent of his daddy's voice. *Ya finish what ya start, son.*

~~~~~~~~

Manny was waiting on the sidewalk when Kate pulled up in front of the apartment building.

"Talked to the manager," he said. "He's already re-rented the apartment. He gave the storage unit key to the new tenant. I knocked on the guy's door. He said he hadn't gotten around to cleaning out Pete's stuff yet." Manny held up a small padlock key.

"I take it the new tenant hadn't seen any signs of him today," Kate said.

"Nope."

They went into the building and down the stairwell to the basement. The door to a large laundry room was propped open with a brick. Several washers and dryers were chugging away at their duties, but no one was in the laundry area. Beyond it were the storage units, floor-to-ceiling wire cages with padlocks on the doors.

They found the one that corresponded with Pete's apartment number. It was half full of boxes and exercise equipment.

They rummaged through the stuff for a few minutes but found

nothing informative.

"Now what?" Manny asked.

Kate was thinking she had no clue when she heard the words, "Let's go down to Jimmy Matthews' old place," come out of her mouth. *Where the hell'd that come from?*

Manny shrugged.

Thirty minutes later they were standing outside the door of what had been Matthews' apartment. It too had been rented to a new tenant.

Manny banged on the door. No response. He banged again.

"Go away," came faintly from the other side.

He banged a third time.

The door opened a crack, a night chain in place. Half a pale face stared out, stringy black hair hanging down a stubbled cheek. "What daya want?"

"Jimmy Matthews used to live here," Manny said. "Did you know him?"

"Nah." The owner of the pale face tried to close the door but Manny had his foot wedged against it.

"What da hell is this? Yer the second sonavabitch today to ask 'bout that asshole."

"Who was the first son of a bitch?" Manny asked, his foot still firmly in place.

"Dunno. Kept sayin' I had to let him in so's he could look for evidence of somethin'. Tole him to take a hike."

"Did he have sandy hair?" Kate asked.

Pale Face seemed to notice her for the first time. A creepy smile spread across his face. Ignoring her question, he said, "Hey there, mama. Ya wanna rock an' roll?"

Kate suppressed a shudder.

"Seriously, man, you need to get some new material." Manny took her elbow. "Let's get the hell outta here."

On the next landing, she stopped. "Wait, let me think." The elusive thought in the back of her brain finally stepped forward into the light. "Pete had storage units on his mind. Let's check the basement."

Manny looked resistant.

"Come on. He's not looking for drugs. He's trying to solve the case." She headed down the stairs.

Manny followed.

The basement of this building was much more chaotic. There was no door on the laundry/storage room, only hinges hanging where a door had once been. Two ancient washers and an even older dryer lined one wall. None were currently in operation. Kate wondered if they even worked. The area was lit by a single lightbulb hanging from a wire in the middle of the ceiling.

The smell was almost unbearable. Kate held her nose.

There were storage units, more or less. The wire partitions were rusty and many were doorless. Boxes with layers of dust inches thick were scattered about. It seemed the more recent tenants of the building were not particularly concerned with storing their more precious belongings.

Kate ventured forward into the storage area. There was one compartment ahead of them that had an open lock looped through a shiny new hasp on the rusty door.

In the dim light, she saw a second bulb dangling down, cobwebs hanging from its grimy string. Manny reached past her and pulled on it. The dusty bulb came on but did little to improve the poor lighting.

A rat scuttled past Kate's foot. She stifled a scream.

"Kate, maybe–"

They both froze. Just beyond the open compartment, a sneakered foot was sticking out from between some boxes.

Manny pushed her aside and drew his gun. He eased forward and around the stack of boxes blocking their view of the shoe's owner.

"Aw, shit. Man, what've ya done?"

Heart in her throat, Kate raced over and peered around the boxes. Pete's still body was stretched out on the floor. She dropped to her knees, almost landing on the syringe next to his hand.

"Careful, Kate!" Manny kicked at the drug paraphernalia near the body. The syringe skittered across the floor.

"Call 911!"

Manny already had his cell phone in his hand. "Damn! No signal. I gotta go outside. You gonna be okay?"

Kate nodded even though it was a lie. Between the fear and the stench, she was in serious danger of losing her breakfast. She swallowed hard and reminded herself to breathe through her mouth.

She felt for and found a faint pulse in his neck. Her fingers came away sticky with blood. Probing gently, she found a knot on his skull, just behind his ear.

He must have hit his head when he passed out.

Her mind belatedly registered that his skin was clammy.

Shock! She frantically looked around for something to cover him with. *Your jacket, dummy!*

She stood up and yanked it off, then tucked it around him. Looking around again, she spotted a rolled up tarp or tent, covered in dust. She dragged it over and gently lifted his feet onto it.

She looked down at his pale, still face, and the rest of the drug paraphernalia scattered around him–a metal spoon, disposable lighter and a small vial.

Please God! I can't help him anymore. He's in Your hands. A mental pause, then she added, *Get me the hell out of this! Please!*

A huge dark shadow fell over her and Pete. Kate jumped and twisted around. A large form, too tall to be Manny, was blocking the light as it lumbered around the pile of boxes.

She screamed.

CHAPTER TWENTY-FOUR

The form jumped. "It's me."

Kate squinted. She was just barely able to make out the features of the broad face in the dim light. "What are you doing here?"

Rob stepped closer, looking down at Pete. "My God, what happened?"

"It looks like he's overdosed."

Rob scowled. "Damn it! We've been killing ourselves trying to help him and he's using again."

Again, something was flitting around the edges of Kate's brain. Her instincts were trying to tell her something, but the turmoil of emotions was getting in the way.

They heard a clatter out in the laundry area and Manny's voice calling, "EMTs are here."

They stepped back so the EMTs could go to work on Pete. Clutching Rob's big hand in both of her own, Kate's mind flitted back and forth between praying and trying to grab the phantom idea floating just out of reach. She looked around the cluttered storage area.

The shovel?

It had just barely registered during the previous sweeps of the room. Its handle was splintered in several places, black strings hanging from one of the rough sections. And it was clean!

She stared at it. The blade was rusty but it wasn't coated in dust like everything else.

Looking around yet again, she saw that some of the boxes

had the dust knocked off of them while others didn't. A few were sitting open. She examined the floor. It was swept clean. Not far from the shovel, a ratty broom also leaned against the wall.

She turned to Rob "What brought you down here anyway?"

"Pete called. He was talking fast, not totally making sense. I couldn't tell if he was excited or scared or what. Now I know he was high." His tone was disgusted.

"Hang on. What did he say?"

"He told me he was down here, that he'd found something that could be evidence, a box of something. He wanted to know if he should bring it to me or call the police. Then I heard a weird noise and the phone went dead."

Kate's eyes swept across the floor. "Do you see a phone?"

Rob looked around. "No, but–"

"Let's go outside. I need to make a call."

Out on the sidewalk, Kate spotted a rusty red splotch, several inches in diameter, a few feet from the door. She gestured to Manny who had followed them out.

"Do me a favor and stand over that." She pointed to the sidewalk. "When the EMTs come out, tell them it's evidence and to try not to step there."

Manny looked down at the spot and nodded. Rob tilted his head at Kate, his eyebrows raised.

"I'll explain in a minute. I need to call Tyrell and get this area processed as a crime scene." Rob followed as she walked away from the building to place the call.

~~~~~~~~~

Halfway through Kate's description to the police detective of what she had seen, and not seen, in the building's basement, Rob had figured it out. He felt a jolt of guilt for jumping to conclusions.

"Oh, and Detective," Kate said into her phone, "Peter Jamieson has never injected drugs, and I have reason to believe he never would." A pause. "Okay, one of us will stay here." She disconnected.

"He's on his way and he's ordering a crime scene team."

Rob grimaced. "He's gonna have a rebellion on his hands

when they see that mess downstairs. That's a CSI nightmare. Why are you so sure Pete wouldn't shoot up?"

Kate seemed to hesitate.

"We've got a waiver," he reminded her.

"He's phobic of needles."

A few minutes later the EMTs brought Pete out, strapped to a gurney. He was still unconscious but not quite as pale. As they were loading him in the ambulance, Kate and Rob walked over to Manny.

"Can you stay here and try to keep people out of the basement?" Kate asked. "Tell them it's a crime scene and the police are on the way."

Manny chuckled. "In this neighborhood, that'll make 'em scatter like roaches in daylight."

Kate smiled at him. "Thanks so much for coming down here with me. I hate to think what would've happened if we hadn't found him."

Manny's expression sobered. "I'll come over to the hospital once the cops arrive. We need somebody on his hospital room door."

Rob was impressed. The bodyguard had also put together the pieces.

"We'll follow the ambulance," Kate said. "I'll call Skip and fill him in."

~~~~~~~~~

"We've been spending far too much time in hospital waiting rooms lately," Rob muttered.

Kate picked up a tattered magazine from the small table beside her chair and handed it to him. "Here, find out what Angelina Jolie's been up to. It'll take your mind off things."

He took the magazine and rolled it into a tube, grasping it like a baseball bat.

"You look like you're gonna take a swing at somebody with that thing. What are you so pissed about?"

"I'm not mad." Rob dropped the magazine back on the table and crossed his arms.

Kate just looked at him, then snorted. She mimicked his body language. "I'm not mad," she said in a low gruff voice.

"Okay, now I'm mad," he said, but his mouth quirked up a little on one end.

Kate let the silence sit between them. When it was obvious he wasn't going to elaborate, she asked, "Who or what are you mad at?"

"I wish to hell I knew." Rob looked away. "I was mad at Pete, when I thought he'd started using. Now I don't know who I'm mad at. I guess whoever's screwing with him. Again."

So you haven't stopped caring after all, my friend.

After a few seconds, she said in a soft voice, "Or at the world, maybe?"

"Yeah, at the world." His tone was sharp. "There's so much damn evil. We're like that guy in those stables in the Greek myth. Constantly shoveling the shit, but the pile never gets any lower."

Kate paused, trying to decide what to say. She could think of several other myths with the same theme, like the guy pushing the rock that kept rolling back down the hill. She felt that way herself often enough.

"How long have you been a lawyer?"

Rob stared at the ceiling, calculating, then looked at her. "Close to twenty-six years."

"That's a lot of shit you've already shoveled. It would be okay if you put down your shovel. You've done your part and then some."

Rob turned away again, but not before she saw the scowl return. "What the hell would I do?"

"Maybe you should explore that. Open your mind to other possibilities."

He was still looking across the crowded ER waiting room. "I'm too young to retire."

"So don't retire. People change careers all the time." She decided on the indirect approach. "I've been talking to Pete about career options. It's becoming obvious he's not going to be able to fight fires anymore. Too much risk of retriggering the PTSD. One option we've been tossing around is teaching at the fire academy. He's excited about that idea."

Which is why, she realized belatedly, she'd been willing to ditch her family obligations today and chase Pete down. He was so close to getting his life back on track. And as it turned out, he'd been trying to be proactive in clearing himself.

She turned her attention back to Rob. There was a glimmer of interest in his eye. Perhaps her tactic had worked.

"Maybe I could teach law school."

"Hey, that's a good idea."

He narrowed his eyes at her. "It ought to be against the law for therapists to use their techniques on friends and family members."

She snorted softly. "We use whatever tools we've got. How many times have you twisted me in a knot in an argument, with your lawyer logic?"

"I do not. I present my case clearly and succinctly."

She grinned at him.

His face finally relaxed and he smiled back.

Kate caught sight of a doctor headed toward them. She jumped up and met him halfway. Rob was right behind her.

"Are you all related to Peter Jamieson?"

"No." Kate pointed to Rob. "But he's Pete's lawyer. I'm a... a friend. I found him."

"I'm also his medical surrogate," Rob said.

Kate gave him a startled look. "You are?"

"It was just a precaution, since there's nobody else in town. I'll fax over the paperwork this afternoon, doctor, but for now, tell us how he is."

The doctor still looked hesitant.

Rob's face turned red. "Dammit, I've had it up to my eyebrows with bureaucracy. We're not waiting until I can get to the office and get the papers. Tell us how the kid's doing!"

Kate put a restraining hand on his arm. He was starting to scare her. "Doctor, what's Pete's status?" That much information was released to the general public.

"He's still critical."

Kate's throat closed. Tears pooled in her eyes. "Is he going to make it?" she managed to get out.

Rob opened his mouth but the doctor held up his hand. He took Kate's elbow and steered them to a less populated corner of the waiting room. Then he held out his hand to Rob.

"Let's start over, Mr...?"

Rob blew out air. He shook the doctor's hand. "Franklin. Rob Franklin. Sorry, it's been a rough day."

"And I'm Kate, uh, Canfield." She wasn't allowed to even admit that her clients were seeing her, since that could carry a stigma. Having two last names to choose from came in handy sometimes.

"To answer your question, Ms. Canfield, yes, he's probably going to make it. The question is how much damage he's done to his brain with drugs. How long has he been an addict?"

"There's a lot more to this than meets the eye, doctor," Rob said. "We have reason to believe this was not a self-inflicted overdose. It was attempted murder."

"He's never used heroin, or anything injectable," Kate said. "He's been clean and sober for nine months now."

The doctor nodded, with a slight smile that Kate found reassuring. "Are the police involved?"

"Yes, a Detective Tyrell Cooper will be in touch with you," Rob said.

At that moment, Manny came through the ER doors. Kate waved him over and introduced him. "There will be bodyguards on Pete's room 24/7."

After saying their goodbyes, Kate and Rob headed out of the hospital. "Did you notice," Rob said, "that doctor didn't even bat an eye when I said it was attempted murder?"

"He works in an ER in Baltimore City. He's seen it all."

Rob snorted. "Talk about shitty stables."

~~~~~~~~~

Skip's mood had gone from bad to downright foul. They had wasted most of a Saturday on a fool's errand. They'd talked to over a dozen of the gals on the street and had garnered practically nothing for their efforts. Only one of them had offered anything the least bit useful.

Elsie was a little older than the others and was starting to go to fat. The evening when Matthews was killed, she'd gone to his apartment to turn in some of her proceeds. She'd had a good afternoon, she told them, and didn't like carrying around too much money. When she heard Jimmy yelling and banging around inside the apartment, she decided to come back later.

About ten minutes after that, she'd been standing near the building when she heard what could have been a gunshot or a car backfiring. She wasn't sure which it was, nor which direction the sound had come from.

She was the only one of the women who hadn't given Skip a disdainful look when he'd suggested now was a good time to get out of this particular profession, while there was no pimp on the scene. "Already thought of that. Saved me some money while I was workin' for Jimmy. I'm gettin' on a bus tomorrow to anywhere but here. Slingin' hash in some diner is better'n this."

There'd been no sign of Roxie all day.

They were walking back toward Dolph's car when there she was, coming toward them, looking like a little girl in her mother's clothes. Her black bra showed through the too-big semi-sheer white blouse that was tucked into a black leather miniskirt. Short lace gloves, black net stockings that bagged a little at the knees and stiletto heels completed the outfit.

Correction. Her mother's clothes if her mother was a slut. Recalling his conversation with Kate last night, he realized that was a possibility.

Roxie had spotted them. She stopped and put her hands on her hips.

As they got closer, she sneered at Skip. "Well, if it isn't Mr. High-and-Mighty Married Man."

"We've been looking for you. We wanted to talk to you about one of your johns, a Mr. Paul Polinski."

"I ain't talkin' to you 'bout nothin' or nobody." She started to walk past him.

Skip stepped into her path.

Fear flickered in her eyes but she kept up the bravado. "You touch me and I'll press charges for assault."

"Look, Miss Roxie," Dolph said. "We're not trying to harass you. We're just trying to find out who killed Jimmy Matthews. You said you liked him, that you wanted his killer brought to justice."

"I done told you Frederico killed him."

"He denies it," Dolph said. "And he's willing to take a lie detector test."

"That lyin' scumbag." Her sneer was back. "Those damned tests ain't worth shit. My stepfather passed one, when I turned him in for pesterin' me, and the sheriff told me to stop tellin' lies 'bout my daddy and go home like a good girl." Despite her best efforts to maintain a tough front, a tear snuck down Roxie's cheek. She swiped at it with lace-covered fingers.

Skip had no idea what expression he had on his face at that moment, but whatever it was, it triggered a nasty reaction.

"Don't you fuckin' look at me that way, you sonofabitch! Don't you *dare* pity me, you limpdick asshole..."

The rest of what she said was lost in the roar of blood rushing to his head. He clenched his fists. Then he turned and walked away, before he broke one of his cardinal rules and struck a woman.

Halfway down the block, he glanced back over his shoulder. Dolph was still talking to Roxie, trying to play the good cop. After a minute, he headed in Skip's direction.

Skip slowed down to let him catch up. "You get anything out of her?"

"Nope," Dolph huffed out. "She claims the names of johns are confidential information."

Skip let out a derisive snort. "This whole damn day has been a colossal waste of time."

The ride back to Towson gave him time to think, which today wasn't really a good thing. A lethargy spread over him. With a small jolt, he realized he was depressed. And he truly hated this case.

So what did he want to do, besides nap for a month? A vague thought had been bouncing around in the back of his head for the last week or so. This time when it surfaced, instead of pushing it aside, he lassoed it and brought it in closer.

The agency was now big enough that he and Rose spent half their time on administrative duties. They split them based on their strengths. But Rose would much prefer to be out in the field more. If he took over most or even all of the administrative stuff...

Shame burned his cheeks. He was going to let Rose and Mac, and Dolph, take all the risks, while he sat back cozy and safe in the office?

He glanced over at gray-haired Dolph and sank down further in his seat. A memory flashed into his mind, of his father driving him to school. And giving him advice on how to deal with the bullies who loved to pick on the scrawny sixteen-year-old named Skippy.

He'd thought he'd left that scared teenager behind decades ago. Apparently not. The kid was still lurking inside. Had all those years of calmly facing down danger been false bravado?

A small part of his brain told him he was being too hard on himself.

His phone vibrated in his pocket. He fished it out. The caller ID said it was Kate.

Finally!

They'd been playing telephone tag all day. A good dose of Kate was just what he needed right now to get himself centered. The knot in his stomach started to loosen even before he answered the call. "Hey darlin'. What's up?"

"Pete's in the hospital."

"Say what?"

"He slipped away from Manny this morning. We found him in the basement of Jimmy's old building. It looked like he'd overdosed but–"

Skip's stomach tightened. The blood was pounding in his ears so badly he couldn't hear her. "After all we've done for this jackass and he's using again–"

"He isn't using. I told you it was a set-up. We found–"

"We who?"

"Rob and I–"

"What the hell was Rob doing there?"

"Pete called him. He was on the phone with him when somebody–"

"I'm not doing this anymore. I'm done with this case."

Silence. "Skip, I'm trying to explain what happened."

"I don't give a shit what happened. I'm done."

This time the silence sounded different. "Kate? Are you there?"

More silence. Skip pulled the phone away from his ear and stared at the screen. It noted the time of disconnect and length of the call.

"What's the matter?" Dolph asked from the driver's seat.

"Lost the signal," Skip muttered, still staring at his phone. He knew there'd be hell to pay when he got home. For the first time in their relationship, his wife had hung up on him.

CHAPTER TWENTY-FIVE

After relieving Maria of childcare duty, Kate kicked off her shoes and dropped onto the sofa. Across the room, Edie and Billy were playing a board game on the old rug Skip had dragged out of the attic to cover where the carpet had been removed. For once the kids weren't squabbling.

She shuddered at the memory of what had happened in that section of the room not quite a week ago. *The week from hell!*

Laying her head back and closing her eyes, she was determined not to think about Skip, Rob or Pete for the next few minutes.

She heard a key turning in the front door lock and felt a draft of cool air as the door opened.

Crap! She opened one eye. Skip was walking toward her, his gait a bit tentative. She closed her eye and let out a sigh.

"Can we talk?" he asked.

"No."

"What?"

Eyes still closed, she said, "I don't think it's a good idea right now."

"Why not?"

She opened her eyes and lifted her head slightly. Working hard to keep her voice even, she said, "Because I'm exhausted and you're... tense. We'll talk later."

He glanced toward the children, then walked over and sat in one of the overstuffed armchairs that faced the sofa.

"Can you tell me what happened at least?"

Kate sighed. "I tried to tell you what happened. You didn't

seem to be in the mood to listen."

"I'm listening now."

Her temper flared. She struggled to tamp it down. "And I'm exhausted now. We'll talk later."

He sat for a moment, his jaw clenched. Then he pushed himself to a stand. "I'm gonna make coffee. You want some?"

She stifled another sigh. It was a peace offering. After a beat, she said, "Sure. I'll be there in a minute."

Skip headed for the kitchen.

She dropped her head back against the sofa again. Reasonableness struggled against fatigue and anger. She was tired of being the reasonable one while everyone else seemed to be losing it.

Okay, that was pretty damn holier than thou. Her reaction to this case was anything but reasonable. She'd lost her detachment and had broken almost all her own rules about compartmentalizing her work so it didn't affect her private life and her family.

With a flash of insight, she realized it wasn't even Pete at the heart of all this for her. Yeah, he was a sweet guy and she felt bad for him. But she often felt bad for her clients. That didn't usually make her jump into the middle of their lives and try to fix things for them.

The next insight hit her with such force, her eyes flew open. Helplessness. She was always telling everyone how that was the worst feeling ever, how people would do just about anything to avoid or overcome it.

Pete's case had stirred up those old helpless feelings she'd felt on 9/11. Her unconscious fantasy had been that if she could make him better, then she'd somehow recover her sense of control over life that had been shaken so badly that day. And then shaken again a few years later when Eddie was killed.

The fragrance of freshly-brewed coffee tickled her nose. Skip was waiting for her. She sighed and struggled to her feet.

Amazingly, the kids were still playing nicely with each other. She'd have to check their temperatures later, make sure they weren't coming down with something.

In the kitchen, Skip had laid out spoons, sugar and cream on the table. Kate sat down. He brought two steaming mugs over.

Kate took a sip of coffee to fortify herself, then told him where she and Manny had found Pete and the indicators that it was a set-up. "We need to put the other guard back on him. Manny said he could stay until this evening."

"So it was a set-up to look like an overdose," Skip said. "That doesn't change the fact that he slipped out on his guard to go looking for drugs."

She took a deep breath to tamp down her temper. She'd had a stressful day but so had he apparently. Neither one of them needed the added stress of an argument. "I don't believe he was looking for drugs. He went looking for evidence, and from the sound of his call to Rob, he may have found some."

"Which is now gone."

"Yeah, but he thought to look in a place we hadn't."

Skip looked away from her. His jaw was tight, never a good sign.

"Look, sweetheart, I know this case has turned out to be a lot more stressful than we thought it would be–"

"And dangerous," he said, still without looking at her.

"Yes, and dangerous. But I don't feel like I can just abandon Pete at this point. Someone's still trying to kill him and there's the little matter of murder charges against him. But you got into this at my request. I'm totally fine with hiring somebody else to–"

His head jerked back in her direction. He opened his mouth and then closed it again.

"What?" Kate asked, her tone sharper than she'd intended.

Skip blew out air, then ran long slender fingers through his hair. "I don't know. I can't seem to think straight."

Kate took a sip of her coffee, waiting. The last of her anger had evaporated. There was definitely something more going on here than just frustration with this case.

Her stomach growled. She realized she'd never had any lunch. Glancing at the clock on the kitchen wall, she discovered it was after four. No wonder she was hungry. "Did you eat?"

Skip shook his head.

She got up and pulled cold cuts and condiments from the refrigerator. She intentionally kept her back to him as she started making sandwiches at the counter. Sometimes he could open up easier when she wasn't looking at him.

"I don't know what's got into me today," Skip said. "I've been, I don't know... off balance all day."

Kate nodded without turning around. She slathered mayonnaise on pieces of bread.

"I was okay yesterday, pleased even that we had a new lead. Although I wasn't looking forward to going downtown today. But ever since I got up this morning, I've..." His voice trailed off.

Kate brought his plate to the table, then kissed his cheek before going back to the counter to finish making her own sandwich.

"I told Dolph to turn around halfway there."

She turned to look at him. "You didn't go downtown?"

"No, we went. He ignored me. But we didn't find out much for all our effort."

Kate sat down at the table and took a bite of her sandwich.

"I'm sorry I went off on you like that, darlin'. Didn't give you a chance to tell me what happened."

She chewed slowly, buying time, deciding what to say. "Skip, this isn't like you. You're so... reactive to this case."

He got up and paced a few steps away, then turned back toward her. "I know it's not like me. I don't get... what's happening."

Kate's chest ached at the confusion in his eyes, turned muddy brown from emotion. "It's been a bad case. You've been shot at. Mac was hurt. I've been attacked. The kids have been in danger."

Skip was shaking his head. "I've been scared witless before because you and the kids were at risk. It hasn't stopped me from functioning. I feel... I can't focus." He ran fingers through his hair again.

He broke eye contact. While staring at the refrigerator, he said, "Today, before you called, I was thinking maybe I should stop doing field work."

Kate sucked in air. She hadn't seen that coming.

He glanced at her, then away again. "I... I've lost my nerve. As we were headed downtown today, my stomach was heaving at the mere thought of going back down there. Which makes no sense since it's not really all that dangerous anymore, not with Frederico and his boys and Samuelson locked up."

Kate felt the familiar click she often experienced in her office, the sense of clarity and small surge of excitement as the psychological pieces fall into place. "Sit down, sweetheart. Let me run something past you."

He took his seat. She put her sandwich down and picked up one of his hands. "I think there's two things going on here. One's complicated and it's affecting all of us to some degree. The other's maybe a simple thing. I think you may have developed a phobia of going downtown."

He gave her an odd look. "That's what I just said. I'm scared."

"Yes but phobias aren't like other fears. They're often quite irrational, based solely on conditioning. Our brains are programmed to make associations between things that happen together. You've had some nasty things happen when you were downtown so now going down there is associated with those unpleasant feelings. That's not your natural territory. Maybe if those same things had happened out here in the county, well, you probably would've still reacted negatively to them. But not necessarily to the *place* where they happened."

His face brightened a little. "That makes sense." He thought for a moment. "So now that I know what's going on, will I be able to control it?"

Kate really hated to tell him that it wasn't quite *that* simple. "Understanding it will help, but conditioned associations don't always respond to logic. The emotions have become hardwired to the situation. You may feel just as bad, just not be as thrown by it."

He squeezed her hand, then let go to pick up his sandwich. "It's good to know I'm not going crazy, at least, or turning into a total coward."

"Hardly. There are a couple things that may help. One is to watch your self-talk, what you're saying to yourself in your head.

If you're telling yourself it's going to be horrible, then it will be."

"Which was what I was doing today, on our way down there." Skip took a bite of his sandwich.

"When you catch yourself thinking like that, change it to something like 'This is no big deal' or even 'I'm Mr. Cool.'"

Skip chuckled.

"It may sound silly but it works, and if it amuses you so much the better. That will help you relax. So will taking a couple deep breaths. Again, it sounds overly simple. Deep breathing and tense muscles are mutually exclusive, so a deep breath will force your body to relax, for a few seconds at least."

"Is that why it's hard to take a deep breath when you're extremely tense?"

"You know, I never thought about that before, but yeah, probably."

Skip grinned at her. "It *is* handy sometimes having a therapist in the house."

She laughed. "Makes up for the times when I annoy you with my analyzing everything to death."

Skip held out his hands, his sandwich in one of them. He moved them up and down as if he were weighing two objects. "Yup, pretty much balances out, I think."

They ate for a few minutes, Kate's ear attuned to the living room for signs that the children's truce had broken down. Sure enough, Edie's voice was starting to rise. Her brother apparently wasn't following the rules, in her opinion.

"You said two things might be going on here. What's the other one?" Skip asked.

Kate decided to ignore the children for now. If she could hear them squabbling, then she knew where they were.

"I don't have it completely sorted out myself. I think this mess with Pete has brought all of us a little closer to burnout." That was an understatement in Rob's case, but she couldn't violate his confidence. Rob would probably tell Skip about it eventually. They were friends in their own right. But it wasn't her story to tell.

"We're all, in our own way, trying to help people, do our small part to make the world a better place. But ironically by trying to do that, we're exposed all the time to the things that hurt people. Every day, I witness the harm dysfunctional families can do, plus disasters like 9/11 and all kinds of other trauma. Rob has to deal with... uncooperative bureaucracies. And you sometimes end up rubbing elbows–"

"With scumbags like Frederico. I get where you're going. We see too much of the ugly stuff."

"Way more than most people see, and also how the system doesn't always help like it's supposed to."

"That prostitute, Roxie. The one that, you know... She told me today that she turned her stepfather in for molesting her, and he passed a lie detector test. So he got off and she got a lecture from the local sheriff."

Kate felt the sadness wrap around her heart and squeeze. The sensation was a familiar one. She used to wish she didn't feel it when clients told her their horror stories. But after Rob's comment about not caring anymore, maybe it was a good thing that she still felt it.

"I've seen that before. Some psychopaths can pass them with flying colors while they're lying through their teeth. Those tests pick up on anxiety so they're not that hard to fool if you can keep your cool."

Skip scratched his head. "Yeah well, my cool isn't something I've seen much of lately."

Kate patted his hand. "There's not really anything more we can do today. Let's try to have a relaxing evening and look at things fresh tomorrow."

Skip groaned, then his face brightened. "I've got a counteroffer for you. We relax for the rest of the weekend and on Monday I'll see if everybody can get together for a brainstorming session. Hopefully Tyrell will have some info back from the lab about that basement by then. I've got a niggly feeling we've got most of the pieces. We just need to put them all on the same table and see how they fit together."

"That sounds good." Irate screaming issued from the living

room. Kate grinned at her husband. "I'll go break up World War III while you make the calls to set that up."

~~~~~~~~~~

At lunchtime on Monday, those who were available gathered to brainstorm at Tyrell's precinct. "Rose is on a surveillance case. I'll have to fill her in later," Skip told Kate as he opened the conference room door for her. Dolph and Judith were already sitting at the table, perusing the interview reports from Judith's case file.

Tyrell came in with a pot of coffee and a stack of styrofoam cups in his hands. He put them on a side table and sat down. Only Dolph and Judith got up to pour cups of the mud-colored brew.

"Why is it that cop shop coffee is always bad?" Skip said.

"Machine's in constant use and it never gets cleaned," Tyrell said.

He pulled a large thermos out from under his arm, took the top off, loosened the stopper and poured. "Sorry, I like you all but I'm not sharing."

Kate breathed in the rich coffee fragrance. Was that a hint of vanilla? "Hm, smells heavenly."

"Okay, for the lovely lady visitor, I'll make an exception." Tyrell reached back to snag a styrofoam cup.

"Hey, no flirting with my wife," Skip said good-naturedly.

Judith's voice cut across the banter. She held up a piece of paper. "That prostitute, Elsie, didn't say anything about hearing a commotion in Matthews' apartment when my men talked to her."

"I figured she might not have admitted it to a cop," Skip said. "She didn't remember the exact time but said it hadn't been dark for long."

"That time of year, we're probably talking between five and six." Judith made a note on the pad in front of her.

"Blood on the sidewalk outside that basement door was Jamieson's blood type," Tyrell said. "Also traces on that shovel. No needle tracks anywhere on him, according to the doc at the hospital, which confirms what you said, Kate. He's not a heroin user. But there was definitely heroin in his system, enough to kill him. We're treating it as assault and attempted homicide."

Kate felt a stab of guilt that she hadn't gone to visit Pete yesterday, but she and her family had needed a day off from the stress. She'd called Mercy Hospital late Saturday afternoon and had been told his condition had stabilized. Yesterday he'd been transferred to the Center for Addiction Medicine on Linden Avenue. Ironically his medical insurance would pay for their detox program when they wouldn't pay for his ongoing therapy.

"Did Pete remember anything about who might have hit him?" Skip asked.

"No. He said he'd pulled a box out of Matthews' storage unit that had some DVDs in it. He thought they might have something useful on them. The last thing he remembered was going outside to get a signal to call Rob."

"I take it you didn't find the box," Dolph said.

Tyrell shook his head.

"How'd he get into the storage unit?" Kate asked. "It had a newish-looking lock dangling from the door."

It's one of those locks where you set your own combination," Tyrell said. "The combo Matthews had used was Jamieson's birthday."

Grief slammed Kate in the chest and closed her throat. Grief for Pete and for the young man she'd never met, and for a friendship that close, a rare gift that had gotten lost along the way.

Rob pushed open the conference room door. "Sorry I'm late, gang. I was in court this morning."

Kate looked at him and felt a rush of gratitude. She blinked back tears.

"You are right on time, my man," Tyrell said. "Have a seat. You want some coffee?" He pointed toward the pot on the side table.

Rob shuddered and sat down next to Kate. He sniffed at her cup, then eyed Tyrell's thermos. "How'd you rate the good stuff?"

"I'll share," she pushed past the lump in her throat.

He took the cup she offered and drank a healthy swig. She gave him a lopsided smile.

"Can you recall exactly what Jamieson said to you on the phone Saturday?" Tyrell asked.

Rob closed his eyes. "He was talking fast and breathing hard. Something like 'Hey, it's Pete. I'm down at Jimmy's building and I found something in the basement.' A box, and he seemed to think whatever was in it had something to do with Matthews' murder." Rob opened his eyes. "Then something about labels in Jimmy's handwriting, but they didn't make sense. Then there were some muffled noises and the phone went dead."

"Jamieson couldn't remember what was on the labels," Tyrell said. "But we found half of a broken jewel case in the basement. Label read, 'RO-PP-SM' and a date."

Skip sat up straighter in his chair. "Roxie and her john, Paul Polinski."

Judith rooted through the papers in front of her. "Here it is. Roxie said Matthews was going to make her a porn star."

"SM," Dolph said. "Chains and whips?"

Skip snorted. "Polinski's the type, and not for the dominant role. Your people find anything else interesting in that basement?"

"No, but the lab's still processing stuff. May take them awhile."

Judith read to the bottom of the report in her hand, a frown growing on her face. "Roxie's alibied for Matthews' TOD window. She named three johns who all verified she was with them that afternoon and evening, with not much time in between."

"Why would she kill Matthews? He was her gravy train," Skip said. "She would, however, have a motive for conking Pete over the head to get her hands on those DVDs."

"But then why shoot drugs into him?" Kate asked.

"And if she wanted those DVDs she could've gotten them out of there a long time before this," Rob said.

"Maybe she didn't know where they were," Dolph said.

"So she's just hanging around Matthews' building," Judith said, "and Petey shows up, and then what? They stumble on the box and she clobbers him to get it."

"He didn't say anything about talking to any of the hookers," Tyrell said. "And I'm a little surprised three johns admitted to being with her?"

"There was some reluctance, until I reassured them their names would be kept out of it," Judith said.

"So maybe Roxie followed Pete for some reason," Skip said. "And when he found the box, she hit him and took it."

"That still doesn't explain the overdose set-up." Kate was beginning to think this brainstorming session was producing more questions than answers.

"Maybe somebody else decided to take advantage of the fact that he was out cold to finish the job," Rob said.

"But who, and why?" Kate asked.

Dolph was scratching the back of his head. "Where's the M.E.'s report again?"

Judith dug through the pile and pulled out a clump of papers. Dolph leafed through them, then stopped. "Here it is. 'Lividity was consistent with the position of the body. Contamination of the scene made it difficult to ascertain the degree of bleeding that had occurred at that location.' Doesn't sound like the M.E. was completely convinced Matthews was killed there."

Dolph looked at his former partner.

"EMTs got there before our guys," Judith said. "They stomped around a bit before they determined he was beyond saving. And it had rained that evening. M.E. said the blood could have washed away."

"Or he could've been killed elsewhere," Dolph said.

She rooted again through the papers and pulled out another report. "The techs checked Jamieson's apartment thoroughly. No signs of blood but they did find some of Matthews' hair."

"Which could've been dropped there at any time," Kate said. "Since they were friends. How good a housekeeper was Pete?"

Judith grimaced. "About as good as you'd expect a guy struggling with addiction to be." After a moment, she asked, "Anybody got anything else to add?"

Something had been nagging at the corner of Kate's mind. "Strings." They all looked at her. "On the shovel. There were some black strings hanging from a splinter."

Tyrell cocked his head. "I'll check with the lab on that. And also take another look at Matthews' apartment, although it's got a new tenant now."

"There's a good chance the apartment is rented furnished so you still might find something." Judith pushed up from the table. "I'm gonna have me another little talk with Mr. Polinski."

"I thought you weren't supposed to be pursuing new leads," Dolph said.

"Screw that. If Matthews made that video without Polinski's knowledge and then he found out about it, he has a much better motive than Jamieson. *And* he was on the scene." She started gathering up the papers from her case file.

Tyrell stood up. "And I think I'll be talking to our little Roxie. See where she was when Jamieson was attacked Saturday."

"Mind if we tag along?" Dolph said, gesturing toward Skip. "Not a bit."

Kate glanced over at Skip. His jaw was tight but he stood to join the other two men as they headed for the door. She fervently hoped her feeble little suggestions helped him deal with his anxiety. When all this was over, if he was still struggling with it, she'd recommend he see a colleague who specialized in phobias.

She turned to Judith who was sliding the last of the papers into their folder. "Did anyone report shots fired around Pete's building that night?"

"No, and the gun didn't have a silencer."

"That's not the nicest neighborhood in Towson, but it's not one where gunshots would go unnoticed either."

"I know." Judith's lips were set in a grim line as she walked past Kate and Rob. "Thanks for your help, guys. If you all hadn't been willing to go to bat for Jamieson..." She let the sentence dangle as she walked out the conference room door.

"Looks like it's just you and me, schweetheart." Rob faked a Bogart accent. "I'll buy you a quick lunch before we have to go back to our offices."

Kate's stomach growled by way of an answer. She grinned at him, relieved that he seemed to be in a good mood today.

~~~~~~~~

After a hurried stop at Rob's favorite deli, Kate made it back to her office with just minutes to spare before her first afternoon client was due. She picked up her phone to check her office voicemail. "Mrs. Huntington," the first message began. "I'm Dr. Andrew Bering from the Center for Addiction Medicine. You're listed as Peter Jamieson's therapist on his intake sheet. I wanted to inform you that he has left our detox program against medical advice. He did sign a waiver upon admission so if you have any questions feel free to call." Kate grabbed a pencil to scribble down his number.

The next message surprised her even more than the first. It was Pete. "I checked out of detox. I really don't think I need it." Kate didn't totally disagree with that assessment, but where the hell was he going to stay now? At least in detox, he was safe in a locked ward.

"I hope you'll understand. I can't just sit around letting you all deal with my problems anymore. I'm gonna check out a hunch. I'll call you later on your cell to let you know what I find out."

Kate groaned out loud in the empty office. If she'd been there when he called she might have been able to talk him out of whatever foolhardy thing he had in mind.

Why didn't he call my cell phone?

Then it dawned on her. He'd intentionally called the office phone hoping she wouldn't answer. He didn't *want* her to talk him out of whatever he had planned. She checked caller ID. It just said *PAYPHONE*.

Where'd he find a working payphone? There was probably one in the detox center, no doubt carefully monitored by the staff. But if he was checking himself out, he would've been allowed to use it.

She glanced at her watch. Two minutes past one. Her client was most likely already out in the waiting room. She quickly called Skip's cell phone. It went straight to voicemail. "Hey there, Pete's checked himself out of detox. He left me a message that he has a hunch he's going to investigate. I've got a funny feeling he may be headed downtown so keep an eye out for him, would you? Love you!"

As Kate disconnected she had a minor epiphany. She'd come to think of Pete as addict Pete, someone who needed to be protected from his demons. But the real Pete was a firefighter courageous enough to run into a collapsing skyscraper to save people he didn't know.

His desire to investigate for himself was a sign of recovery, of his returning emotional strength. She said a silent prayer that it wouldn't get him killed.

CHAPTER TWENTY-SIX

The deep breathing and talking to himself was helping, but Skip still couldn't wait to get out of the city. They hadn't had any luck locating Roxie. He and Dolph had split up to keep looking while Tyrell went to check out Matthews' old apartment.

Skip was toying with the idea of giving up. They'd been over the ten square blocks where she was likely to be twice and had gone to the room she rented in the flophouse. Another young woman had answered their knock and told them Roxie had moved out. Maybe she had left town now.

He spotted a group of gals on the next street corner. Taking a deep breath, he headed in their direction. As he neared them, he saw a flash of a pale elbow, at about thigh height of the women clustered around. At first he thought a child was amongst them.

Roxie! He quickened his pace.

The women were having a rather animated conversation. Skip realized Roxie was trying to recruit the others to make porn movies. "I've got the equipment. Jimmy gave it to me, you know, before–"

"Gave it to you, or you stole it from the basement?"

Skip's question had Roxie whirling around and the others taking a few steps back. The child-woman tried to take off but Skip caught her by the upper arm. The others scattered.

"Where were you Saturday?" Skip asked. "We were looking for you for a long time."

"As I recall you found me. Now let go." Roxie tried to tug her arm loose.

"Not until I get some answers. Where were you earlier that day?"

"With a john, of course. He wanted an all-day exclusive."

"Mr. Polinski by any chance?"

Roxie stopped squirming. Her pale face went even whiter. "Yeah, what's it to you?"

"And he's gonna swear to that if I call him right now? I have his home number, by the way. Maybe I should ask his wife first whether or not he was home on Saturday."

Horror washed over Roxie's face, then was gone, replaced with a sneer. "You sonofabitch! You'd ruin the poor man's life just like that."

"No, actually I wouldn't. He seems to be doing a fine job of ruining it without my help. But I am hanging onto you so you can't call him and arrange your alibi. Detective Cooper wants to have a chat with you."

Roxie renewed her squirming and trying to yank her arm loose. She looked up at him and curled her lip. "Let go of me, you bastard! You men are all the same. Just manhandle a woman, make her do whatever you want."

"Oh really, you just called Polinski a 'poor man.' He's not a bastard like the rest of us?"

If he kept her talking, maybe she'd let something slip. He gave her a little shake to settle her down.

It didn't work. She dug in her heels on the sidewalk and leaned back, trying to use her weight to pull him off balance. "No, he's not a bastard. He's pathetic." She spat out the last word.

"You like that word *pathetic* don't you? You bandy it about a good bit."

"Yeah, well that's what most men are–pathetic bastards."

A combination of cheap perfume and body odor assaulted Skip's nostrils. His stomach threatened to rebel. He took in a couple deep breaths through his mouth.

Roxie narrowed her eyes at him. "Don't you be panting after me, Mr. Limp-dick Married Man. I ain't givin' ya none. And if ya try to take it, I'll scream rape."

Part of him wanted to laugh out loud. Another part wanted to smack her. He decided neither would be a useful response. "Trust me, I'm not the least bit interested in your favors."

"Don't you be lookin' down your high-'n-mighty nose at me, you pathetic slime ball!"

"Now there you go with that word *pathetic* again."

"Yeah, well that's what my bastard stepfather used to call me." She was yelling now. "Right after he beat the shit outta me and raped me. Then *he'd* call *me* pathetic. Well, I showed him. Who's the pathetic one now?"

Skip's shock at her bluntness must have registered on his face because hers turned into a mask of fury. It took a second for the last part of her tirade to register in his mind.

But before he could process what it meant, Roxie had launched herself at him. "Don't you dare pity me!" she screamed, spittle flying, hitting him in the face. "You're just like him. You're probably diddling your daughters while your pathetic wife watches."

Rage exploded in his chest. His fist came up and he just barely managed not to slug her. Instead he swiped his sleeve across his face. Then he grasped both her shoulders and shook her. "You need to shut up now," he said through clenched teeth.

"Let her go, man," a heavily accented voice said from behind him.

Skip whirled around, hanging onto Roxie with one hand. Standing less than ten feet away were one of Freddie's men and a scrawny white dude Skip didn't recognize.

Did these guys get missed in the police sweep, or had they made bail?

"I said let her go."

"She's under arrest."

The Hispanic dude took a step toward him. "You ain't no cop."

Skip was trying to tamp down his anger, as well as the urge to pull his gun and shoot these bastards. Probably not a good idea.

Unfortunately while contemplating his options, he'd loosened his grip on Roxie's shoulder. She yanked away from him and took off down the sidewalk.

He started after her but the Hispanic dude stepped into his path. "We need to teach ya a lesson, man. Can't have ya manhandlin' de merchandise."

Skip's gut twisted. His mouth went dry. This was Freddie's replacement. And the man had something to prove. He was marking his territory.

Skip's sheer size was apparently enough to make scrawny white dude nervous. He plucked at his buddy's arm. "Come on, he let her go."

Skip's brain had frozen. No strategy for what to do next came to mind. He continued to stare at the short but beefy Hispanic guy, hoping his fear wasn't showing on his face.

He let out a fake growl. That was enough for the white guy. He took off.

To his right, Skip caught a glimpse of Roxie rounding the corner half a block away. *Damn!* He'd finally caught up with her and these bastards made him lose her again.

Anger surged through him, burning his cheeks. He narrowed his eyes at the man in front of him. "Now what, asshole?"

The man was opening and closing his hands. The muscles in his meaty arms–bare despite the chilly day–rippled each time he clenched his fists. But his eyes were showing a lot of white around dark brown pupils. He backed away. "Just show de girls a little respect an' we'll leave ya alone, man."

Skip swallowed the desire to tell him he had no interest in showing the girls anything. He turned to his left to watch the man swagger away, then pulled out his cell phone and called Tyrell.

"Hey, I had Roxie but she got away from me. She just turned the corner from North Eutaw, west on Fayette."

"Hang on. I'll get some uniforms to chase her down." Skip heard the crackle of a police band radio in the background, then the detective giving the dispatcher Roxie's description.

"The furniture in Matthews' apartment was still there," Tyrell said. "I found what might be tiny blood splatters on the wall, low near the floor. Got a crime scene unit on the way."

"Your people didn't catch that before?" Skip heard the sharpness in his tone. "Sorry, man, I just had a confrontation with a couple of lowlifes. That's how Roxie got away from me."

"No problem, and it's a good question. The place isn't all that clean and these spots could be something other than blood. Hate to think about what. The techs will spray it will luminol and see what they get."

"Okay, I'll–"

"Look out!" A male voice from behind him.

Skip whirled. Sunlight flashed off a blade. He threw up his arm.

He'd partially deflected the blow but a searing pain erupted in his bicep.

The child in front of him raised her arm, a knife in her hand. "I'll kill you too, you pathetic bastard!"

A blur to his right. A man's body slammed into the girl.

Skip was knocked off his feet. His head cracked against the cement sidewalk. An explosion of pain.

Roxie! The girl with the knife was Roxie.

The world went dark.

CHAPTER TWENTY-SEVEN

Skip had no idea how much time had passed when he looked up into Dolph's sagging face. He'd never noticed before how much the man resembled a basset hound.

"If this is heaven, I want a transfer," he muttered.

Dolph laughed. "He'll live."

A paramedic's face replaced Dolph's. He helped Skip sit up.

"What happened?" Skip asked.

"I was coming around the corner back there." Dolph gestured behind him. "Best I could tell Roxie tried to skewer you and Pete jumped her."

Nearby was a gurney. From the ground, Skip couldn't make out who was lying on it. He used his good arm to push himself up to a stand, despite the paramedic's efforts to discourage this. He swayed a little on his feet, then took a couple steps toward the gurney.

The left shoulder of Pete's shirt was bloody. A second paramedic was in the process of wrapping a bandage around his right hand.

"He gonna be okay?" Skip asked the paramedic.

"Yeah, she just grazed my shoulder," Pete answered him. "My hand got cut when I grabbed the knife from her."

"Thanks, man. You saved my life."

Pete grinned up at him. "Figured I owed you one."

Skip put a hand on Pete's uninjured shoulder and squeezed gently.

The world tilted a little. Dolph reached out to steady him.

"You're bleedin' all over the sidewalk, son. Let these boys patch you up."

"Over here, sir." A paramedic led Skip toward an ambulance and had him sit in the open doorway. He squirted something into the wound on his arm.

It stung like hell. He winced and tried not to pull away. "Did Roxie get away?"

"Nope," Dolph said. "Tyrell has her in custody. Judith's on her way down. He's gonna let her have first crack at the kid. See if a woman's touch can get more outta her. He said I could observe."

Skip was amazed at how calm he felt. Was it real or just endorphins?

Could be real. The worst had happened. He'd been attacked, knocked out, could've been killed. But he woke up. And if he hadn't, he'd be dead and wouldn't be able to feel afraid anymore.

He wasn't sure how logical all that was, but it felt like something had shifted and he wasn't about to look that gift horse in the mouth.

The second paramedic had finished with Pete. He came over to the ambulance. Tilting Skip's head down a little, he started probing the lump on the back of it. Skip winced again.

"Don't poke at his brain too hard there, young man," Dolph said. "He ain't got no brain cells to spare. What the hell were you doing letting a little gal like that get the drop on you?"

"She'd twisted loose from me and took off. I thought she was long gone. Tyrell said you could observe, but not me?"

"You're gonna be on your way to the hospital, son."

Skip looked at the paramedic who was now wrapping a gauze bandage around his bicep. The guy was pretty beefy, looked like he was into body-building. Nodding down at his arm, Skip asked, "How bad is it?"

The paramedic hesitated. Skip narrowed his eyes at him. Finally the man said, "Not too bad. Docs at the hospital will put some stitches in the muscle to make sure it heals right, before they close up the wound."

Skip debated for a second. He *really* wanted to be there when

Judith interviewed Roxie. "You cleaned it out good?"

"Irrigated as best I could, but they'll work on it some more at the hospital. Get you on antibiotics, to be on the safe side."

"It gonna make any difference whether those things are done right away? Or can they wait an hour or two?"

"Are you crazy?" Dolph yelled.

Skip ignored him. He held the paramedic's gaze as the latter hesitated. Finally the man said, "I can't make you go to the hospital... Uh, I wouldn't push it much past an hour. Let me get you a sling to keep it still, so the bleeding doesn't start up again."

"I take it you didn't find anything back there," Skip said to the paramedic who'd been checking his head.

"How could he? Your brains already fell out of your head!"

"Ease up, Dolph. Can't you have some pity for a poor injured man here."

In the next instant, pain shot through Skip's arm as the body-builder paramedic slid it into a sling, then passed a strap around his body to immobilize the arm.

"I'll go to the hospital," he managed to push past gritted teeth. "But I wanna hear what Roxie has to say for herself first."

Skip, Dolph and Tyrell were jammed into the observation area behind a one-way mirror. Judith settled into a chair in the interrogation room next door. Roxie, sitting across the table from her, looked like a scared child.

Judith ran through the preliminaries, reminding the young woman of her rights and identifying who was present and why they were there for the sake of the recorder. Then she asked, almost conversationally, "So Roxie, why'd you go after Mr. Canfield with a knife?"

"I was just defendin' myself."

"Against what? The witnesses said he was turned away from you."

"Oh, well... I thought he was gonna slug me."

That didn't even vaguely resemble reality but Judith let it go. "So that's why you yelled something to the effect that you were gonna kill him too?"

"I... I didn't say that."

"I've got several witnesses that say you did."

"It was noisy, cars honkin', people makin' noise. Somebody else musta yelled somethin' like that and people thought it was me."

Judith gave her a sympathetic nod. "Well, while you're here could I ask you a few things about Jimmy Matthews? I know you were interviewed right after he was killed, but we're still tying up some loose ends on that case. You said you liked Matthews. That's pretty unusual. I mean sometimes hookers fall in love with their pimps, or they hate and fear him..."

Roxie shrugged. "Jimmy was a lot better'n most pimps. He never beat us, and he let us keep 'nough money to live on."

"I thought she'd claimed this was her first gig," Dolph whispered in the observation room.

Tyrell just snorted.

"I know pimps sometimes rape their girls." Judith's voice was soft. She leaned forward. "Did Jimmy ever force you to have sex with him?"

"Well, no, ma'am. I mean I had sex with him sometimes, but he didn't have to force me. Ya know, it's part of the deal. Pimps fuck their girls."

"So Jimmy was a prince among pimps," Judith said, not a trace of sarcasm in her tone. "He was nice to you. Let you keep a decent share of your proceeds. Didn't hit you."

A shadow passed across the prostitute's face.

"He did hit you, didn't he, Roxie? At least once."

"Well, yeah, once. I mean a few times, but only when he was doped up. He didn't mean no harm by it."

"Did he hit all his girls when he was doped up?" Judith's voice was incredibly gentle.

"Uh, no." Roxie's eyes darted back and forth, then she dropped her gaze to the table. "Just me," she said, in a small voice. "I was the only one he did drugs with. I was kinda his girlfriend." She looked up again. "But I didn't do the drugs, just pretended to, honest. I was just tryin' to keep him happy, 'cause when he was happy, he was nice to me."

Judith nodded sympathetically. "The medical examiner found a lot of drugs in his bloodstream. He must've been pretty high when he died. Did he beat up on you that day?"

"I, uh... What are you talkin' about? I wasn't around when Jimmy was killed. I was workin'."

"Okay, but see, I still don't understand why you said you'd kill Mr. Canfield *too*."

"I didn't say that!"

"Do you know Jimmy's friend, Peter Jamieson?"

Roxie narrowed her eyes. "The guy you arrested? Yeah, I've seen him around some."

"Did you see him around on Saturday?"

"No."

"Where were you on Saturday morning?" Judith voice was still gentle, as if she was making conversation rather than interrogating a suspect.

"Workin'."

"Who were you with?"

"Don't know. A couple different guys. They weren't regulars."

"Mr. Canfield claimed you said you were with a Mr. Polinski Saturday, all morning."

"I never said that. Canfield's just another lying cheatin' bastard," Roxie spat out. "Comin' downtown to find a hooker 'cause he can't get it up no more with his frigid wife."

Skip clenched his fists, then wished he hadn't when pain shot through his injured arm.

Roxie leaned forward. "He's tryin' to set me up, Detective."

"Set you up for what?"

"For Jimmy's murder, that's what. He's tryin' to get his client off by framin' me. 'Cause a jury'd much rather convict a hooker than a hero."

"How's Canfield trying to frame you?" Judith sounded genuinely interested.

"Well, he... he was sayin' stuff to me. Out there on the street, you know, insultin' me. Tryin' to get me to lose my temper so I'd look like a killer."

It was getting stuffy in the observation room. Skip fished out his handkerchief and wiped the sweat off his face. He wished there was a chair so he could sit down.

Judith was nodding, as if she agreed with Roxie's version of reality. "Did he do anything else, you know, to set you up?"

"Well..." Roxie's gaze darted around the room again, as if looking for inspiration. "He came downtown a couple weeks ago. Said he just wanted information. He was goin' on about my hair and fingerprints bein' in Jimmy's apartment. I laughed and said of course they were, since I was one of Jimmy's girls. I went there, to turn in money and all."

What the... That doesn't even make sense.

Dolph stirred beside him. Tyrell leaned forward.

Am I missing something here?

Judith nodded solemnly, as if Roxie's story was perfectly logical.

"Then he... Canfield, he said he wouldn't turn me in to the cops if I'd give him a blow job, ya know, for free. I knew I hadn't done nothin'. But I thought, what the hey, he's a handsome guy. So I offered to do more than blow him off, ya know, give him the whole package. But then he couldn't get it up."

Skip clenched his jaw. Dolph and Tyrell studiously kept their eyes glued to the window.

"I didn't mean to laugh, but he just looked so silly. That big mountain of a man and his little willie just hangin' there."

Skip felt heat rising in his cheeks. He silently urged Judith to move on.

"I thought he was gonna kill me, he was so mad," Roxie was saying. "But just then one of my friends came in and started yellin' at him to leave me alone, and he took off. That's why I drew my knife, Detective, honest. 'Cause I'd had that fracas with him before and I was afraid of him, but I didn't yell that I'd kill him *too*. I didn't say that. He'd just gotten me so riled up, with his insults."

"So did you pull your knife because you were scared or angry?"

"Well, scared, of course. But he'd got me all shook, that's all. Ya know, rattled."

Nodding again as if she believed Roxie, Judith said, "So Saturday, when you finished up with those johns, about what time was that?"

Roxie made a show of thinking about the question. "I don't know exactly. I guess around one or so."

Dolph glanced sideways at him. "You okay, son?"

"Yeah." Skip stepped back and leaned on the cement wall behind him. It felt cool against his sweaty shirt.

Ah! Much better.

"So were you at your place, with these johns?" Judith asked. Roxie nodded.

"That's real close to where Jimmy used to live. When you came out, did you see anybody running away from his building, or acting suspicious?"

Roxie let out a noise that was probably meant to be a fake laugh. It sounded more like she was choking on something. "Down here? Somebody's actin' suspicious most of the time. Uh, why do you ask?"

"Peter Jamieson was attacked Saturday morning, near where you were."

"Oh, my." Roxie raised a hand to her mouth and tried to look upset. The black lace glove on her hand had a hole in it, at the base of her thumb.

Tyrell leaned forward to reach for the button on a microphone in front of him. Before he could open his mouth, Judith raised a hand in a stop gesture, then moved the hand around as if she were swatting at a fly.

"She caught it," Dolph whispered.

Judith had never taken her eyes off the girl. "Roxie, could you put your hands on the table for a minute, please."

She looked confused but complied.

"Those are really cute lace gloves," Judith said.

"They were a present from Jimmy," the girl said softly. "He said I looked pretty in lace."

"They are pretty," Judith said. "And black is so nice. It's not only sexy looking, but it doesn't show the dirt. I'll bet those gloves can go a long time between washings."

Roxie looked down at her hands in horror, then snatched them off the table.

"Put your hands back on the table, please." Judith's voice now had a touch of steel under the surface.

Roxie reluctantly did so.

Judith carefully took each glove by its edge around the girl's wrist and peeled the glove off inside out. "I could use an evidence bag here."

Tyrell darted from the observation room. A moment later Skip saw him enter the interview room and hand Judith a large brown paper envelope. She carefully dropped the gloves in it and handed it back to him.

Roxie hadn't seemed to even registered that Tyrell had been there. She'd crossed her arms on the table and put her forehead down on them.

"You want to tell me what happened, Roxie?" Judith asked softly.

"I didn't mean to hurt him," the woman sobbed. "He was crazy from the drugs. Started beatin' me."

She lifted her face to Judith, tears making rivulets in her make-up. "Then he hit me in the face. I knew it was gonna be really bad. Pimps never hit ya in the face, 'cause then ya can't work 'til the bruises go away. Johns don't care about bruises nowhere else. Once they got ya undressed, they don't care about nothin' but gettin' off, but they're turned off by a bruised face."

Judith was nodding sympathetically, handing the young woman tissues.

Skip shook his head to clear it. Which turned out to be a really bad idea. Pain shot through his skull. Had he heard right? Judith was getting a *confession* out of this woman!

"It was self-defense, I swear it was. He kept comin' at me,

punchin' me, and I saw the gun. I thought if I pointed it at him, he'd stop, but he just laughed at me and he... he said I was pathetic. And that he'd kill me for pointin' his own gun at him. He came at me, and I had to fire. I had to..."

Skip shook his head, more gingerly this time. Roxie's lips were still moving but he couldn't hear her. What happened to the volume?

His wounded arm was aching. He looked down at the sling. The light navy cloth had turned a deep purple all the way down to his elbow. He touched the bandage around his bicep. His hand came away wet and sticky.

"Dolph, you'd better take me to the hospital."

Dolph didn't respond. Skip realized he hadn't said the words, only thought them.

Then something else nudged at the edge of his brain. This time he did manage to get the words out. "Check on her stepfather. I think she did something to him."

Tyrell nodded without taking his eyes off the window.

Skip stretched out his good arm. His fingers grazed Dolph's shoulder.

The older man turned around. His eyes went wide. He grabbed for Skip as the big man slid down to the floor, leaving a streak of blood on the wall.

CHAPTER TWENTY-EIGHT

Skip could see a faint light. It grew brighter, expanding. He heard a voice but couldn't make out the words. But he'd know that pitch and cadence anywhere. It was his Kate's sweet voice.

He heard Rose's clipped tone as the light expanded, filling his vision, making him squint. Then Dolph's deeper timbre.

Rob's voice in the background. Again no words, more an impression of tone and cadence.

He couldn't see anything but the light. *Shit, am I dead?* Was this his wake with everyone gathered around talking about him?

The light was so bright, it hurt his eyes. He felt them watering. *Wait a minute, dead people's eyes don't water, do they?*

He heard someone say, "I think he's coming around."

Skip blinked, then turned his head away from the blinding light. Kate's face swam into view. She was smiling at him.

~~~~~~~~~

The next time he opened his eyes, Kate was reading, the floor lamp next to her turned away from the bed. The room was dim. Night had fallen outside the one large window.

She looked up from her book and smiled. "How are you feeling?"

He tried to answer her but his dry mouth wouldn't let him. She poured water into a plastic cup, then held it so he could drink from the straw.

He gave her a crooked grin. "I'm having *deja vu* here," he croaked out. Early on in their courtship, he'd had a close encounter with a killer. When he woke up in the hospital that time, she'd also helped him drink some water. But other than that, she'd kept her distance, a little afraid of the powerful attraction between them so soon after Ed Huntington's death.

This time she sat down on the side of the bed and brushed the hair off his forehead. "How are you feeling?" she asked again.

How was he feeling? He took inventory. "I'm okay. No pain."

Actually he felt numb physically. They must have him on the good drugs. Emotionally he was downright euphoric. Was that the drugs too? He was trying to lasso a thought that was skittering around the edge of his brain.

"They did a CAT scan. That thick head of yours is okay." Kate gave him a mock scowl, but her voice was gentle. "You lost a lot of blood though. That was pretty damn dumb of you to refuse to go to the hospital."

"I was pissed. I just wanted to..." The thought pranced by again. *Damn!*

She was frowning for real now, her eyes worried.

This time he caught hold of the thought as it flitted by. "Darlin', can anger cancel out fear?"

Her eyebrows shot up. "Yeah. Well, I don't know if I'd use the words *cancel out*. But when we're angry, we don't care so much about the consequences. Anger can make us brave."

"Today, I was afraid but then I got pissed, when those..." He caught himself. He'd been about to tell her about the two thugs he'd faced down. No need to worry her.

Wait! He wasn't supposed to be thinking like that now. But he couldn't remember why not.

"Did you freak out when you heard?" He gestured toward his injured arm.

"I was scared but Dolph told me you were stable."

"Will you be freaked out, if I keep doing this?"

"Well, I'd prefer that you try a bit harder to stay out of the way of knives and bullets in the future. But no, I won't freak out if you stay in detective work. If anything, I'm less scared now than I used to be."

He snorted. "You're less scared and I'm more scared. Kickass

Kate and Scared Shitless Skip. We're quite a team."

She laughed out loud. "It doesn't sound like you were scared shitless today, just appropriately nervous. Enough to make you cautious."

He picked up her hand in his good one and brought it to his lips. Turning it over, he kissed her palm.

Kate sucked in her breath.

"Ahem."

Dolph, Judith and Tyrell Cooper were crowded in the doorway.

"Well if it isn't the legal beagles triumpherant."

Kate laughed again. "I think you mean *triumvirate*. Come on in, guys. If you've got questions, you probably need to keep them simple. He's a little loopy."

They gathered around the bed.

"I'll need an official statement when you're up for it," Tyrell said. "For now I just want to ask how you knew about the stepfather."

Skip shrugged with his good shoulder. "Something Roxie said, about showing him in the end. What'd you find out?"

"Took some doing since everything about her was a lie. She'd established a whole new identity with forged birth certificate and all. But we finally connected her to a case from last year. Small town in Indiana. Man was found in his stepdaughter's bed, stabbed to death. No knife, no stepdaughter."

"Lemme guess. The stepdaughter's description matches Roxie."

"Yeah, except for the hair color. Real name's Roseanne Brown."

"Did you find out what was in that box?" Kate asked. "What was she so bent on covering up?"

Judith nodded. "She hadn't gotten rid of the box but there was nothing all that incriminating in it. The dumpster behind her building was another story. It gets emptied on Tuesdays and Fridays." She gave Tyrell a wicked grin.

"She made me do the dumpster diving since it's in my jurisdiction." Tyrell directed a mock glare at Judith. "And after all the unofficial help I gave you on this case."

"Come on, so what'd you find?" Skip asked.

"Two DVDs," Tyrell said. "One starring Roxie and Paul Polinski as we'd suspected. And one with her and Jimmy Matthews. Looked like the camera had been set up on a tripod. They started out just playing around, mock S and M. Then Matthews called her pathetic and Roxie went ballistic. She almost strangled him before he finally got her off of him."

"She and I had another little chat," Judith said. "Seems Jimmy didn't threaten her or come at her. He was lying on his bed laughing at her, called her pathetic and she shot him."

"You're the shrink, Kate," Tyrell said. "Could one word really be that big a deal?"

Skip jumped in before she could answer. "She said her stepfather used to call her that after he'd beaten and molested her."

Kate nodded. "Yes, then that word could definitely be a trigger for extreme rage, all the anger that had built up over years of abuse."

"Did you catch up with Polinski?" Skip asked.

"Oh, yeah." Judith grinned at him. "He squealed like a stuck pig. He really was working late. Roxie called him after she shot Matthews. He went to a car rental place and rented an SUV, then helped her move the body and get rid of the bloody bedding. They knew enough from watching CSI on TV to know they had to keep the body in the same position, so it wouldn't be obvious it had been moved.

"He helped on Saturday too, to drag Jamieson back behind the storage area. But he swears he was just knocked out when he left and he knows nothing about any drug overdose."

Skip opened his mouth to ask another question. But his eyes were drooping shut. He fought to keep them open.

"He's fading, you all," Kate said from a distance. "Best we call it a night."

~~~~~~~~~

Kate was struggling to stay awake. Which was not a good thing when one is driving a car. She turned on the radio, hoping that would help.

She hadn't wanted to leave the hospital, especially since Mac and Rose had volunteered to go to the house to help Maria with the kids. She'd been contemplating sleeping in the bedside chair when one of the nurses came in to check Skip's IV. "You go on home, hon. With the pain meds he's on, he'll be out 'til morning."

Kate pulled up in front of her house. A faint light came from the living room window. She had told Rose to feel free to use the guest bedroom upstairs. Mac would be on the sofa since he still wasn't supposed to climb stairs. She hoped she could sneak in without disturbing him, but somehow she doubted it.

Reaching for the radio to turn it off, she paused when a male voice abruptly broke into the middle of a song. "Sorry to interrupt, folks, but we have a special bulletin. Earlier this evening, a prisoner escaped after being transported to the hospital for an emergency appendectomy. Phillip Murrell, who was awaiting trial for assault and attempted murder, complained of abdominal pains earlier this evening. He and his guards had just arrived at the emergency room at St. Joseph's Hospital in—"

Kate pushed the button. It wasn't the hospital where Skip was. That's all she cared about.

She got out of the car and started toward the porch, fumbling in her purse for her house keys.

Man, am I tired.

Finally her fingers connected with the desired object, just as she felt more than saw movement on the path in front of her.

She looked up. Her feet and her heart froze.

The grin on David Samuelson's face looked quite macabre in the dull light from a nearby streetlamp. "Good evening, Mrs. Huntington-Canfield. Such a pleasure to see you again."

Kate shook her head. *I'm hallucinating.*

She willed her knees not to give out on her. She opened her mouth but nothing came out. Swallowing hard, she tried again. "I thought you were in jail."

"I was until just a few hours ago. I'll tell you all about it once we're settled in the car."

"I'm not going anywhere with you." It registered that he was wearing a white jacket over dark pants. He held his left arm tightly against his ribcage.

It was him! The guy who escaped from the hospital.

"Who's Phillip Murrell?"

"Me, of course. That's my real name." He raised his right arm. In his hand was a gun. "If you scream or do anything other than exactly what I tell you, I'll shoot you right here. Then I'll go in your house and kill your children."

Kate hadn't thought her mouth could get any drier. She nodded mutely.

He gestured toward her car. She turned and started walking, her mind racing. She knew she shouldn't get in the car with him. From that point on, he would have the complete upper hand.

But what was she to do against a gun? She couldn't fight him and risk failure. He'd break into the house, and this time Mac and Rose wouldn't be expecting trouble. He'd kill them and her babies. She choked back a sob.

This can't be happening.

"Gimme your purse."

She slid the strap from her shoulder and handed it over. He fumbled in it without taking his eyes off of her. He found the key fob and clicked the doors open.

"Get in the back seat, passenger side, and put your seat belt on."

After a moment's hesitation, she complied.

He held out a hand to stop her from closing the door. Squatting down, he looked at the lever that engaged the childproof mode so the door couldn't be opened from the inside. He nodded, then manually locked her door and closed it.

Walking around the back of the car, he paused to open the trunk and toss her purse inside. After checking that the other back door was also set to childproof mode, he slid behind the wheel.

He looked at her in the rearview mirror. "Put your hands in your lap, clasped together. You move them and I'll come back for the kids." He started the car.

"Where are we going?" She was surprised at how calm she sounded.

"West."

He negotiated his way through the streets of Towson, glancing frequently in the mirror. Then he turned onto the ramp for the Beltway.

Kate's mind was racing, grasping for a plan. It wouldn't be enough to get out of the car. She had to be able to get to a phone before he could get back to the house. She'd have to wait until they got off the Beltway. There were bound to be stores still open on any of the major roads that had exits off the highway. She prayed they were headed to someplace far away from Towson.

"So David, or should I call you Phil? How'd you get away from your guards at the hospital?"

"Call me Dave. I never cared for Phillip."

She suppressed the urge to call him Phil. She'd never hated anybody in her life quite like she hated this man.

He glanced in the mirror again. "To answer your question, the dumb doctor asked the guards to step outside. When he leaned over to examine me, I grabbed him around the neck with my good arm and gave it a twist."

Kate cringed, but a seed was planted in her mind.

"Then I borrowed his clothes. After a bit, one of the guards got curious." He held her eyes in the mirror for a long moment. "Scalpels are incredibly sharp." He picked the gun up out of his lap and waved it in the air. "This was his."

"Why didn't you just take off? Why come back after me? I'm not the only one who can identify you now, and even if you kill me, the cops know what you did."

He made eye contact with her in the mirror. "I don't care about the dumb cops. But I've got a reputation to protect. I'm gonna set myself up as a hit man. Hit men don't leave witnesses, ever." He looked back at the road. "It's a shame really. I kinda liked you, 'til you broke my arm." His tone was conversational.

She drew in a deep breath, trying to calm herself so she could think. Once they were off the highway, she'd look for her chance. They were already quite a ways from Towson. The exit for Reisterstown Road had gone by and now they were at Liberty Road.

When he pulled off onto the ramp for I-70, another limited-access highway, her heart sank. He was headed for western Maryland.

Bile rose in the back of her throat. She swallowed hard.

The leaving witnesses made no sense. He'd no doubt left some at the hospital. "I can't imagine your future customers would find out that you'd left witnesses behind. I'm assuming you'll be changing your identity and appearance."

He glanced at her in the mirror. "Of course. I have my emergency kit stashed in a safe place." He looked back at the road before adding, "I'm going back for your buddy and the spic chick too, but I'll get my back-up gun first."

She caught the scream before it left her mouth. It came out as a whimper.

He chuckled. "Don't worry. That gun's got a silencer. I won't hurt the kids or the nanny, not unless they wake up. I'm not into offing kids."

Despite herself, tears streamed down Kate's cheeks. The knuckles of her hands, gripped together in her lap, had turned white. A blast of red hot rage shot through her. She could easily kill this man with her bare hands.

Anger can make us brave.

The seed in the back of her mind germinated.

"Tell you what." Dave/Phil glanced in the mirror again. "You're a good-looking woman and I haven't had any in, let's see, about a week. If you lie still and let me do you, I won't shoot your kids even if they do wake up. Won't really matter if they see me, since I won't look the same by morning." He chuckled.

For a moment, Kate's vision blurred. Fury and nauseating terror waged a war inside her body. Fury won. "Let me get this straight." Her voice was low and even.

No, it would be better if I sound scared.

"If I let you... r-rape me, you'll spare my children?"

"Who said anything about rape? I don't need to force women. Like I said, if you let me, then..." He shrugged and looked back at the road.

She felt the click in her brain. This wasn't about not leaving witnesses behind. It was about power. She had bested him, broken his arm. Now he wanted her submissive to prove he was in control.

She waited until he looked in the mirror again, then nodded.

She marveled at how calm she felt. She was going to find a way to kill this man.

CHAPTER TWENTY-NINE

The highway was dark and mostly deserted. Kate had no idea what time it was. She was trying to keep the fires of anger stoked to combat the terror.

Her mind reviewed the various holds she'd learned in aikido. The intention of the lessons had been to teach the students how to break such holds, but nonetheless they'd had to learn the holds in order to practice on each other.

Her gaze was glued to the rearview mirror, watching for an opportunity to slip a hand down and unlatch her seatbelt.

Dave/Phil looked up and caught her eye. "You might as well relax. We've got a ways to go yet."

She gave him a feeble smile, then saw red taillights in the distance. And, hallelujah, the red and blue pulsating lights of a police car.

Returning his gaze to the road, he also saw the back-up ahead. "What the fuck?" He hit the brakes.

Kate braced herself with her feet as she slipped her left hand down to release the seatbelt. She quickly grasped her hands again in her lap, holding the seatbelt in place.

The Prius slid to a stop. It wasn't an accident as she'd assumed. Bright floodlights lit up a construction area. The police cruiser was parked at their end of it, its lights flashing no doubt to warn drivers of the back-up.

They were roughly twenty cars back from the police car. Kate decided to bide her time.

Dave/Phil looked up in the mirror. "You behave back there."

She hoped she looked sufficiently frightened. Again, she gave a small nod.

As they crept forward, she prayed there was actually a police officer in that cruiser.

When they were two cars back from it, Dave/Phil took the gun from his lap and slid it under his seat.

As he straightened up, Kate made her move. In an instant, she'd wrapped her arm around his neck. She curled her other elbow around that wrist, locking her arm in place, and yanked back hard.

He gasped and clawed at her arm.

She tightened her grip. "Stop or I'll break your neck," she growled in his ear, giving him yet another yank to prove she meant it.

"I can't breathe," he whispered.

"Tough shit! Put your right hand on the steering wheel right now. Use your left to lower the window."

He tried to laugh but it came out as a wheeze. She tightened her hold on him yet again. His right hand instinctively came up to fight her.

"There's nothing I'd like more than an excuse to kill you."

His left hand fumbled for the window button. Then he tried to lurch forward, to reach under the seat for the gun.

She snapped his head back. In the process, her elbow jabbed his injured shoulder. He let out a howl of pain and fought to squirm away from her.

She yanked on his neck again. "Do what I say, shithead."

His right hand dropped to his lap. The window whirred down. Cars behind them were now honking their horns.

"Put the car in park. Try for a different gear and you'll be dead before the car moves."

He complied.

A warm stickiness under her elbow. She glanced down. A circle of red had blossomed on the shoulder of his white jacket.

That's for Mac, asshole!

"Now put your right hand on the horn and press, and keep

pressing until I say stop."

He didn't move. She tightened her arm around his neck and ground her teeth in his ear.

He laid on the horn.

A police officer suddenly appeared outside the window.

"You can't stop here. Move a..." His voice trailed off when he saw Kate's death hold on her captor's neck.

"Stop," she ordered. "This guy kidnapped me—"

Dave/Phil interrupted. "She's a crazy woman," he wheezed. "Get her off me."

The officer had unsnapped his holster, but his expression said he wasn't at all sure what was going on.

"He's got a gun under the seat," Kate yelled. "He kidnapped me and was planning to kill me. He's the asshole who escaped police custody earlier tonight, at the hospital."

Something shifted on the officer's face. He drew his gun. "You can let him go, lady."

"No I can't. He's a stone-cold killer. He'll go for his gun and try to shoot you."

Despite the pressure on his neck, Dave/Phil smiled at the cop. "Officer, this lady is my wife. She's a paranoid schizophrenic. She has spells like this."

Kate yanked. "Shut up, asshole, and put your hands on the wheel so the officer can handcuff you. Make a false move and I'll snap your neck."

Dave/Phil made a gurgling noise in his throat. He went limp against her arm.

"Look, lady, I believe you," the cop said. "I heard the BOLO earlier. But you might want to let up some, before you choke him."

"Not if you and I want to live."

The cop now had handcuffs in one hand, his gun in the other. His face was a study in indecision.

"Uh, you might actually want to holster your gun before you get too close to his hands," Kate said.

The cop still hesitated.

Kate heard a gruff voice from behind him. "We got your back,

Bob." She glanced over to the side of the road. A half-dozen construction workers were lined up, most carrying wrenches or other lethal-looking tools. Several of them slapped their weapons against their gloved hands.

Kate smiled for the first time in hours. "Now you play nice, *Phillip*, or I *will* break your neck! And these nice gentlemen will testify that it was justifiable homicide."

The officer holstered his gun, then stepped forward and opened the driver's door.

Dave/Phil came to life and tried to lunge sideways for the officer's holster. Kate started to pull back again on his neck, but he was ripped from her grasp.

The next thing she knew he was lying on the gravel shoulder, howling. The officer had planted one knee in the middle of his back and was yanking his arms behind him to cuff him.

The construction workers closed in around them, blocking Kate's view. She heard the slap of metal against work-gloved palms.

"He's probably got a scalpel on him somewhere," Kate yelled as she scrambled over into the front seat. She reached under the driver's seat and felt around. Pulling out the gun, she opened the passenger door and got out on that side.

The cop had pulled Dave/Phil to a stand and was eyeing her nervously.

Kate turned the gun around and handed it butt first to the nearest construction worker. "You might want to cover him while the officer searches him. He killed a doctor and a guard at the hospital, even with an injured shoulder."

The cop nodded. "Cover him." He pushed Dave/Phil up against his cruiser and patted him down. He pulled a bloody scalpel from his sock.

Opening the back door of the car, he put a hand on his prisoner's head and shoved him down into the backseat. Dave/Phil let out another yelp of pain. The officer ignored him. He slammed the door closed.

Keeping one eye on his prisoner, he half turned back toward Kate. "How'd he kidnap you?"

"I'm one of the people he attempted to kill before. He came to my house tonight for a second crack at me."

She heard a low chuckle from the cluster of construction workers. "Looks like he messed with the wrong woman, don't it, Bobby?"

The officer's mouth quirked up on one end.

"Please don't let him get away again," Kate said. "Next time, I *will* kill him."

The adrenaline suddenly drained out of her system. "I'm going to go sit in my car now." Her own voice sounded faint and far away. Her body trembled as she walked the few feet back to the Prius.

The cop and the construction workers discreetly looked away while Kickass Kate threw up next to her car.

CHAPTER THIRTY

"This is it." Kate pointed to the flyer taped to the window. The glass was fogged with condensation from the muggy June night.

Skip opened the door for her. They were greeted by a blast of air-conditioned chill. The small auditorium in the community center was half full. People of all ages, including a few teenagers were scattered in clumps on the metal folding chairs, chatting.

Kate spotted Manny Ortiz waving to them. He had saved a group of seats three rows back. Rob, Liz and Dolph were already there. Kate slipped into the seat next to Rob. Skip sat down on the other side of her. She glanced at her watch. Ten minutes of eight.

After greeting the others, Kate watched a few people wander over to a refreshment table and pour themselves cups of coffee from one of several pots on hot plates.

Rob leaned over. "The State Attorney's office called me today," he whispered in her ear. "They struck a deal with Phillip Murell, aka David Samuelson."

Her mouth dropped open. She pulled back and stared at him.

"No, no," he quickly added. "It's a good thing. He agreed to life without chance of parole."

She took a deep breath to slow her racing pulse. "Why?"

"Maryland's repeal of the death penalty just went into effect. Pennsylvania still has it. They wanted to extradite him for crimes committed up there."

Kate grinned at him. Then she turned to Skip and whispered the good news in his ear. He gave a thumbs up to Rob.

Kate settled back in her chair.

Rob nudged her shoulder. She turned toward him again.

"I called an old buddy today. He's the dean of the University of Baltimore Law School now. Looks like I might be teaching there part-time this fall."

Kate threw her arms around him. "That's great! What are you going to do about your practice?"

"Cut back some. Be a lot pickier about the cases I take."

"Sounds like a plan."

Mac lowered himself into the seat on the other side of Skip. "Never been to one of these," he growled.

Kate squeezed Rob's hand, then leaned forward to greet Mac and Rose.

A slender, middle-aged man with a pock-marked face stepped up to the podium. He called the meeting to order.

Then the person they were all there to see walked up to the front of the room. He stood at the podium and gave the audience a shy smile. Leaning toward the microphone, he said, "Hi, folks. I'm Pete, and I'm an addict."

"Hi, Pete," the room chorused.

"As of today, I've been clean and sober one year."

Applause broke out, along with several cheers.

"I'm also a recovering firefighter."

A smattering of chuckles.

"Fighting fires was all I ever wanted to do, since I was a little kid. And my best friend wanted to be a cop. We spent hours daydreaming about what it would be like to be heroes someday."

Pete paused. "But when I grew up and became a firefighter, I didn't feel like a hero. I was just doing my job. The job I loved. And I was happy."

Kate swallowed a lump in her throat.

"A little less than twelve years ago, I was on vacation in New York, on September 11th."

Pete looked right at Kate. They'd discussed this. He had never before shared in a twelve-step meeting–even with this, his home group–that he was a 9/11 first responder.

She gave him a nod of encouragement.

"I wasn't on duty but people needed help. I ran into a burning building and rescued people. It's what I do."

Pete cleared his throat. "I won't bore you with the details of the next decade of my life. It was relatively uneventful. But on the tenth anniversary of 9/11, something snapped inside. My official diagnosis was delayed PTSD. I went downhill fast."

He stopped and took a drink of water from a cup on the table beside the podium.

"Meanwhile my best friend and I had grown apart. He didn't become a cop. He became a drug addict and a dealer. I still loved him but I couldn't bear to be around him. We lost touch."

Pete sought her out again in the crowd. One of the tears pooling in her eyes had broken loose but she smiled at him.

"Now I tracked him down. I wanted what he had to offer. Oblivion. I was willing to do anything to make the nightmares and flashbacks stop. He was so happy to see me when I knocked on his door." Pete's voice broke. He turned away for a moment, then leaned back into the microphone. "Jimmy, I'm sorry."

Kate swiped at another runaway tear. The room was absolutely silent.

Pete took a moment to compose himself. "I hit bottom shortly after I lost the job I loved. I was put on admin leave without pay. I had a year to get my act together. I came here. I started going to see a counselor. And I went back to pretending that Jimmy didn't exist." He stopped again, swallowing hard.

"Again, I won't bore you with details, but a lot has happened in the last year. I lost a friend, my best friend. Jimmy didn't make it."

A communal moan rippled through the room.

"But at my lowest point, a bunch of people came out of nowhere to help me. A lawyer, a therapist, and a private detective gave me their services for free. Kinda sounds like a joke, doesn't it? A lawyer, a therapist and a P.I. walked into a bar."

Chuckles rolled through the audience.

"But it wasn't just those three. The people that worked for them also went beyond the call of duty." Pete looked their way again. "One of them almost died trying to get me out of trouble.

And another, a recovering addict himself... well, he helped me a lot."

Kate heard Manny, three seats over, clear his throat.

"They're my heroes, all of them. But none of them would accept that label, any more than I did on 9/11. Because they were all just doing their jobs. Yeah, they weren't getting paid at the moment for doing their jobs. But that's how they saw it, just like I saw it that way. A building was burning and there were still people inside. I did my job."

Pete paused. "Thanks for listening."

"Thanks for sharing," rippled through the audience. Then the room erupted in a standing ovation.

~~~~~◇~~~~~

Author's Notes

Zero Hero was a hard book to write, for several reasons. The characters were going through such emotional changes that I was sometimes not sure how they should be reacting to events and to each other. Ironically, Pete Jamieson was the easiest of the characters to portray. And I, like Kate, learned some things from him about heroism.

9/11 has left considerable emotional scar tissue on the American psyche. Our society's 'healthy denial' about our security in the world was shaken to the core. As I listened in on Kate's 'sessions' with Pete and watched her struggle with her feelings about his case, I was reminded of just how helpless I felt on that day in 2001.

Even though it was difficult at times, the telling of this story ended up being therapeutic for me. I hope that it has had a similar healing effect for you, the reader.

Moving on to other topics, I'd like to point out that yes, the characters of Benito and Tony Donati, and Benito's Plumbing Supplies, are total figments of my imagination and any resemblance to real people or business establishments is purely coincidental. If your name happens to be Tony Donati, please accept my apologies for making your namesake in this book one of those criminals who is dumb as a rock.

There was, however, a real mob family, the Bufalino family, that was based in Scranton, Pennsylvania. And it did meet its demise when its boss was arrested and turned state's evidence against some of his own people. William 'Big Billy' D'Elia will indeed be released from prison in 2014.

And there really is a Methodist church on Pocahontas Road near Finzel, Maryland, but I have no idea whether or not they hold AA meetings there.

To paraphrase an old saying, it takes a village to produce a book. As always, I am exceedingly grateful to my wonderful beta readers–Angi, Gina, Sue and Ralph–and to my proofreader, Kirsten Weiss, and especially to my critique partner and co-founder at *misterio press*, Shannon Esposito. After struggling so much to write this book, I was sure it was worthy only of the circular file. Imagine my amazement when they all–even my toughest betas–told me this was the best book yet in the series.

Also a huge thank you to my editor, Marcy Kennedy, whose advice has helped me to become a better writer in so many ways, and to Melinda VanLone, who produced a book cover that was exactly what I had envisioned in my mind's eye.

And now a synopsis of the next book in the series:

FATAL FORTY-EIGHT
A Kate Huntington Mystery

Kate's former boss, Sally Ford, is retiring. The new man in her life, Charles Tolliver, has convinced her to turn over the reins of The Trauma Recovery Center to others and spend her golden years with him.

But instead of many golden years, she may only have forty-eight hours. On the evening of her retirement party, she is kidnapped by a serial killer.

Normally the disappearance of an adult would be treated as a missing person's case, but Lieutenant Judith Anderson of the Baltimore County Police Department realizes the MO is similar to a rash of kidnappings/murders that occurred in New York the previous year. When Kate and her P.I. husband insist on being part of the investigation, Judith's hesitation is brief. A woman's life is at stake and there is no time to lose.

Unfortunately the pair of FBI agents who arrive from New York have mixed emotions about civilian involvement. The middle-aged male agent is happy to have Kate's assistance as he fine-tunes his psychological profile of the 'unsub' the New York press has dubbed the Forty-Eight Hour Killer. But the voluptuous, young female agent believes in doing things by the book.

As she locks horns out in the field with Skip, misunderstandings abound back at headquarters. But there's no time for these innuendoes and jealousies. Sally has less than forty-eight hours to live.

About the Author

Kassandra Lamb was a psychotherapist for over two decades, specializing in trauma recovery. She has also taught psychopathology at Towson University and at other colleges. Now retired, she devotes the majority of her time to her other greatest passion, writing. The magic portal to the world of Kate and her friends (i.e., Kassandra's computer) is located in Florida, where Kassandra's husband and dog catch occasional glimpses of her.

She has completed six books in the Kate Huntington series and one Kate on Vacation novella. She is currently working on book seven in the series and a second novella.

You can read and see more about Kassandra and the Kate Huntington series (including photo galleries) at **http://kassandralamb.com**. Please sign up for the newsletter to get updates regarding future releases and other interesting tidbits about the series.

You can contact Kassandra at **lambkassandra3@gmail.com** or visit her blog at **http://misteriopress.com**. She also hangs out at Twitter and on Facebook so feel free to track her down there **@KassandraLamb** and **http://www.facebook.com/kassandralambauthor**

At *misterio press*, we take pride in producing top quality books for our readers. All manuscripts are proofread several times, but proofreaders are human. If you discover any errors in this book, please e-mail the author at lambkassandra3@gmail.com. Thank you!

Look for these other great *misterio press* titles:

Karma's A Bitch (Pet Psychic Mysteries)
by Shannon Esposito
Maui Widow Waltz (Islands of Aloha Mysteries)
by JoAnn Bassett
The Metaphysical Detective (Riga Hayworth Mysteries)
by Kirsten Weiss
Dangerous and Unseemly (Concordia Wells Mysteries)
by K.B. Owen
Forever Road (Peri Jean Mace Mysteries)
by Catie Rhodes
Tin God (Delta Crossroads Mysteries)
by Stacy Green

plus other stories by these authors!